2017 YOUNG EXPLORER'S ADVENTURE GUIDE

dreaming robot press

quality middle grade and young adult
science fiction and fantasy stories

1 3 5 7 9 10 8 6 4 2

First published in the United States by Dreaming Robot Press. 2016

Copyright © 2016 by Corie J. Weaver. All rights reserved

Publisher's Cataloging-in- Publication data

Names: Weaver, Sean, 1968- , editor. | Weaver, Corie, 1970- , editor.

Title: 2017 Young explorer's adventure guide / edited by Sean and Corie Weaver.

Description: Las Vegas, NM: Dreaming Robot Press, 2016.

Identifiers: ISBN 978-1- 940924-21- 2 | LCCN 2016952327

Subjects: LCSH Short stories. | Science Fiction. | Children's stories, American. | BISAC JUVENILE FICTION
/ Science Fiction | JUVENILE FICTION / Short Stories

Classification: LCC PZ7 .T9332 Tw 2016 | DCC [Fic]—dc236

ISBN: 978-1-940924-21-2

Published by Dreaming Robot Press
1214 San Francisco Avenue
Las Vegas, NM 87701
www.dreamingrobotpress.com

Acknowledgements

Thanks to our families for putting up with all the madness, our authors for believing in our dream, and our friends for helping spread the word. We'd also ask for a round of applause for our editorial team of Amanda Coffin and Nicole Brugger-Dethmers. Together, I think we've done something amazing.

Permissions

Contents

Introduction

I read science fiction far before I knew what science fiction was. It may have started with Madeleine L'Engle's *A Wrinkle in Time*. Or perhaps Lois Lowry's *The Giver*. Maybe even before that, with Bruce Coville or Ursula K. Le Guin or Isaac Asimov...I don't know which story I first picked up that introduced me to worlds far different from our own, but I do know I didn't read them because they were science fiction. I read them because they were good.

That's one of the magics of reading while young: You're not reading because of labels. You're just looking for a good story.

As I grew older, I started introducing false boundaries to the book I chose. I can't read this; it's a boy book, or, I can't read this; I don't look like the girl on the cover, or I can't read this; it's too childish. At the end of the day, I was filling my bookshelves with a lot of I can'ts, and that, quite honestly, is a terrible way to approach books. And life.

It took growing up a little more for me to return to books for youths, both as a reader and a writer. I was never more concerned about appearances than I was as a teenager. I wanted to seem older and wiser, and so I surrounded myself with books I didn't really like all that much; I just thought they were "literary." I forgot for a time that the value of the book is in the magic of the words, not in whether or not the book was wrapped in a leather-bound cover stamped in gold foil.

I had also forgotten the value of stories written for young people. I was so busy trying not to be a young person myself that, much like Susan in Narnia, I'd thrown aside all my childish things and forgotten what was really important. There is a sort of truth that exists in books for young people that doesn't exist anywhere else. Maybe it's because, as Nancy Kress's narrator says in "The Robot Did It," adults' brains are "less plastic" and that, for children, the truth is right now, such as in R.W.W. Greene's "I Will. Not." Regardless, in many ways, Madeleine L'Engle's words on the matter are truer now than ever before:

"You have to write the book that wants to be written. And if the book will be too difficult for grown-ups, then you write it for children."

This collection of science fiction contains stories ranging from robots to space travel, with characters that embody many different walks of life and attitudes, and each one contains the sort of truth that you can only find in stories for young people. And—as with all good stories—the heart of each one is that of discovery and adventure, strength and courage. So whether you're a kid yourself, or smart enough to have returned to liking the same sort of stories you liked as a kid, you're sure to find something here that will remind you of the magic of reading.

This collection is for the people whose bookshelves are filled with I can.

Beth Revis,
New York Times bestselling author of the
Across the Universe series,
The Body Electric *and A* World Without You

The Robot Did It

by Nancy Kress

Nancy Kress is the author of thirty-three books, including twenty-six novels, four collections of short stories, and three books on writing. Her work has won six Nebulas, two Hugos, a Sturgeon, and the John W. Campbell Memorial Award. Most recent works are the Nebula-winning Yesterday's Kin *(Tachyon, 2014) and* The Best of Nancy Kress *(Subterranean, 2015). Her work has been translated into Swedish, Danish, French, Italian, German, Spanish, Polish, Croatian, Chinese, Lithuanian, Romanian, Japanese, Korean, Hebrew, Russian, and Klingon, none of which she can read.*

In addition to writing, Kress often teaches at various venues around the country and abroad, including Clarion; in 2008 she was the Picador visiting lecturer at the University of Leipzig. Kress lives in Seattle with her husband, writer Jack Skillingstead, and Cosette, the world's most spoiled toy poodle.

My name is Nia. I am ten years old. Robots *suck*. That is all I am going to say right now because I am too mad to say anything else.

Okay, it is later and I have calmed down. A little bit,

anyway—enough to say this: It was not my fault. It wasn't H'raf's fault, either, no matter what Mom says. The whole thing was the robot's fault. *Totally*. To blame H'raf and me is just wrong!

Now I'm more calm. Maybe it was a little bit my fault, and a little bit H'raf's. But mostly the robot's. And it isn't even fair to blame H'raf and me because we didn't mean it to happen. I would never deliberately almost destroy Moon Colony Alpha! I love Alpha! I grew up there! The part that was H'raf's and my fault wasn't planned, it just sort of happened. And all because of language.

Mostly.

This is what happened: As soon as summer vacation started in Colesville, Illinois, my family traveled back to Moon Base Alpha, where I used to live. We went back because some aliens had landed on the moon. Their scientists were working with our scientists, which included my mom because she's an important biologist. Also, the aliens wanted their kids to play with human kids because kids can learn each other's languages more easily than adults can. Dad says that's because after twelve or so, human brains get "less plastic" and don't pick up foreign languages as easily. Every time he says that, I think of plastic Tupperware in my head and start laughing. Dad laughs, too, but it annoys Mom. She thinks I should be more serious. Also more careful and less impulsive and a lot of other things I'm mostly not.

But the three alien kids and us three human kids on Alpha liked each other. We played together all summer. Not that you can tell it's summer on the moon; we don't have seasons. We played tag in the rock corridors of Alpha, which is underground, and we had picnics above ground under the Dome, where you can see a gazillion stars all the time and Earth hangs in the sky like a big blue-and-white ball.

We played in the aliens' apartments, too. They breathe different air than we do, so when we were in their homes, Ben and Jillian and I had to wear space suits with air packs on our backs, and when we were all in human spaces—which was most of the time—the alien kids wore their space suits, which were a lot lighter and better looking than ours, and which somehow turned our air into their air without air packs. Our scientists studied that a lot.

It was a good summer, even though I missed my friends on Earth and my dad's dog, Bandit. We played basketball and tag and a weird alien game that involved blinking lights and a lot of somersaults. H'raf, an alien boy, and I got to be good friends. They look a little weird—bluish, with six tentacles where we have five fingers. They also have tails. But you get used to all that, and H'raf, Jinfroh, and B-b-b-jump! were nice. We three human kids learned to speak a lot of their language, which we called Alienese. Well, you don't just speak it, which is why their names are so strange.

It's also what caused all the trouble later on.

"Tell me again how to say his name," Dad said, after H'raf left our apartment to go home for dinner. We can't ever eat together. Our food would make them sick, and theirs would sicken us. Still, anything they eat can't be any worse than broccoli. I hate broccoli.

I told Dad a lot of times already how to say H'raf's name, but he can't seem to get it right. "You blow air out your lips real fast, say 'raf,' and raise up your left pinkie." All words in Alienese use both sound and body movements. "Try it."

Dad tried it.

I said, "No, you just said 'sleeping mat.' H'raf is not a sleeping mat. Like *this*." I showed him again.

This time he did better. He said, "And how do you say the girl's name?"

"Jinfroh. Sort of gargle on the 'Jin' part, then spit out 'froh' real fast while you twist your right wrist to the left."

Dad didn't gargle right. I said, "You just said 'rock head.'"

"I give up. I never was much good at languages!"

Actually it's a good thing that Dad gave up, because the littlest alien kid's name is the hardest: B-b-b-jump! You stutter with your lips, jump up, and make a clicking sound. If you make the click wrong, you end up calling him a toilet and he doesn't like it.

The aliens say my name perfectly, only they add a little thumb flick on the end. I didn't ask them what I would be called if they left out the thumb flick. Sometimes it's better to not know things.

"Can I go now? I told H'raf I'll meet him in the gym."

"Yes, but just one more thing." Dad ran his hand through his hair. He should really stop doing that—I think it's what's making him go bald. "Dr. Porter wanted me to ask you this."

Dr. Porter is the chief language scientist on Alpha. He's making a video dictionary of Alienese. I have to meet with him every few days and answer a gazillion questions. We don't like each other. He thinks I'm badly behaved and too sassy. I think he's the kind of adult that talks all fake-sweet to kids but doesn't really like them.

Dad took out his phone and ran a video of H'raf's mom saying something. She raised her ring finger, said "clanth!" twisted her thumb, and said, "pof," very softly.

"Dad, I have no idea what that means."

"Dr. Porter says it's important. Could you ask H'raf?"

He still wasn't pronouncing it right. This time he called H'raf a metal chair. I said, "Why doesn't Dr. Porter ask H'raf himself?"

"He did. But the answer wasn't clear. I don't think H'raf likes Dr. Porter much."

I grinned. Dad gave me a fake swat on the bottom, and I ran off to meet H'raf in the gym. We were going to program Luna, my robot dog, to do some new tricks. H'raf learned really fast to program human computers, but we can't do anything with theirs. Mom says they use completely different physics. Then she said a whole lot of long words I didn't understand, so I stopped listening.

Also, H'raf was going to bring his bic!dul, which is maybe the coolest toy in the whole universe. It looks like a green blob, but you talk to it and tell it what you want it to turn into, and it *does*. It can look like him, or me, or Luna, or a coffee pot, or the Dome—anything. We are only supposed to play with it when adults are around. Mom says that until she understands the science behind it, it could have "dangerous aspects." But the bic!dul fits in H'raf's pocket, and so sometimes we sneak into a storage closet to play with it. What's dangerous about a green blob that turns into the shape of a coffee pot? It's not like you can make hot coffee in it.

"C'mon, Luna! Let's go!" She scampered after me as I ran along the smooth rock corridors to the gym. Alpha Colony is always growing; big machines bore through rock to make new tunnels and rooms. I was looking forward to having H'raf all to myself. Jillian and Ben both had to make up time they missed on the exercise machines—it's important to exercise a lot, because if you don't, the moon's lower gravity turns your muscles to mush. I liked Jinfroh and B-b-b-jump!, but they didn't approve of H'raf smuggling the bic!dul out of his quarters for us to play with. Jinfroh can be too big-sisterish sometimes. B-b-b-jump! is still sort of a baby.

I burst into the gym. H'raf was there, but I knew right away that something was wrong. He was making the pattern with his feet that meant he was upset. "Nia!" he said in English, but with the thumb twist on the end. "We must to go!"

"Go where?"

"We have trouble!"

I looked around the empty gym—I didn't see any trouble.

"Not at Alpha," H'raf said. "Trouble at home!"

"Home? You mean, your home? Your planet? You're leaving?"

"Yes! Big trouble! We must to go today!"

"What trouble?" I asked. But when H'raf started to explain, I didn't understand any of the words. All at once I got mad, which is what I do when I'm scared. Mom says it's a bad habit. Dr. Porter says I'm undisciplined. I didn't care. I said, "You can't go! Make them leave you here!"

H'raf raised his right arm, which is sort of like us shaking our head *no*. "Can't."

"Will you be coming back? When?"

"I don't know."

Well, of course he didn't know—nobody tells kids anything. They just order us around. *Move to Earth, Nia. Leave your friends. Move back to Alpha, Nia. Make new friends.* Now it would probably be: *Move back to Earth, Nia.* And this new friend leaves.

I shouted, "I'm sick and tired of good-byes!"

"Yes. Me. Also," H'raf said. "I must to go now." Then he leaned toward me and whispered, "Before I must to go, I give to Nia a present. Only not here."

I knew immediately what he meant. We held hands—he has one more tentacle than I have fingers, but it doesn't matter—and ran out of the gym, away from the security cameras. My phone was ringing wildly: Mom or Dad calling me. I ignored the phone. In the storage closet, H'raf pulled out the bic!dul. "Look, Nia."

The green blob sat on his hand. He said to it, "H'raf." The blob changed shape and in a minute there was a little green H'raf sitting on his palm. "To remember of me."

"I would remember you anyway, H'raf. Forever."

"Yes. I remember Nia for all time of all stars. But one more important, Nia. If this bic!dul makes trouble, you must to say this three turns." H'raf raised his ring finger, said "clanth!"

twisted his thumb and said, "pof," very softly, and then he said, "tarn!-dal!-jump."

It started with the same words that Dad said Dr. Porter wanted to know, but then went on longer. I said in Alienese, "What does it mean?"

H'raf looked like he was searching his memory for the right words. He didn't find them. The storage closet door flew open. I snatched the bic!dul from H'raf's hand and shoved it in my pocket.

A security officer stood there, looking really mad. He wasn't one of Alpha's security team; he'd come up from Earth when the aliens first showed up. Serious security. He grabbed me by the arm but didn't touch H'raf. "What are you doing here? Didn't you hear your phone? Everybody's looking for you two!"

"Let go! I'm coming!"

H'raf flicked both wrists upward and made a snorting noise in his nose. That all added up to a very bad word in Alienese. I couldn't help it; I grinned at him.

It was my last smile for a long time.

There was a quick going-away ceremony under the Dome, and then the aliens were gone. I sat in our apartment with Mom and Dad. "What happened? Why did they have to go?"

"There is a crisis on one of their colony worlds," Dad said. He ran his hand through his hair.

"*One* of their colony worlds? You mean they have a lot of colonies? How many?" We only have two: Alpha and the Mars colony. My friend Rosa's family moved to Mars last year.

Mom said, "It's not clear how many colonies they have."

"Why not? Can't they count? Can't *you* count?"

"Nia," Dad said, "don't take that tone with your mother. I know you're upset, but it's not her fault."

That was true. It didn't make me feel any better. I said,

"Everybody leaves! Or you make me leave them!"

Luna rushed up to me and whimpered. I programmed her to do that when I'm upset. She climbed into my lap.

Mom said, "Nia, you need to learn to accept things that you can't control. Now I need to ask you something. Please think about it carefully. Those words that Dr. Porter asked you to have H'raf explain—"

"Angela," Dad said, "maybe this isn't the best time. She's pretty upset."

But there is no stopping Mom when anything scientific is involved. She barreled ahead. "I know. But this is really important. What did H'raf say?"

"I didn't get a chance to ask him!"

There was a long silence. Finally Mom said, "Nia, we trusted you with this."

It was too much. I said, "Well, I trusted you to not tell me to make friends with H'raf, and then when I do, to just care about what information I can get out of him! I'm not some sort of *spy*!"

Dad said, "Of course you're not, honey," at the same moment that Mom said, "Nia, nobody said anything about—"

"I don't feel good," I said and threw up on the kitchen floor.

Then everybody got concerned and put me to bed and got the doctor. It turned out I had the flu, which must have come up to Alpha with one of the new government people or security guys or scientists, because it wasn't here before. Jillian and Ben got it, too, and a whole lot of other people, including Dr. Porter. Mom brought me chicken soup and put cold cloths on my head. Dad read me stories. They both forgave me for yelling at them because, after all, I had been coming down with the flu and wasn't really myself. Sickness has some good points.

Too bad you have to feel so rotten to take advantage of them.

After a few days, the fever and achiness and throwing up stopped. I still felt yukky, though. Nothing was any fun. Jillian and Ben were still sick. Most of the people who came up to Alpha while the aliens were here had gone back down to Earth. I messaged with Kezia and Alice on Earth, but I couldn't call H'raf because once the alien ship left, we couldn't contact them. Dad says their spaceship isn't in normal space, but I think their cell plan just has really poor coverage.

Luna and I went every day to the storage closet so I could play with the bic!dul that H'raf gave me. The bic!dul wasn't H'raf, or anybody else I could play with. But H'raf made it for me, and so it was a piece of him, like a memory is a piece of somebody. I didn't want a piece of H'raf, I wanted the whole alien. But this is what I got.

Then the storage closet got filled up with new supplies from Earth, big crates of something or other, and there was no room for us. So Luna and the bic!dul H'raf and I went down to a new bore tunnel.

I was not supposed to be there. The bore machinery is big and loud and dangerous. It works all the time, all by itself, cutting through rock to make new tunnels and new rooms. Then robot arms load the rock onto little train cars and take it up to the surface to dump. Other robots, which are mostly arms attached to weird-looking machines, smooth out the tunnel floors and put in lights and air ducts and stuff like that. The robots install security cameras, too, but this tunnel didn't have them yet.

Which is why I went there.

I sat on the rough rock floor of the new tunnel and played with the bic!dul. "Be H'raf," I told it in Alienese. The blob melted and then reformed into the shape of a little green H'raf.

"Be a phone."

It did, although of course the phone didn't work. But, then, neither did the green H'raf.

"Be a ball."

The bic!dul became a ball and Luna barked at it. "Fetch, Luna!" I threw the ball down the tunnel, away from the bore machine. It bounced off the wall. Before Luna could grab it, a robot arm installing air ducts picked it up.

I jumped up, scraping my knee on the rough rock. "Give that back! It's not an air duct, you stupid robot!"

The robot squashed the bic!dul flat—robots are really strong—and cemented it into the ceiling, which was what it was programmed to do, and reached down for another air duct.

"Give it back! It's mine!"

The robot cemented a second air duct over the ball. I hit the robot, which did no good at all. Luna barked and jumped. My phone rang. Shouting and barks and phone chimes echoed off the stone walls.

"Nia," Dad said, on audio override, "where are you? Come back to the apartment. Your mother is sick."

Mom had the flu. She was sicker than I had been, but not dangerously sick. The doctor said so. Here's what I didn't know before: It's not so bad to have someone in your family sick if you're not. I got to help take care of Mom, which had never ever happened before because Mom was always the strong one. Now she wasn't. I made her soup—Dad showed me how—and I put cold cloths on her forehead and I read to her, because it hurt her eyes to read. It cheered me up a lot, especially since Dad was often gone. There was something going on at the Moon Council. He's not a member, but Mom is and he was filling in for her. So I took care of Mom—I was important!

And she didn't once tell me to clean my room or stand up straighter or not be so impulsive. It was great.

Until she got better.

After lunch one day, she put on her glasses, blinked, and said to Dad, "Wayne, fill me in on the crisis."

I looked up from carrying away the tray with her lunch dishes. Did she mean the crisis on the alien colony world? Was it over, and maybe H'raf was coming back?

But it wasn't the aliens' crisis. It was a crisis on Alpha. Dad glanced at me and ran his hand through his hair. "I haven't wanted to worry Nia."

Mom said, "Nia is old enough to understand. She's learned a lot of self-control, and she's been so mature during my illness."

I put the tray down, looking mature and self-controlled and old enough to understand anything.

Dad said to Mom, "Haven't you kept up with the Council bulletins?"

"Reading still gives me a headache, Wayne—tell us."

Us. I looked even more mature. I did this by nodding seriously and sort of squinting up my eyes, like I was gazing at A Really Important Crisis.

Dad still looked uncertain. But he said, "Nia—do you know what disassemblers are?"

"No." Six words into the crisis, and already I didn't understand.

"Well—everything in the world is made up of atoms, right? The bed, the dishes, you and me—everything."

"I know *that.*" Sometimes they treat me like I'm six.

"Do you know what an atom is made up of?"

"It's got, uh, stuff in the middle and electrons go whizzing around the center."

"Close enough. Have you ever heard of nanotechnology?"

It sounded familiar, but I couldn't remember what it was. I said, "Sort of."

Mom said, "Nanotech is building up things atom by atom, kind of like the 3-D printer does, but on a more basic level. A nanotech machine could build anything out of the right materials."

"*Really?*" I pictured a big box that could make anything: ice cream cones, cell phones, robot dogs like Luna. "Do we have one?"

"No. Human technology is only as far as 3-D printers."

Too bad. Our 3-D printer was only programmed to make boring things like cups and socks and parts for other machines. I said, "But how is nanotechnology a crisis right now on Alpha?"

Dad said, "Nanotech builds things using tiny little machines called 'assemblers.'"

"Because they assemble atoms," I said, feeling smart.

"Right. But—"

All at once I got it. I jumped up, spilling the rest of the soup and water from Mom's tray. "You said 'disassemblers,' not 'assemblers'! Do disassemblers take things apart?"

"Yes. Atom by atom," Mom said. Dad was wiping up the spills on the floor.

"And we have disassemblers on Alpha? That's the crisis?"

"Yes."

"But...what are the disassemblers taking apart atom by atom?"

Long silence. Then Mom said, "The moon."

It wasn't quite as bad as that—at least, not yet. The disassemblers were in only one spot and were so far taking apart only a few rocks. But—get this!—they were spreading. The disassemblers had assemblers with them, and the assemblers were making more disassemblers so that they could take apart more things! What kind of stupid idea is that? It's like my bratty cousin Jason could make more and more Jasons until the whole world was filled with whining, bratty little cousins.

Nobody knew where the disassemblers came from. So far, they were in only one place on the moon. All the scientists were working to keep them there, and more scientists were coming up on shuttles from Earth. Pretty soon we might have as many scientists as atoms.

Dad and I were having cocoa at our tiny kitchen table when I asked him about the worst-case scenario. That's the most terrible thing that can ever happen. I thought the worst-case scenario would be that the whole moon is dissembled, but Dad said no.

"We wouldn't let it get that far. If necessary, the Moon-NASA Council will authorize blowing up part of Alpha Colony, using bombs big enough to destroy all the disassemblers."

"Blow up how much of Alpha?"

"As much as necessary," he said.

"Dad—*how much?*"

"A lot. But if that happens, we'll already have been evacuated to Earth. We'll be safe."

"But Alpha Colony won't! It will be blown up!"

"Nia, you really don't have to worry about this. The Council will come up with a solution. Meanwhile, Dr. Porter wants to see you for another language session."

I groaned. "I already told him all the Alienese I know! Jillian told him, and Ben told him, and he recorded everything, and anyway I don't like him!"

"Why don't you like him?"

That's the sort of question Dad always asks. Mom would just have said, "I don't care if you like him or not. You're going." I said, "He treats me like a baby. He even treats Jillian like a baby and she's *thirteen.*"

Mom came into the kitchen, dressed for work. "Nia, don't you have a language session with Dr. Porter?"

"No," I said.

"Yes," Dad said.

"I don't like him," I said.

Mom said, "I don't care if you like him or not. This is important. You're going."

"Nia!" said Dr. Porter in his worst fake-syrupy voice. "How good of you to come! And only fifteen minutes late!"

Julia Liu, who operates the recording equipment, grinned at me. I don't think she likes Dr. Porter, either.

He said, "Are you ready, dear? Don't be nervous, now."

"I'm not nervous." Why would I be nervous? We've done this a gazillion times before.

"Fine. I want to talk about the alien-language phrase that has been giving us so much trouble." Dr. Porter raised his ring finger, said "clanth!" twisted his thumb, and said, "pof," very softly.

"I already told you that I don't know what it means." I told him and told him!

"Ah, but we have made some progress with the phrase. We've studied every single occasion that anyone used it, and 'clanth' with the thumb twist seems to indicate a problem or trouble that hasn't arrived yet. There are English phrases that people say to ward off bad luck—you have probably heard adults say some of them. 'Knock on wood,' or 'God willing and the creek don't rise'—have you ever heard those phrases, Nia?"

"No," I said, although I had. His whole voice was fake-syrupy.

"They're superstitious phrases, and most people don't really think they'll keep away problems, but the alien phrase might mean something like that."

"What do the other parts of it mean?" I was getting sort of interested.

"We're not sure, but raising the ring finger starts a lot of alien sentences and seems to have something to do with... not luck, exactly, not fate, not victory, but all three rolled together, and all influenced by some other untranslatable concept."

Dr. Porter didn't know what it meant. Clueless, but he didn't want to say so. I said, "Uh huh."

"Try again, dear," he said, like he was telling a first-grader to color inside the lines. "What else can you remember about this phrase?"

"Nothing," I said.

And then—in the middle of the night—I did remember. I remembered H'raf giving me the bic!dul. He handed me the green blob and said, "But one more important, Nia. If this bic!dul makes trouble, you must to say this three turns." H'raf raised his ring finger, said "clanth!" and twisted his thumb, said, "pof," very softly, and said….some other words. What words? I couldn't remember. I'd been too upset about his going away.

If this bic!dul makes trouble….

No. It couldn't be. No.

H'raf and I weren't supposed to play with the bic!dul away from adults. He wasn't supposed to give it to me as a going-away gift.

No.

How exactly did the bic!dul work? How did it change shape?

And what part of Alpha Colony was being disassembled?

Nooooooo…

I stumbled out of bed and put on my clothes, feeling around in the dark for my shoes. Luna was turned off, in the corner. I crept through the kitchen, unlocked the door, and ran as fast as I could through Alpha Colony's tunnels. Security cameras were watching me, of course, but maybe I could get where I needed to go before anyone noticed.

Maybe a different part of Alpha was being disassembled. Oh, please, let it be a different part of Alpha….

It wasn't. I got to where the new bore tunnel started, and there were barriers and computers and a lot of machines I didn't recognize and three people, even though it was the middle of the night.

"Hey!" Security said. "Who are you? What are you doing here?"

"It was me!" I gasped. "I started the disassemblers! I threw the bic!dul and a construction robot cemented it into the ceiling and it started to disassemble atoms! It was me!"

They stared at me like I was a zombie about to eat their brains. "The bic!dul!" I screamed. "It was the bic!dul! Don't any of you speak Alienese?"

None of them did. They were one Security and two scientists from Earth, maybe experts about things that were coming apart. Which, right then, included me.

One of the scientists, a man with a beard that really needed combing, said, "Who are you? How did you get here?"

"I live here! I'm Nia Philips, and I started all this!"

"Come with me, miss," Security said, grabbing my arm. "You don't belong here."

"Wait," Uncombed Beard said. "Philips? The Angela Philips that's on the Moon-NASA Council?"

"That's my mom. But don't call her! I can fix this! We don't need Mom." She would ground me for 50 years. "Just let me go into the tunnel!"

They didn't, of course. They called Mom. They called Dr. Porter to find out what "bic!dul" meant. They probably would have called every single person on Alpha if Mom and Dad hadn't shown up, panting and in their bathrobes.

"Nia!" Dad said. "Are you all right?"

Mom said "What is going on here? Nia, what have you done now?"

How unfair! I said hotly, "I didn't do it—the robot did! I'm trying to fix it!"

"Fix what?" Dad said, just as Dr. Porter came riding up on one of the little train cars that carries rocks away from the new tunnel. He was all crammed in and peeking over the top. That would have been funny if I could have laughed right then.

Which I couldn't.

I said, "I was playing with the bic!dul down here—you know, the green blob that can change shape. H'raf gave it to me. I threw it for Luna when it was a ball. A robot picked it up and cemented it into the ceiling all sort of smashed flat, and now I think it's up there making new baby disassemblers and taking apart the moon!"

Total silence. You never heard such silence—more quiet than outer space, more quiet than death. Until I burst into tears.

Dad put his arm around me. Mom turned red, trying to hold in her anger. The scientists turned pale. It was Dr. Porter, who I don't even like, who said the only sensible thing. It was so sensible that I didn't even care that he said it all fake-sweet.

"Nia—think hard, dear. The bic!dul is controlled by voice, isn't it? That's how you make it change shape? Did H'raf tell you any words to say if the bic!dul malfunctioned?"

"Yes!" I sobbed. "But I can't remember all of the words! And anyway, the bic!dul won't listen to me because it's all smashed flat by your stupid robot!" The robot wasn't really Dr. Porter's, but by that time, I didn't care.

A pale scientist said, "There may be an intact central mechanism. Or each disassembler may have the capacity to respond to reprogramming. It's alien tech—we just don't know!"

Dr. Porter said, "What part of the words do you remember?"

"You know—the words about luck and problems! The ones we talked about!"

"And there were more words, as well."

His voice was soothing; I stopped sobbing, as long as I didn't look at Mom. She was going to ground me for a *century*. "Yes," I said, "more words at the end, but I don't remember them."

"I know, dear. Listen to me. I'm going to say some words that we linguists have learned in Alienese, and I want you to tell me if any of them were what H'raf said to stop the bic!dul. Ready?"

"Y-yes."

"Jelp click."

"No, H'raf didn't say that."

"Kulpar with a wrist twist like this."

"No."

"Tarn."

"Yes! What does it mean?"

"We aren't sure. But it seems to have something to do with the way machinery operates in—"

"I remember!" I shouted. Dr. Porter's questions squashed H'raf's whole sentence back into my head, just like that stupid robot squashed the bic!dul into the tunnel ceiling. I raised my ring finger, said "clanth!" twisted my thumb, said, "pof," very softly, and then, "tarn!-dal!-jump. You have to say the whole thing three times!"

Dr. Porter said to Security, "Did you record that?" She nodded. Dr. Porter went to the security screen, nodded, and told her to push aside the barrier in front of the tunnel. He stepped over the fallen rocks and stopped at the place where I said, "There." Then he looked up at the ceiling, raised his ring finger, said "clanth!" twisted his thumb, said, "pof," very softly and then, "tarn!-dal!-jump." He did it three times.

And I *laughed*.

Everybody looked shocked and Mom said, "Nia!" But I couldn't stop laughing—he looked so funny, and he was doing it all wrong, and Heaven knows what he actually said. I couldn't stop laughing! Later, Dad told me that was just a response to tension, but I think it was because Dr. Porter—serious, solemn, fake-sweet Dr. Porter—was talking to a ceiling with commands it could never understand in a million years. He jumped wrong, he clicked with his tongue wrong, he said the words wrong.

Dad said quietly, "Nia—you do it. Go on."

The scientist without a beard said, "I don't think—"

"Yes," Mom said, "Nia will have the right accent."

"Really, Dr. Philips, there is no—"

"*Yes*," Mom said, in her Council voice. The scientist didn't argue anymore.

Dad went with me into the tunnel. What if it picked that minute to disassemble more, and rocks fell on us? But it didn't. I turned my face toward the ceiling, raised my ring finger, said "clanth!" twisted my thumb, said, "pof," very softly and then, "tarn!-dal!" while I jumped just right. Three times.

Nothing happened.

"It's still disassembling!" I cried.

"Maybe not," a scientist said, studying his computer screen. "It may take a minute for the embedded instruments to register any change….wait….*yes*. Fracture 16A is no longer widening!"

Nobody said anything else. The silence bit me, sort of like when you know there's a mosquito sucking your blood but you can't reach it to swat it away. I had to say something. So I said, "Can we get the bic!dul out of the cement so I can have it back to play with?"

Wrong thing to say.

So I saved Alpha Base. I stopped the moon from disassembling.

Of course, I also had started the moon disassembling. Mom didn't forget that. She didn't ground me for a century, but it felt that long. Also, I had to apologize to everybody in the known universe. Also, I had to write an essay on what I learned from this whole thing. I wrote that I learned three things:

• Never play with alien toys that you aren't supposed to have.

• Language and accents really are learned better by kids than adults.

• If you have an alien friend who takes off for his people's colony world, so that he can't share in the blame for something he did just as much as you, don't whine about it because you have to take responsibility for the part you did. That's being mature.

• Don't trust robots because they don't get blamed for anything *even when it's their fault*!

Mom made me take that last one out.

But it's still true.

In the Middle Gray
by Valerie Hunter

Valerie Hunter is a high school English teacher as well as a graduate student at Vermont College of Fine Arts' Writing for Children and Young Adults program. Her short stories have appeared in anthologies including Real Girls Don't Rust, Cleavage: Real Fiction for Real Girls, One Thousand Words for War, Brave New Girls, *and* (Re)Sisters.

Cal had walked with Reg to town on three August tenths in a row, but this was the first time he felt nervous.

He tried to hide it. Reg never looked nervous at all, with her chin held high and her shoulders squared. Then again, Reg had nothing to worry about.

His older sister was the most brilliant tinker Cal knew, and also the most enterprising. Three years ago, when Reg was barely ten but already able to make or fix anything, a neighbor hired her to go to Hartland and pretend to be his son and take the exam to get into the Mechanical Institute in the States. Reg had passed both the written and practical tests with flying colors, and every year after that, she'd been hired by someone else and had been just as successful, getting paid more each year.

This year, now that Cal was ten, she'd gotten him hired, as well. Cal knew he wasn't nearly as brilliant as Reg, but she'd been convinced he was ready. "You're up against amateurs who've never seen real competition and rich kids who see this as their ticket out of the Territories but who can't tell a flit sprocket from a tomb wheel. You'll have no difficulty getting Winston Kearns in."

Winston Kearns was the boy Cal had been hired to be. Winston had tried to get in himself last year, when he was eleven, and failed.

Reg prepared Cal for the written test, quizzing him on questions until he had them memorized. They were mostly common sense.

Reg designed the practical component for him, too: a contraption that measured and poured flour very precisely. Cal thought it was stupid— it took at least as long as it would for a person to do the same task, if not longer— but Reg said it was exactly the type of machine the competition judges liked. So Cal built it to Reg's specifications, and it worked well, even if it was stupid.

The competition had been three weeks ago. Cal knew he'd done well on the written test, and his machine had worked just fine and hadn't looked any more pointless than most of the other gadgets there. But he'd fumbled and flustered his way through the interview even though he'd known all the answers, and he'd been clumsy disassembling and reassembling the machine.

Now he and Reg were walking to town to get the newspaper that printed the list of who had been accepted to the Institute, and despite Reg's reassurances that Winston Kearns' name would be there, Cal wasn't sure.

"I don't know why you're so worried," Reg said for the hundredth time. "You were taught by the best—me. Next year you can take over my business altogether, and I can get in as myself."

Reg would be thirteen next year, the oldest age the Institute accepted. It made Cal happy to think of her going, but he didn't like thinking about pretending to be someone else again. The whole idea of getting someone else into the Institute muddled his head. Lying and cheating were wrong, and what Reg and he were doing seemed like both. Yet here were adults hiring them to do it, and their own parents allowing it like it was nothing at all.

When Cal mentioned this to Reg, she snorted. "Are you five years old? Haven't you figured out that's the way of things in the Territories? If you're not willing to lie and cheat a little, you'll never get anywhere."

When Cal just looked at her, not really sure what she meant but unwilling to ask, Reg's expression softened. "The Institute accepts anyone from the States without even a test. It's only in the Territories that they have these silly competitions, because they think we're backwards riff-raff who shouldn't be allowed to go east unless we're something truly special."

"But that's not fair," Cal blurted out.

"Obviously! So what's wrong with cheating a system that's already unfair?"

He didn't answer because he didn't have an answer. He knew it wasn't right, the people of the Territories always being treated like second-class citizens, but Ma was fond of saying two wrongs didn't make a right.

So he asked Ma about it. She didn't snort at him. Instead she looked thoughtful.

"It doesn't entirely sit right with me, either," she said finally. "But sometimes things aren't as black and white as we'd like them to be. Maybe we just have to get used to living in the middle gray."

Cal pictured a great rolling fog. It was easy to be confused in a fog like that.

"Anyhow," Ma said, "I trust you and Reg to make your own decisions on the matter."

Cal wasn't sure he had made the decision, though. Reg had made it for him. The fog continued to swirl around him, even now as they walked to town. Maybe it would clear if Winston Kearns' name was on the list.

When they got to town, Reg bought a copy of the *Prairie Sentinel*. Just like every year, she waited until they were back out on the prairie to look at it, but this time she passed it to Cal rather than opening it herself.

Cal turned to page eight. Twenty names. Albert Brunner, the boy Reg had pretended to be, was right at the top.

Cal read the list three times. Winston Kearns' name was not there.

The fog thickened until the entire world felt gray. He'd failed.

No one said much after. Not Reg. Not Ma or Pa or his little sister Agatha. Cal didn't even hear from Winston Kearns' father, since Reg took care of that correspondence.

He wished someone would say *something*, but maybe, like him, they didn't know what to say.

Reg kept working with him in their workshop in the barn like nothing was different. In October, she shoved a newspaper at him. "Look."

Cal had been avoiding newspapers since August, but he took it and looked where she pointed. The article was about a clock being installed in Boston near the Mechanical Institute. The senior students had designed it, creating different figures to emerge at each hour.

The article wasn't long enough to excite Cal's imagination. "Maybe you'll get to see it when you go to the Institute," he said.

"Never mind that. Let's build a clock like that ourselves."

"Us?" Was she pure crazy?

"Not an enormous public clock, but a little one. You're good with miniatures, and I'm good with plans. I bet we can do it."

"What about your entry for the competition?" Reg usually

spent months planning and building her new invention. Last year she'd started even earlier, since they had both his and hers to work on. "Or is this going to be your entry?"

"I've got plenty of time to think about the competition," Reg said. "This is just for us."

So Reg made the plans, and Cal helped with everything else—cleaning and fixing an old mantel clock and building the frame to go around it with twelve doors and twelve little rooms inside to hold the figures. He came up with the figures himself, fashioning them from tin, painting on the tiny details, and then rigging them up with the mechanisms he and Reg designed to make them move.

Every day the hour between the end of school and the beginning of their chores was filled with their clock, and Cal remembered just how satisfying Reg's projects were. When he was working on the clock, he didn't think about failing or whether or not he'd be hired for the competition again or anything else that troubled him the rest of the time. He just focused on the task in front of him, and if something didn't work the first time, well, he just kept trying till it did.

When the weather got cold, they moved from their workshop to the house, and even though Ma complained about the mess, she marveled at those tiny figures in a way that made Cal feel proud. Even Agatha, who previously thought all of Reg's and Cal's work to be dirty and boring, watched him paint and offered opinions on color choices.

The article about the clock in Boston hadn't said what the figures were, so Cal made up his own, everything from a queen and a knight to a farmer and a steam locomotive engineer. He tried to give the queen Reg's fierce expression, but in the end she just had beady eyes and a bit of a frown as she thumped her staff emphatically.

"You could have picked one theme and stuck to it," Reg said as they worked at attaching the figures.

Cal shrugged. He liked the randomness of the figures. It was their clock, after all.

When they finished, Reg showed it off to the whole family, nudging the hour hand forward so they could see all twelve figures in quick succession. Cal watched with wonder, as though he hadn't helped make it.

Afterwards, Reg hung it in their workshop. "Because it's ours, and we should never forget how good we are at tinkering," she said, and Cal nodded even though he knew he wasn't half the tinker she was.

"All right, time to apply ourselves," said Reg, like the clock hadn't been work. Well, maybe it hadn't been; it had been fun. "This is the year we get Winston Kearns into the Institute."

Time seemed to stutter a moment, and Cal had to swallow a few times before he could speak. "They've hired me again?"

Reg avoided his eyes. "They've hired *me*."

No. No, that was all wrong. This was the last year Reg was eligible to get into the Institute. This was the year she was supposed to be herself.

He tried to say that, but the words wouldn't come out right. "But you... what...? You can't..."

Reg raised her eyebrows. "Sure I can. I've done it for the past three years, haven't I? And I can pass for a thirteen-year-old boy for another few years after this, at least. Think of the money I'll make!"

The money she would have been happy to have him earn, if he'd been able to. This was *his* fault.

"You should enter for yourself," he insisted. "Let me be Winston Kearns."

As soon as the words were out of his mouth, he felt foolish. He hadn't been good enough last year, and now it was too late.

"You need another year apprenticing with me," Reg said.

"We'll hire you out again next year. Now let's go. I've got a plan for a mechanical churn..."

Ma tried to talk her out of it at supper. "You're being short-sighted, Regina. Think of the money you'll make down the road with a proper education. We can get by fine without your money, right, John?"

"Yes," Pa said, his tone neutral.

"But an education is no guarantee," Reg argued. "How many people around here would be looking to hire a mechanical engineer? They'd think me too posh. And in the States, even with an education they might still think I'm some know-nothing girl from the Territories. A bird in the hand is worth two in the bush—I can keep making money this way for a few more years, and once I'm grown I can get all sorts of jobs as a tinker."

Cal waited for Ma to keep arguing, to tell Reg she shouldn't do it. But Ma just frowned. "If you're sure..."

"I am," Reg said. "There's nothing more to say about it."

Cal thought there was, but he couldn't seem to find the words.

They set to work on the churn, even though Cal hated every moment of it. It made a clattery racket that gave him a headache, even though Reg kept trying to make it quieter.

"Anyhow, it works. That's all that matters. The judges won't care about the noise."

"How do you know?" he asked.

"Those judges don't care a whit about how good a mechanic you are or what wonderful things you can make. All they care about is that you come with something practical and that you sound smart when you explain it."

He had failed miserably at that, at sounding posh and polished. He'd practiced everything else, but he hadn't been able to practice not being nervous.

"That's why there's no sense in my attending the Institute," Reg went on, cranking her wrench so hard that Cal was afraid she might break the churn handle. "Who wants to go to a school where they expect everyone to be automatons? Where they don't want creative mechanics?"

"They let their senior students make that clock," Cal said.

Reg frowned. "The Institute would never let the likes of you or me in with our clock, no matter how splendid. And it is splendid, no doubt about that. So why should I want to go there and stop making splendid things of my own?"

Her expression was so fierce that Cal had to look away. In that moment he knew just how badly she wanted to go. Not because she wanted to stop making splendid things, but because she wanted to keep making them, to make them even better, and deep down she knew the Institute might actually be a place where she could do that, even if she was trying really hard to convince herself it wasn't.

The plan sprouted in Cal's mind at that moment, and it grew as crazily as a weed. He had to get her in. His job this year was to be Regina Robbins.

He tried to uproot this idea. He wasn't a girl. He didn't have an invention, and it was less than a month till the competition. He could hardly build something wonderful in that time, especially without Reg seeing. He would need a parent to accompany him to the competition, and Pa would think the idea pure nonsense. And even if he managed to do all that, the fact remained that he was the same tongue-tied simpleton as last year.

It was a horrible idea, an impossible idea, yet he couldn't stop thinking about it. He was the reason Reg wasn't trying to get into the Institute, so he had to be the one to do it for her.

One problem at a time. If he needed to look like a girl, he would need a girl's help. The only girls he knew well enough to trust with a secret like this were his sisters, and he couldn't very well tell Reg. It would have to be Agatha.

His younger sister was tricky. She liked to tattle, but it also puffed her up to be trusted. If she thought she was the only one he trusted enough to tell, she might feel too honored to tattle.

He grabbed her after supper that evening. "I need your help," he said, both because he knew it would make her feel important and because it was true.

Agatha smiled. "With what?"

"It's a secret. I'm trusting you, all right?"

She nodded, her smile growing.

He'd thought this next part over carefully. Agatha and Reg didn't get on. They were too different—Reg with her gears and clutter and Agatha all neat and proper—but they were also similar. They were both stubborn, and they both liked having their own way. Agatha enjoyed getting Reg in trouble whenever she could because Reg was always nasty to Agatha. Or maybe Reg was always nasty to Agatha because Agatha was always tattling on Reg. Cal couldn't quite tell.

But both his sisters got along with him, and right now that was all that mattered.

"I got hired to get someone into the Institute. A girl."

Agatha's eyes got wider, and then they narrowed. "A girl? Why didn't they hire Reg?"

"She was already hired."

Agatha continued to look at him. Cal waited for her to ask why anyone would hire the likes of him, but maybe she was too nice to say that. Instead she said, "Reg doesn't know?"

He nodded.

"Who arranged it?"

"I did. On the sly."

Agatha's eyebrows knit together. She knew as well as Cal did that he was not a sneaky person.

"I want to prove Reg wrong," he blurted out. "That I can do this as well as she can. But on the off chance I don't get in... I don't want her to know I failed again."

These half-truths seemed to make sense to Agatha, just like he figured they would. "How can I help?" she asked.

"Can you help me be a convincing girl?" he asked.

All the skepticism cleared from Agatha's face. "Of course."

Agatha proved an excellent ally. She borrowed one of Ma's old dresses for him, and even though he felt ridiculous in it and Agatha giggled as soon as she saw him, she managed to keep a straight face after that. She also found Reg's braid of hair that Ma had kept when Reg cut it off before that first competition. Cal and Reg had nearly the same shade of hair, and after a lot of hair pins stabbing his scalp, Agatha managed to get it attached.

"Do I look convincing?" Cal asked.

"Maybe... Get up and walk."

Cal walked across his bedroom.

"Why are you walking like a baby who's just learned how?" Agatha asked.

"I don't want to get my legs tangled in the skirt," he admitted.

Agatha snorted. "That's not going to happen. Walk like a normal person."

He did, and sure enough he didn't trip. "Better?" he asked.

She nodded. At her direction, he also practiced sitting down and getting up. He wondered if Reg had felt this strange the first time she'd pretended to be a boy. He bet not. Reg always seemed to know exactly what she was doing.

"Now introduce yourself as whoever it is you're supposed to be," Agatha said.

His mind searched wildly for a name as he stood up and squared his shoulders like Reg. "Hello, I'm Alice Anderson," he said, trying to make his voice higher.

Agatha snorted again. "Girls don't talk like that. And they don't stand with their shoulders like that, either."

"Reg does," he pointed out.

Agatha narrowed her eyes, and for a moment he thought she'd guessed it was Reg he was trying to be. But all she said was, "Reg doesn't count."

"How should I sound?"

"Just talk normally."

So they practiced until bedtime, when he was allowed to be himself again and go to sleep.

Next Cal needed a gadget to bring. There wasn't enough time to make something complicated, something worthy of being entered under Reg's name.

It would have to be the clock.

The idea came to him almost immediately, but he pushed it aside. Reg said the judges would never appreciate the clock, that it was just for themselves. Taking it out of the barn would be all wrong. Reg would never approve.

But Reg wouldn't approve of any part of his plan. And Reg's whole argument against the Institute was that she didn't want to attend a school that wouldn't accept their clock. If he could get her in using the clock, well, that would prove her wrong.

He felt like he was in Ma's middle gray again, choked by a dense fog. But the clock was the only option he had, so it would have to do.

He needed to practice disassembling and reassembling it, which was a problem because Reg was in the barn whenever he was. Of course he knew how to take the clock apart and put it together; after all, he'd helped build it. But he'd known what he was doing with the gadget last year, too, and that hadn't kept him from looking like a fumbling fool at the competition. This time he wanted to practice till his hands knew exactly what to do without even having to think about it, because his head would probably be in a muddle.

The only time he had a moment in the barn alone was when

he milked the cows morning and night, so he did that quickly and then popped out and put back in one of the clock's twelve figures, each of which had its own unique little mechanism. It didn't seem like enough practice, so he started getting up and sneaking out to the barn after everyone had gone to sleep, taking apart the whole clock, gears, figures, and all, and then putting it back together by lantern light.

Reg noticed. Not the clock, but him, how tired he was. She glared at him with her sharp eyes.

"Are you ill?"

"No," he said, stifling a yawn.

"What's the matter, then? You look dreadful!"

"I'm fine," he mumbled.

"You're really not," she said, but to his relief she didn't say anything else.

Ma noticed, too, and dosed him with her foul castor oil. He told himself it was worth it even though it made him want to puke.

He knew he was going to have to tell his parents. He'd need Pa to take him to the competition and swear he was Reg to the person who did the signing in. Parents had to show their Territorial identification cards, too.

Somehow, though, telling Pa what he was doing seemed a bigger obstacle than convincing Agatha to help him or learning to walk in a dress or knowing every last detail of the clock. Because if Pa said no—and that was a very real possibility—that would be it. Reg would never get into the Institute, and it would be all Cal's fault.

Cal knew Pa loved them and wanted what was best for them. Pa had been the one to set up their barn stall workshop. He always appreciated Cal's and Reg's help with the farm machinery, readily admitting he didn't know the first thing about fixing a mechanical thresher or a steam combine.

Cal got the feeling, though, that Pa had the same mistrust of gadgetry that many of their neighbors had, and that while he may have been glad for their help, he really didn't see it as a job, not one Reg should go to school for. It seemed like Pa might prefer Reg to stick around and keep bringing in money rather than going off and doing something he didn't understand.

But Cal also knew that Pa could sometimes be made to change his mind. Cal had seen Ma do this with Pa, and he'd even see Reg do it a time or two, but he'd never been brave enough to try it himself. He'd always figured Pa was bound to know best because Pa was grown and Cal wasn't. Thinking otherwise made Cal feel funny, like the earth was a little less solid beneath his feet.

Three days before the competition, when they were alone in the cornfield, Cal finally asked Pa, "Could you take me to Hartland on Monday?"

Pa's eyes seemed to bore right into Cal. "Why?"

Cal took a deep breath. "For Reg. I want to get her into the Institute. She's going to pretend to be Winston Kearns, so I'm going to pretend to be her."

Pa's eyebrows rose. "This is Reg's plan?"

"No, sir. She doesn't know."

"But Reg said she doesn't want to go."

"I think she's only saying that. We can do all right without the money she brings in, can't we?"

Pa nodded. "Truth be told, your ma and I held onto most of that money. Figured we'd save it for Reg's dowry. It could do just as well for her education. But are you sure about her feelings on this?"

"She was set on going last year, before I failed. So it's my fault. I need to make this right."

Pa gave him another piercing look. "Who's to say you won't fail again?"

The words threatened to bowl him over, but Cal stood firm. "I might, but I have to try. Nothing ventured, nothing gained."

It was one of Ma's expressions, and Pa smiled slightly. "What does your ma think about this?"

"I didn't tell her yet," he said. It dawned on him that he could have—Ma was more likely to be on Cal's side, and she could have convinced Pa—but it wouldn't have been right. He needed to convince Pa himself.

Pa stood there awhile longer looking at Cal. An appraising look. "All right," he said finally. "Nothing ventured, nothing gained."

The final days before the competition flew. Cal told Ma the plan, and he practiced explaining the clock, taking it apart, and acting like Reg, all while holding tight to the secret. Now that Reg was the only one not to know, it seemed even harder to keep quiet.

On Monday morning, after Mr. Kearns had left with Reg, Cal got into the dress and had Agatha pin on the braid. She was quiet and seemed extra jabby with the pins. "It's Reg you're pretending to be, isn't it?" she finally said.

He turned to look at her, and nearly got stuck in the eye. Agatha scowled, and Cal tried to find the words to explain himself.

"Turn around. I'm not done," Agatha said. Once he did, she added, "You could've told me."

"I wasn't sure if you'd want to help if you knew it was Reg," he mumbled.

Agatha paused. "Do you really think I'm that mean?"

"No," he said honestly.

She jammed in one last pin. "Besides, if Reg goes to the Institute, I'll have my own room." She smiled at Cal. "Get her in!"

Cal had forgotten just how many people came to the competition. Hartland's main street was packed with people, and he tried not to think about the likelihood of his failure.

He reached the registration desk, placing the clock down carefully as he signed Reg's name and Pa vouched for him. The man behind the desk told him where to go to for the written test, and Pa squeezed Cal's shoulder before he left in a way that made Cal feel a little more confident.

He'd been nervous he'd be in the same room as Reg, but he was in a small room with only girls. Did they get a different test? A harder one, because the Institute thought a girl would have to be truly exceptional in order to deserve a place there? Or easier, because they thought girls were capable of less to begin with and were therefore impressed if a girl exceeded these low expectations?

He hoped it was neither. He wanted to be judged—he wanted *Reg* to be judged—as any other tinker.

They were given tests and told to begin. It didn't seem any different than the one he'd taken last year. He knew most of the answers because Reg had taught him.

Afterwards they were sent to another room, still all the girls together. Everyone looked calm. Maybe they were hiding their nerves, like he was, or maybe they were just naturally confident, like Reg.

He wondered how many of them would end up getting in, and then he shut that thought away and eyed their inventions. Many of the girls had all manner of big, brassy contraptions with them, the purposes of which Cal couldn't guess. All practical and impressive, surely. A wave of doubt crashed over him—the clock was nothing special, he'd be laughed out of the room—but he took a deep breath and tried to shut that thought away, too.

The girls were called individually to another room, alphabetically, so Cal knew he'd be toward the end. None of the girls returned. There must be another exit from the room they were being called into, but as girl after girl disappeared, he couldn't help feeling there was some kind of dragon in there eating each of them in turn.

When there were only two others left, the man at the door called, "Regina Robbins."

Cal marched into the room, his chin up. Reg wouldn't be scared of any dragon.

The room was tiny. Sure enough there was another door at the opposite side and no dragon, just a table with four chairs and a woman and two men, all frowning.

Cal sat, putting the clock in front of him.

"What's this?" asked one of the men.

"A clock I made," he said.

"A clock?" said the woman, her voice dripping scorn.

Something inside Cal began to shrivel, but when he opened his mouth it was Reg's voice that came out, bold as brass. "A clock," he repeated. "Like the one the senior students at the Institute made. There's a figure for each hour."

"Let's see," said the second man.

He wound the clock, and then pushed the minute hand ahead to the next hour, over and over, so they could see all twelve figures.

He couldn't tell if they were impressed or not, but Reg wouldn't care, so Cal tried not to, either. One of the men jotted something down in a ledger.

"All right," the man said. "Let's see its guts."

Cal grinned, because it sounded like something Reg would say. He began to disassemble the clock while they fired questions at him, all the same questions as last year, all the same questions he'd practiced. He stumbled over a few of his answers, but he kept going. More importantly, he kept his hands steady as he showed off the inner workings of all those tiny figures and then put them back together again.

He had no sooner breathed a very tiny sigh of relief when the woman said, "Tell us, Miss Robbins— how will you benefit from attending the Mechanical Institute?"

Cal fumbled the screwdriver in his hand. It was hardly the most difficult question he'd been asked, but it was the only one he hadn't been prepared for. Maybe it was new this year, or maybe they only asked it to girls, or—

"Miss Robbins?" the woman prompted.

A dozen answers rolled through his head, all of them about what a wonderful opportunity it would be, but when he opened his mouth he said, "Truth be told, you can accept me or not. Even if I don't end up going to your posh school, I'm still a mechanic, and I'll still go on tinkering. It would be nice to learn things official-like, but if you don't end up taking me, that's your own loss. Because I'm a fine mechanic."

Somewhere deep inside, Cal cringed a little, but he smiled Reg's fierce smile and didn't let it waver, even when no one smiled back.

"Thank you. You're dismissed," the woman said, and Cal strode out of the room.

Out in the crowded hall, he faltered. What had he done? Hadn't Reg herself said that the judges didn't want anyone's true self, just automatons? Here he'd gone and ruined everything.

But somehow, it didn't seem ruined. Somehow he thought Reg might even approve.

The weeks after the competition felt impossibly long. Cal changed his mind about whether Reg would get in every other minute till he thought he'd go crazy.

On August tenth, he and Reg walked to town to get the newspaper, Agatha tagging along. Once again, Reg waited till they were outside of town to look at the list. Cal wanted to rip it out of her hand.

Reg opened the paper, then grinned. "Winston Kearns is going to the Institute," she said, letting the paper fall to her side.

Cal couldn't breathe. He'd failed, and now he had to pretend everything was fine, because Reg could never know—

Agatha elbowed past him. She snatched the paper, looked at it, and then handed it back to Reg. "Did you read the whole list?"

Reg looked at her like she was crazy. "Why would I?"

"Just read it," Agatha said, her voice as fierce as Reg's at her fiercest.

Reg looked at the paper again, and her face went still, like it had somehow frozen. Cal felt frozen, too, because hope was rising all around him but he couldn't quite believe it. He managed to look over Reg's shoulder at the list, at her name on the list, Regina Robbins, really there, and surely they couldn't take it back, couldn't—

Reg's head came up slowly, swiveling from Agatha to Cal. "How...?"

It was the first time he'd ever heard Reg speechless.

Agatha was all but dancing. "Cal did it! Cal was you!" Her eyes widened, and she turned to Cal. "It's not a secret anymore, right?"

"No," he managed to say.

"Good." Agatha nudged Reg. "You should thank him."

Reg still didn't say anything. Cal wondered if she ever would. The euphoric feeling of his victory faded into a cold dread that what he'd done was all wrong.

Agatha sighed. "Can I go tell Ma and Pa?"

Neither of them said anything, so Agatha ran ahead.

"Are you mad?" Cal asked.

"No. I... How did you manage?"

He told her everything. "So it mostly wasn't me. Pa brought me there, and Agatha made sure I looked like a girl, and it was your clock—"

"Hush!" Reg said so fiercely that Cal immediately stopped talking. "It was you. You're the one who did it." She didn't sound upset. She sounded like she did when they were in the barn struggling over some mechanical problem, and she'd finally grasped it and was excited to show him.

She grabbed him in a hug so tight that he could feel just how badly she'd wanted this, how happy she was.

"Do you know why I said I didn't want to go?" she asked, releasing him so she could look him in the eyes.

"Because I failed last year, and you wanted to keep making money. And because you thought the Institute would be an awful place that wouldn't let you make fun things, like the clock," he said. "I think the judges liked it, by the way."

"Of course they did," she said. "It's a very impressive clock. And it's yours as much as mine, don't ever forget that. But the reason I didn't want to go was because they couldn't see the brilliance in *you*."

He stared at her, not understanding.

"You still don't get it, do you? I thought the Institute must not be worth it because you couldn't get in, and you're so talented, Cal. And now you've gone and proved it and gotten in, you've gotten *me* in, and I want to go…" She laughed, a pure whoop of joy that seemed to fly across the fields like a bird. "It's like some kind of fairy tale."

"I don't think most fairy tales have gears and sprockets," Cal said, grinning.

"Then they're missing out," Reg said. She grinned back at him. "Next year you can hire yourself out again, and the year after that you can get in yourself…"

Her words deflated something inside him. He toed at the dirt. When he was pretending to be Reg, he could say anything. Maybe it was time to do the same as himself.

He took a deep breath. "I'm not sure if I'll go myself, but I don't want to pretend to be anyone else again."

Reg frowned at him. Cal thought she was going to erupt, but she sounded quite calm as she said, "What do you mean you're not going yourself?"

"Well, I don't know. I mean, Pa might not..."

"You just found a way to get me into the Institute, which was darned near impossible. I think you can find a way to convince Pa to let you go, too."

"Maybe."

"You're going!" she said. "We're going to be unstoppable there!"

He pictured it, their bright future. No fog in sight. "We will," he agreed, and they walked home.

Rela

by Marilag Angway

Marilag Angway started her foray into science fiction and fantasy sometime in the early '90s by reading books written by females for females. She had no idea that these books were far and few at the time and feels lucky to have had the opportunity to be inspired by female authors to think big and never stop imagining. Her various fantasy and science fiction scribbles can be found in publications such as Ticonderoga Publications, Rosarium Publishing, Bards and Sages Publishing, Hadley Rille Books, and Deepwood Publishing, among other places. You can find Marilag's bookish and writing and randomy ramblings at http://storyandsomnomancy.wordpress.com.

There were two things Rela loved most when it came to being a delivery girl.

The first was the opportunity for travel, mostly travel out of the city and back without being constantly pursued by government-folk who thought she was "trouble." Government-folk believed northerners to be "trouble," and she was as northern as she could get, with her dark, sun-kissed skin and her drab, homespun clothing (though she was only half-northern, as her father was so very much a southerner). But she was a child. Even government-folk were lenient with children. She was also a delivery girl. There was some respect given to Rela's job, because delivery boys and girls took risks most soft city-dwellers would never take on a regular basis.

She went outside the city borders and survived. Every time.

Travel was less frightening to a young girl of eleven, and with Rela, well... Rela was fearless. She knew exactly what she wanted out of being a delivery girl, knew what she would get in return.

Nothing ventured, nothing gained, her mother always said. Rela took those words to heart.

Which led to the second thing she loved as a delivery girl: her bright pink hoverbike, Iring.

Rela loved her hoverbike as much as she loved the feel of the wind whipping at her hair as she sped through the countryside. She loved it as much as she loved the taste of freshly-harvested mangosteen, a rarity even in Cebu City, with its lackluster farms and poor soil quality. Iring had taken Rela many places by her sixth month as a delivery girl, and everyone who'd seen the bright pink contraption would know which girl had come to give them the goods.

Her father called Iring a monstrosity, though he supposed a girl like Rela *would* like the color pink. ("And why not? It's a bright color that you can see from kilometers away," she'd told him.) Her mother had wrinkled her nose and commented on the smell, saying nothing about whether or not it was fitting for her daughter. Her mother did not like the contraption, either.

Neither parent, however, stopped her from using it to bring goods to villages outside Cebu City's borders. She loved them both for not judging her too harshly. She hated that she was not interested in growing up as they wanted her to, but that was how it was with Rela.

Aim for something great, her father always said. Rela also took those words to heart.

It was the thought of her parents that made her remember

how far away she was from the city. It was the immediate
thought of being far away and stranded that made her frown
at one of the things she loved about her job.

Rela wiped her arm across her face, dragging the soot and
grime and grease as she did. Sweat poured off her forehead,
a combination of heat and hard work setting the downward
turn of her brow. She grumbled and reached, stretched and
mechanicked.

She kicked the hoverbike once, then twice for good measure.
"Silly thing," she muttered, tired.

As much as Rela loved her hoverbike, it had its sheer
amount of wear and tear. Iring was a hand-me-down, passed
to her from the last delivery girl who'd grown too old and
too cautious to make the journey north. When Rela had been
given the bike, the first thing she'd done was repair it. Iring
was a volcanic gas-guzzler, and it took a great deal of time to
finally get it running to Rela's tastes. She'd painted it pink as a
sign of victory. She'd named it Iring for the way it purred like
an overgrown, monstrous cat with a large toothy smile and a
puffy coat of white.

Unfortunately, not even Rela's mechanicking skills could
have prepared her for Iring's constant moaning and sputtering,
groaning and keeling over. This had been the third time it had
happened since she'd begun her journey north. She could only
imagine her week's ride back.

She reached a hand between the hover plates, her other
hand tapping the tool-belt that was always strapped to her
waist. She tried to figure out what had gone wrong this time.
She hoped it was fixable. Especially when she was stranded in
the middle of nowhere.

Rela was farther north than her regular routes normally
took her. Not many Cebu City-dwellers paid to have things
delivered so far, especially when most of the southern city folk
tended to stay in the south. The north had plenty of its own

dangers, like poisonous sea-creatures, volcano-mining bandits, and erupting volcanoes. Most delivery girls and boys did not take on north-bound jobs for this reason.

The job was a favor to her mother, who had a friend living in a village on a large island near the coast of Masbate. It had been an urgent one and something her mother could only entrust to Rela.

If she'd known Iring was going to strand her in the middle of nowhere, though, Rela would have thought better of it. She kicked her hoverbike again and began tightening the bike's pistons. She was sure that was what had been giving her the problem.

Rela squinted as the sun peeked out of the ash-gray clouds. It was a little past noon, and she was thirsty. She took a small swig from her last bottle of water, too little to quench her thirst but too big a drain on her resources. She had a mind to turn back, but it was a long travel south, and her water would not last. Her chances were better if she found the village, and *soon*.

The engine whirred, and Rela stepped back to admire her handiwork. "*Hala*! Back in business!"

She wiped her hands clean and placed the tools back in her belt. With one final inspection and a gentle, loving kick, she got on Iring, pulled the pedal, and hovered toward the horizon.

The village was empty.

This annoyed Rela more than it surprised her. She'd left her hoverbike parked on the outskirts, thinking she had to be considerate of the people who got nervous around volcano-tech. Most people *knew* about volcano-tech, of course, and likely some knew how to operate the hoverbikes. But that didn't stop the more superstitious bunch from hurling curses at her and gesturing the sign of the cross whenever she passed by. Rela wasn't very religious, but seeing the villagers' scared faces made her uncomfortable.

She wasn't a demon. She wasn't evil. She was just a delivery girl.

She should have known that northern villagers tended to live a nomadic life, moving from one place to another in search of fertile, farmable land. While the south had plenty such land, the north contained promises of even better crops amidst the danger. Likely the villagers had scarpered off, leaving empty shells of houses in their wake.

Rela sniffed the air and touched the soil. She stood still for long moments, feeling the warm wind on her arms and the humid draft stuffing her nose. She sneezed once. Twice. Wiped the tears that leaked out of her eyes.

Farther into the village, she could see the deep-grooved tracks on the muddy road. Carabao, she thought. They dragged wagons and wagons of heavy loads. She noticed the tracks had been overused, as though the carabao made several trips back and forth to carry things up.

Up?

"There was a plank," Rela said aloud, touching the ground again, her hand rubbing at the long, rectangular recess that began right where the muddy tracks stopped. "Here. They were boarding a ship. They were in a hurry."

There were a few reasons for villages to empty out. There was the possibility that the land was not fertile enough, the soil too poor or the waters too poisonous. There was the possibility that the whole village was a settlement of escaped Cebu City convicts, forever hunted, forever moving away, away, away. There was the possibility that it was the time of the season where villagers moved on because it was the natural thing to do.

But the land was not infertile. As Rela continued to walk farther into the village, she noticed the farms behind the houses. She saw the trenches of rice paddies, the plots of rambutan trees mounted on higher, hillier terraces. She saw the way the area had been carefully cultivated, and she knew that no nomad or settler would have given up so quickly on the land. She knew the people who lived there were not criminals. Criminals did not have the time to grow trees.

There was something else that made the people leave. Scared them enough to abandon the ripe fruits that littered the ground.

She didn't think the reasons mattered now. The only problem she saw was that nobody was there for her to deliver to.

"Matikason," she groaned. Deceitful. "How do I explain this to Nanay?"

Rela sighed and moved on. She plucked the unopened though overripe rambutans off the ground, pocketing a few. There would be no use in fiddling with the rice paddies, because she would have no time to sift through rice, let alone boil it.

She drew some comfort from the fact that she'd finally come across a functional water pump. Rela tasted the water—cold and fresh, soothing to a parched throat—and began to fill her water bottles one at a time.

It hadn't occurred to her that there was another reason the villagers had disappeared, why it looked as though everyone had been eager to leave their houses and their farms. Why, not even the carabao were left behind.

It hadn't occurred to her because she'd never been this far north. Whatever stories she'd heard about Northern Pinas she'd gotten from the old tigsugilon who visited the Cebu City taverns. He had many tales to recount, and often Rela had listened intently to them. Her favorite was always the tale of the ancient northerners and how they had stolen their god's treasures from the mountains. For that they had been punished, and most of the north had been destroyed as a result.

Memory of the tigsugilon's latest story brought Rela to attention, but it was the tremor in the ground that had shaken her out of her remembering. It was the heat and the smell of smoke and sulfur that made her jump away from the pump, that made her drop her third water bottle, its contents spilling onto the soil beneath her feet.

The ground quaked again, and she looked for the tell-tale signs of smoke. She saw it past the first mountain at the northeastern side of the village. It made her realize the exact reason why the villagers left.

An active volcano was about to erupt.

She ran.

At first she ran back to the rice paddies and the rambutan fruits. When she realized that she'd been running the opposite direction of her hoverbike, Rela turned herself around and ran back to the other side of the village.

The ground shook again, and she knew that the mountain before her would soon be covered by fire and flame and spewing rocks. Rela did not want to be within a kilometer of the village when the lava began to flow. Lava was a slow-moving fluid, but it would not be the lava that would ultimately kill her.

The sulfur would suffocate her first.

Rela found her hoverbike and revved the engine. Iring sputtered once, twice, and—Rela held her breath because she did *not* have the time to fix the darned pistons again—jumped off the ground.

"Go, go, go!" Rela coaxed. "*Go!*"

The hoverbike sped off, its loud rumble muted in comparison to the great, booming grumble of the mountain behind her. It was like listening to the sound of thunder, only in this case, the oncoming storm would not bring rain, wet and warm, clear and welcome. Volcanic rain would be hard and scorching hot, merciless red and deep-black ash.

Iring continued to speed through unpaved roads that Rela had just passed some half hour ago. The hoverbike did not stop, not with Rela controlling the helm.

Not until she saw the airship docking perilously by the

craggy hillside.

When Rela turned six, she had asked for an airship as a birthday present. At least, that's what her father had told her years later. He'd laughed it off the first time she'd asked, but when it looked like she was completely serious, he'd recanted his amusement.

"You'd need a lot of people to help you fly one," her father had said. "More than the friends you have now."

"You and Nanay can help," she'd said. "And Paolo and Promil."

Paolo and Promil were two of the dogs her mother kept in the kennel. Her parents were dog-breeders and often sold their litters of pups to city-folk who wanted a dog of their own. Only Paolo and Promil remained in the household, which Rela was fine with.

"Paolo and Promil are too old," her father had said. "Besides, they don't really think like you and I do. They think like dogs, and dogs don't like airships."

That had not stopped Rela from wanting an airship the year after that and the year after that. She had continued to ask for one up until her mother decided enough was enough and dissuaded her from asking with one simple phrase.

"Build yourself one then."

That had opened up a whole new world of possibility. But Rela knew she was beaten. For the moment.

The sight of the airship was not something Rela had expected in an area that was about to give way to a natural disaster. She knew only two types of folk who neared places primed for volcanic eruption: government-sanctioned volcano chasers and non-government-sanctioned volcano chasers (the bandits her father had warned her about).

She hoped against hope that these were not bandits.

Rela looked behind her and saw the volcano's rising smoke.

She gulped and looked up again at the airship that stood resolute and grand, the dark gray sky in turmoil behind it. It was then that she decided something.

She wanted to be *on* that ship.

With one last look behind her, she revved the engine again, and she took her hoverbike higher and higher, toward the airship's gangplank.

Towards a crew she desperately hoped weren't bandits.

She was wrong. It was known to happen.

"What in Maria Makiling are you doing on *my* ship?"

The woman had growled it. Rela was not so much threatened as impressed. She did not know how many female captains there were out in the Pinas, but she was sure it was only a handful of them. And by the way the woman had been scarred, Rela knew she wasn't one of the Cebu City folk, either.

Yep, Rela thought. *Definitely bandits.*

Which meant the ship wasn't the best place to be as a half-southerner.

"There's an exploding volcano," Rela said, pointing to the direction of the smoke.

The woman narrowed her eyes. "That is obvious."

"Then why are you still docked?"

The woman did not reply. Instead, she turned to the man next to her, who looked as equally shocked that a girl Rela's age would even find her way on board their ship.

She was sure, though, it wasn't her age the captain had taken issue with. It might have been the hoverbike she'd almost crashed onto the ship. It might also have been the way Rela had jumped off the hoverbike—while it was in the middle of *docking*—walked straight toward the woman, and asked to join her crew.

Nothing ventured, nothing gained.

"That isn't really a girl's business," the woman said. She

turned away, rasping sharply at the man next to her. "I've got no time for this. Throw her—"

Rela didn't know where exactly the woman had planned to *throw* her, because it was then that everyone felt the airship move. No, not move. Rela knew the ground had been the one doing the moving. Because the ground was likely to crack around them, especially with a volcano nearby bursting to its limit.

The woman never finished the sentence. Her eyes focused on the horizon, toward the direction of the smoke and fire-spewing rocks. She'd forgotten there was a girl attempting to stow away on her ship.

Yet the man remembered, for he glanced her way.

"What do we do with this one, then?" the man said, jerking his head toward Rela.

The woman looked at Rela again and frowned. "How much time before we can get the thrusters repaired?"

The man shrugged, bit his lip. Rela didn't really understand much of what he'd said, but she did know that something needed fixing and that they were having trouble getting it done quickly enough.

Rela may have been young and small, but she did know how to fix things.

"I can do it," she said.

The man and woman turned to look at her. It was the woman who raised an eyebrow and spoke. "Do what?"

"I can fix it. I know how."

"So can many of my other crew members. What makes you *special?*"

What did make her special? She wasn't. Not really. She knew how to put things together, knew how to take them apart. She'd learned these things by watching and listening, by skulking in corners of repair shops and dallying in places where people chased her whenever she got caught.

She watched fingers at work with a focus that could rival

the most meditative of priests. She paid attention to parts that made things move and work, and she pieced things together. She learned a lot just by keeping herself as small as possible, by using her eyes and observing, observing, observing.

She was small and useful, and she knew people always overlooked the small and useful.

"I can help," she said resolutely. Almost petulantly.

The woman remained silent, and below them, the ship moved again. This time, the shaking earth was followed by a distant rumble and a shout of warning. The man sprang to action, yelling and waving his arms to the crew below. The woman did the same, though she glanced back at Rela and tilted her head. "Kid, get yourself up towards the northeast thruster. Fix what's broken, and I might think about your request."

It was motivation enough, and Rela beamed at the woman, even as she worried what her next step would be.

She went straight for Iring, got on again, and flew toward the northeast corner of the ship.

Rela got to work.

At first it had been more difficult persuading the engineers to let her help. But it had become clear to them that perhaps she could, after all, and they gave way to her as she pressed her hands to the side of the cylindrical thruster to feel her way down to the broken parts.

Having small and steady fingers certainly helped. Having the brains to tell a piston from a bolt, a screw, and a cog clinched the deal. While Rela wasn't sure how the mechanics of airship thrust worked, the engineers around her were more than happy to give her some help as she started feeling the pieces with her hand.

Eventually, she found the problem. A stray piece had lodged itself into the cogs that turned and churned and allowed the volcanic gas to ignite into fire and flame. Taking it off required precision tools and small fingers. Without wasting any time, Rela used one hand to grab at her belt, releasing the small tongs. She reached toward the thrusters again.

The ship quaked.

Rela stumbled and would have fallen off the narrow platform if not for a steady hand at her back. She did not have the time to thank the engineer who kept her up. She did not think she could, with her heart thudding so loud that it overtook the noise of the volcano. She was thankful for the support, even more thankful that her fingers did not tremble even as she did inside.

Tongs gripped the piece between the cogs, and she pulled. The piece—a piece of metal Rela did not recognize—came free, and she began the next part of the repairs. She put her tongs away and this time plunged both hands into the thruster, almost as though she meant to crawl inside like it was a large air duct.

It wasn't very large, and she certainly didn't fully fit inside. It felt like it swallowed her up, though, and she gulped with a little bit of nervousness.

Not the time to be afraid, she thought.

Nothing ventured, nothing gained.

Rela gritted her teeth and used her hands to feel her way through the mechanicking.

"*Hala!*" she cried as she heard the *clink* and the *whirr*. "Done!"

It was right on time, because another quake took form, and this time, even the engineers' hands slipped from her back and her waist. It was time to go.

Someone gripped Rela's shoulder, urging her out of the thruster and back onto the hoverbike. She scrambled toward Iring, revving the engine, only to find—with panic now rushing in—that her bike had run out of fuel.

"Mabilis, mabilis!" the engineers screamed. One by one,

they hauled themselves up on coils of rope, and like monkeys, started swinging themselves across to make it back onto the deck. Faster and faster they went, until it was just Rela.

In their hurry toward the deck, they had forgotten her. Forgotten the little delivery girl with the pink hoverbike. The pink hoverbike that had stopped working.

Rela did not know how to make it away from the thrusters without Iring, and she refused to leave her hoverbike on the platform. But if she stayed nearby when the airship began its ascent...she gulped. She'd be burnt as crisp as if she'd jumped straight into the mouth of the erupting volcano.

Aim for something great. Her father's words drummed inside her head as her heart continued to beat quickly through her chest. Her palms became sweaty, and her head began to ache. There must be some way to...

She saw the rope that the engineers used to make it onto the deck. Coils and coils of rope that could carry her weight and much more. Rela looked over at the deck and tried to gauge the proper distance between the thrusters and the next landing.

"Far," she muttered. "Much too far."

It would take her several broken cords to do what she needed to do.

Rela revved up Iring one more time in hopes that the hoverbike would give one final thrust. No luck. She bit her lip and loosened the sharp knife in her tool belt.

Still seated on the hoverbike, Rela lifted herself up, hands reaching toward the rope. She began to cut.

A brilliant idea was one thing. Executing it wonderfully was a whole thing in itself.

Rela kept her grip on the rope as she swung her hoverbike—and herself—across. Within moments she was swinging toward the next piece of hanging rope, and after a great deal of concentration—and timing—she'd cut the next line of rope and grabbed the two strands. She tied them around Iring, cut the previous pieces of rope, and swung again.

She did this three times. Then four. Then five.

The sixth time she almost missed, for that was when the thrusters came on, and the ship began to float up, up, up.

Rela gritted her teeth and focused. She cut the next rope, tied it around the hoverbike, cut off the previous rope, swung to the next. Cut, tie, cut, swing. Cut, tie, cut, swing.

It never seemed to end.

Until it finally did, and one final swing brought her—and Iring—crashing down onto the deck, this time with Rela hurtling downward with sheer gracelessness. She smacked onto the surface with a loud *thwap* as she rolled to the side and finally landed on her back, arms splayed out. She breathed once, twice.

Then she groaned and tried to get up.

The woman—the captain—helped her up, yelling words and phrases she could not quite hear. Rela's ears rang with the noise of the volcano and the thrusters, and she steadied herself before trying to speak. When she finally *did* open her mouth, it wasn't a line of thanks to the woman or the engineers. It wasn't to ask to be added to the woman's crew.

"My hoverbike," Rela said. Her eyes landed on Iring and she felt her heart explode into a million tiny pieces.

Iring had made it onto the deck as well, pink and brown and altogether very grimy. It had snapped into two pieces.

The hoverbike had broken on the last swing.

There were two things Rela loved most when it came to riding on an airship.

The first was the opportunity for travel. The airship in flight was a beautiful thing, passing through the skies with ease. It had moved north, following the flow of the wind for a time before it doubled back in a southerly direction. The islands below had been specks of brown and black and gray, the water almost luminescent at night, filled with jellyfish that made Rela shudder with dread. It wasn't until they were moving south that she could see the stark difference between the lands in the north and the lands she'd been more familiar with, mostly green and pale, muddy brown, numerous plants and rice paddies growing in the distance.

The captain, Caliso, had been grateful for Rela's help and had promised to take her where she needed to go. After the initial shock over her hoverbike, Rela had asked Caliso again for a place on her crew, though this time around, her heart wasn't really in it.

She'd missed her parents by then. It had taken one more glance at her broken hoverbike and the feel of the letter inside her vest pocket to remind her that she still had a mission to undertake before heading home, and she would need to find a way to get to the villagers who had gone missing. Perhaps they'd moved south. Most villagers tended to move south.

Rela refused to give up, so she'd pored over a map of Southern Pinas. When she'd asked the captain where the villagers would likely go, Caliso had pointed at a place on the map near Cebu City.

"Refugee Hills," Caliso said, wrinkling her nose. "Too close to Cebu City for my taste. But if that's where you want to go, we can take you there."

The captain had stayed silent for a time before she tilted her head, almost like an owl when it's glancing curiously at something in front of it. "Perhaps..."

Rela's ears twitched, and she tried not to blush.

"Perhaps in a few years, when you're *ready*." Caliso smiled. It wasn't a mocking smile or a malicious smile. It was a normal, natural smile. A comforting smile. "I may be persuaded to accept you on board. We could use another mechanic with us. Maria Makiling knows a lot of things break down in an airship, even one as advanced as mine."

It was a promise, Rela knew. And one day, Rela would eventually seek out that promise. When she stopped being a delivery girl.

But for the moment, while she waited to get to Refugee Hills to find the missing villagers, to deliver her mother's urgent letter, she still had one more thing to do.

Which led to her second favorite thing about riding on that airship: having access to a room full of scrap and volcano-tech.

She had lugged Iring's pieces into the workroom and had asked Caliso for full use of the parts there. The captain readily agreed, and Rela had gone to work.

"Build yourself one then," her mother had said.

Rela's mouth curled into a smile. One day, she would ride Caliso's airship again. One day, she would move on to build one herself. *Aim for something great.*

But first...

She twirled the wrench in her hand and looked at the parts on the table, already thinking about what pieces should go where, already recalling the times she'd watched repairmen and women mechanicking away in their workshops. She hummed as she did so, eyes focused on the problem at hand.

First, she was going to rebuild her hoverbike.

Blaze-of-Glory Shoes
by Brandon Crilly

An Ottawa teacher by day, Brandon Crilly has been published in On Spec, Solarpunk Press, Third Flatiron Anthologies *and other markets. His short story "Rainclouds" earned a semi-finalist spot in the fourth quarter of Writers of the Future 32. He has also released several SF chapbooks, including* Science is for Real, *which asks the question, "What would happen if Hollywood blockbusters followed actual science?" Find out more about Brandon's work at brandoncrilly.wordpress. com or by following him on Twitter: @B_Crilly.*

Powaw had never seen a pair of shoes like the ones hanging above him.

They were suspended from one of the colony's power lines, tied together by their laces, unmoving in the windless air. Even through the glare of his radiation suit's helmet, Powaw could see the patterns of blue and yellow along the sides, and the logo for a company that didn't exist anymore.

He glanced up and down the street again. The Old Colonies all looked the same these days: gray, abandoned and empty of life. The buildings in Nebula-Eight were squat, metal structures with very little color, and most only one story tall; the power line holding the shoes was strung between the only two-story buildings on the street. Powaw guessed that one was a general store of some sort, because of the sign out front showing a jolly, overweight figure in an apron. The building across from it looked like an office.

There were probably things they could use in the general store. If any supply containers were properly sealed when Nebula-Eight was attacked, the rations or basic materials inside would have been protected from the radiation. That was what the crew of the starship *Aldrin* looked for when they hopped from one colony to the next. He and his friends needed to finish examining the rest of this tiny side street, like Lieutenant Hayvers instructed, but their attention right now was just on the shoes.

Or at least Kelsi's was. She was tapping her fingers together as her eyes flicked from the shoes to the power line and back again. Beside her, Tarek was standing perfectly still in his green radiation suit, seemingly staring at the open doorway of the office. It was difficult to tell where his eyes were pointed, thanks to the dark glasses they had found for him back on Nebula-Five.

He asked, "What do they look like?" His voice always sounded a bit tinny over their suits' com system.

"Blue and yellow," Powaw said, and he tried to describe the swirling designs in a way that Tarek would understand. His friend had been able to see when he was really young, so Powaw never had to explain what colors looked like, but he wasn't an artist, and he wasn't sure if he got the description right.

"They sound awesome," Tarek said when he was finished. He tilted his head and smiled. "Good condition?"

"I don't think anybody wore them before they got thrown up there," Kelsi said. "Why would anybody do that to a perfectly good pair of shoes?"

Powaw shook his head. "Maybe they didn't need them?"

"Remember that time Yoon tossed your set of styluses into the waste recycler?" Tarek said. "This is probably the same thing."

"Huh. Yeah, could be." Powaw tried to imagine kids like them running around Nebula-Eight, pulling pranks on each other, knowing that they could waste something like a pair of shoes because there would be another shipment of supplies on the way. Nobody on the *Aldrin* wasted anything if they could avoid it; they needed all the supplies they could make or scrounge.

Like a new pair of shoes, he thought, and imagined returning to Lieutenant Hayvers and the rest of the group—including his aunt, who was out collecting plant samples—and showing them that he and his friends could handle scavenging on their own.

"How are we going to get them down, though?" he asked.

"Working on it," Kelsi murmured as her eyes kept flicking around.

"Is the line close to any windows?" Tarek asked.

Powaw shook his head. "No, I don't think we'd be able to reach." When Tarek waved his metal cane, Powaw added, "The lines look like they're bolted in place. Sorry."

Some of the adults had laser cutters that could break the power line, but Powaw didn't want to go back and ask for their help. Lieutenant Hayvers had been against letting them go off alone—"We're going to trust the kids to spot something useful on their own?" he had said—and even though his aunt and some of the others had defended them, Powaw felt the need to prove that he and his friends could pull their own weight.

He had overheard his aunt and one of the engineers, Luke Reed, talking in the galley a few weeks ago, and he hadn't been able to get the conversation out of his head. Luke had said, "We're stretching everything to the limit. The engines, the shields … the *Aldrin* wasn't supposed to be out this long without a proper stay at a space dock."

"We'll make do," his aunt had said, calm as always.

"Yeah, I guess so," Luke had muttered. Powaw had been about to slink back to his cabin when he said, "You ever get tired of this? Jumping from one colony to the next, scrounging what we can, knowing that we'll just be jumping again in a few days?"

"What do you mean?"

"You don't ever want to maybe relax for a day? Have a little fun?"

His aunt had laughed. "We still have fun sometimes. We just have different priorities. That will change eventually."

"Here's hoping…"

It had never dawned on Powaw before how much stress the adults must be under. Not only did they have to maintain the *Aldrin*, but there were sixteen young people on the ship as well, most of them younger than Powaw and his friends. As he stared at the shoes, he realized that he didn't want to collect them just because someone would be able to wear them. He wanted to walk back to the others, holding the shoes up in the air and grinning like an idiot, just to see the adults smile—maybe even laugh. That had to be a contribution that was worth it.

"We need a ladder or something," Kelsi said, breaking his thoughts.

"I haven't seen one yet."

"We could stack some boxes. Maybe bring a table out here and put the boxes on top. It's only … eight meters up, I think."

Powaw checked the clock on his helmet's HUD. They only had twenty minutes before they were supposed to report back to Lieutenant Hayvers. "Do we have enough time?"

"Not if we keep standing around!" Kelsi said and dashed off toward the office.

Powaw sighed and turned to the general store, just as Tarek asked, "Okay, where do we go?"

He paused, not sure what to say. This was always the issue when Tarek went along on a mission. Powaw admired his friend's intelligence and his eagerness to help, but there was only so much that he could really do. He would never suggest that Tarek stay back on the ship, but he had heard Lieutenant Hayvers refer to Tarek as a liability once, and part of him couldn't help but agree.

But he and Tarek had been friends long before the Old Colonies were attacked, and so he said, "The general store. We might get lucky and find a ladder. Come on."

They walked side-by-side, Tarek's metal cane brushing back and forth over the ground. He tapped it against the general store's front step and then the entrance to guide his way through, and Powaw followed behind him.

"Don't get eaten!" Kelsi's voice chimed over the com.

Powaw shook his head. The adults liked to tell stories about monsters that lived in the Old Colonies, describing bizarre creatures mutated by the radiation. The younger children on the *Aldrin* still got frightened, but Powaw and his friends were old enough to laugh the stories off; there were no such things as monsters. Just whoever had attacked the Old Colonies, and that definitely wasn't some eight-tentacled octopus thing that spewed fire.

Everything in the general store was coated in dust. There was a long counter at the back; behind it, a sign listed different goods and their prices. Metal containers were arranged in groups around the space to show the colonists what had been delivered; some of it could have been collected for free as part of the colonists' weekly ration, but the rest would have been bought, usually on credit. Most of this was useless now: food turned to ash, electronics fried and so on. Any basic materials the *Aldrin* could use would be stored in a warehouse elsewhere for the others to find.

Tarek rapped the side of the containers with his cane and cocked his head. "We won't be able to drag these outside before we have to report back."

"How can you tell?"

"I'm getting better at listening to vibrations, even through the suit," Tarek said with a smile. "A full container rattles differently than an empty one."

"Huh. Very cool." Powaw looked around the store but didn't see a ladder or anything they could move quickly. There was a doorway beside the counter, leading farther into the store, and a staircase at the back. "You want to help me check the back?"

Tarek led the way again. A window to the right caught Powaw's eye, and he wandered over to examine it. The glass had been blown out long ago, probably during the attack, but something had left a stain around the outside. At first Powaw thought the metal was scorched, but when he ran his gloved hand over it, he thought it felt sticky. *Weird.*

He was about to ask Kelsi over the com system, since she was better at science than he was, when he heard Tarek's voice: "Hey, I might have found something."

The back room was crowded with sealed containers, just like Powaw had hoped. He scanned the labels and saw several marked FOOD, plus a few other materials the *Aldrin* could use. "Good find! Did you just guess what's in these?"

"That's not what I meant," Tarek said. His friend was in a far corner of the room, facing away. "I was going to wait for you to tell me. What's in them?"

"Food, other stuff." Powaw frowned as he approached his friend. "What were you talking about?"

"Take a look."

There was a sealed plastic case hanging from the wall. Powaw studied the object inside and gulped. It was a long, metal rod about the same length as Tarek's cane, but with plastic grips for both hands and a few buttons and switches between them. On one end, the rod split into four rounded points, almost like a claw. Powaw recognized it immediately: an energy lance, almost identical to the ones that Lieutenant Hayvers and the *Aldrin's* security team carried.

"There's a lance in there, right?"

"Yeah," Powaw said. "How'd you know?"

Tarek tapped the side of the case. The model name and manufacturer of the lance were stamped into the plastic. "The letters are raised a bit. I could sort of make them out, but I wasn't sure."

"Good guess."

"Do you think it still works?"

"Yeah." Powaw studied the case more closely, confirming that it wasn't damaged. "The military used to transport weapons in containers that protected them from anything— heat, electricity, radiation, you name it. This thing wouldn't have been fried in the attack."

"How do you know that?"

"Research," Powaw said. Tarek turned a little to face him, a motion that Powaw still didn't really understand from his friend. "Lieutenant Hayvers said I might be a good fit for security—when I 'grow up a little more.' I've been doing a little research."

"Maybe we can see if the lieutenant is right."

"What do you mean?"

"If the lance works, we can shoot out that cable and get the shoes."

For a moment, Powaw was going to tell Tarek he was insane. Then he looked at the clock on his HUD, pictured his aunt and the others laughing and said, "Let's do it."

It took a couple minutes to find the switch to open the case. The front cover slid aside, and Powaw carefully removed the lance. Lieutenant Hayvers had shown him the *Aldrin*'s energy lances a couple of times; he thought he knew how to check its power level and settings and, most importantly, how to operate the safety.

The safety was a tiny button beside the higher of the two grips, almost in line with the trigger. He pressed it, and a tiny bar started to glow blue on the side of the lance; that meant it was close to fully charged. There were two square, metal objects in the case—extra power packs—and he scooped them up, knowing that Lieutenant Hayvers would want them.

"Okay. Let's do this."

Tarek followed him back outside, where Kelsi was waiting below the shoes. "So you think you can actually hit the cable?"

Powaw forgot that she would've heard his entire conversation with Tarek over the suits' com. "I don't know. We couldn't find a ladder or anything, though."

"Me neither. Just don't shoot me with that thing, okay?"

"Should we make sure it works first?" Tarek asked.

"It looks like it has a full charge still, but … yeah, you're probably right." Powaw looked around the street, trying to find something he could use as a practice target. "You think the others will hear the shot?" The range on their suits' com was pretty short, but the sound of the lance would carry.

"Yes, knowing our luck, and they'll probably come running. I wish we had found a ladder," Kelsi said.

Powaw eyed the sign above the general store. He brought the lance as close to level with his eye as he could, which was a little awkward with his helmet. He was trying to remember the stance that he had been taught. The lance wobbled a little in his hands until he balanced the bottom on his shoulder. He took a few long, steadying breaths and closed one eye, using the rounded points at the top of the lance to aim at the tubby figure in the apron.

There was a sharp whine when he squeezed the trigger. A bright red bolt shot out from the lance and missed the sign by at least a foot, burning a hole through the metal wall beside it. He heard Kelsi snicker. His second shot soared under the sign, burning another hole. Tarek tapped his cane a couple times against the ground but didn't say anything.

Powaw took another couple of breaths and aimed again, trying to put all of his focus on the tubby figure's belly.

This time, the shot pinged against the sign. Instead of burning it or melting it, the shot ricocheted off and plunged down the street. It soared through the broken window of another building, two down from the general store. Something inside crashed loudly enough for them to hear through their helmets.

"Holy crap," Kelsi said.

"What did you hit?" Tarek asked.

"The sign."

"So the sign must be made of ... something."

Kelsi snorted. "Thanks for that. At least you hit what you were aiming at, Pow. Now you just need to do the same thing again."

"Right." Powaw's shoulders felt tense—because of the thrill of hitting his target, or the idea of bringing back those shoes, or because he knew he really wasn't supposed to be using an energy lance. He tried to shrug the tension away, which didn't work, and settled on a few more deep breaths as he aimed at the spot where the power cable connected to the general store's roof.

"You can do this," Tarek said quietly.

He took longer to aim this time. His aunt liked to tell him stories when he was younger, the Algonquin legends she could remember from when she was a kid. She said it was important to keep them alive, since they might be the last two Algonquin left after the attack. He knew the legends weren't real, but his aunt also told him about how their people used to survive: living off the land, hunting wild animals and shepherding the environment. He was about as far from a hunter as someone could get, but his aunt did say that the spirit of their people was still inside them, and he wondered if that could help him here.

When he squeezed the trigger, the shot missed by at least a few centimeters. Powaw shifted his aim slightly and fired again.

There was a loud pop as the power cable was severed. The line sprang free from the roof, whipped through the air and then plunged to the ground. The shoes were jostled off at the same time, and Kelsi rushed toward them. They hit the ground beside the cable before she made it; she scooped them up and waved them in the air in triumph, letting out a long whoop.

Behind her, something roared.

Powaw froze. He thought the sound had come from the same building where his ricochet had disappeared.

"Guys?" Tarek asked, and Kelsi shushed him.

Powaw's mind flashed back to the monster stories the adults told, and he reminded himself that they were just stories to scare children.

And then something burst through the doorway of the building, and he knew they weren't.

The creature landed in the center of the street. It stood on two spindly legs and raised three arms into the air; each one ended in long, irregularly-shaped claws. Another roar came from a massive jaw that reminded Powaw of a picture he'd seen of a dragon. Something thick and slimy dripped from its teeth, its claws, and other random spots on its body, and he thought of the stain he had seen in the general store, around the broken window. About a half-dozen tiny yellow dots were scattered around the creature's face, and when they blinked, Powaw realized these were its eyes.

Kelsi screamed. Powaw grabbed Tarek's arm and shouted, "Run!"

He dragged Tarek toward the general store. His friend kept asking what was going on, but Powaw didn't have the breath to explain. He just knew they needed to get away from whatever that thing was. He glanced behind him, expecting Kelsi to be following, but instead he saw her disappear into the office building. The creature stood in the center of the street, looking back and forth, as if deciding who to follow.

"Kelsi, find somewhere to hide," Powaw said into his com. As he pushed Tarek into the store, he raised the lance one-handed, fumbled with the trigger, and fired a wild shot into the air.

As he followed Tarek through the door, he heard the creature roar again.

"Where do we go?" Tarek asked.

Powaw pulled his friend to the back room where they had found the lance. He shut the door and yanked Tarek to the ground behind one of the rows of crates. Their breath seemed to echo loudly in his ears; he hoped the creature wouldn't be able to hear it through their suits.

"Lieutenant Hayvers, Auntie Nuna—we need help. Please, you have to come get us right now." There was a code the security officers on the *Aldrin* used when one of them was in serious danger, but he couldn't remember it. With the coms' short range, he knew it might not even matter.

"Kelsi, are you okay?" he said, but there was no response from her, either. He hoped that meant she was hiding behind something that was blocking the signal. "The creature might have followed her, Tarek."

"It didn't."

"How do you know?"

"I can feel its footsteps." Tarek had both hands pressed to the plastic floorboards. "It's just outside."

Powaw pressed his gloves against the floor, but he couldn't feel anything besides the pumping of his heartbeat. "You can feel its footsteps?"

"Vibrations, remember? They're faint, but each step is pretty heavy. I can just feel enough to know it's out there." To his surprise, Tarek smiled. "Being blind can come in handy, I guess."

Powaw's head was spinning. There was an actual monster out there, hunting for them. Monsters were supposed to be things from stories. They showed up in some of the legends his aunt told him, like the Mishibijiw, a sort-of dragon thing that drowned people, or the Widjigo, a man-eating spirit that used to be human before it committed an evil act and got turned into a monster. His aunt said the Widjigo was so hungry all the time that it kept chewing off its own lips. Picturing that still gave Powaw the occasional nightmare—but the Widjigo was nothing compared to the thing out there.

He tried to think of a way out of this. With any luck, the adults had heard the shots or the creature roaring and were on their way. If they hadn't, they would be there shortly; according to the clock on his HUD, Powaw and his friends were already late. All they had to do was wait, and someone would be along to rescue them.

Except that the creature knew he and Tarek were in the store.

"We need to figure out how to get out of here," Tarek said softly.

"I'll think of something."

"I can help."

"Just let me think…"

"I said I can help, Pow."

"How?" Powaw asked, more heatedly than he meant it. His heart was still hammering. "I just … there's only so much you can do, right?"

Tarek frowned. "I can do *something*. There's two of us, and we need a plan. Do you still have the lance?"

"Yeah. I'm not that good a shot, though, remember?"

"Maybe I can line him up for you."

"What?"

Tarek tapped his cane, and Powaw realized what he meant. "No way."

"It's something I can do."

"It'll tear you apart. You didn't see its—"

"Don't tell me. You'll freak me out." Tarek pointed across the room. "Go find somewhere you can see the doorway."

"I'm not—"

"Would you rather wait for it to find us on its own?"

Powaw tried to listen for the creature, but he couldn't hear anything. "Fine. Just … if this doesn't work…"

"We'll be the first people to go out in a blaze of glory because of a pair of shoes?"

Powaw held back a nervous laugh. He got to his feet as quietly as he could and scuttled across the room to a spot between two crates where he was directly facing the door. If the creature came through, he thought he might actually be able to hit it. And if he missed, he hoped the creature would come right at him and ignore Tarek.

He heard a soft, metallic sound, and through the darkness he saw Tarek tapping his metal cane against the ground. Powaw's shoulders tensed again as he aimed the energy lance at the doorway.

A few seconds went by before something struck the other side of the door. The noise made Powaw jump.

He corrected his aim just as the door burst open.

Powaw didn't wait. Red bolts of energy spewed from the energy lance as he squeezed the trigger, and in their glare he saw the creature standing in the doorway, all claws and spindly limbs and oozing, gray skin. Every shot seemed to miss, and the creature roared as it took a step forward. Powaw screamed something back and kept firing, until one of the shots grazed the creature's side. The creature backed away, flailing its arms, and Powaw fired some more. There was one last cry and the creature disappeared.

Powaw heard a loud crash from somewhere. He stood there in the dark room, waiting for the creature to come back, but it didn't. He could hear Tarek's heavy breathing over the com.

"Did you hit it?"

"Yeah," Powaw said. "It's gone, I think. Good idea."

"Someone has to be the brains, right?" Tarek shuffled to his feet. "We should find Kelsi."

This time, Powaw led the way out of the general store. There was no sign of the creature. Powaw wondered if it went out through a window or the door.

And realized neither, when he saw the creature flying down the staircase toward them.

Powaw shoved Tarek to the floor. He tried to raise the lance, but the creature was too fast; one arm struck him in the chest so hard that he fell onto his back. The lance fell out of his hands, and the creature appeared above him. It clacked its teeth together and flexed all three of its massive, mutated claws. When the creature roared, Powaw shut his eyes.

"Get away from him!" he heard Tarek shout. Powaw opened his eyes in time to see the creature cry out as something hit it in the back. Tarek's cane spun away into the darkness, and Powaw realized his friend had thrown it.

Which meant he had nothing to defend himself with as the creature turned on him.

Powaw knew there wasn't enough time to do anything.

Over the com, he heard a new voice bellow: "Stay down!"

Bright flashes of energy filled the room. The creature roared and backed away from the front entrance where three figures in radiation suits had appeared. Each figure held an energy lance, and they kept firing as the creature tried to flee farther into the general store. Lasers cut into its skin, leaving deep, smoking burns, and the creature finally turned and ran.

One of the figures, Lieutenant Hayvers, fired three shots into its back, and it dropped to the ground. It didn't move again.

This time it was Lieutenant Hayvers standing over Powaw, one hand extended to help him up. "You all right, son?"

"Yeah," Powaw said. He looked for Tarek and saw someone else helping his friend up and handing him his cane. "Thanks."

"Let's get you outside before your aunt comes rushing in here…"

They stepped out into the sunlight, and Powaw saw Auntie Nuna standing with the rest of their group from the *Aldrin*. Kelsi was with them. When she saw Powaw and Tarek, she let out a long, relieved breath.

And then she grinned and held up the pair of blue-and-yellow shoes. There were murmurs from some of the adults, and Powaw started to worry that he had done the opposite of what he wanted.

The only person who hadn't seen the shoes yet was Lieutenant Hayvers, since he was scanning the street with his eyes. When they landed on Kelsi, his grizzled face twisted into an expression Powaw didn't understand.

Until the lieutenant's booming laugh echoed through the suits' coms.

They told the adults everything that happened. Hayvers directed two of his security people to watch for other creatures while the rest of the adults went to inspect the supplies in the general store. Powaw handed the energy lance and the extra power packs over to the lieutenant. He wasn't sure he wanted to hold them again.

"Not bad, son," Hayvers said.

"It wasn't just me," Powaw said, glancing over at Tarek and Kelsi. "Sir ... what do you think that creature was?"

Hayvers shrugged. "Something for the scientists to figure out. They've told me some about what radiation can do to people..."

"You think that was a person?"

"Been a long time since Nebula-Eight was attacked. Who knows?"

He wandered away to check in with the others. Powaw remembered the story of the Widjigo again, and he couldn't decide whether imagining that spindly creature as a human being made him feel better or worse.

Tarek came over as the lieutenant walked away. "So, security still in your future?"

"Maybe if I can drag you around with me." When his friend looked confused, Powaw said, "You figured out how to get us out of there, Tarek. What I said in the store—"

Tarek shrugged. "Don't worry about it. There's more important stuff than that."

"Like?"

"Who's going to get those shoes."

Powaw grinned and steered his friend toward where Kelsi was showing them off to Aunt Nuna. "If they fit you, I'd say you deserve them."

Trench 42

by Sherry D. Ramsey

Sherry D. Ramsey is a writer, editor, publisher, creativity addict and self-confessed Internet geek. Her books and stories range from middle grade to adult and delve into all corners of the speculative fiction realm. Sherry lives in Nova Scotia with her husband, children, and dogs, where she consumes far more coffee and chocolate than is likely good for her. You can visit her online at www.sherrydramsey. com and keep up with her much more pithy musings on Twitter @sdramsey.

Amari stared out the viewport wall at the graceful, gliding shapes in the water. The exterior lights on the *Llyr*, casting a shadowed glow on its surroundings, provided the only illumination at this depth. The underwater research station was on the move, its caterpillar-like legs trundling toward Trench 42 for a two-week stay. Amari had heard her mother and father discussing the studies the station might undertake at the trench, and now she sighed. All the scientists aboard the *Llyr* would be lining up to do their research, so there wouldn't be a spare gillsuit available for her own expeditions for a while.

It was going to be a long, boring stop at Trench 42.

A cluster of pop-eyed fish, no longer than Amari's thumb, sidled up to the viewport and peered inside, mouths pursing and relaxing as if they wanted to kiss her. Their unblinking eyes were huge in comparison to their bodies, and their dark scales flickered in the station's lights. Amari put a finger against the glass, opposite one fish's tiny face. It focused on the movement but didn't seem afraid. Then the station lurched in its sea-floor walk, and the school of fish skittered away. Outside, the station lights clawed a high column of rock and coral out of the shadows.

"Hey!"

Amari jumped, knowing, even as she whirled around, that it was Lem. If she'd been paying attention to anything other than the fish, she would have seen his reflection in the thick acrylic viewport as he crept up behind her. Her twin grinned, not at all sorry for startling her.

"What's so interesting?" he asked. "You look like you want to go right through the wall and out into the water. I don't recommend it without a gillsuit," he added with a knowing wink.

"Just some fish." Though she and Lem were alike in many ways, he loved the geology of the deep ocean—the trenches, the layers of sediment, the slow grinding of tectonic plates far below them—while Amari loved everything that lived here.

They started for the stairs up to their apartment in the habitat pod. The station had a central hub, where the science labs, hydroponics, algae beds, administration, and recreational facilities occupied five levels. Ten domed pods surrounded the hub, each of which held nine living units and a viewport lounge. The pods attached to the central hub via flexible accordion tubes, large enough for two adults to walk through side-by-side, but able to shift up, down, and sideways as the station plodded across the uneven geography of the ocean floor. Amari's and Lem's family lived in Pod 6,

Unit 2, Level 3. The viewport room was on Level 1, so they had to take the central stairs up in order to get home.

"We got a mail drop yesterday," Lem said as they climbed the spiral staircase. Their footfalls echoed off the metal steps. Packages and supplies came down to the *Llyr* periodically by mini submersible.

"I know. I didn't get anything."

"Are you sure?" Lem asked.

Amari turned to frown down at him. He was grinning. "What's that supposed to mean?"

"Keep going," he told her, pointing upward. "You'll see."

Lem was such a tease! But Amari was eager to find out what he meant. She ran up the steps, Lem keeping pace behind her, their clatter filling the stairwell.

Their parents were still at work, their mom in the science lab, their dad in admin, so the unit was quiet when Amari opened the door.

"This way!" Lem pushed past her. They passed the doors to their parents' and Lem's bedrooms and went into Amari's.

"Ta-daa!" Lem said with a flourish.

On Amari's desk sat one of the small plastic aquarium tanks from the labs, filled with a few cups of water and a floating plant, the top covered with a bright orange lid. A paper packet leaned against the outside. It read, "Sea Monkeys."

"Sea monkeys?" Amari asked, picking up the packet.

Lem sat in her desk chair and spun around. "Technically, a species of brine shrimp. Since you can't bring any of the fish from these depths into the pods, I thought I'd get you a different kind of pet." He stopped spinning and grinned. "It's an early birthday present!"

Amari shook the envelope gently and heard only a harsh, scratchy sound, as if the packet were filled with sand. She eyed her brother doubtfully. "And these shrimp are in here?" This must be one of Lem's elaborate jokes.

But he nodded. "Their eggs can go dormant for long periods of time and even dry out completely. When you put them in water, they'll hatch!"

Amari looked at her brother closely, but his brown eyes seemed more excited than teasing. "I just dump them into the water?"

"You have to purify the water first," Lem said, "but Mom and I did that in the lab. So yeah, dump them in any time you want!"

Amari tore the package open carefully and scattered the dust-like contents across the surface of the water. The flecks settled quickly to the bottom, lodging among the covering of small white pebbles.

"Now give it all a good stir, and tomorrow they should start to hatch," Lem said. Amari did, swirling the water around with the long stylus from her tablet.

"Tomorrow? That soon?"

"Twenty-four hours or less, supposedly," Lem said, peering into the tank.

"Hey," Amari said, "thank you. But now I have to come up with something amazing for your birthday present."

He grinned. "Yep. And you have only a week to do it. Anyway, I figure this will give you something else to do when you can't grab a gillsuit and go swim with your fish outside."

"That's really nice of you," Amari said. She eyed her brother skeptically. "What's the catch?"

Lem shook his head. "No catch. I just want to keep you busy so I can have some peace."

He laughed and dodged away when she pretended to smack him. Down the hall, they heard the unit door opening and went to tell their parents that the sea monkey project was underway.

Amari awoke the next morning to the realization that the habitat had stopped moving. In the two years that they'd lived

on the *Llyr*, the motion of the station as it explored the deep
ocean had become normal; it seemed weird to be motionless.
The station moved slowly—you could swim ahead of it in a
gillsuit, so you'd never be left behind. For the first year, Amari's
mother had insisted that she and Lem wear tethers anytime
they went outside the habitat, but when they'd turned twelve
on their last birthday, she'd said they didn't need them anymore.

Amari turned her head to see the little aquarium tank
on her desk and sighed. They must have reached Trench
42, so she'd be stuck inside. She squinted at the tank; no
evidence of hatched sea monkeys yet. It was strange to think
of them, trapped inside their tiny environment, inside her
small environment, where she felt a little trapped, too. She
loved living on the *Llyr*, despite the tiny living units and lack
of many other kids. It let her get out into the ocean almost
every single day to study its creatures. Now she'd have to be
content with sea monkeys for a while.

There was a knock on her door. "You awake in there?"

Amari smiled. "Sure, come on in!"

Her father pushed the door open and stuck his head in.
"Mrs. Cho is sick today, so she can't go exo. That means
there's a spare gillsuit. Want to suit up and come with me for
security sweep?"

"Yes!" Amari didn't spare more than a second feeling sorry
for Mrs. Cho, who was a deep-sea marine biologist and a
really sweet lady. She threw back the covers. "Give me five
minutes—"

"Whoa, slow down," her dad said, the skin around his
dark eyes crinkling as he laughed and put up his hands. "We
have time for breakfast. Just get dressed and come join us."

Amari was at the counter in their tiny kitchen in under
five minutes. Her mother passed her a plate of scrambled
eggs and fresh sea-kale. The eggs were reconstituted from
powder, but the greens were grown fresh in the hydroponics

lab. Amari smothered the whole thing with ketchup and began to eat. Between mouthfuls, she asked, "Who's doing the site plan today?"

"I think Dr. Peirce and Dr. Lagunov."

Two things happened when the *Llyr* arrived in a new place—security sweep and the creation of a site plan. Outside teams would explore the new area and map it in detail, noting anything that might be of interest to the crew, or dangerous to them. From there, the scientists would decide what to study. While the instruments and cameras aboard the habitat could gather a lot of information, Dad always said, "There's nothing like getting a look with your own eyes."

Lem strolled in from his room just as Amari finished her eggs and bolted down a glass of orange juice. He looked at his twin suspiciously. "What are you doing up this early?"

She smiled. "I'm going with Dad to do security sweep. Mrs. Cho is sick."

Lem looked like he was about to protest, but their father said, "I've already arranged for you to spend some time with Dr. Hodge in the geology lab. Mr. Cho has the same stomach bug as his wife, so they're short-handed there today, too."

Her brother's complaint was replaced by a wide grin. Both twins would be perfectly happy with their jobs for the day.

A few minutes later, walking through the flexible tube-tunnel that connected their habitat pod to the main hub, Amari asked her father if he had known about the sea monkeys. He smiled.

"Lem told me about the idea a few weeks ago, and we ordered them. I guess you'll be anxious to get back inside and see if they're hatching today."

"They'll keep," she told him. "I want to see everything that's outside first."

"I think you were meant to be mer-folk, not human," her dad teased.

"But here I am, stuck with legs instead of a tail." Amari grinned back.

"Best I can offer you is a gillsuit," he said, and they clattered down to the lowest level of the main hub, where the moon pool waited.

The moon pool was a rectangular, water-filled opening in the bottom of the *Llyr*. The gillsuits hung in alcoves around the sides of the room. Air pressure was carefully set so that the sea water didn't rush in and fill up the room. This meant that the crew could slip into gillsuits, slide into the pool, and be outside the *Llyr* in moments. Amari thought of the pool as a magic portal, connecting the dry world inside the *Llyr* to the undersea world outside.

Two other people were in the room; Salak Peirce, a plant biologist who looked after the algae beds that supplied the *Llyr*'s oxygen, and Miranda Lagunov, a biologist who specialized in extremophiles, creatures who thrived in places where almost nothing else on Earth could live. They both wore gillsuits and sleek, transparent helmets with their water-to-air filtration units on either side. These were the "gills." The filters worked like a fish's gills, allowing humans to breathe the oxygen they removed from the water. Oxygen was scarce in water, especially this deep in the bathypelagic zone, but the gills processed huge amounts of water in a short amount of time. The gillsuits themselves were made of a flexible, un-crushable graphene polymer fabric, protection against the incredible pressure at extreme ocean depths.

Amari got into her gillsuit quickly while Dr. Peirce and Dr. Lagunov said good morning and got into a discussion with Amari's father about the site plan. Amari sat on the edge of the pool, dangling her feet in the water, and waited impatiently to put on her helmet. She was burning to explore the new area. Finally she said, "I'm ready, Dad!"

He turned to her with a smile. "And there's our

timekeeper. She won't let us stand around here talking all day when there's real work to be done." He slipped his helmet on, the bonding edges meeting his suit to form a waterproof seal, and Amari did the same. Then they checked each other's suits, and once her dad nodded to her, they slid into the water together.

Amari pushed along the walls to guide herself down and out from beneath the base of the hub, then floated up a few feet from the ocean floor to have a good look around. The exterior lights on the main hub burned at full power and illuminated all the habitat pods and the area around the *Llyr* with a green-tinged glow. A bright red crab, disturbed by Amari's sudden appearance, scuttled away through a waving patch of orange feather stars and disappeared at the edge of the light. The Llyr had stopped with the leading habitat pod about ten feet from the edge of the trench, where the floor sloped downward into the dark depths.

Her dad signaled to get Amari's attention, and she pressed the helmet's communicator switch just above her left ear.

"Perimeter sweep," her dad said. Amari nodded. They swam in a counter-clockwise direction, away from the trench, from one pod to the next. Someone in the viewport lounge of a pod waved to them. Amari lifted a hand in return, but her attention was fixed on their surroundings—the ocean floor, the water as far as the lights illuminated it—checking for anything that could cause problems for the *Llyr* or the crew. And of course, any sea creatures in the area. Drifting silt clouded the water. The *Llyr* had thrown up sand and debris upon stopping and driving the station's stabilizer rods several feet into the seafloor. The rods anchored the *Llyr,* an extra bit of insurance when they stopped somewhere potentially dangerous—like the edge of a trench.

"All clear," her dad said over the comm, "but one of the rods on the next pod seems to have malfunctioned, so we have to check it out."

"Okay," Amari answered. They'd passed the second pod and headed for the third—their own.

This brought them about halfway around the *Llyr*. On this side, a high rock and coral formation towered. It was probably what she'd seen in the distance as the station approached the trench. It reached up half as high as their five-level habitat. The rock was pitted and rough, riddled with holes and small passages. Amari saw movement as fish darted in and out of the openings. A cluster of jellyfish undulated across the surface. Amari smiled. She'd love a chance to explore this more closely.

"I see the problem," her father said, drawing her attention away from the coral. He'd settled his feet on the seafloor and leaned in to look underneath the habitat pod, switching on the light embedded in the chest of his gillsuit. It shone a bright beam where the external lights on the habitat didn't quite reach.

When Amari joined him, she saw it, too. Two of the stabilizer rods burrowed straight down into the sandy floor, but one veered off at a wild angle. It must have hit something buried in the silt and slid off, bending the rod.

"Odd," Amari's father said, swimming under the pod to test the bent piece of metal. "These will usually drive through rock or just stop if they meet too much resistance."

"It won't retract inside the pod like that," Amari said. "Will you have to cut it off?"

"I think so. I'll report to maintenance." He huddled under the pod, snapping pictures of the damage with his helmet's top-mounted camera, and then set off around the rest of the perimeter. Amari lingered for a minute, resting her feet on the silty bottom and examining the coral spire, watching a school of dark fish the length of her hand hover near the sea floor. She wished she could turn off the *Llyr*'s external lights for a few minutes to see if the fish were bioluminescent—at these depths they'd glow blue. She loved watching the almost magical colors transform a dull outline of fins and tail.

A tremble shook the seafloor, and the fish flashed away. The rumble shivered up Amari's legs.

"Amari? Are you coming?" Her father's voice sounded inside her helmet.

"Coming, Dad. Did you just feel that?"

"Feel what?"

She swam up to him and told him about the tremor.

"I didn't notice it," he said, "but the sensors would have picked it up. We'll check the readings when we get back inside." His voice didn't give anything away, but Amari knew that earthquakes happened frequently on the sea floor. It might be dangerous if there was a big one while they were stopped so close to a trench.

The rest of their survey showed nothing else that might be troublesome. Peirce and Lagunov now wore tethers and had ventured out over the edge of the trench, shining large halolamps down into the depths and recording video and still photos. Later, after all the data had been viewed and evaluated and the plan assembled, the scientists would venture deeper into the trench.

"Hey, Jak, can you come over here?" Lagunov's voice sounded on their frequency. "Something strange here."

"Just wait here," Amari's dad told her, but she followed him. If they had discovered something strange in the trench, she wasn't going to miss out on it.

Her father pulled a retractable tether hook from his gillsuit's belt and clipped it to Dr. Lagunov's tether. Amari did the same onto Dr. Peirce's tether. As they swam out over the edge of the trench, her dad looked back and saw that Amari had followed him. He shook his head slightly, but he didn't say anything. Amari grinned. He probably hadn't expected her to stay behind, anyway.

Dr. Lagunov peered at a hand-held device in a special crush-resistant case. "There's something half sticking out of the wall of the trench," she said. "The halolamp's light barely reaches it."

Looking down, Amari glimpsed a reflective surface glinting far below them. The outline seemed rounded, but the distance and low light made it hard to see any details.

"Didn't we get any readings on it from the *Llyr*'s sonar?" her father asked. "We should have known this was here."

"We didn't," Dr. Peirce said, "and what's really strange is that we're still not reading it, even this close. The sonar doesn't see it, even though we can. That doesn't make sense."

Amari considered some of the possibilities. A shipwreck. A natural rock or coral formation. A plane that had crashed into the water and settled into the trench, to be partially covered by silt and sand over many years. But any of those things would have appeared on the *Llyr*'s sonar as sound waves bounced off it and echoed back.

Amari's father glanced back at the *Llyr*. She knew he'd like to get more tethers and descend right this minute to investigate—just as Amari would. But he was in charge of security, so safety protocol won out.

"Get whatever pictures you can, and we'll discuss it inside," he said finally. "We have to tell maintenance about the broken stabilizer rod, too. Amari, let's get going."

Amari felt a sharp pang of disappointment. In her imagination, she saw herself descending to the odd shape, halolamp in hand, ready to discover the answer to this minor mystery. She took one long, final look at the dim shape below. Something fluoresced briefly as it swam toward the thing and then veered off, giving it a wide berth. Amari frowned. What would spook the fish away from it?

"Amari," her dad said, in the voice that meant he was serious.

With a sigh, she turned and swam after him, back toward the boring safety of the *Llyr*.

They re-entered the *Llyr* and stripped out of their gillsuits. The suits went into the decon locker for five minutes to be dried and decontaminated for the next wearers. It was protocol to wait for one's suit to be ready and then hang it back on one of the waiting hooks so that the next person would find a clean and dry one. It was the longest five minutes Amari could remember. She couldn't wait to go with her father into the science labs and discuss the strange shape in the trench.

While they waited, Lem clattered down the stairs. "Did you feel anything out there?" he demanded breathlessly.

"I did! I was standing on the seafloor and felt a tremor," Amari told him. Of course Lem would be excited about it.

"We don't know what caused it," he said, practically hopping from one foot to the other.

Their dad frowned. "What do you mean, you don't know what caused it?"

"It wasn't like a normal quake," Lem said. "We didn't measure any plate movement."

"Okay, Lem, since you're here, take over my gillsuit," their father said, moving to the stairs. "Wait with Amari until the cycle finishes, and then you two head back to the apartment."

"What? I want to come with you!" Amari squeaked.

Lem protested, too. "I told Dr. Hodge I'd be right back!"

Their father shook his head. "I don't know what's going on, and the safest place for you is back at home. I'll tell you everything when I get back." *We don't need you underfoot*, he didn't say, but Amari heard the unspoken words as he turned and left.

"Grrr," Lem said, balling his fists. "I hate it when he does that. I was actually helping Dr. Hodge!"

"I know. I was right there looking at the thing in the trench, and I didn't get in anyone's way," Amari said, indignant.

"What thing in the trench?"

"I'll tell you in a minute. How can you not know what made the tremor?"

Lem shrugged. "Quakes are caused when the earth's plates move against each other, but not this time. Everything shook, but that wasn't the cause."

Amari frowned. "What else could shake us up like that? Something big hitting the sea floor, like a submarine or a sinking ship? But the sensors would pick that up."

Lem pointed a finger at her. "Right. We wouldn't even need the sensors. It would have been right on top of us."

The decon locker beeped, and Amari and Lem hung up the suits, then started back to the family's living unit. Amari told Lem about the strange round shape lying deeper in the trench.

"A shipwreck?" he asked. "If it lodged against the wall of the trench, years of sand and silt could have drifted over it."

Amari shook her head. "I don't think so. It didn't have the right shape."

"I wonder who'll go down to get a closer look, and when?"

"They won't let anyone go into the trench if we're having tremors." They'd reached the main lounge for their pod and began climbing the stairs, Amari in the lead. "Some of the gillsuits will be tied up with whoever fixes the stabilizer rod, too. But hey!" she said, brightening. "I wonder if anything's happening with my sea monkeys?"

"I didn't even look at them today," Lem said, and they pounded up the stairs.

In Amari's room, she turned on the light and peered in through the tank wall. One section was curved to form a magnifying lens for the interior. If she looked closely, she could just see tiny forms moving around in the water.

They looked like fuzzy specks with tiny tails, but they were definitely moving on their own, not just floating.

"They're alive," she whispered, "and they're exploring the tank!"

"Of course they're alive!" Lem said, nudging her aside so he could see, too. "I wouldn't buy you bad sea monkey eggs!"

Amari smiled. "I know. It's just so amazing how they can be dormant for so long—"

Her words cut off as a violent lurch shook the pod. The tank of sea monkeys slid across Amari's desk. She made a grab for it even as she stumbled on the unstable floor. Lem clutched at the desk with one hand and Amari's arm with the other, and they managed not to fall. When the shaking stopped, Amari had the sea monkey tank in one hand. The water inside sloshed around, but the bright orange cover stayed tight. The tiny creatures were safe.

For now.

"What was that?" Lem's voice sounded a little unsteady.

"Another not-quake?" Amari suggested, breathless herself. Nothing had ever shaken the habitat pod like that before.

Amari's room had only one smallish window above her bed. The twins ran out to the living room, where a bigger window looked out on their watery world. There was nothing to see there, only clouds of sand and silt whirling in the current. Anything else that might have been down there was obscured.

Lem hit the communicator pad. There were buttons for all the main areas in the hub, the other living units, and one for each family member of their own unit. "Dad? What's happening?"

Only the crackle of static came in response. He tried another button. "Mom? You there?"

Nothing.

"Maybe one of the quakes damaged communications?"

"They're not quakes," Lem said stubbornly, "but you could be right."

"The view lounge," Amari said, but Lem's voice stopped her as she reached for the door latch.

"Dad said to come here and wait. Will we get in trouble for going out?"

As if in answer, the pod lurched again, tossing Amari against the wall. She clutched the sea monkey tank tighter. Lem went down on his knees. He looked up at her.

"I think we should go and see what's happening," Amari said. "The comm pad in the lounge might still work. And what if we have to leave the pod? The only way is through the tube to the hub."

Lem nodded and climbed to his feet. With her sea monkey tank cradled in one arm, Amari opened the door. They hurried down the spiral steps and emerged into the viewport lounge, meeting none of the other residents of the pod. Everyone must be in their units or already gone to the hub. Amari went immediately to the window and peered outside. She gasped.

The tower of rock and coral tilted sideways now, as if something large had pushed it askew. Pieces had broken off and tumbled down to the seafloor. Some of the corals had been broken as well, their fan-like branches shattered. The fish and jellyfish from earlier had fled.

Amari squinted down at the seafloor. Something large and reddish-brown lay in a shallow depression at the base of the coral spire. It looked like a six-foot rock split in half, except the inside was hollowed-out, making it more like a shell, or a container for something. A large hole had splintered open in one side. Lem joined Amari at the window.

"What's that?"

Amari shook her head. "It wasn't there when Dad and I were outside earlier. It almost looks like a big, cracked eggshell, only made of rock."

"Is it part of that coral formation? That looks all busted up."

Amari pressed her forehead against the viewport, wishing she could get into a gillsuit and go outside for a closer look. "No, it's not made of the same stuff at all. The outside of it looks a little like brain coral, but we're way too deep for that. And it's blue. Most things that live and grow at this depth are black or red because there's so little light. It doesn't make sense."

Lem pressed the comm pad, trying again to reach their parents, but the same static hiss emerged.

Amari was about to say they should go to the hub when movement outside the viewport caught her eye. Fish returning to the coral refuge? But no, it was bigger than any of the fish known to live at this depth. Amari knew that sperm whales could dive this deep sometimes, but it wasn't that big. It seemed about human-sized. Maybe someone had ventured outside in a gillsuit, even though that seemed like a dangerous risk with the seafloor so unstable.

Then it swam right up to the viewport, and Amari saw that it wasn't human at all.

The creature outside the viewport was so startling, so alien, Amari screamed. Lem ran to join her, and they both stared at the creature.

It was the size of an adult human, and humanoid in shape, but it had rough-looking bluish skin, not scaly, but pebbled with bumps. Its head, tilted curiously as the creature regarded them, seemed over-large for its body, and many fine, waving tendrils took the place of hair. Two large eyes, dark and bulbous as those of the fish Amari had seen yesterday, stared in at the twins. Its mouth was a horizontal, almost lipless slit across the bottom third of its face. Two arms ended in long-fingered hands with softly undulating webbing stretched between each digit. Its legs were finned on the sides and back, with flipper-like feet that fluttered gently in the current, holding the creature in place.

"That is not a fish," Lem said in a strangled voice. "That's not any kind of fish, is it, Amari?"

She swallowed. "No. Not a fish." Not any kind of a fish or underwater creature that she'd ever seen or heard of...or even imagined.

The creature startled them by curling away from the viewport and gliding back to the broken coral spire. It darted around the wreckage, picking up bits of broken coral and rock, examining and then discarding them.

"What's it doing?" Lem whispered.

Amari stared at the creature, wondering the same thing. This didn't make sense. How could such a creature exist without anyone knowing about it? Of course, the *Llyr* was here to explore, to investigate and maybe discover new creatures and habitats, but how was it possible that they'd missed these creatures in all the previous years and years of sea exploration?

Exploring. The word echoed in her mind, bouncing off ideas and bits of information and linking them together into something that made sense. She looked down at the tank of newly-hatched sea monkeys in her hand, and at the broken, hollow rock lying on the seafloor below them. She thought about the shadow in the trench, something buried under sand and silt for a long time in the darkness. She thought about the *Llyr* trundling along, stirring things up, the stabilizer rod hitting something buried. *Waking it up?*

"It's exploring! Lem, look!" She pointed to the broken rock halves. "It's not a rock, not coral—it's...a shell! That thing just came out of it!"

"But what is it?" Lem looked at her, puzzled.

"Remember the shape in the trench? What if it's a ship, a

space ship that crashed down here a long time ago—"

Lem's eyes lit up. "And the tremors weren't quakes, they were buried eggs, or pods, or something—"

"Oh, no!" Amari's hand flew to her mouth. Her eyes were very wide.

"What?"

Amari grabbed Lem's arm with her free one. "Come on!" Dragging her brother, she ran into the flexible tube connecting the habitat pod to the main hub. But instead of heading up to the labs or admin levels, Amari started down the stairs.

"Where are we going?" Lem shouted. "We should tell Dad—"

"The moon pool!" Amari's steps didn't slow. She threw words back over her shoulder to Lem. "That creature is exploring. If it finds the moon pool—"

"It could come right into the *Llyr*!" Lem finished for her.

"Lem! Amari!" Their mother's voice echoed down the stairwell, but she was too far away for them to explain that they couldn't wait for her.

They both knew that a possibly alien creature inside the *Llyr* could be a very bad idea. And the creature could find the entrance at any moment. They ran down the stairs.

"Even if it's not dangerous to us, the air in here could be dangerous to it," Amari said as they slid into the moon pool room. "It doesn't know anything about us or the *Llyr*."

"What if—" Lem's words died as they both saw something floating in the moon pool. It was still below the surface of the water, but only by a few inches. The alien's blue face and floating tendrils were clearly visible through the water. Its bulbous eyes peered up into the room, as if it were trying to make sense of it. They turned in the direction of Lem and Amari.

Amari's mind raced. She was not so much afraid for herself or the station as she was for the alien creature. Obviously the salt ocean water and the enormous pressure at this depth wasn't harmful to it. It must have come from a world with similar conditions. But even though their technology allowed humans to venture into this world, too, they couldn't survive in it without that technology. If the alien ventured into the world of the *Llyr*, Amari didn't think it would survive long.

Holding up a hand in a "stop" kind of way, and hoping it understood, she took a few steps toward the moon pool.

"Amari!" Lem hissed. "What are you—"

She shook her head and took another step, motioning the creature to stay underwater. "Get ready to close the pool door," she told her brother out of the corner of her mouth. "I'll tell you if it drops down far enough to close it safely."

At the edge of her vision she saw Lem sidle toward the control panel. One push of the button would slide the pool door over the opening. Amari walked toward the pool, step by careful step, motioning the creature to stay. Did it understand? It hadn't come up out of the water yet.

"Lem? Amari?" Their mother's voice came again, closer now.

"We should get this closed before she gets here," Lem warned in a low voice.

"I know." Amari had reached the edge of the moon pool. The alien creature looked up at her through a few scant inches of water. Her eyes met the bulbous, unblinking ones. She tried to tell the creature *go, please go, it's not safe here.*

For a long moment their eyes held, and Amari held her breath. She felt a strange thrill of communication pass between them. Even without words, she thought the alien might understand her message. *Be safe. I want to help you.*

In a flash of blue and fins, the alien darted down and away.

"Now!" Amari hissed, and Lem hit the button. The door slid soundlessly over the moon pool, shutting the water out of sight. The latches clicked into place. Amari felt her body go weak with relief.

"Lem! Amari! What are you doing down here? This is no time to be playing around the moon pool!" Their mother stood in the doorway, hands on her hips.

Amari turned, the sea monkey tank with its tiny new life still clutched to her chest. She smiled at her mother. This was going to take a while to tell.

It was not going to be such a boring stop at Trench 42, after all.

After the Fall
by Mike Barretta

Mike Barretta is a retired U.S. naval aviator who works for a defense contractor as a pilot. He holds a master's degree in strategic planning and international negotiation from the Naval Post-Graduate School and a master's in English from the University of West Florida. His wife Mary, to whom he has been married to for 23 years, is living proof that he is not such a bad guy once you get to know him. His stories have appeared in Baen's Universe, *Redstone,* New Scientist, Orson Scott Card's Intergalactic Medicine Show *and various anthologies.*

Lucy Cardiff daydreamed of dragons. Not the fantasy fire-breathing kind that hoarded treasure and fought off armies of dwarves, but the practical kind, long in limb with gracefully tapered wings designed to soar, the kind that plucked fish from the sea or snatched pigeons on the wing.

In that regard, she was definitely her mother's daughter.

She turned her attention back to the task at hand, making a dragon, and opened the plastic cover of her portfolio. Dr. Rebecca Nelms' famously unreadable cursive script filled the title page. At the bottom, though, clear as day, was, "See me!" Lucy didn't worry too much about it. At least three quarters of the students in the class probably had a "See me!" Dr. Nelms was a bit of a throwback. Unlike the other teachers who used content analysis tools to grade work submitted on-line, Dr. Nelms preferred her students to submit printed work. She believed students took much more care when they brought their work into the real world.

"OK, class," said Dr. Nelms. "Good job on your preliminary design work. I can tell you guys have put in a lot of effort on your concepts. Some of you have your work cut out for you. Big dreams, I like to see that." She passed out her responses to their capstone projects. "But now, it's time to turn those dreams into reality. Did anybody not get their project portfolio back yet?"

As a talented artist, Lucy thought Dr. Nelms was right. She took as much care in creating her AP Biology portfolio as the paintings that consumed the majority of her time. When you held something in your hand and turned it over to someone else, responsibility for it was unavoidable.

"Now, open up the refrigerators at your workstations and take out the packages inside. We are going to inventory the contents and register your Neosaur so as to not confuse it with anyone else's," said Dr. Nelms.

Lucy went to her workstation, a black-surfaced lab bench plumbed with water, gas, electricity, and fiber. She opened the refrigerator and took out her cardboard box. The only thing on the box was a shipping label to the school.

"Okay, open your shipping boxes. Be gentle—the contents are not particularly fragile, but they are expensive. We still want to exercise care. Take out the smaller box inside. If you have trouble with the tape, go ahead and use your obsidian scalpels. Carefully, please."

Lucy touched her lab bench drawer, and the biometric lock opened. She took out the stone-bladed scalpel, sharper than any metal blade ever made, and slit the packing tape. She folded back the flaps.

"Go ahead and open up your kit box and inventory it. Make sure everything is inside. You should have four amino acid vials, recombinator medium, a viral delivery injector and a Neosaur egg. Make sure the barcodes and numbers are the same on all of the kit's contents. Make sure the egg is not cracked. Raise your hand if you find anything wrong."

Neosaur, thought Lucy. It certainly sounded sexier than chicken. She lifted the Bioscholastic Neosaur egg from the kit and inspected it. It looked just like a chicken egg because that is exactly what it was, a genuine chicken egg from a cloned, germline-patented chicken. The egg had a barcode printed on it and what looked to be a small Lego glued on the small end. The Lego thing was an injector port where she would inject the egg with a retrovirus, which would rewrite the DNA of the cloned chicken embryo inside so something she'd designed would hatch.

"Take the plastic card inside the kit and register your kit with Bioscholastic's website. This will give you access to tutorials and the genetic compilers. Let's do it now, so I know we all have access."

Lucy slid the card into the tablet reader, and the Bioscholastic site registered her kit. It asked her if she wanted to continue. She selected no.

"Log out, and put your kits back in the refrigerator. Recycle the shipping boxes in the back of the classroom. Then we are done for the day."

Lucy put her kit away, tucked her tablet under her arm, and retrieved her backpack from her class chair. She waited in line to see Dr. Nelms. With any other teacher, most students would bolt for the door rather than spend an extra minute in class, but Dr. Nelms was different. She had been a soldier in the Bio-terror wars and later, a lab director at Anthrodynamics, a major bio-defense corporation. She had been there and done that. Not only was she interesting, she genuinely cared about the students and the subject matter.

"Dr. Nelms, you wrote 'See me' on my project folder," said Lucy.

"Lucy dear, I need to talk to you about managing your expectations. I think you might be biting off more than you can chew," said Dr. Nelms.

"I don't understand."

"You are a very talented and ambitious designer, but this is a capstone project. We are pulling together everything we have learned about evolutionary pressures, genetic activation, and biosynthesis. Nature gets to eat its mistakes, but we have to live with ours. Your proposal is extravagant. At the very least, it is university-level work, and I don't know if you have the time or the skills to manage it. Flight is a very hard problem. There are not many people who can design a flying creature."

"It's a chicken. I think I have a good start. It has wings," said Lucy.

"Chickens have wings, but they don't really fly. They flap and jump to roost out of reach of predators, and that is typically the best that any student at your level can accomplish."

"I still want to try."

"Lucy, you wouldn't be trying to make a dragon now, would you?" asked Dr. Nelms.

"Dragons aren't terribly practical," said Lucy

"No, they're not.'"

Lucy left the room cautioned yet resolved. She could visualize what she wanted to create, and in her experience as an artist, that was the toughest battle. She was optimistic because she took to the subject so well that Dr. Nelms insinuated that she might have a career in the field of genetic engineering. Dr. Nelms said that all of life was art, and Earth was its canvas. She liked that idea, and it changed the way she viewed the world. Whenever she saw an opossum waddling across the road or a raccoon digging in a garbage can, she saw them as something special, like a carefully laid brushstroke, rather than just blurry background objects in her life. Lucy figured that for some part of the day, she could trade the feel of a brush in her hand and the rich smell of oil paints for the soft whir of sequencers and compilers.

She caught the bus.

It dropped her off, and she walked the rest of the way to her home, a cottage tucked inside a half acre of ancient live oak, a microcosm untouched by developers. Her mom inherited the cottage from her parents and made it her permanent residence after the divorce.

Lucy's mother was a talented artist. With art came financial uncertainty, and her mother's anxiety transferred to her in the form of conflicting advice. "Follow your heart," her mother said, right up until the past-due notices showed up, and then her tune changed to, "Do something practical." Her senior year, Lucy realized she had enough science, math, and English credits to follow her heart with a schedule heavy in art classes and study halls, but it was over a stack of bills that her mother badgered her into taking the practical AP biology class.

She was so angry at her mother's meddling that she did not bother to point out the $3000 lab fee associated with the course. If her mom was going to pick her courses, then her mom could pay for them, and when the bill came due, her mom had to empty the savings account to cover it.

Lucy didn't care all that much. Another job would come along, and her mother would paint her way out of the hole. In book cover art circles, her mother was a bit of legend. She painted gorgeous scenes pulled from the book's pages. But the fantasy and science fiction books she illustrated shifted away from traditional media to the digital. Digital art was faster and cheaper, and nearly anyone could hang out a shingle and call themselves an artist. Her mother competed with a lot of talented amateurs who undervalued their own work and undercut hers.

Still, Lucy felt pretty good. She enjoyed the class, had plenty of time for her own artwork, and got to teach her mom a little lesson about interfering with her life.

Everything was cool until her mother was diagnosed with pancreatic cancer.

Her father's car, a shiny black Lexus, menaced the dirt driveway with its sleek form. Her mother and father had a good relationship since their divorce. Her mother had a casual, barefoot kind of attitude, while her father, a partner in a law firm, was serious and professional. She could not fathom the universe that brought them together.

Two suitcases stood guard in the living room. She went out the back door to the studio.

She walked into the studio and inhaled the comforting scent of oil paints. The smell always said home to her. Her mother slept in the recliner under a blanket, her bald head covered with a black knit watch cap. Her father sat at the small breakfast table, sifting through her mom's reference materials for her current project.

"Dad, what are you doing here?" Lucy asked. She kept her voice low.

"Hey, how about 'Hi, Dad—glad to see you'?" asked David Cardiff.

"Hi, Dad—glad to see you."

"Your mom had an oncology appointment, and she asked me to take her. And then we talked."

"What does that mean?" asked Lucy.

"Maybe we should wait for her to wake up."

"No, tell me now."

"I'm coming back for a while," said her father.

"Why?" Lucy always thought she would want him to come back, but she had grown so used to his just visiting that having him under the same roof would be weird.

"To help take care of your mother."

"She is getting better."

"She's not, Lucy. We should wait for her to wake up."

"Tell me, Dad." Her lips trembled and her eyes watered. Her mother was prone to tiny white lies, while her father was relentlessly truthful. She took a look at her mom, so small in the oversized chair, and thought that if there was any time for a comforting lie, it would be right now.

"The chemotherapy and radiation aren't working anymore. She doesn't want to go to a hospice and be sick until... She wants to stay here, and I am going to help her. She's decided to try a new therapy. It can't stop the disease, but it will make her feel healthy, it will give her the energy she wants. She'll be able to finish her painting."

For how long? were the first words that came to Lucy's mind, but instead she lashed out, "Why do you care? You left." The moment those words left her mouth she wanted to pull them back. Her father did care, and the divorce was mutual, but she was too angry and upset to apologize.

"Lucy, I never stopped caring."

"Then why did you..."

"Lucy, I don't want to rehash a decade-old divorce. This is the wrong time. Your mom asked me to stay, and I am. Now, please keep your voice down. She is sleeping. We can talk about it when she wakes."

"Fine."

She held it in because that is what she did. She wiped her eyes before a tear could fall. She knew what her father was saying and understood why he was here, but it seemed so wrong that she was left out of the decision.

"She is going to be fine," said Lucy.

She left the cottage, careful not to slam the door, though she wanted to. She would slam the door right off its hinges. She would slam it so hard it would burst into splinters. Outside under the covered walkway that connected the cottage to the studio, bees buzzed in the tangles of honeysuckle and wisteria. A gentle wind rustled the pine and oak. Her heart pounded louder and louder, drowning out the buzz of stupid insects going about their stupid lives. She felt her father watching her, and to his credit he did not chase her down to hold her and say stupid things to her like how it was going to be all right. She left, walking head down along the dirt driveway to the road and then to the bluffs where the aeronauts flung themselves into the sky to catch the rising thermals. She turned away from the few cars that passed so they would not see her face.

At the bluffs, she sat on the rickety bench, and it sagged beneath her weight. The aeronauts launched themselves over the edge, falling into space until their translucent wings caught the air and cast them into the sky. She sat on the bench and held it in, even as she wanted to scream.

Saturday morning was usually breakfast-in-bed day. Her mom would make bacon and eggs, and then they would lounge on the bed, eating and talking to late morning, but her father's moving back had disrupted the usual routine. He was an early riser even on the weekend and had stepped out to go shopping.

Sometimes she felt like a spy in her own house. Lucy watched her mother and father and captured glimpses of what they must have been like before she ever graced the world. He held her and rubbed her back, and she seemed to sink into him. He kept her warm and brought her what she needed without complaint. How could they ever fall apart?

Once she saw her father lean in and kiss her mother on the cheek. He spoke to her so softly that Lucy couldn't hear what he said. Her mother smiled. If he could make her smile like that, create a moment between them, precious and sacred, then he could stay as long as he liked, as far as Lucy was concerned.

Her mother rallied, but the doctor had said she would. The

new therapy took away the pain and gave her new energy, but it could not cure the disease. The doctor said she would run strong until the end. Lucy imagined it like running towards a cliff, faster and faster, picking up speed until the ground dropped away from beneath your feet.

And then the long, terrible fall.

She made her mom some coffee and brought it in.

"Mom, made you some."

"Lucy, thank you. You are reading my mind."

Her mom set her brush down and took the cup; she wrapped her hands around the warmth and sipped. "Good."

"Can I see?"

"No, not yet, no peeking."

With her renewed energy, her mom had returned to painting, and Lucy enjoyed nothing more than to watch her mother paint and sketch, but this time her mom had spun her easel away from general view and tucked herself in a corner.

When her mom was a student she studied painting in France and the Netherlands. She audited medical and veterinary classes to learn about anatomy and dug up dinosaur bones in the Gobi Desert and the American Midwest. Her mother's imagination lived and breathed on the canvas. Her creatures swam in alien seas, stampeded across grassy plains, and soared across lightning-split storm clouds. There was a depth and realism about her paintings that made them true. They were situated in a world. It was what Lucy aspired to in her own art.

"Lucy, we need to talk about after."

"I don't want to. Not now."

She didn't have anything else to do. She wanted to be with her mother, but she couldn't talk about what her mother wanted to talk about. "I have to work on my Neosaur. Can I take the jeep?" Anxiety clawed at her insides; she just needed to leave and avoid the conversation. If she didn't hear or didn't know, then it couldn't be real.

"We don't have to talk, not right now, but stay with me until your father gets back."

She sat. "Okay."

"It's nice having him around, isn't it?" asked her mother.

"It is," she conceded. Having her father lunk around the house in his underwear took some getting used to, but overall it was not as bad as she expected. She found herself drawn into conversations that she never suspected she would have with him. She and her mom talked about the same things, but they were always theoretical questions framed in metaphor, and the answer always revolved around trusting your instincts. What if she didn't have any instincts? Not to worry, her father had a plan. He would flat out ask about boys, sex, and drugs. He outlined strategies for her to avoid the pitfalls of the teenage years. Her father's you-need-to-have-a- plan mentality conflicted with her mom's trust-yourself attitude. Both systems had their merits, but until her father moved back, her mom's held sway. Her father's infuriatingly logical way of viewing the world challenged issues that she thought had been long settled.

"Why did you get divorced?"

"Oh goodness, the real question is how we ever got together!"

"How did you get together then?"

"Have you ever looked at your father? I mean, come on, he's gorgeous. Those blue eyes..."

"Mom!" Lucy's face flushed with embarrassment. She couldn't think of her father as anything but her father. "He does have pretty eyes. Tell me."

"Well, besides the obvious physical thing..."

"Okay, Mom, I get it."

"I don't know. Opposites attract. He was determined and focused. Grim, even. He had a way of making you feel safe. And I was a bit, I don't know..."

"A free spirit."

"I guess that's the nice way of putting it."

"So, why did you get divorced?"

"The opposites-attract thing works out great for a while. We complemented each other, but when life got serious, when you had to choose a direction or a philosophy, an approach to how to face the world, we couldn't agree."

"When I came along?"

"No, you were the only thing we could agree on."

"Then why?"

"First, we grated on each other and then...well, if we didn't... if we didn't divorce, I think we might have learned to hate each other, and I love him too much for that. If you ask me, we divorced in the nick of time."

"Why did you ask him to come back?"

"For you."

With their student ID Cards, AP Biology students had access to the school lab after hours. Lucy would much rather be anywhere else on a Sunday afternoon, but final coding was due in a week, and her genetic program was riddled with errors and incompatibilities. If she wasn't careful, she would turn a perfectly good chicken embryo into a rotted puddle of slime.

She leaned back in the lab chair and took out her tablet. Though she had not seen her mom's painting, she had seen and photographed some of her reference sketches of a feathered dragon. The sketches were energetic gray-scale slashes of paint, full of life and energy. Scribbled on one of the pages was a URL. Lucy typed it in and it brought up an academic article from *The Journal of Chinese Paleontology*.

The authors had discovered the fossilized remains of a giant maniraptoran theropod, a flying, bat-winged dinosaur. It seemed that at one time China really did have dragons, and they had the bones in the ground to prove it. The dinosaur stood five meters tall, the height of a giraffe, and had a nineteen-meter wingspan, the length of two school buses. They were the biggest known animals to ever take to the sky, larger even than a Quetzalcoatlus, an extinct pterosaur and the previous record holder.

A photograph showed the find, a set of dark fossilized bones set in dun-colored desert stone. The creature's neck was stretched back, its mouth frozen open in a carnivorous smile. One of the long-fingered wings was fully extended. A man, dwarfed by the size of the animal, lay on the ground to lend a sense of scale.

Lucy sat down at her workstation and opened the Bionics programming language.

Her mom's sketches and the single fossil photograph did not fill her with any workable inspiration. She wiped her previous changes and stared at the baseline Neosaur code. Her mom said that a mature artist did not rely upon inspiration to simply appear, but got to work so inspiration had no choice but to show up. It took an act of faith to believe that her imagination could be translated into a concoction of amino acids and proteins that could result in a living breathing creature. Act as if you have talent, said her mother, and it will be granted to you.

She read through the baseline Neosaur code, seeing the overlapping patterns and intertwined genetic compositions. She started typing, altering the Neosaur egg's destiny. There was a rhythm to coding that was like painting. She layered protein sequences like she layered rich oil colors on a canvas, adding depth and style to bring the vision in her head to life.

Flying creatures were engineering marvels, frighteningly strong yet delicate. Weight needed to be distributed considering a center of gravity and the aerodynamic center of pressure. They needed powerful immune systems and fast recovery times to repair the physical wear and tear of flight. She knit contradictory requirements together to find a balance. Nature had eons to experiment; she had a weekend. It didn't seem possible, but there she was, in the zone, coding a dragon. A secondary monitor updated the morphology of the animal. She could see her mistakes in real time. The system tried to drive her towards the easy answers encoded in the drop down menus. Most of the students would let the machine do the hard creative work. They would compile a selection of compatible choices from the menus and create an imitation of originality. She despised the idea.

She had to create something unique and beautiful.

She was doing it for her mother.

When she was done, she ran her final program through the compiler. The Bioscholastics computers would take an in-depth look and give a refined analysis of her dragon's viability. She waited. Chugging on the novel genetic code of a new creature took more than a few minutes. The machine displayed the results—a cryptic assortment of access or parameter errors without any amplifying explanation. She Googled the errors and discovered that the Bioscholastics Neosaur kit used a truncated version of the Bionics programming language to keep young bioengineers within safe guidelines. No one wanted a high school kid to unleash a venomous devil chicken on an unsuspecting public.

The student version of the program would not let her make what she wanted. She sat back in her lab chair and spun. Her code was good. She was sure of it. She had divined the recipe for a Chinese dragon dinosaur. She just had to prove it.

She snooped at Dr. Nelms' lab table. Her teacher had a successful career in the industry and still consulted on the side. Consequently she had access to the full-powered genetic compiler programs at three different design houses. The drawers were locked, but the slide-out desk extension pulled out. A piece of paper with URLs and passwords was taped to the extension.

She logged into Anthrodynamics Inc. as Dr. Nelms and ran her program.

Her mother wanted to watch the aeronauts, so her father helped her into the Jeep. Lucy drove all three of them to the bluffs. Late it in the evening the wind died down, so only the most skilled aeronauts, those who could handle light winds and five-meter wings without a safety parachute, took to the sky. They parked and watched the flyers surf the currents, spiraling higher and then diving towards the dark water, building speed to swoop up the face of the bluffs and alight on the edge. They watched until her mother tired. They drove home and put her in the daybed in the studio. Her father sat on one side of her, and Lucy sat on the other.

Her mother closed her eyes, her breathing slow and shallow. The hospice bracelet sent telemetry to the hospital. The hospital pinged her father's phone.

Just like the aeronauts, it was like running towards a cliff, faster and faster, until you found yourself alone and unsupported, over the edge with nothing but wide open uncertainty above, below, and ahead.

"Nothing left but the rising," said her mother, barely above a whisper. "Thank you."

"For what, Mom?"

"For being my daughter."

They sat, Lucy and her father, and waited, and after a short while they were the only two in the room.

"What do I do now?" asked Lucy.

"Lucy," said her father, "let's go for a walk."

She nodded, unable to speak. If she were to make a sound, it would be something terrible and unfitting. She held it in, turning away from the pain. Her father took her hand, and they walked back to the bluffs to sit on the sagging bench and figure out what was to come after.

The aeronauts, like dragons, wheeled in the sky, calling to each other.

Her Neosaur, a drab chicken-lizard devoid of any of the form and style she saw in her imagination, hatched. She did not know what had gone wrong. It looked like she felt, sad and gray and tiny. Even after it fledged, it still looked like a feathery, gray lizard with translucent flaps of skin draped between the long fingers of its wings. It cried constantly, so she took to carrying it around. It clung to her clothes, nestled on her chest and nuzzled on her cheek, occasionally nipping at her earlobes. She called the little Neosaur Artemis, after the Greek goddess of the hunt, a completely unfitting name for such a sad little creature.

At breakfast one morning, she placed Artemis on the breakfast table, and the tiny Neosaur plucked at her gray feathers, pulling them out. They stuck to the edges of her tiny toothed mouth. Lucy picked her up, dusting the tiny feathers from her muzzle. Artemis felt heavier, likes she had put on a bit more weight. Given the amount of food she ate, she ought to be. With the tip of her finger, Lucy parted the soft downy feathers and felt the tips of immature pin feathers dotting the Neosaur's body.

Over the next two months, Artemis grew to about two feet tall. Her elegant, raptorian body was covered in sleek, interlocking, fan-shaped feathers in iridescent green, blue, gold, and red. Her coloration had the jewel-like intensity of a hummingbird. The leading edges of her membranous wings were densely layered with tiny, blade-like feathers that she could flex independently. She had a fearsome appearance, but her disposition was gentle. She ate everything. Bugs, lizards, field mice, table scraps, nuts, acorns, and berries went down her gullet with equal enthusiasm. She took to a high protein dog food with gusto, and Lucy's father complained that she was worse than a teenager.

Artemis refused to be separated from Lucy and followed her

around, heeling by instinct. She was smart, at least as smart as a dog, and maybe as smart as those sarcastic gene-crafted parrots at the pet store. She climbed up the rough bark of the live oaks, clinging with the two dagger-like phalanges that did not have wing skin stretched between them, but she would not fly.

It was as if something was holding her down.

Lucy sat next to her father in the school principal's office. Artemis sniffed a potted palm tree in the corner.

"Artemis, no," said Lucy.

Artemis squawked and returned to her side, rubbing her feathered cheek against Lucy's own.

"Mr. Cardiff," said Principal DeMaria. "Lucy is a wonderful student, but her Neosaur distracts the other students. I can't have it following her around the school all day. It needs to be returned to the pens. Some of the parents are concerned. They don't like their children in the company of a dinosaur."

"Artemis is not a dinosaur. She is a service animal as defined by the Americans with Disabilities Act."

"Your daughter is not disabled," said Principal DeMaria, "and service animals are registered."

Lucy's father reached into his briefcase and brought out a manila folder. "I'm sure you will find the paperwork in order. Artemis is registered with the US Service Animal Registry as an emotional support animal. If you have any questions, you can contact my firm." He slid over his business card.

"It's a bit unorthodox. Service animals are usually dogs."

"The law does not limit the kind of animal. I'll admit there is room for legal interpretations, but interpretations are expensive. I'm sure the school district would prefer to avoid any legal or financial complications that might arise from objections to Artemis."

"I am going to table this decision for the moment. Artemis can stay without a fight, providing she is muzzled…"

"Dad," protested Lucy.

"Loosely," added Mr. DeMaria. "I mean, look at those teeth. And she needs her claws blunted for safety."

"We can work with that," said Mr. Cardiff.

"There is another matter, Mr. Cardiff. It seems that there was an intrusion into Anthrodynamics' computer systems that emanated from this school, coincidentally the same day your daughter was registered in the AP Biology lab. The school board is cooperating in an investigation into the matter. The company has expressed an interest in speaking to your daughter and taking a look at Artemis."

"Why would they want to do that?"

"Dad, I…"

"Not another word," said her father.

"The Bionics programming language used in the Neosaur kit is a truncated version. It is incapable of creating a creature like Artemis. There is the matter of the computer intrusion itself and the potential hazard of a gene-crafted creature of unknown capability. The end-user license agreement for the Neosaur kits gives Bioscholastics a claim on Artemis. It doesn't happen often, but the company could take her away," said Principal DeMaria.

Lucy walked down to the bluffs to watch the aeronauts. Artemis followed and trilled at every new sight and sound. Her father was dealing with her use of Dr. Nelms' account at Anthrodynamics and was working on an agreement that would let her keep Artemis. Anthrodynamics might settle for access to her DNA and source code. It seemed Artemis' hybrid wing design, particularly the independently moving feathers at the leading edge, had bio-mimetic applications in the aerospace industry worth billions of dollars, and Lucy was the only one with the source code.

If only Artemis would fly.

It was a beautiful, breezy day, the kind the aeronauts favored. She watched them vanish over the edge and then soar skyward, wings spread, stroking the air. They whooped and called to one another. So much joy, she thought, all for one small price of simply falling over the edge.

"You could do that," said Lucy to Artemis. "You have wings. Wouldn't you want to?"

Artemis trilled, an all-purpose response to the sound of Lucy's voice. The raptor watched the flyers tracking skyward and then preened herself.

Lucy heard a car door close and turned to look. Her father and the Anthrodynamics lawyer walked towards her. Panic surged. What if they were taking Artemis away?

"We have to fly, Artemis."

She stood and walked towards a group of aeronauts eating lunch. Artemis followed. They didn't see her, and she slipped on a wing pack.

"Hey," said an aeronaut.

"Lucy," said her father.

"Run!" said Lucy.

She ran toward the edge. Artemis kept pace, leaning forward, wings half-spread. The aeronaut whose wings she borrowed ran after her, half a step behind. Artemis dodged towards him, and the man veered away.

"Whoa, you crazy bird," he said. He stopped running and called to her. "You'll kill yourself!"

The ground rushed beneath her feet in a blur of green. She heard her father's faraway voice, and then the ground was gone, lost behind her, and she was over the edge, alone and unsupported.

She fell.

This is what it is to die, she thought: the long pointless plummet of panicked life and then the sudden, just as meaningless, stop.

She swept her arms forward and the aeronaut wings unfurled, catching air, turning her reckless plummet into a glide. She pulled her legs together and arched her back. The wings changed camber, generating lift. She rose and banked towards the cliff. The wind rising off the face of the rock caught her and swept her upwards at dizzying speed.

She rose higher, as if an invisible hand had cradled her body and pulled her skyward. Her heart pounded with fear and joy.

Before you can rise, you have to fall.

She looked over her shoulder.

Artemis soared. Ungainly on the ground, in flight Artemis was the definition of grace. The Neosaur's wings flexed, fully extended and spangled with reflected sun light. Artemis took the lead and Lucy followed, matching Artemis's wingbeats stroke for stroke. The powerful myoplastic muscles built into the aeronaut's wings augmented her strength. She glanced below. Her father, the Anthrodynamics lawyer, and the aeronauts looked up at her. Artemis let out a wild screech of joy, and Lucy did the same.

Lucy closed her eyes and experienced the rush of the wind and warmth of the sun.

She soared unafraid and un-alone.

Light flashed from their wings as they flew in tandem, one next to the other.

In comparison, leaping from the cliff was easy. Her landing was ungraceful and bruising. She flared her feet dragging along the ground, lift dumped from the wings, and she tumbled. Her father took her up in his arms. Drooping wings dragged the ground behind her.

Artemis alighted next to her.

"I'm sorry for scaring you," she said.

"We'll talk later," said her father.

"First time! That was awesome," said the aeronaut. "Can I have my wings back?"

"Am I going to keep Artemis?"

"Yes," said her father.

Lucy lifted the canvas that shrouded her mother's painting. Sometime between stepping off the cliff and catching the air, she found enough courage to see her mother's last painting.

She saw herself standing at the bluffs, poised to take a step over the edge into the unknown. Her hair and dress billowed into the wind. The sky was thick with sunlit clouds of orange and gold and red. Rays of light from a shrouded sun fanned out across the sky. Dark waves capped with white marched across the ocean surface. A dragon, in the colors of Artemis, rose into the sky, wings outstretched.

"She loves you so much," said her father.

Lucy ran to him, and he wrapped his arms around her.

"I know," said Lucy.

The Fantastic Tale of Miss Arney's Doubloon

by Zach Shephard

Zach Shephard's fiction has appeared in places like Galaxy's Edge, Intergalactic Medicine Show *and the* Unidentified Funny Objects *anthology series. He likes Halloween and Christmas more than any thirty-four-year-old probably should, and hibernates in the summer to avoid his nemesis, the sun. With enough donuts handy, you can bribe him to do pretty much anything. For a complete bibliography of Zach's stories, check out www.zachshephard.com.*

"Let's go to Miss Arney's house next!" Jenny said.

Nicole rolled her eyes at her cousin's suggestion. "Miss Arney doesn't even give out candy. If we went down Main Street we'd get *tons* of candy."

"That's not how trick-or-treating works," Jenny said. "Walking past the shops and letting store-owners dump stuff into your bag isn't fun. You've got to go to neighborhoods! To houses! To scary dark doors with spiders guarding the way!" She drew her plastic cutlass and sliced at the air, flipping her pirate-patch over her eye.

None of that sounded any good to Nicole. She just wanted to go home, cuddle up with the dog and play games on her phone. And maybe eat candy—the only good part about Halloween. Even dressing up wasn't fun, which was why Nicole had thrown together a fortune-teller outfit from her mom's scarves and jewelry with as little effort as possible.

But of course the other kids would want to do whatever Jenny did. After all, she was the one who'd seen a spaceship the other day—or so she'd claimed. Nicole didn't believe her for a second. The "spaceship" was probably just a weird-looking cloud. And besides, even if aliens *were* real, why would they visit a tiny little town like Greensburg? They should be meeting with the President or something. It didn't make any sense.

As expected, Nicole's idea to go down Main Street was overruled. The group of fifth-graders, escorted by Li's parents, made for Miss Arney's house. They squished together on the tiny porch, kicking aside crisped autumn leaves in the darkness. Jenny rang the bell, and as the door opened, their voices carried through the cool October air:

"*Trick or treat!*"

Miss Arney, wearing plastic devil-horns and a shiny red cape, smiled with delight.

"Look at all of you! Such lovely costumes."

She held out a sack. *The* sack. Everyone knew about the treasures you could get from Miss Arney: she had a great big collection of board games she'd played when she was younger, and every year she'd throw pawns and cards and other bits into her sack for kids to claim. The girls thrust their hands in and fished around. Nicole joined reluctantly, secretly hoping a stray peanut butter cup had made its way into the bag.

She got her fingers around something that was almost the right shape and pulled it out. It wasn't a peanut butter cup— just a dumb coaster or something. She dropped it into her bag without giving it a second look.

Everyone thanked Miss Arney (even Nicole, who didn't forget her manners despite her disappointment) and shuffled down the sidewalk.

"What'd you get?" Jenny asked.

"Nothing cool."

"I got a *dragon!* Isn't it awesome?" Jenny showed the figurine.

"Sure. When can we go home?"

"It's Halloween, 'Cole! Aren't you having fun?"

How was this fun? Things were so much better inside. Leave the trick-or-treating, softball and camping to Jenny.

"Okay," Jenny said, flipping her patch over her eye. "If ye won't be havin' any fun here, we'll try the high seas!" She grabbed Nicole's hand.

"What are you—"

Jenny yanked them behind a bush when Li's parents weren't looking. She peeked down the sidewalk.

"Those scurvy dogs won't even know we're gone. Come on!"

Jenny pulled Nicole through a dark yard, across a street and into a field. They stopped in the middle, breathing heavily. Between moon-silvered cloud streaks, the stars shone brightly.

"We're going to get in trouble," Nicole said.

"Good! Pirates live for trouble. Now show us yer booty, sailor." Jenny took the dragon figurine from her bag and made some dragon noises, which sounded to Nicole like a chicken auditioning for the opera.

Nicole pulled out the item she'd gotten from Miss Arney. The golden disc was about the size of her palm and half an inch thick.

"Yar!" Jenny said. "It be a doubloon!"

"It's way too big for a doubloon."

Jenny's posture slumped in overdramatic fashion. "Use your imagination, dorkbutt. Tonight I'm a pirate, and that's a doubloon. And you! You're not a fortune-teller—you're Lady Dracona, the gypsy queen cursed by Baron McSnotfart to transform into a dragon whenever you're mad!" She swung the figurine through the air, making more noises. "Here—

try it out." Jenny gave Nicole the figurine and accepted the doubloon in exchange.

Nicole examined the dragon, but its details were lost in the dark. A moment later a golden light covered it.

"Whoa!" Jenny said. "Check it out!"

The doubloon glowed in her palms. The girls huddled over it, staring into its translucent surface. Its guts were full of circuitry, and on the surface was an animation of a twisty ladder.

"That ladder must lead to treasure," Jenny said.

"It's not a ladder. It's one of those DNA things. And where'd it come from, anyway?"

"I flicked this switch on the back and everything lit up. This is the coolest thing anyone has *ever* gotten from Miss Arney."

Jenny ran circles through the field, swinging the coin high and low like a ship atop stormy waves. Nicole sighed and pocketed her dragon, wishing her dad hadn't made her leave her phone with Li's parents.

She watched Jenny play, wondering when her cousin would get bored so they could leave. As the glowing doubloon swept through the field, Nicole noticed something in the background.

"Jenny," she whispered, "come here."

"What be the problem, Lady Dracona?"

"Shh! Does that bush look weird to you?" She pointed at a large, distant shape.

Jenny lifted her patch and squinted into the darkness. She shrugged.

"I don't—wait! Did it just move?"

The girls stared. Was the bush growing? Swelling like a balloon? No—it was just the wind pushing things around. Except there *was* no wind.

Nicole focused on the stars behind the bush. One by one, they were covered by the expanding shape.

"Turn the doubloon off. I can't see with the light in my face."

Jenny flicked the switch. Right away Nicole noticed two

dim lights hanging high in the bush, like reflective purple marbles.

The lights blinked.

The girls squealed. The bush expanded into a huge shape, blotting out more stars. There was a screech that put Jenny's dragon noises to shame, followed by a loud beating of wings. The girls ran in the opposite direction.

"What the heck is that?" Nicole asked.

"Down!" Jenny tackled her to the ground, a rush of air passing over them. Nicole looked up just in time to see a dark shape soaring into the distance, rising higher and—

"Turning! It's turning!"

The purple-eyed thing screeched, swooping back toward Nicole and Jenny. They scrambled to their feet and ran.

"Split!" Jenny yelled, pushing Nicole away. They dove and rolled in opposite directions, the dark thing coming down like a giant scythe to scrape the grass between them.

Nicole sprinted off, her heart pounding. Was Jenny okay? She checked over her shoulder and ran right into something.

Oof! She fell. Rolling onto her belly, she saw a pair of hooves before her.

"Careful, lass! It's dangerous out here."

Nicole looked up. The red-bearded man was like any other adult she'd ever seen, except—*hooves!* The legs coming out of his ragged shorts were thin but toned, and their color reminded her of the dark, polished dresser in her parents' bedroom.

"Don't worry," the man said. "Cap'n Mard's here!"

He pulled a weird-looking pistol from his holster and fired at the far-off flying thing. Nicole expected a *bang* and some smoke, but instead there was a static-crackle and a flash of orange light.

Two more hoof-footed people in ragged clothes came to Captain Mard's side. All three fired laser-shots at the swooping shape. It kept its distance, diving at something in the field.

"Jenny!" Nicole said. Jenny screamed something back, just as the shape lifted her from the ground.

Nicole ran after the retreating sky-thing, her shouts competing with the sounds of laser-blasts and beating wings. Jenny's screams faded into the distance as the dark shape carried her away.

Nicole stumbled to a halt. The laser-fire stopped. Captain Mard came up to her.

"Do you have the disc, lass?"

"It took Jenny! We have to find her. We have to—"

Captain Mard knelt and held her by the shoulders, looking into her eyes. His hands were weird: only three fingers on each, plus a big bony hook growing out the back of the left one.

"Calm down, lass. We can find your friend. But we'll need the disc."

Nicole sniffled, her eyes wet. "The doubloon?"

"Yes—I suppose that is how it looks. Do you have it?"

"Jenny does."

"Bah! No matter. We can still get your friend back. I just need to know where you got the doubloon."

Nicole pointed toward the neighborhood, half-lit with the glow-sticks and flashlights of trick-or-treaters. "Miss Arney's house."

"Very well. To Miss Arney's house!"

Captain Mard insisted they go to the back door instead of the front. Miss Arney answered, still wearing her devil costume.

"Nicole!" she said. "Where's the rest of your group? And who're these gentlemen?"

"Something took Jenny. We need your help!"

Miss Arney looked the group over, her dark eyes framed by strands of graying brown hair. She seemed to realize this definitely wasn't a Halloween trick.

"Come in," she said. "I'll get some drinks."

They sat in the kitchen. The porch light was off and Miss Arney ignored the doorbell. She stared into her tea, digesting Nicole's story about the doubloon.

"That wasn't supposed to be in the sack," Miss Arney said. "I don't know how it got there."

"Doesn't matter now," Captain Mard said. "We just need to know where you found it."

Miss Arney scratched at a brown stain on the tablecloth, her eyes glazed by memory. "It happened a few months ago," she said. "I was hiking in the hills when I came across an overgrown path I'd never noticed before. The sun was getting low, but I decided I could spend a few minutes exploring. At the base of a pine tree, I found the doubloon.

"It was beautiful," she said, her face alight with wonder. "And halfway to my car, it got even better: I found the switch that lit it up. It was so gorgeous I didn't even look away until I heard the screech."

Nicole shivered. She knew that screech all too well.

"Something huge soared overhead, scraping the treetops. I flicked the doubloon off to kill the light and ducked into a bush. I squatted there for a long time, holding my breath and watching the sky. Everything was calm and quiet, and then, *wham!* The thing landed in a clearing, maybe fifty feet away. There wasn't enough sunlight left for me to make out its shape, but I heard it sniffing about. I held my breath and didn't move a muscle. Eventually, the thing screeched and took off. When it seemed safe to come out, I ran to my car and drove home."

"It didn't chase you?" Nicole asked.

"No, but that wasn't the last I saw of it. A few days later I turned the doubloon on again. I figured I was safe at home, right? Wrong: before long I heard the screech, out in the hills. I switched the doubloon off and peeked out my window. The sun was low, but there was just enough light to see *something* circling the sky: a black shape against purple clouds." Miss

Arney rubbed her arms like she'd suddenly gone cold. "I never turned the doubloon on again."

Captain Mard wagged a finger at his crew. "I knew we were close. Should have kept poking around those hills when we picked up the signal. Miss Arney, can you take us to where you found the doubloon?"

"Shouldn't we let the police take care of this?"

"Believe me, my men can handle that beastie better than anyone else."

Miss Arney chewed her lip. "Okay, how about this: I'll draw you a map, but then I'm calling the police."

"Fair enough." Captain Mard handed her a napkin, and she started sketching.

"There," she said, sliding the map across the table. "Now if you'll excuse me, I have to use the phone."

Miss Arney left the kitchen. Captain Mard turned the napkin in his hands, tilting his head to the side. "Do you know where this is?" he asked Nicole.

"Yeah. Jenny dragged me up there once."

Captain Mard nodded sharply. "A moment, please."

He exited the room. Jenny heard a brief zapping sound and a yelp. Captain Mard came back with Miss Arney in his arms, sleeping peacefully.

"Don't suppose you know where her bedroom is, do you?" he asked. "I'd like her to be comfortable when she wakes."

"Did you hurt her?"

"Of course not! But I couldn't risk the police fouling things up. If we're going to save your friend and get that doubloon back, we'll have to do it ourselves."

Jenny helped Captain Mard find the bedroom. They set Miss Arney down, pulled a blanket over her and left the house.

The group walked back to the field where Nicole and Jenny had activated the doubloon. Captain Mard led everyone behind some trees, where a long silver ship stood.

"Wow!" Nicole said. "It's like a boat, but without the sails. Are you guys pirates or something?"

"Ha!" Captain Mard said. "Pirates—I like that. But no, we're aliens."

Aliens! Real-life aliens. And Nicole had thought this Halloween couldn't get any weirder.

A gangway descended from the side of the ship. Everyone climbed aboard, where more of Captain Mard's crew waited.

The ship's engines fired up, but they didn't sound like any engines Nicole was used to. They made a sort of swooshing sound, like waves brushing the shore.

The ship rose above the trees and lurched forward. Nicole stumbled, and Captain Mard laughed.

"Need to work on your sky-legs, lass!"

Nicole latched onto a post in the middle of the deck. Her parents had tried to make her go on a hot-air balloon once, which sounded like the scariest thing ever. This was somehow worse.

"Something wrong?" Captain Mard asked.

"We're going to crash."

Captain Mard laughed. "There's nothing to fear, lass. Think of it this way: if we were in danger, wouldn't my men be panicked?"

"I guess."

"So look around."

All across the deck, space-pirates were laughing and playing board games. A group at the far end performed something like a sea shanty on strange instruments. No one seemed to care they were flying.

"Go along," Captain Mard said, moving toward a staircase in the floor. "Have a look around while I take care of some things." He went below the deck.

This wasn't Nicole's idea of a good time—it was more like Jenny's. Her cousin would've been right at home, running across the ship, shouting orders like she were a sea captain.

Of course—that was it! To forget about how high she was, Nicole just needed to pretend this was a seagoing ship. After all, Jenny was always telling her to use her imagination more.

Nicole closed her eyes. She listened to the accordion-style sea shanty and the churning-wave sound of the engines. She felt the ship moving as if it were rocking on the water, and she even thought she smelled salt on the air.

Everything came together in her mind. She was on a *real* pirate ship, sailing under a gorgeous starry sky. Waves lapped against the hull, while far-off dolphins breached and cackled in the dark.

She opened her eyes. One slow step at a time, she moved to the rail and looked out. Down below, the trees were bare. Except they *weren't* trees: they were kelp, drifting on the seafloor. And the tiny town in the distance, full of twinkles from flashlights and porch bulbs, was actually a merfolk village: the trick-or-treaters there dressed as sharks and got sunken treasures instead of candy. Nicole smiled at the thought.

The ship sailed toward the hills. Nicole gazed into the imagined underwater world, her trance broken by a series of barks.

A dog! The space-pirates had a *dog!* Nicole ran down the stairs into the bowels of the ship, following the barks through dim, narrow corridors. After a few turns she saw an open door up ahead, on the right, an orange light coming through. Something snarled from within.

"Quiet down, you brainless beast!" It was Captain Mard's voice, and it was followed by a crackle of electricity. The barking stopped, replaced by a whimper.

Captain Mard exited the room, closing the door and mopping his brow. He deactivated his electrified baton and stowed it in a secret panel on the wall.

"Ah!" he said, noticing Nicole down the hall and smiling. "Glad to see you've left your post."

"Were you hitting that dog?"

Captain Mard laughed. "Oh, that was no dog. Just a simple beast from a planet you've never heard of. We've got a pair of them in there, and the bigger one acts up whenever it hears our favorite song. Now come along, lass—we're surely close to the hills by now." He draped a hand over Nicole's shoulder and guided her down the hall. Something whimpered softly behind them.

The ship landed in a clearing on the wooded hill. Everyone disembarked and Captain Mard addressed the crew.

"Weapons ready, boys!" There was a rattle of metal as the dozen space-pirates checked their armaments. Some weapons emitted a high-pitched whine as they powered up, while others sounded like traditional Earth-guns being cocked. One space-pirate pointed his pistol skyward and shot a bright plume of flame into the night, nodding to himself in approval.

Nicole led the way. They climbed a slope and came to a wall of bushes, taller than the tallest space-pirate. She pushed twigs aside and ventured into a narrow, tree-strangled path.

It was dark and eerily quiet. Nicole struck up conversation to break the silence.

"Your doubloon isn't really a coin, is it?" she asked. "It looked like a computer or something."

"Very observant!" Captain Mard said. "The doubloons are data discs. Each contains the genome of an alien species—all the information our machine needs to create life."

"Do you have one for humans?" Nicole asked. "Can you make *people?*"

Captain Mard laughed. "Don't you worry, lass. We only deal in exotic beasts. Galactic circuses pay out the nose for attractions from other solar systems."

Nicole thought about how poorly most Earth circuses treated their animals. Then she remembered the thing on the ship, getting zapped by Captain Mard's baton. It made her want to hug her dog.

The trees became less dense and everyone was able to stand straight. Nicole slipped around a rock the size of a recliner, brushing ferns as she passed.

"Why'd you come to Earth?" she asked. "Are you here for more animals?"

"Ha! Far from it. If people saw Earth animals, they'd come looking for Earth. My crew's the only one to stumble across this rock, and we'd like to keep it that way. Unknown planets are nice places for conducting business."

"If no one knows you're here, how'd you lose your doubloons?"

"One of the beasties we cooked up got away. Darned rascal snatched the doubloons on his way out."

The sky thing! Nicole thought. With its purple-marble eyes and terrible screech. The thing that had Jenny. Gosh—she hoped her cousin was okay.

The trees thinned enough to reveal a cloud-striped sky. Ferns and shrubs gave way to dirt and fallen pinecones. Nicole led everyone uphill.

"I think we're almost there," she said. "I haven't been this far before, but—*Jenny!*"

The pirate-costumed girl stopped in her tracks. She flipped up her eye patch, spotted the group and came skipping down.

Nicole charged uphill and threw her arms around her cousin.

"You're alive! How'd you escape?"

Jenny pulled back from the hug. "Escape? Oh—it's not like that. I'm just exploring. Gerald's super nice."

"Who's Gerald?"

"The big scary winged thing! Except he's not actually scary. He just wanted his doubloon back."

Captain Mard butted in: "*Our* doubloon. Where's this Gerald character?"

Jenny pointed to a cave up the hill.

"Thanks, lass." Captain Mard turned to his crew. "All right, boys—let's do this!" They drew their weapons.

"Wait!" Jenny said, blocking their way. "You're not going to hurt Gerald, are you?"

Captain Mard sighed, in the condescending-but-patient way adults sometimes do. He bent down to Jenny's eye-level. "Gerald may seem nice, but he's just a witless beast. And a thieving one, at that. You're lucky he didn't chomp you."

"He's not witless. If you're taking guns up there, you'll have to go through me." She crossed her arms.

Captain Mard beckoned two of his men over. "Take them back to the ship. I don't want anyone fouling things up."

The space-pirates approached. One was bald except for a ponytail atop his head, while the other had a red complexion and a jaw so square he looked like a brick.

"Come along," Ponytail said, taking Nicole gently by the arm. Brick got some resistance from Jenny, but she was half his size and couldn't do much. They escorted the girls back to the path while Captain Mard's group began their ascent.

"They're not going to kill Gerald, are they?" Jenny asked.

"Not if they can avoid it," Ponytail said. "We don't have anything against him—we just want our doubloons back."

Jenny let out a relieved breath, relaxing enough for Brick to let her walk freely. "I think we're okay then. Gerald wouldn't start a fight—he's too cool for that. You've got to meet him, 'Cole. He's like a pterodactyl, but all splotchy black and orange, with a huge crocodile tail. And he's smart! He built a machine that lets him talk, and I used it to make my voice sound like a dinosaur's. So cool."

"Wait," Brick said, stopping the group. "Did he build any other machines?"

"Sure. He's got all sorts of junk up there."

"Does he have anything with a slot the size of the doubloon?"

"I don't know. Maybe?"

Brick rubbed his huge, square chin. He took Ponytail aside to confer.

"What's the deal?" Jenny whispered to Nicole.

"The doubloons are data discs. They're worried Gerald built a machine that can read them. I don't like this, Jenny. We've got to get out of here."

"We could jet now, while they're talking."

"We'd never outrun them. Just try to come up with a plan while we walk."

The journey resumed. Nicole wracked her brain the entire way, looking for a plan that could set them free. What did she know about the space-pirates? They had hooves for feet and hooks on their hands; they played board games while sailing and treated animals poorly. But how could she use any of that? She squeezed her eyes shut. Think! There had to be *something!*

They reached the ship and ascended the gangplank.

"Any ideas?" Jenny whispered.

"No," Nicole said. "I just—wait!"

They'd reached the deck, where Nicole saw the instruments the space-pirates had used for their sea-shanty.

"I think I've got a plan," she said. "No time to explain. Just be ready when something happens."

The space-pirates escorted them below the deck, into the narrow corridors. Nicole whistled a tune.

"Hey," Ponytail said, "that's our favorite song!" He and Brick started singing along, dancing as they walked, their hooves clopping against the metal floor. Before long, an animal's barking carried through the ship.

"Miserable beast!" Brick said. "We'd better go quiet him down."

They took a left into the corridor where the animal's room

was located. When they reached the door Nicole pulled the dragon figurine from her pocket, swinging it through the air and doing her very best to imitate Jenny's bestial roars.

"What've you got there?" Ponytail asked.

"A game piece."

"Really!" Brick said, exchanging an excited look with his partner. "From what game?"

"Jenny could probably tell you more about it." She handed Brick the dragon. He examined it with the wonder of a kid who'd dug up buried treasure. Jenny, catching Nicole's wink, made up all sorts of rules for a game she'd never played. Both space-pirates listened intently.

Nicole edged toward the wall, inching out of her captors' vision. If she made any sudden movements, they might look her way, and they'd surely know what she was up to. One step at a time. Just a little closer . . .

Brick looked up from the figurine.

"Hey! Stay away from there!"

Nicole lunged the final distance, opened the secret panel on the wall and whipped out the electric baton. She flicked its switch and pointed its crackling end at Brick, stopping him in his tracks.

"Careful with that thing," he said, his hands raised in surrender. "You could hurt someone."

"Jenny," Nicole said, "get their weapons."

"Way ahead of you." Jenny was already pulling Ponytail's handgun from his holster. She took Brick's next.

"Where were you going to put us?" Nicole asked.

"That room," Ponytail said. "End of the hall, on the left."

"Cool. Lead the way."

The girls escorted the space-pirates to the room. They shuffled their prisoners inside the cell at the back and locked the door, then returned to the corridor. Nicole scooped her dragon figurine off the floor and pocketed it.

"We've got to save Gerald," Jenny said.

"Not before we free the animals here," Nicole replied.

She opened the door from which the barking had come. Inside was a room with a hot orange light and two big cages, and inside those cages were the most beautiful creatures Nicole had ever seen.

They had the bodies of tigers and heads of zebras. Their coats were striped in different colors: one sparkled blue and gold, like ocean waves and pirate booty; the other, snarling and barking through its zebra mouth, was the same purple and pink as Nicole's gypsy scarves.

Nicole realized she was still holding the baton that had been used to zap those poor animals. She tossed it aside and the snarling stopped. Both zebra-cats wagged their tails and hopped around like excited puppies.

Nicole dug into her pocket for some candy and unwrapped a mini Milky Way bar. She offered it through the bars to the purple and pink animal.

It gobbled the snack up, its wet sponge of a tongue licking Nicole's hand and making her giggle. The thing smacked its lips like a dog with peanut butter on its teeth.

Nicole gave some candy to Jenny, who fed the other animal. Soon enough, both zebra-cats were panting happily.

"I'm letting mine out," Nicole said. She did, and was immediately slurped on the face by a sloppy tongue. Jenny followed suit with similar results.

"Let's get going," Jenny said. "Gerald needs us!"

The girls sped through the corridors with their new friends in tow. They disembarked from the ship. Nicole looked up the hill, letting out a big breath. "This is a lot of climbing for one day."

"Pshaw!" Jenny said. "Climbing's for suckers!"

Nicole turned to see her cousin sitting triumphantly atop the blue-and-gold zebra-cat.

"What're you waiting for?" Jenny asked. "Get moving!"

Nicole mounted her own new friend, and they tore up the hill.

Those things were *fast!* Nimble, too—they darted from side to side, avoiding trees and branches like they were dodging bullets. Nicole kept her head low, a tuft of fur in either hand, her eyes narrowed against the wind.

"I'm going to name you Crystal," she said, "like a gypsy's crystal ball." Her mount barked happily.

In no time at all they reached the cave mouth, where the zebra-cats stopped for a breather. Jenny pulled out her stolen guns, a determined look on her face.

"Are you crazy?" Nicole asked. "Our parents would kill us if they knew we were running around with guns."

"Well what do *you* think we should do?"

"You said Gerald wouldn't pick a fight, right? I don't think the pirates would either—they just want their doubloons back. We can probably talk to Captain Mard and work something out. But if you run in there shooting lasers all over the place, it'll ruin everything."

"Ugh, *fine.*" Jenny tossed the weapons aside. "You ready to do this, Lady Dracona?"

"You bet, Pirate Queen."

The cave was dark, but the tunnel at the back glowed faintly yellow. Jenny led the way, her zebra-cat pawing quietly.

The tunnel was huge. It bent to the right almost immediately, and around the curve Nicole saw the source of the light: lamps on the ground, connected by long cables.

They continued on. After two more twists of the tunnel, Nicole heard something up ahead.

"That crackle! It sounds like the captain's gun."

"And that's Gerald's screech!" Jenny said. "Hurry!"

The zebra-cats sprinted. Soon enough the tunnel opened into a well-lit cavern with machines and parts stacked throughout. The place was the size of an NBA arena, with a crack in the ceiling big enough to fly a helicopter through.

At the far end was Gerald, exactly as Jenny had described: a pterodactyl with a crocodile's tail, all splotchy black and orange. He swooped around the cavern, avoiding laser-blasts from the pirates who took cover behind junk piles and machines.

"Sorry, Nicole," Jenny said, "but I don't think they're willing to talk."

She flipped down her eye patch and shouted a war-cry, charging toward Gerald's side of the cavern. Nicole tried to follow but couldn't control Crystal: the zebra-cat veered to the right, barking and snarling, making a straight line for the man who'd caged and shocked it.

Captain Mard, huddled behind a machine that looked like a NASA command console, saw the purple-pink blur coming. He swung his gun and fired an orange blast that hit the ground at Crystal's feet. Rocks exploded upward and Nicole was flung from her mount, rolling into the cavern wall. She smacked her head, and everything went black.

When she came around, the battle was still raging. It looked like she'd only been out a few seconds—maybe a minute, tops—but things had gotten ugly since then. Jenny zipped around on her mount, trying to avoid the crossfire. Gerald was backed into a far corner, no longer airborne, guarding a mound of bright doubloons. As Nicole rubbed her sore head and regained her footing, the space-pirates organized into a tight group that advanced on the pterodactyl. Jenny swung her mount around and stood before Gerald.

"There's no need for you to get involved," Captain Mard said. "Just step aside so we can put this thing out of its misery."

"You don't have to hurt him!" Jenny said.

"As long as he's around, our doubloons won't be safe. Now move out of the way, or you're going down with him!"

Nicole had to do something. The pirates were far away and not facing her, so she had the chance to act without being seen.

She looked to the console where Captain Mard had been. Nearby, on the ground, was the flame-spewing pistol that had been tested before everyone journeyed up the hill. She ran over and picked it up.

With the space-pirates clustered so closely, Nicole could probably hit them all at once. But she couldn't set anyone on fire—what a terrible thought! There had to be some other way.

"I'm giving you thirty seconds," Captain Mard said to Jenny. "If you haven't moved by then, you've chosen your own fate."

Nicole's mind scrambled. If she couldn't use the pistol, there had to be something else. The console, maybe—but what did it do?

She couldn't read the symbols on the sliders and buttons, but she did recognize something that looked like a microphone. This must have been the machine Jenny had told her about— the one that let Gerald talk, and turned Jenny's voice into a dinosaur's.

"Ten seconds!" Captain Mard said.

Nicole felt the dragon figurine in her pocket. *Use your imagination*, she thought.

"Five seconds!"

Nicole found a big red knob that could only be the machine's volume control. She cranked it all the way up, grabbed the microphone and ran into an unlit side-tunnel.

"Four! Three! Two!"

Aiming the fire-pistol at the tunnel mouth, Nicole unleashed a huge jet of flame into the cavern.

"Stand down, alien scum!" she said into the microphone, her amplified dinosaur-voice shaking the rock walls. "Or suffer the wrath of Lady Dracona!"

She shot more fire into the cavern, then released the trigger and peeked out from the darkness of her tunnel.

"A dragon!" Captain Mard said, dropping his gun and stumbling backward. "This crazy beast used our doubloons to make a *dragon!* No fortune is worth our lives, boys—I'm done with this planet. Run!"

The space-pirates sprinted to the main tunnel and disappeared. Nicole ran from the shadows to meet Jenny.

"That was you, 'Cole?"

"Of course not. That was Lady Dracona!" Nicole shot a brief flame-jet into the air.

Gerald stared at Nicole with those shiny purple eyes. He held up a finger on his wing, as if requesting her patience.

The pterodactyl waddled over to the machine Nicole had used. He placed a sort of mechanical crown on his head, plugged it into the machine and fiddled with some controls.

"Thank you, friend Nicole," a voice said. It came from the machine, accented in British. "Your quick thinking saved not only us, but also the poor animals that would have been crafted from the information in those doubloons."

"I'm just glad I could help. What's going to happen to the doubloons now?"

"Ideally, I'd like to deliver them into the hands of someone trustworthy. Someone who will use the information to preserve these beautiful species, rather than enslave them. There are surely races beyond the stars that would do such a thing, but—unfortunately—I haven't yet built a machine capable of interstellar travel. This may take some time."

"So you're going to stay here and work on it?"

"If you two would be so kind as to keep my secret, yes."

The girls jumped with joy, assuring Gerald they'd never tell anyone about the genius space-pterodactyl living in the cave. Their celebration was interrupted when a big, spongy tongue assaulted Nicole.

"Crystal! You're okay!" She hugged the zebra-cat's neck. It barked and wagged its tail.

"Now," Gerald said, "it's time we got you two home. Your parents must be worried sick."

"Can I ride Crystal?" Nicole asked. "It'd be faster!"

"Perhaps next time. For now, I must insist we employ an even quicker method of travel." He removed the headset and spread his wings wide, exposing his belly.

"Oh my gosh," Jenny said. "This part is the *best!*" She climbed into Gerald's belly-pouch like he was a giant kangaroo. "Wait," she said then, "this won't work. 'Cole's afraid of heights."

Nicole thought back to the pirate ship, with the kelp-trees and merfolk village down below.

"Nicole might be," she said, "but Lady Dracona isn't!" She climbed inside with Jenny, and *whoosh!* They were up and away, through the crack in the cavern's ceiling, climbing way up high.

They soared over the countryside, screaming with delight as the wind rushed their faces. Below, the land was a patchwork of blue and black, half-lit by the moon. Tiny trees and fences zipped by, while beetle-sized cows glanced up curiously.

"Look!" Nicole yelled. "Mister Weston's scarecrow! I think it just waved at us!"

"It totally did!" Jenny replied.

They laughed and cheered the whole way, these witches riding the sky on a magical Halloween night.

Weeds
by Dianna Sanchez

Dianna Sanchez is the not-so-secret identity of Jenise Aminoff, whose superpower is cooking with small children. She is an MIT alumna, graduate of the 1995 Clarion Workshop and Odyssey Online, active member of SCBWI, and a former editor of New Myths *magazine (www.newmyths.com). Aside from eighteen years as a technical and science writer, she has taught science in Boston Public Schools, developed curricula for STEM education, and taught Preschool Chef, a cooking class for children ages 3-5. A Latina geek born in Albuquerque, New Mexico, she now lives near Boston, Massachusetts, with her husband and two daughters. Her debut novel,* A Witch's Kitchen, *is available from Dreaming Robot Press.*

I could be back on Mars, I think, looking up at the flaming pink range of the Sandia Mountains. Homesickness hits me with at least as much force as the gravity. I could be home, but I'm not. There's a faint smear of green along the top of the Sandias, something I have never seen outside of a dome. And the sky above is a deep, surreal blue, the kind of sky I've only ever seen in photos or paintings. Still, I can see why Abuelo said he felt right at home when he moved from Albuquerque to Mars. To the east, above the mountains, I can just make out the faint streak of the comet, moving slowly towards Earth.

The Earthborn guy at the car rental counter behind us clears his throat.

"Oh, sorry," Mom tells him, tearing herself away from the sunset. "It's been a long, long time since I've been home."

This is still home for her, after all these years. I pull away to stare at the mountains again. I never should have agreed to come with her.

The guy behind the counter stares at me. I can feel it, like a hot wind on my neck. "Here you are, ma'am," he says, handing my mother the keys. "Are you sure you wouldn't prefer a fully automated model?"

Mom laughs her short, sarcastic bark. "You think driving on Mars is any different from driving on Earth? Relax, amigo, I bought your insurance."

"And will your, ah, daughter be driving? Is she old enough?" He paused, then asked delicately, "Can she drive wearing that thing?"

"Of course she can drive in that thing, but I don't think she's old enough here. She's fourteen."

He gapes at me, and Mom bursts out laughing. "Martian children grow fast. Less gravity to keep them down. Come on, Lupe, let's go."

We head for the doors, my exoskeleton whirring softly, walking for me, our luggage following dutifully behind us. The doors open automatically, and I cringe. I know it's safe, I know this world has air, but I have to convince myself, step by step, to walk outside. And then I stand still for a moment and think, *I'm not in a dome. I am standing outside, unprotected, and I'm alive.*

My mom says, "It's okay, Lupe. The gravity's tough for me, too. Espera aquí, I'll go get the car." She walks away in a weird, flat shuffle and leaves me there under the crazy, bruise-colored sky. It's true, the gravity is crushing me, despite my exoskeleton supporting my skinny, Marsborn bones. It hurts to stand, to move, to breathe. The air is so thick and heavy and full of weird smells: dust and exhaust and something vaguely herbal. Sagebrush? Manzanita? I have no idea.

The car pulls up, a good big one. They still make them big here. The front seat is more than roomy enough to accommodate me and my exo. I slide in and sit gratefully. My feet begin to throb.

Mom eases us out of the rental lot and down the short drive to the highway. The city's lighting up around us, a tattered blanket of glittering light stretching from the mesa to the Sandias. It makes me dizzy. The total population of Mars could fit inside Albuquerque.

As Mom drives us through the city, the restaurants and office buildings and mercados get farther apart, giving way to squat adobe homes. Traffic thins out. We can see open fields on either side of the road, glittering in the city light, covered with solar panels. Once, these fields were full of corn, tomatoes, chiles, or maybe alfalfa for pasture. Once, there was water to irrigate them all. Once, water ran freely on the surface. The thought makes me shiver.

A flock of black birds rises from the branches of a dead tree, and I squeal. I've never seen an animal outside of a zoo. How can they fly in this gravity? "Mom, are those crows?" I ask.

"Mm-hmm."

"They're bigger than I imagined." Abuelo had tried to show me, spreading his hands like wings. His hands are so small, though. Strong, rough, with dirt under the nails, but tiny, like all Earthborn hands.

"Venga, Lupe," Abuelo called. "You know the corn won't grow unless you plant it."

"Coming," I yelled back. "I have to suit up!" I hurried to the airlock and struggled into my big, crinkly dustsuit, checked my breather mask, then strapped it to my face. I pulled on a hat my mother knitted for me, decorated with cats and stiff with Marsdust.

Abuelo stepped in after me, already in his suit, and sat to tug on his work boots. I slipped my feet into my boots—they were my brother Jaime's before, a little big, but I didn't care. I tugged the straps as tight as I could and then hopped up.

"I'm ready, I'm ready!"

Abuelo grinned at me, his chin grizzled with gray and black stubble, his face like wrinkled brown leather. "Let me put my breather on." He pulled on the mask and a wide-brimmed hat, then picked up a sack of seed corn and stood up. At eight years old, I was already his height. "Okay, vamos." He closed one airlock door behind us and hit the cycler. The little airlock grew cold, and my ears popped. A green light flashed, and Abuelo pushed open the outer door.

The dome covered five acres of beige soil. It was like a park inside an enormous glass balloon. We walked past the rows of early spring crops: broccoli, chard, lettuce, peas, and my grandfather's favorite, quelites, also known as lamb's quarters. "They're weeds," he'd told me proudly. "Easy to grow, don't need much water, perfectly edible. No one else thought of bringing edible weeds."

That day, though, we were planting corn. We headed out to where the bot was buzzing back and forth across the field, digging furrows and laying drip-tape alongside them. Each drip spot was marked with a bright yellow dot, so we'd know just where to plant.

"Okay, nieta," Abuelo said. "Ready to plant?"

"How many?" I asked, though I knew. It was part of the ritual.

"Just two," he told me, smiling. "We used to put three, two to grow and one for the crow…"

"...but there are no crows on Mars!" we finished together, and I laughed.

He sighed. "No crows, no caterpillars, no grasshoppers, but also no earthworms, no bees." We kept the CO_2 content too high in the dome, to help the plants grow. It would kill any insects.

"Dad's working on the bees, Abuelo," I told him. I actually hoped he wouldn't succeed in adapting the little microdrones. I liked hand-pollinating the crops.

"I know, nieta," he told me. "Come on, we have work to do."

I held out my hand in its skin-tight glove for the seed corn. He spilled some into my hand. Carefully, I dropped two kernels into the furrow beside the first yellow dot. Then I moved on exactly half a meter to the next dot and dropped two more. Behind me, with a small trowel, Abuelo covered the corn.

A bot buzzed up to him and stopped. "All furrows are ready, señor."

"Bien," he said. "Here you go." Abuelo poured most of the seed into the bot's funnel. "When this runs out, come back, and I'll fill you up with the blue corn seed."

"Sí, señor." It backed up to the row next to us and started depositing seed corn, following the dots just as I did, and covering the seed. It zoomed on past us. We would only do one row.

"What's the point?" Jaime had asked us at breakfast. "The bots do it faster and better."

"The only way to know the soil is to be down in it," my grandfather had told him. "If you're not getting dirty, you're not doing it right."

I held out my hand, and he filled it again. The sun broke over the lip of Tharsis crater and filled the dome with a rosy glow. I dropped two kernels into the soil.

We turn west onto a small side street, Calle Otero. Panels

stretch away on either side of us, green LEDs like eyes in the darkness. Maybe a hundred meters farther, I spot Abuelo's house. Not his now, of course, but the home where he grew up. I recognize it from the photos in his scrapbook, the casement windows lit up under the protruding roof beams, the concrete block wall marking the edge of the property. All the climbing roses are gone, along with the apricot and plum trees, the grape arbor. The stump of a huge cottonwood tree still stands in the yard, surrounded by yucca and cacti and gravel. Behind the house, the fields are full of solar panels.

Mom pulls the car onto the gravel driveway and parks. "Well, we're here."

I can smell food as I exit the car, scents I've never smelled before. I'm ravenous, I realize. Mom gets to the door first, a cast-iron grillwork protecting a solid slab behind it, and rings the bell. I'm still making my way around the car when I hear the door open.

"Hola," Mom says. "I'm Elena. Are you Miguelito?"

A boy's voice pipes up, scornful. "Only my grandma calls me that. I'm Mikey."

I turn the corner and face the open doorway. Mikey is tiny. On Mars I'd guess he was two or three, but here, I have no idea. Old enough to be trusted with opening the front door.

He spots me, his eyes go wide. He shrieks, "A monster!" and runs screaming from the door. Great. So much for first impressions.

Mom bursts out laughing, which just completely makes my day. "God, Mom, didn't you tell them about me?" She just looks at me, with that sly grin on her face, and I feel my stomach sink. "You didn't, did you? Oh, fantastic."

A woman hurries up to the door. "Elena? Is that you?"

I have to blink. She looks so much like Mom. Slightly shorter, with a mad bush of hair tinted red, unlike Mom's salt-and-pepper bob. Older, more wrinkled, and plump, rounded in every curve where Mom is slender, like all Martians. The same cheekbones, the same chocolate eyes, darker skin.

"Rita," Mom says. "God! It's so good to see you again!" And she grabs her sister in an enormous hug, yelling, "Omigod! Omigod!" while Rita hugs her back and says, "Díos mio mi vida! I can't believe you're back."

Finally, Mom peels an arm loose and reaches for me. "Lupe, come here and meet your Tía Rita."

Rita stares up at me, color draining from her face. "Miguelito wasn't lying, then. I was gonna paddle him and send him to his room. What...." She glances at my mom. "You could have warned us."

"I agree," I tell her.

Mom shrugs. "What difference would it have made? If I told you before we came, everybody would have been whispering and gossiping and coming by to sneak a peek at her. I wanted tonight to be just family."

Rita folds her arms and clenches her jaw, exactly the way Mom does when she's mad but doesn't want to yell. She nods, once, and steps aside. "Well, then, come on in."

"Thanks," I say. I have to duck my head to get in the door. My great-grandfather, who built the house, was a very small man, perhaps one-point-five meters, and though I am small for a Marsborn, with the exo adding to my height, my hair brushes the ceiling. I'm in the kitchen, beside a dining table set for six, with the sink and stove on the opposite side. A refrigerator hums in the corner.

Several pots simmer on the stove, filling the kitchen with those marvelous smells. There's the tang of Mexican oregano, the bite of red chile, the rich, earthy aroma of corn, a sweet hint of tomato. My mouth begins to water.

I extend my hand to Tía Rita and pop it out of the exo. "Hi. It's nice to meet you," I say. "I've heard a lot about you from Mom and Abuelo. And I always wanted to see his house."

Tía Rita blinks, surprised. She reaches out and grips my bare hand. "Of course, Lupe," she says. "I'm glad you came. You should know where you come from."

Hmph. I know where I come from.

"Please, come sit down," Rita says, pulling out a chair for Mom and another for me.

I sit carefully at the table and stroke the wood. We have no wood on Mars; a table like this would be hideously expensive.

"Would you like something to drink?"

"Water, please."

She bustles away, rummaging in the cabinet for a good glass. I hear a rustle at my feet. Mikey is staring up at me from under the table with large brown eyes. There's a faint slant to his eyes I hadn't noticed before.

"You're green!" he whispers urgently to me. "And you're all covered in metal."

"I know," I whisper back.

He stares at me, wide-eyed. "Are you a monster?"

"Maybe," I tell him conspiratorially, "but I am definitely your cousin."

Mikey considers this. "Will I turn green? Am I a monster, too?"

"Only if you want to be," I say.

"If I were a monster," he says slowly, "maybe Paula would stop beating me up on the way home from school."

"There are other ways to make her stop besides turning yourself green," I tell him.

"Like wearing all that metal?"

"The exo is here to protect my bones because they're too weak for Earth gravity. See how each piece follows one of my bones?" I tap the strut along my shin. Dad printed it specifically to fit me. "Without that, I could break my leg just by stepping too hard."

Tía Rita sets a glass down in front of me. "Is that Mikey

down there? Miguelito, come out. She's not going to eat you."

Mikey scuttles back out of sight and emerges on the other side of the table. "Of course she's not going to eat me," he says, suddenly bold. "She's a *plant*. She doesn't eat food."

My mother laughs. "She does eat, chico. Just not as much as you do, and not all the same things you do."

"Not meat," he says.

"No, not meat," I confirm. I do eat insects, but Mom warned me that's considered gross on Earth. Like eating animals is totally normal?

"Then you can't eat me!" he cries triumphantly.

"You're being rude," Tía Rita chides.

"Am not." He disappears under the table again.

"Aí, Díos mio," Tía Rita says. "That boy gets more stubborn every day." She sits down with her own glass. "Are you staying here tonight?"

Mom shakes her head. "We'll stay at the Dorado Inn. They have low-gravity gel beds for us. It's going to take me a while to get used to the gravity again." She glances at me. I say nothing.

"Oh," Tía Rita says, visibly relieved. "Yes, that would probably be better."

The front door opens. "I'm home!" A man walks in, closing the door behind him. He's Asian, and I understand the slant to Mikey's eyes. He blinks at me, then smiles. "So you're our Martian relations? I'm Andy Liao." He holds out a hand to Mom, who rises to take his hand, and then to me. His grip is gentle. "I guess you're Guadalupe."

"Call me Lupe, please," I tell him.

"That's a sweet exosuit you've got there. Series V?"

I nod. "Dad modified the design a little for me." Mom shifts uncomfortably beside me.

Andy glances around. "Where's Mikey?"

Tía Rita huffs and nods at the table.

Andy sits down and peers under the table. "Mikey? Come

on out, buddy."

Mikey clambers out, sulky. "Abuela said I was being rude."

"Asking too many questions again?"

Mikey shrugged.

"Go ahead," I invite him. "Preguntame. I know you have questions. Everybody does."

Mikey cocks his head. "Did it… hurt?"

"It itched like crazy for about a week, but otherwise, no."

"Is it growing on you, like a fungus or something? Or is it part of your suit?"

"The exosuit's separate. I need it because my bones aren't strong enough for Earth gravity. The green stuff is part of my skin." I hold out my arm to him. "Touch it, you'll see."

Tía Rita calls out, "It's not catching, is it?"

Mom laughs. "Not at all. It's just algae, one of the oldest organisms on Earth, the first plant life to venture out of the ocean. It partnered with a fungus and became lichen. That lichen broke down rocks and created the first soil. In Lupe, it does the same thing as it did in lichen. It creates food from sunlight in exchange for minerals and nitrogen from her body."

Andy reaches out and touches my arm through a gap in the exo's struts, then chuckles. "Feels just like my skin," he says. "Dry as paper, tough as leather."

"Mars is a desert," I tell him. "Just like here."

"And you grow crops there?" he asks, suddenly alert.

"Yes, we did," Mom says.

"We do," I correct her.

Jaime chased me through the sunflowers, just like old times, just like he wasn't already in college. It was a whole new field, ten more acres, a fresh dome next to our old home dome. The sunflowers were taller than me, just opening their buds to the sun. We wouldn't be able to eat their seeds—they'd be full of lead and other heavy metals—but they'd make the soil better, get it ready for edible crops. My dustsuit crinkled as I ran, dodging and weaving between the rows.

"Ha!" Jaime yelled, lunging for me. "Got you!"

But I twisted out of his grasp. "Can't catch me, shorty! Earthborn!"

"Jaime! Lupe!" Abuelo's voice rang in my breather's earbuds. "Come on in. We have something to talk about."

Mom and Dad were sitting in the kitchen. Abuelo stood at the sink.

"We're getting divorced," Mom said.

My parents wouldn't look at each other. Jaime looked shocked but not all that surprised. I clenched my fists. "You can't get divorced."

Dad looked away from me. "Lupe, I'm sorry. We tried to work things out. Your mother wants to return to Earth, and I want to stay here."

I turned to Mom. "So, you're just going to leave us?"

"I'm taking you with me." Mom tried to take my hand, but I pulled it away. "Lupe," she said, "this is a wonderful opportunity. The ISA has snagged a comet, a big one, and they're bringing it back to Earth. Some of that water is coming to New Mexico. We can farm again, on our own land. We can go home."

"Your home, not mine."

Mom turns back to Jaime. "This would be easier if you would come with us."

Jaime's face is streaked with tears. He shakes his head. "I'm halfway through college in Bradbury. Mars is a much better place for astronomy than Earth—less atmosphere in the way."

"But don't you miss it? Don't you want to see Earth again?"

"Mom, I was four when we moved. I don't even remember Earth. I may not be Marsborn, but this is my home."

"Well, I was born here," I declare loudly. "Look at me! I started my skin treatments already. I'd be a freak there."

Dad says, "She's right. It would be incredibly hard for her, Elena. Her bones will be so brittle, her muscles weak. It will take years of serious therapy for her to acclimate to the gravity, and even then, she'll probably need an exosuit for the rest of her life."

"She'll be among family," Mom pointed out. "We're so isolated here. She would have a chance to reconnect with our culture."

Dad folded his arms. "Her eyesight will deteriorate. She'll sprain ankles and break bones, over and over again. What kind of life is that?"

"What kind of life is this?" Mom yelled back at him. "No breathable atmosphere. The water's full of perchlorates, the soil's full of heavy metals, all trying to poison us. And best of all, we're constantly bombarded by cosmic rays that give us cancer and destroy our brains. Do you remember when our magnetic shielding failed, and we had to stay in the basement for a week while the bots fixed it?"

Abuelo speaks up, finally. "It's not that bad, Elena. We've found solutions for all these problems. We're improving on them all the time, expanding."

"Don't you start," Mom said. "I believed you when you said this would be better, that we'd be helping to save humanity from itself. But there's no reason for it now, when Earth's carbon dioxide levels are falling and there's water coming. We have a chance to revive our way of life, to live as our ancestors did."

Abuelo considered this. "De seguro. But I don't believe in going backwards. We've built something amazing. I'm going to see it through. I'll need help, though. Enrique?"

Dad shook his head. "I've got my business in Bradbury. Sorry, Ramon."

"Then that just leaves Lupe."

Mom bristled. "Lupe is coming with me."

"No, I'm not," I screamed at her. "You can't make me! I

want to stay here, with Abuelo."

"Lupe, on Earth, you'll never have to wear a breather again. You can walk in the open air, eat all you want. You can go to a real university, not that teensy little excuse for a college in Bradbury."

"Hey!" Jaime said.

"I don't care," I said. "I want to stay here with Abuelo. I want to make this the biggest farm on Mars. Dad, tell her I can stay here." But Dad just looked away.

"I'll file abuse charges! I'll file for emancipation!" I told them. "You can't make me go!"

Still in my dustsuit, I grabbed my breather and slammed through the airlock door. I've always done that, whenever I got angry. I'd head out to the dome and work it off.

A minute later, I heard the airlock cycle behind me. It didn't take Abuelo long to find me among the cornstalks.

"Lupe," Abuelo said in his soft voice, "I know you're mad."

"Of course I'm mad! She makes decisions for me, like I have no brain of my own. It's not fair! I don't want to go. I want to stay here with you."

"I want you to stay, too," he told me. "You have a real gift for farming, a love of the soil, just like me. You could make a huge difference here."

"Then convince her to let me stay!"

Abuelo was quiet for a moment, then he said, "You could also farm on Earth. They need you, too."

"Ha. Farming on Earth is easy. Any idiot could do it."

"But you might learn something new, something you can bring back here to me." He gave me a hug. "Venga con tu madre. You can't make this decision without knowing what you're giving up. Go to Earth, see what all the fuss is about. Then decide. I'll convince Elena to respect your decision."

I have never seen so much food before. One after another,

Tía Rita lays the dishes out on the table. Chiles rellenos – green chiles stuffed with cheese, battered, fried, and smothered with red chile sauce. Blue corn enchiladas. Pinto beans and Spanish rice. Guacamole and tortilla chips. Sopapillas and honey.

"I made it all vegetarian for you," Tía Rita says. "I hope it's okay."

"It's amazing, Rita!" my mother gushes. "God, I'd forgotten how good rice is."

"She broke out the last of the Chimayo chile powder for you," Andy confides, helping himself to a large portion of enchiladas.

Mom's jaw drops. "Rita, you shouldn't have! It's so expensive now."

"Worth its weight in gold," Mikey quips.

"Not every day we get visitors from Mars," Tía Rita replies, glaring at her grandson, then turning her glare on me. "Lupe, you're hardly eating anything. Don't you like chile?"

I have taken less than a third of what everyone else has on their plate. "I love it," I say truthfully. The red chile on the enchiladas dances on my tongue. "This is just a lot more than I'm used to eating."

"Don't you need to eat more in higher gravity?" Andy asks.

"She's a plant, Dad," Mikey says. "She doesn't have to eat much." He held a spoon next to my arm. "Look, she's the same color as the guacamole! You should be named Guacamole instead of Guadalupe."

"Miguelito!" Tía Rita says sharply. "Cierra la boca y no entra moscas."

Shut your mouth and you'll swallow no flies, something Abuelo said to me at least once a week, as long as I lived with him. I choke back tears. "It's okay, he's right. I'm like a giant walking avocado. I didn't know that before. I've never eaten an avocado."

"You have to have some!" Mikey cries. "I love guacamole."

He spoons a generous dollop onto my plate. I dip a tortilla chip in and taste it: smooth, mellow, a little like tofu but slightly spicy with chunks of tomato, onion, garlic.

"It's delicious," I tell him. "Thank you."

"So you can't grow avocados on Mars?" Tía Rita asks.

"No trees," Mom replies. "They take too long to mature. They need food now, not five years from now."

"But you grew other things, like chile?" Andy asks.

"Enough for family, not enough to sell. Conditioning the soil for nightshades is hard. They take up too many heavy metals," Mom explains. "Greens, too."

"Then why didn't you use hydroponics?" Andy asks.

Mom pushes her plate away. "Stubborn pig-headedness."

"Flavor," I retort. "Vegetables grown in water taste like water. It takes soil to grow really good food."

"It's stupid," Mom said. "Growing food in poisoned soil with poisoned water in poisoned air. If we'd done hydroponics, we could have lived in Bradbury, not out in the middle of nowhere. We could have grown twice as much. And your father would never have convinced me we should turn you into a green freak, just to reduce your need to eat. Now we can stop the treatments, and you'll go back to normal."

I push away from the table. "I AM normal!" I yell at her. "On Mars, I'm normal. You're the one who brought me here and made me a freak." And before she can reply, I get up and walk out the front door.

I'm thirty meters down the road, pacing along the fence, kicking up dust, wishing for a decent cornfield, when Mikey comes up behind me, swinging a flashlight. Redundant. The exo has plenty of exterior lighting.

"That was mean, what your mom said."

"Nothing I haven't heard before," I tell him, though that's not really true.

I stop, realizing suddenly that there's no dome, I'm in open air. Unprotected. I shiver all over.

"Look," Mikey says, "there's the Big Dipper. Do you have that on Mars?"

I look up. I can barely see it, with all the city light, but he's right. "Of course we do. The stars are the same on Mars. My brother Jaime studies them. Sometimes, in the summer, we'd go out in the dome at night and lie on the soil, looking up between cornstalks at the stars. We'd try to guess where Earth was, and sometimes we'd even find it." And suddenly, I'm okay again, because I'm under the same old sky.

Mikey looks out at the rows of solar panels. "I think it would be cool, growing stuff again. I want to grow grapes, like Abuelito did. Do you think we can?"

I look down at him. He looks so hopeful, one corner of his mouth trying to edge up into a smile. "Maybe. It depends on a lot of things: the condition of the soil, the availability of water."

"Could you check it? Tomorrow, maybe?"

"Sure, why not?" I look down at him. "You're the only one who doesn't think I'm a freak. Why is that?"

His shoulders start shaking, silently laughing. "Have you seen my eyes? I've been the family freak up until you came along."

I run the exo's gloves along the fence, bumping over the rusted barbs in the wire. I wonder where his mom is. "Tía Rita doesn't seem to mind."

"No, but other people do." He paused to pick up an empty can from the ground. "They don't know what to make of you, or where you fit in."

"We're malezas," I say, thinking of Abuelo. "Weeds. No one wants us, but we grow all the same."

"Heh. That's better than guacamole, I guess."

We laugh.

"Let's go back and have dessert." Mikey turns back to the house.

The alarm goes off at seven a.m. on the dot. I wake up in the gel bed feeling like I'd been beaten. Every joint in my body screams in protest. In the bed next to me, Mom moans. "Oh, god, why did I ever think this was a good idea?"

By the time we emerge from the hotel, the sun has risen well above the Sandia Mountains. I'm shocked to see that they are bluish-grey in this light, fringed and dotted with green. Nothing like Martian mountains. I feel betrayed somehow.

Today, in daylight, I see nothing but wasteland, everything brown and dead, the Rio Grande dry as a bone, as it has been for fifty years. Empty buildings stare at me as we drive down into the valley. Broken windows gape open, adobe walls crumble. Sand piles in corners.

At the farm, I find the same thing. I look at the fields and want to cry. Beneath the solar panels, in the perpetual shade, I can see that the topsoil is gone, used up or scoured away down to the parched clay beneath.

Mom parks the car in the driveway. "Come on, Lupe."

"I told Mikey I'd check out the farm," I reply. "I'll meet you out here when you're ready."

"But Lupe…"

I stride away. Behind me, I hear the door open and close.

I rev up my exo, hop right over the barbed wire fence, and prowl around the grounds, beside the neat, reflective rows of panels. I pass the bones of a toolshed, corrals for cattle, old cast iron bathtubs used as troughs, an ancient manual tractor, its tires all rotted. Shovel blades, their handles broken. A ditch, half full of sand. My feet raise puffs of dust as I walk. Everything is dead, I think.

Out of the corner of my eye, I spy movement. A bird darts under the fence in front of me. It pauses, cocking its head at me for a moment, its crest pointing back like its long tail. And then it darts forward under a row of solar panels to pull a wriggling beetle from the sand and gulp it down. Off it dashes, like a tumbleweed on the wind.

A roadrunner, alive, breathing. Now I see small signs of life everywhere. A grasshopper, a bird, the curving tracks of a snake. Tiny specks of green in hollows and along the ditches. And there, just beginning to push its way up, a spear of asparagus. How is that even possible?

I crouch down, free my hand from the exo, and push my fingers into the sand. To my surprise, it isn't all sand, not here along the ditch. There's still some soil, still some life. I feel an insect wriggle against my skin, something I've only ever felt in science class or a lab.

If you don't get dirty, you're not doing it right.

"Lupe," my mother says behind me.

I stand up, turn to her. Tía Rita has come with her.

"What did you find?" she asks.

I show them the asparagus, and they both gasp. "I had no idea anything could still grow out here," Tía Rita says.

"I'm amazed, too," I tell her. "I think you're in better shape than I thought."

She squints at me, the sun in her face. "You believe that? You think we can farm here again?"

"You'll need new topsoil, some amendments, and drip irrigation equipment. Some agricultural bots would help."

Mom looks at me. "Will you do it?"

I take a deep breath. "No. I'm going home, Mom, you know that. I hurt everywhere. The sky is too weird. And every time I step outside without a suit or a dome, I have a panic attack. I hate it here. I want to go home."

Mom stares at me. "I didn't really think what it would be like for you," she said. "I love being home, even with the gravity. Everything smells right again, everything tastes right. And there are people, family! I have been so lonely, for so long. I guess I assumed you'd feel the same way. But I was wrong. I was thinking about me, not you. I... I didn't want to leave you behind. I'll miss you so much." She wiped a tear from her eye.

"Me, too," I told her. "So how about a compromise? I'll stay long enough to help you get the farm going again. But then, I'm going home."

She smiled at me. "Sounds good."

"So where do we start?" Tía Rita asks.

"Have you considered planting weeds?"

Builders for the Future
by Salena Casha

Salena Casha's work has appeared in over thirty publications. She was a finalist for the 2013-2014 Boston Public Library's Children's Writer-in-Residence. Her first three picture books were published by MeeGenius Books. One of them, Nuwa and the Great Wall, *was featured in the 2014 PBS Summer Learning Project for kids and won honorable mention in the 2014 Hollywood Halloween Book Festival. When not writing, she can be found editing math books, carving pumpkins and traveling the world. Check out her website at www.salenacasha.com.*

Seraphina's little brother was the first to notice when things changed. Maybe it was because he spent most of his days by himself in his family's house on Mars trying to outwit the babysitter bots assigned to him. Or maybe he was in fact a better observer than anyone ever gave him credit for—a strange byproduct of his "condition."

So of course he was the one who first saw it during a snack break. The hologram floated in the traction tube and pinged under warped glass. It didn't matter who the letter was for. He wanted to read it.

He poked at the fingerprint sensor. It glowed red.

Incorrect match.

He frowned and punched the button again.

Incorrect match.

Even though he was persistent for an eight-year-old, after fifteen minutes of pressing, squeezing, and sticking his hand into the tube itself, he gave up. Whatever the letter said, it wasn't worth losing fingers for.

When Seraphina came home from school that day, about four hours after her brother found the letter, she saw it the moment she walked into their living pod. She knew the letter was supposed to arrive because Mark hadn't been able to shut up about it during their year eleven science class.

How he'd gotten his letter.

How he already knew what the competition task would be.

How he was going to be the first person in a hundred years from their school to be selected as a Builder for the Future.

It wasn't curiosity that Seraphina felt when she walked straight past the traction tube and up to her room. Yes, her hands itched to wind the message into playback, but she didn't. Instead, she sat down at her work desk, popped out her building set and took apart the hovercraft miniature she'd skimmed together the previous night.

The sleek hull shone in the limited glo-light of her overhead. It wouldn't be like those huge ones that bobbed along Mars' streets. It could never hold a person or a full-sized animal.

Maybe a baby mouse. Someday. When it was good enough.

With the sleek pin of her skimmer, she split the hovercraft into the strangest shapes and bits that she could, carving it into a massive puzzle of cubes and circles that hadn't existed before. One-handed, she grabbed her timer. For a moment, she closed her eyes and took a quick, quiet breath.

Her fingers found the clock and she punched start.

It took her five minutes and twenty-four seconds to rebuild the craft, slightly different than the last. A little thinner around the edges with sharper propellers. She'd done it about a minute slower than the night before, so she took apart the spacecraft, skimmed it into different pieces and began again.

Her fingers moved easily between the blocks. They were titanium, no tick marks or buttons to show where or how they fit together. Like a bike without training wheels. Her dad had used them at work to build structures, the kind that people lived in on Colony M. Once he built the miniature, he'd take it to the lab. They'd blow up the little pieces of matter until they were big enough to fit an entire person. The new building or craft or piece of equipment would then be assigned a place in Colony M. Easy to take apart if you had a giant skimmer, which the government definitely did.

She'd taken the blocks from her father's toolbox after he'd floated away. No one, not her mother, not her brother, not even those strange government men in suits who gave her family the news, had tried to take them away from her. They were hers just as much as they had once been his. Grown-up toys, they'd called them. But to her, they were more than that.

After two hours, she'd gotten her time down to four minutes and twenty-six seconds. Good enough for now. She stretched, her neck aching, and then walked downstairs and ordered a snack pack from the kitchen bot, chocolate chip flavored. She sat by herself at the counter, her legs swinging in the air from the stool, gravity meter ticking steadily at her hip.

"Fina, Fina! It's broken!"

Her brother rushed into the kitchen waving something that looked like an old Earth egg-beater. Seraphina had given it to him for his fifth birthday. It was a handheld gaming console, something he could sneak after lights-out and play. The Sleep Police couldn't pick up on it because it operated on a secret wavelength. It projected a hologram of the game onto any flat surface and, if he wore it with the virtual glasses he had, it could take him anywhere he wanted.

Once she'd caught him using it to go to virtual school at Seraphina's instruction center which, given his position, wasn't allowed.

"What are you doing?" she'd asked.

"Being normal," he'd replied. "I just like to stand in the back and watch."

Sometimes, if she closed her eyes hard enough, she could feel him in the back of the classroom. One of the invisible.

His dark curls fell into his eyes, and he brushed them away.

"What happened?" she asked, setting down her chocolate-chip bar. He eyed the snack before handing over the toy.

"It stopped lighting up, and now it just fizzles every time I try to turn it on."

She frowned, shook it, turned it upside down, and punched a few buttons. It whined. She'd need to take a closer look at the wires.

"I'll fix it tonight," she said.

"Caleb, please return to the nursery," a robotic voice resounded through the halls.

"Just one second," Caleb called over his shoulder before turning to Seraphina.

Something in his eyes told her that he hadn't come out here at all to have her fix his toy. No. He was curious about something else. She didn't need to look closer at the device to know he'd sabotaged it on purpose, just so he could talk to her.

"You got a message you know. In the tube," he said.

"So?" Seraphina said, her mouth full of chocolate chips.

"Can I watch you open it?"

She waited for him to get bored with her and just walk away. She ate the entire bar, slowly.

He didn't move.

Her mother often joked that it was his curiosity and persistence that got him banned from school. Seraphina knew the world didn't work that way; the doctors said he had some sort of genetic mutation that made him different from everyone else. She had it, too, not enough to keep her from going to school, but she always knew what she was. And whatever it was that they both had, it gave them things other people didn't see or understand. Like super-powered brains. And for Seraphina, a few other not-so-nice things.

"Fine," she said. "I'll open it."

She pushed off from the table and landed on the floor, the gravity sensors pulling at her bare toes. Their home on Mars, according to the chart readouts, had a far lighter gravity than her ancestors' original home on Earth. The first settlers had coated the planet in some sort of gravity paint that helped hold everyone in place. Or at least that was what it was supposed to do.

She'd once found a corner of her instruction center in the cafeteria that had a little less gravity than normal. She wouldn't have noticed except for the fact that her toes floated an inch above the ground before she righted herself. After that, she'd designed her own personal gravity meter and kept an eye on the readouts. She didn't want to just start floating away into the hazy purple sky in the middle of an afternoon.

Caleb followed her back to the front room, the message pinging insistently as she neared.

She took a deep breath and swiped her finger across the monitor. A flash of fear went through her.

What if she didn't get in?

What if Mark was the only one in her class allowed to go?

What if *she*, Seraphina Saff, wasn't good enough?

The letter folded out in front of her in the air, the robotic voice of the holomail reverberating in space. She wanted to tell it to be quiet, but her tongue was heavy in her mouth.

"Dear Ms. Seraphina Saff,

We are pleased to inform you that you have been accepted into this year's Builders for the Future competition. You were one of 20 selections within Colony M.

The competition will be 24 hours in total and will take place in the Central Mars Natatorium on West Street two days from now at 12:00 Lunar Time. You are not allowed to bring anything with you, and you will be scanned for tools, data chips, and blueprints upon arrival.

Best of luck."

Caleb whooped, jumping up and down. "You made it, you made it!"

Seraphina didn't move. She didn't even smile. Her hands started to shake, though, and the urge she'd been fighting all her life, the urge to destroy something out of pure joy struck her in the chest.

"I need to practice," she blurted out as Caleb wrapped his arms around her middle.

"Can I come watch?" Caleb asked, his arms still locked tightly around her.

She wasn't sure if he meant watching her practice or watching her competition. With her right hand, she gently pushed him away.

"No," she said, even though something in her chest pulled, and she knew she shouldn't have said it.

Caleb frowned, crossing his arms in front of his chest. "But…"

Seraphina did not wait for him to finish his sentence. Clutching the hologram chip to her chest, she walked back upstairs and locked her bedroom door behind her.

She had made it. At eleven, she was one of the youngest Mars pioneers to be selected for the program. The first woman who orbited Jupiter had won the competition years ago. Famous people were made in the builders' competition.

Like her dad.

The urge to break something pinged through her like a zip of electricity, and she headed for the desk. Placing the letter on the table, she reached for the mini hovercraft she'd built. Her skimmer tore it to pieces, fingers finding every dent and crack. It felt good to destroy something, to reduce it to nothing. The letter on her desk pulsed with energy as she took a deep breath and eyed the timer beside her. She needed to practice.

Making it into the BFF competition wasn't enough for her, she decided, her hand hovering over the punch clock. She needed to beat Mark.

She needed to win.

By the time she got to school the next day, everyone already knew she'd been selected. A hush descended over the classroom pod as she entered. No one talked to her in school anyway, so walking into the classroom was the worst part of every day. Her stomach curled, and her fingers itched, and she wished she was back in her room with her model. Wished she could have just switched with Caleb for the day and stayed home.

She sat down at her desk.

Greetings, Ms. Saff. Today, we will continue your lesson in geometry.

She rolled her eyes. She'd covered this weeks ago when she couldn't fall asleep. Numbly, her fingers moved across the screen, answering before the computer could finish asking her the question.

After her classmates tired of staring at her, they faced their own desks and commenced their lessons.

Maybe, if she was very quiet and careful about it, she could take one of her "sick day" pills she'd self-engineered and get released early for the day. She needed to practice, after all.

A throat cleared somewhere above her, and she looked up to see Mark smirking at her. He folded his grasshopper-thin arms in front of his chest, his greasy black hair shining in the LED light. Like the rest of them, he wore a normal silver jumpsuit with an orange stripe around the right bicep and an emergency oxygen machine pinholed to the back, just in case the oxygen bubble that covered all of Colony M popped.

"Heard we were the only two who made it into the competition from our sector," he said casually.

She did not look up at him.

"Interesting," she replied.

"Aren't you going to congratulate me?" he asked.

Her fingers paused and she glared at her screen. "Not unless you're going to congratulate me."

He snickered, his eyes narrowing.

"Fine," he said. "I'm surprised you made it at all, really. With that held-back brother of yours and the rumors I hear about you, I didn't think they'd let people like you in."

Seraphina's fists clenched, her heart racing.

Don't, she told herself. She pressed her lips together hard, her blood beating fiercely in her ears.

"Maybe they just felt bad for your family. I mean, your dad won years ago, right? He was older than us, but we can't all be prodigies. Maybe they feel bad for you after his little accident and all. Trying to make up for the fact that one of his kids won't ever amount to anything, that he never really got to leave anything behind that was worthwhile."

She couldn't feel her hands as she stood up, the chair whirring away from her.

Ms. Saff, please return to your seat, her monitor spoke aloud.

She ignored it.

"Don't," she warned.

Everyone else in the class had stopped working to watch the pair. If by the third warning neither of them had sat down, the AI would call a monitor. They had minutes.

"Don't what? I'm only telling the truth," Mark said. "You're probably just as stupid as your slow brother."

She wouldn't have cared if Mark had just insulted her personally. She knew she was smarter than him, and she felt nothing at all for him. But Mark had never met Caleb, didn't know the things he could do. Because of some test Caleb hadn't passed but couldn't study for, he'd never be allowed to show them.

Her clenched fist connected with Mark's nose before she even knew what happened. It crunched beneath her hand.

Mark yelped, a high-pitched screech. Pain exploded over her knuckles but she didn't even flinch.

An alarm sounded somewhere nearby, and she wasn't sure if one of her classmates had pulled the alert, or if they'd exceeded their number of warnings.

"You broke my nose!" Mark grunted, hands still covering his face.

"I hope it hurt," she replied. It didn't even sound like her, tinny and far away.

Inside though, she was shaking. She'd barely ever touched another human being. Hugs made her squirm, and even when she'd been a mini-kid, she hated holding her mother's hand. Which was one of her superpowers, her mother always said.

Blood from Mark's nose dripped off her finger, and she wiped it on the shoulder of his jumpsuit.

"Don't ever insult my brother again," she added. The threat sounded weird when she said it out loud, not like herself, but what was she supposed to do? It was her brother!

The metal door of the class pod screeched open, and two large AIs entered and stalked toward them. They were seven feet tall with blue-gray laser eyes. All four narrowed in on Mark and Seraphina.

"Step away from one another and put your hands on the desk in front of you," the first AI instructed.

Seraphina held Mark's eyes as she put her hands on her keypad. He wiped his nose before setting his palms down on the panel in front of him. Scarlet smeared the white surface. Her punch still crackled across her knuckles.

She wasn't sorry.

The first AI approached. "You, come with me," it said to Seraphina.

"And you, with me," the second said to Mark.

As they walked down the aisle of desks, Seraphina held Mark's gaze and didn't let him see how terrified she was of what was about to happen.

The AI replayed the video of what happened and, instead of watching a scene she'd already been a part of, Seraphina stared at the shock on the Head of the Pod's face.

At the end, she paused the video and shook her head once, her pixie cut shaking back and forth in a wave of gold. "This isn't good."

"I know," Seraphina said, "but he said terrible things about my brother."

"They're just words, Seraphina. They can't do anything to you," the Head replied.

Deep down, Seraphina knew this wasn't true at all. Sometimes words were the most painful blow. Sometimes they could force people to change their entire life for good and bad. But she didn't want to argue. Not when she was already in trouble.

"Do you know the first rule of Colony M, Seraphina?" the Head asked.

"Yes," Seraphina responded. "Rule Number One of Colony M: No violence allowed."

"And why do we have this rule, Seraphina?" the Head asked.

Seraphina didn't squirm, just looked the Head in the eye and spoke words she'd memorized back in year six.

"Because so few people actually made it here from Earth."

The Head leaned forward, her watery eyes sad. "Every life on Mars matters," the Head said, pointing at the banner above her desk, the exact words blinking in hologram light.

Existence mattered. But living in Colony M—things like

going outside or going to school—had requirements. Ones that Caleb hadn't met. Ones she almost hadn't, either.

"I have to punish you. We have a zero-tolerance policy for violence. And given your background, it worries us."

Background. Genes. Same thing. Seraphina's hands itched to destroy something, but she held steady.

"I understand," Seraphina managed to choke out, even though her eyes had started burning.

"Your invitation to the Build of the Future competition will be revoked. And you're put on a two-week suspension pending a community jury decision and psychological evaluation."

The words almost split Seraphina in half. Her insides burned. She'd worked so hard, putting in years of preparation, and they were going to take BFF away from her just because she'd stood up to a bully? Later, her mother would say it could have been much worse. She could have been detained and put on a watch list. She could have been sent away from her mother and Caleb to an entirely different colony. Her mom said this a lot, and the more adults said something, Seraphina decided, the more you knew they didn't believe it themselves. Could have been worse? Everything was as bad as it could possibly be.

No.

"No, what?" the Head asked.

Did I really say that out loud? Seraphina thought.

"No," Seraphina said again, louder this time, "that's not a fair punishment."

"I think I'm going pretty easy on you actually, given the circumstances," the Head said, her thin eyebrows rising. They weren't the same color as the hair on her head, Seraphina realized.

Once a family had one selection in a generation, it was over. Builders were innovators of the future. They went to special schools. They were the ones who got to take building blocks to labs and create things. They got huge skimmers. Her mother worked in disease research, her father had been a builder. Caleb would never be allowed to work and support any of them. Seraphina had been their only chance.

But maybe not.

"Let Caleb sub in for me. Don't let my family lose our only spot. Please, just let him play instead."

Seraphina couldn't believe she'd said the words.

The Head raised her eyebrows higher. "I'm not sure we can do something like that."

"You can," Seraphina insisted. "Just let Caleb compete for me. I won that spot regardless of what happened today. At least let a Saff into the competition. I know people can only be selected, ever, once."

It was fair. And really, the Head probably thought it would be to her advantage. There was a little bit of shuffling and grumbling, but Seraphina could already see that the Head was thinking about it. She could tell because Caleb's file had popped up on the corner of the Head's eyelet reader. Hyper. Difficulty concentrating. Dyslexic. Unfocused. Slow. Really, what were the odds in the Head's mind that Caleb could win at all?

"He won't be allowed any special considerations," the Head said. "He'll be treated as a normal participant."

If this was the deal, Seraphina had to take it. And it didn't matter, because Seraphina was sure Caleb could show Mark who the real genius was.

"Fine," she said.

"I'll talk it over with the Committee. See what they say," the Head said. "Now the AI will escort you back to your Living Pod."

With a smile and with hands that no longer itched to destroy something, Seraphina walked out of the Learning Center. For the rest of the day, even though she could still see Mark smirking at her in the back of her mind, she already felt like she'd won.

Caleb's letter came the same way Seraphina's had, approximately two hours after her fight with Mark. Caleb didn't know that his sister had stood up for him in school or that people outside of their living pod even knew who he was.

The letter winked at him. His name. Even though a few of the letters danced away from him, he knew it was his. And this time, when he punched the traction tube with his fingerprint, the glass slid open for him.

It took him a few tries to read the whole thing through, but at the end of the letter, his eyes lit up. He was going to get to be like his big sister for once and play the game! He spent the next few hours raiding Seraphina's room for her blocks. It had taken him a half-hour to get into her room, but he'd managed to crack the code on the door and rewire it to use the password "Fart Bubbles".

The blocks were smooth and sleek beneath his fingers. He'd seen her build things with them—planes and cars and hovercrafts and houses. Just like Dad had before he'd floated away into the sky. She'd said they were for practice, and he needed to practice, too.

When Seraphina came home, she walked into her room to find Caleb sitting at her desk, eyes frowning in concentration at the structure in front of him: a strangely tilted silver tower. It was different than what she normally came up with, and she had to bite her tongue to ask him what he was doing with her blocks.

"Congrats!" she said.

He turned, dropping the blocks, rushing to give her a hug. His arms wrapped around her waist, and she was suddenly surprised at how small he was. He smiled a dizzying smile.

"I've been practicing," he said.

Seraphina's gut clenched. She knew what she'd lost, and now all the pressure was on Caleb. She smiled and squeezed him back even though her eyes burned a little with the thought that she'd never get to compete.

"Can you help me get ready?" he asked.

She wanted to, she did, but the Head had said she couldn't help him. Then again, the Head had never really dealt with Saffs before.

"I know you can do it all by yourself," she said.

At the words, he stepped back, arms crossed in front of his chest. He frowned, cheeks reddening. "You're just afraid I'll beat you," he said.

Seraphina shrugged, her chest aching. If she told him the truth, he'd get mad. He wouldn't understand. She hated lying to him, but she couldn't tell him she'd gotten into a fight over something mean someone he didn't even know had said about him.

"I am," she said. She walked over to his old egg-beater toy and turned it on. "Now, as long as we keep it a secret, we can practice."

And even though Caleb didn't understand, he smiled all the same.

Caleb had never seen anything like it. In fact, there were only a few places he'd been to beyond his house in Colony M. Sometimes, he'd go weeks without seeing the purple and orange sky, the double moons. He didn't know so many people even lived in Colony M.

The natatorium was shaped like an old Earth horseshoe. A detector flanked each entrance to the arena. His mother took him to an enormous titanium door. His name was emblazoned on the top of it in large chunky letters: Caleb Stamford Saff.

"Do I get to keep the door because it has my name on it?" he asked.

His mother laughed as she crouched down beside him. "Never hurts to ask. Though I'm not sure where you'd put it."

He nodded seriously as she shuttled him toward his entrance. Seraphina was nowhere to be found.

"Does Seraphina have a door?" he asked, even though he was sure she had the biggest door in the arena.

"Go on," his mother said. "You don't want to be late."

"But she's going to miss it!" he told his mother.

"Don't worry about her. This is about you, Caleb. It's your turn," she said, her eyes fiercely glittering. "Your dad would be so proud of you."

Dad. Caleb only remembered him a little. He was like Seraphina. Always working with blocks. Always away. Maybe, if the natatorium had an open top, he could watch Caleb play the game from up there.

His mother helped him step onto a conveyer belt that led to the first detector. She looked so far away as it swept him away from her.

"Sir, your letter, please," a bot with a sleek, featureless face and a narrow body of connecting bolts and plates said as he approached.

He offered the bot his letter chip to scan, even though he wanted to keep it forever and ever and never let it go. The bot's arms swept around him and boosted him into the detector's seat. A flash of white left spots on his eyes, and then he was moving again.

The conveyor belt slipped underneath his feet, and he was taken through a narrow tunnel, the walls made of thick cushions. It brought him to a room about the size of his bedroom, square, with walls made of the same strange, bouncy cushions. The room was so silent he could hear his stomach growl. He couldn't see the crowd that sat in the amphitheater seats above him, gazing down at his small white box. He didn't know Seraphina was among them, seated at the very front, right next to their mom.

Seraphina pressed her hand to the glass that separated the crowd from the BFF work stations. A bruise still blushed across its knuckles. Her heart held steady. She wondered what it felt like to be Caleb right now in that little box. Did he feel like their dad had when he'd done this?

"I believe in you," she whispered. She didn't even bother looking for Mark's station. He wasn't worth her viewing time.

"He'll be great," her mom whispered to her. "You did such a good thing."

Good was something her genes said she was incapable of doing. It was time to show them all what the Saffs could do. So Seraphina closed her eyes and nodded and wondered what was going on in the box.

"Welcome, Caleb Saff," a voice said. Caleb's head swiveled to watch a part of the puffy wall detach itself, metal eyes blinking to life on the top pillow.

"Hi," Caleb said.

"I will be your assistant for the entirety of the competition," it said. A metal arm reached toward him from its padding and offered him a backpack full of snacks. He peered inside. Seraphina wouldn't be happy with it, because they didn't give them any chocolate chip flavored packs.

He took the pack and placed it against one of the walls, far from him because he knew he'd just eat all the snacks if it was right next to him.

"The competition will begin momentarily," the bot said.

"Is my sister there yet?" Caleb asked. He wondered if she was right next door to him, her fingers itching because she hadn't been allowed to bring her blocks.

"I cannot reveal information about fellow competitors," the bot said.

That was the most annoying thing Caleb had ever heard.

He sighed. There had to be a way that he could get the bot

to tell him about Seraphina. The bots at the house were pretty easy to convince. And by convince, Caleb meant playing with the wiring. When the bot eventually turned its pillow face away from him, maybe Caleb could trick it.

"In thirty seconds, you will be given your assignment," the bot said.

A rumbling overtook the padded box, and a glass plank rose out of a rectangular divot in the floor. Caleb wandered over to it, more curious than afraid. On it were a bunch of tools. He recognized only one, but his eyes lit up. A few moments of silence, and then the box rumbled again. The bot blinked at Caleb.

Little bit little, the pillowed padding of the box slid off the walls, melting and draining until nothing was left but the strange gray color of Mars' gravity paint. Above Caleb, the roof of the box slid away, revealing the far-away open-skied ceiling of the amphitheater.

"Your assignment is to escape this box using only the tools in here," the bot intoned. Before him was a scraper, a wire, a few pieces of magnetic string, a meter, and a set of Seraphina's building blocks.

Caleb smiled wickedly. His focus bounced around the four walls, his mind whirring and fracturing, already working out a way.

And the competition began.

It took Caleb about ten minutes to dismantle the bot. He managed to tie its arms with the magnetic string, his fingers working through the plush to find the battery-operated innards. He hadn't wanted to take it apart, but it kept talking at him, telling him what not to do, and it wasn't helping him focus at all.

He then began with the scraper. Because, if there was one thing Seraphina and Dad had taught him, it was how to fly.

Seraphina watched Caleb. Her fingers traced the gravity meter at her hip, and she smiled. They couldn't have picked a better challenge for him. A part of herself was down there, working with him, beside him, egging him on. He must have seen her make her own gravity meter once. Always watching. Asking questions.

She'd built it, not just because of that one place in her Learning Center, but actually because of their dad. He'd vanished when she was eight due to poor gravity coverage in a neighboring colony. His suit was never found. Out of fear of floating away, she'd built her own meter, even though a part of her had wanted to go up after him, to find him after all those years.

"He's going to do it," she whispered to her mom.

Her mom said nothing, just squeezed her hand.

She watched Caleb chip away at the gravity paint on the bottom of his cube. She watched him attach the magnetic wires on the walls to look like a ladder. With one hand, he fashioned the building blocks into a belt at his waist.

It was funny to watch him work. He flickered across the box, back and forth and back and forth so many times that Seraphina couldn't count. Sure, he should have adjusted a few things and maybe done something with the meter they had given him, but he wasn't her. And she was okay with that.

As the time wore on, she watched him test his device over and over. Each time, he scraped off a little more of the gravity paint until a sizeable section of the rightmost corner of the floor was gone.

On the tenth try, he managed to attach the belt to the magnetic wire stairs and crest the top of the box.

She stood up, a smile on her face, her ears deaf to the announcer saying his name. She turned from the arena and walked to the door.

Never once did she look for Mark.

Caleb and Seraphina stood at the door of their house. It was early, earlier than Caleb had ever woken up in his life. He wanted to hold her hand but didn't, keeping it firmly pressed against his side. A blue armband wrapped around his right bicep; a pack was secured across his back.

"Ready?" Seraphina asked.

He took a deep breath. Even though he hadn't won the BFF, even though he'd been disqualified for dismantling the bot, this was a better reward than he'd ever been given before. And at least Mark hadn't won, either.

Underneath it all, Seraphina knew they didn't need the competition to do great things. She'd already done one so far. Even though she hated touching people, she grabbed his hand.

Caleb ducked his head and smiled.

"You'll do fine, I promise," she said.

Swallowing hard, he nodded. He hadn't even had to dismantle a bot to leave the house this time. They were letting him go to school. Of course he was nervous.

"And if anyone gives you a hard time," Seraphina added, "you tell them I'm your sister." Even though the bruises on her knuckles had faded, she wouldn't forget. Together they moved toward the door, out into the purple hazy sky of colony M. The freedom of this, Caleb decided, was almost as good as flying.

Where Treasure Drifts in Space
by Jeannie Warner

Jeannie Warner spent her formative years in Southern California and Colorado and is not afraid to abandon the most luxurious environs for a chance to travel anywhere. She has a useless degree in musicology, a checkered career in computer security, and aspirations of world domination. Her writing credits include blogs of random musings and cyber security, thriller novel manuscripts, stories in online magazines, stories in various anthologies, a Mad Scientist's Journal, *several police statements, and a collection of snarky notes to a former upstairs neighbor. She lives in the San Francisco Bay area near several of her best friends whom she refers to as "minions."*

"Blast it, Ollie, don't you have that landing strut bolt out yet?" The voice came from inside the *New London's* main cargo bay.

"I'm trying!" Olivia was trying. She was standing on a long, heavy wrench and bouncing a little in the hopes that it might loosen the bolt. "It's rusted on!"

"How can it be rusted? We spend all our time in space!"

"I reckon it's the time *New London* has spent on spaceports, when they hose down the tarmac. Plus space is chock full of corrosion and ice." Jumping down, Olivia tried lying across the bar and lifting her feet up.

"That's very astute, young lady." A deep voice sounded right behind her. She squawked in surprise and fell off the wrench. Looking up from the tarmac, she saw an older man watching her with his hands on his hips. He was heavyset with pale blue eyes in a pale, lined face. He stood fairly straight and tall, which told Olivia he grew up on a planet rather than on a ship or space station. He wore faded brown pants and a long gray jacket, and his knit cap curled over eyebrows that had started to tuft up. "Some people forget and take off right after a cleaning, and space is a cold place." He offered a hand to help her up.

"Y-yes it is." Olivia didn't like being towered over. Although she was small compared to the stranger, she was average in height for her crew. When kids grow up in space, the lack of gravity twists the bones as the muscles develop. Her crewmates, Mattie, Blink, Bongo, and the other crew were all twisty, their shapes dictated by the work they did. Having an adult tower over her brought back recent unpleasant memories of a brush with the group that tried to shut down the Federal Association of Generational Navy or FAGN system. They had wanted to reeducate the youths on the various ships into "more appropriate" jobs like menial labor and office work.

And yet this man met her eyes in a straightforward manner. There wasn't any condescension, and when she accepted his hand and he helped her to her feet, he smiled as though they had both done the right thing. "Want some help with that wrench? Perhaps my extra weight will do the trick."

Olivia liked the way he didn't just rush in and do it for her. She hated that, when people assumed you couldn't do something, when the truth was you could eventually do it just fine if you were patient. "That'd be okay. Thanks." She laid hands on the wrench and waited for his as well before they both yanked downward. With four hands, the wrench turned and the bolt loosened with a grinding squeak. Once moving, it took much less effort to finish, and the stranger stepped back to let Olivia do it all. "The *New London* is a good-looking ship. Decent repairs, clean."

"Eh, not that clean. But it'll do," Olivia said, cocking a tentative smile upward. "What are you doing so far out here, a planet-born fellow like yourself?"

"Well, truth be told, I'm a bit of a treasure seeker these days." The stranger looked over Olivia's ship, craning his neck to look where the numbers used to be painted on the dorsal ridges. "This looks to be an old FAGN ship. Model X4-32 Ballistic, right?"

Olivia's shoulders hunched. "Maybe. I'm not usually the mechanic, but we have a couple crew real sick."

The stranger's gaze didn't miss the reaction. "Oh, I'm not from the Federation, or anything like it." He spread his hands. "I heard about your program being halted, and I was against it. I hoped to find some of the FAGN ships still operating. I hopped a few freighters on the way to this backwater system, paying my way in work on repairs and updates. I figured there might be a captain willing to hear a proposition I have on a… potentially lucrative venture."

"What's your name, then?" Olivia demanded.

"Gold. James Gold," he offered a slight bow. "Are you the captain?"

Olivia liked that he asked. "No. That'd be Dodger. Captain Dodger." She lowered her voice. "Don't ever forget to call him that."

James smiled. "I will not. I would be obliged for an introduction, though."

Nodding, Olivia turned to lead him up the ramp into the main hold. "Captain! We got a visitor!"

The owner of the voice that had accused her of being slow with the wrench appeared at the top of the ramp. Captain

Dodger stood at Olivia's height, clad in a worn-looking captain's jacket. His eyes and hair were dark, his cheek bones were sharp, and his nose was a touch large for his face. Underneath the coat Dodger wore the same overalls as Olivia did—nondescript gray and nigh indestructible. The dark stains on both were a testament to hard work. "Hey now, what's all this? Who's he?" He pointed his screwdriver at the newcomer and scowled.

"This is James Gold," Olivia said. "He has a business proposition." And with that, she let Dodger take over the conversation. He would, anyway.

"What kinda business?" Dodger demanded, fists on hips. He didn't offer a hand right away, nor did James.

"Treasure. Well, salvage, at any rate. I have in my possession information about the last known location of the Federation Exploration vessel, *Gloriana*."

Olivia's eyebrows shot up, but it was Dodger who choked with surprise. "The *Gloriana*? No way. Word is she got caught in the edge of a gravity well near a black hole. That would've ripped everything to shreds. I think someone is pulling your leg."

"Maybe they tried," James lifted one trouser leg slightly, showing what Olivia hadn't noticed at first. His ankle was steel; the foot and who knows how much more was robotic. "I've got some intel that *Gloriana* broke free. But it cost her all her fuel, and she's been caught drifting, orbiting a gas giant in the rings ever since." His grin showed a few gold teeth. "Do you have any idea of her worth? All those star charts, maps, exploration records, just begging to be harvested and sold?"

Dodger's eyes already had a shiny look that Olivia had seen before. "So what's in it for you?" he asked. "What's your angle?"

"Half of the profits from the sale," James said promptly. "I have contacts in the mining and metallurgy corps who have said they'll deal with us for all of the planetary data. The *Gloriana's* databanks on that topic alone will be enough for me to retire."

"One quarter," Olivia stepped forward again. This was her area, once Dodger looked like he wanted the deal. And by the greedy expression growing in his eyes, he was hooked. "There's risk involved if she's anywhere near the gravity well or if that giant has ice rings or risk of radiation. Also fuel and other expenses to run and repair the ship, and manpower. Expenses, ya know."

James' eyebrows shot up a little. "One third. You'll have a harder time selling the data through reputable sources." He paused. "You say you have some sick crew? What sickness are we talking here?"

It was a reasonable question. "Our engineers Paris and Blink are both recovering from radiation sickness. Their treatment is why we were on that station, getting extra injections. Twenty-nine percent," Olivia did a little math in her head. "There could be follow-up medical costs if it's where you say and we have radiation exposure."

James sighed a little. "Fair point. Twenty-nine percent." He held his hand out.

"Agreed," Dodger shook it, then cocked his head. "Olivia, you got all those bolts replaced?"

"Give me a half hour," Olivia promised. "Mr. Gold, do you have bags?"

"I do," James nodded. They agreed on a liftoff time in two hours and went their separate ways, Dodger up to the bridge, Olivia back to finish her maintenance, and James to collect his bags.

The first leg of the journey out of the system and through the next took over a week, longer than expected due to repairs and problems with engineering. Dodger muttered daily about slackers, but no one could fault the boys for being laid up.

Mr. Gold, after providing the first of the coordinates, assisted Olivia with maintenance. "The X4-32s are pretty reliable," he observed, holding a light for Olivia as she compared a printout against a tangle of wires. "And this one looks well-kept."

"Paris and Blink do a good job," Olivia smiled. "Hope they're better soon. How'd you learn ships, being a dirt-licker and all?" She paused, then blushed as she realized how her words sounded. "Sorry. Planet-born. I didn't mean any—"

"I know the term. I grew up by a shipyard on the ground," James said. "My first job was helping site cleaning and fetching meals and such. Space has always been my passion."

"Really? Me, too! Cruise liners, mostly, though. Not these smaller cargo ships—they feel like storage bays with rooms attached. Not that I don't love the *London*!"

"Ah, that's why you're…" James' gesture included the length of Olivia. "Basically straight. Gravity."

The girl shrugged. "I reckon. The others all were born and grew up on ships or orbitals. No regular gravity, no straight bones." It was an old, well-known problem. Dealing with the misshapen children of space is what had spawned the FAGN program originally. "Everyone's useful here."

"Absolutely," James agreed. "Your job must be charming the station crews."

Olivia waved a wrench at him. "I do a heck of a lot more than that. It ain't official, but I'm practically the first mate around here. I can do cargo loads, fuel capacity, and run charts in my head. I'm just doing maintenance because engineering is flat out after their Prussian Blue treatments." She longed for a proper medi-bot and more modern medicines.

The older man looked abashed. "I apologize. No, truly I do." He turned back to studying the circuitry. "And I think I see the problem. You have two connectors here that are hot. I think there's a short. When they expand, they—"

"They move away and lose their connection!" Olivia cut in. "Of course! How could I have missed it?"

"Generally touching wiring isn't a good idea," James said, "but if the casing is warm, it's a quick help for diagnosis." He looked down at the fair-haired girl beside him. "You're not what I expected to find out here."

Olivia looked up. "How do you mean?"

James cleared his throat. "Well, just the whole FAGN program getting shut down. The rebel ships and all that have a certain rep." He grinned. "But you're a bright young thing. What are you, 14? You remind me of me at your age. Capable. Confident. Not at all what the Federation put out that you lot are like. That'll teach me to jump to conclusions, eh?"

"I reckon so!" Olivia grinned back.

Over the loudspeaker just above the engine core came Dodger's voice. "Olivia, you done? I need you up here on the bridge."

James said, "You go on. I'll replace this fuse. Like I said, I'm glad for the partnership, and I am looking forward to spending the loot; helping out is a simple way I can say thanks."

"Thanks back!" Olivia handed over the wrench and waved before ducking through the iris out of the engine room. She cast a couple glances back, but James seemed intent on the aid he'd promised.

Up on the bridge, Dodger had pushed aside the various storage and learning chips that normally littered the nav comp and was hunched over it. He looked up and beckoned Olivia over. "This is going to take some fancy flying. According to the charts your Mr. Gold gave us, we're going to be orbiting a gas giant, searching through heavy ice rings. The notes say there's no clear line of sight on the *Gloriana* to make it show up in infrared, so the approach is going to be tricky." He indicated the rings displayed on the screen. "I'm concerned about our Reaction Control System. Ever since Mouse tried to dock us with that orbital station like a blind minnow humping a whale..."

"Hey now," Olivia protested, "you told him that he could dock us the next time his turn came up."

"Mouse don't practice the sims the way you do," Dodger

growled. "He don't get to try again until he do. But the verniers on the RCS ain't firing perfect." He looked at her. "An' the whole cargo bay smells just a little like pee. Makes me nervous."

"Do you think we've got a hydrazine leak?" Olivia asked. The FAGN's thrusters ran on hydrazine, and when things went wrong you could smell the ammonia in the fuel. Right before you died, if it was strong enough.

Dodger nodded. "I wish Paris and Blink weren't sick."

"Me too," said Olivia. "I'll see what James and I can find."

Dodger nodded and drummed his fingers on the console. Finally, "Do you trust him?"

"I trust our crew," Olivia said slowly. "And haven't we proved the clever ones all along?" She took a breath and tried to focus on the good. "Those charts, that's real money if sold to the right folks. That's enough for a medi-bot for the sick bay. And food that comes in something besides blocks."

Dodger preened, fingering the lapels of his Captain's coat. "And a new uniform. Maybe ion thrusters to replace them verniers. Right. I'll chart us a course through the rocks."

Olivia saluted and headed back down into the engine room.

James was gone by the time she returned to the engine room, but the wiring was tucked away, and things were humming along with the engine's heartbeat. She sniffed the air once but couldn't smell ammonia. Her toolbox sat open, and she packed it up before heading down to the hydrazine tanks.

Olivia spent the next few hours sniffing along the wires and thin tubes that led to the verniers. She found signs of wear, and she made careful notes in the ship's log so that Paris could check her work when he was well.

Dodger's voice came over the ship's loudspeaker. "James Gold to the bridge! We're approaching the gas giant!" Olivia sat back on her heels, wiping her hands on a rag. Looking up, she saw James leave his cabin and climb the metal stairs to the bridge.

People think space is silent—and it is, mostly—but spaceships make little noises in a constant chatter. The hiss of the smaller verniers firing was an old friend as Dodger navigated the ship through the rocky ice orbit, searching for the lost ship.

A faint "*sput*"-like noise and then hissing took Olivia by surprise. She scooted across the main cargo hold like a spider toward the sound as the smell of ammonia started to grow. From her kit she found and slapped on a breather, and she bent to study the lines leading from the tank. With magnified vision, she located where a main line had a tiny but unmistakable pin hole. She pinched it with gloved fingers when an impact against the side of the ship sent her rolling to her knees, tools flying. A moment later the hold lights flickered and went out. Ten seconds later she felt as much as heard the hiss of air circulation fade.

"That's bad," Olivia whispered to herself, thinking over the systems and how they connected. "If we lost engines and life support, that means spin could go next." Now deeply suspicious, she scuttled toward one of Dodger's hidey-holes normally used for hiding cargo during Federal inspections. She had just reached the grate when, true to her prediction, the control-motion gyroscope lost power. Another impact on the ship shook the hull, stopping the spin.

With some effort, she pulled herself inside just as Dodger's voice came over the loudspeaker. "All hands to the life support pods and launch! We've got a huge prob—!" The microphone cut off abruptly as two alarm systems started to blare warnings. Along the catwalks, Olivia heard the sound of feet and shouting as Mattie, Bongo, and the others helped Blink and Paris from the sick bay into the life pods and closed themselves in. Watching through the grate, Olivia wondered if her suspicions were going to get her killed. Her hands were cold with fear and a growing sense of betrayal.

James Gold appeared on a catwalk within her field of vision perhaps two minutes later, toting a limp Dodger over his shoulder. Olivia felt sick to her stomach, watching Gold check each of the hatches to be sure the pods had launched before pushing the boy into an empty one and punching the launch button for him from the inside.

The girl gritted her teeth as she watched Gold moving like an old hand in zero-gee, launching across the cargo bay straight for the faulty RCS line. He uncoiled a new line out of his pocket as he flew. He landed and with expert speed replaced the hose before pushing off again through space to the bridge door. He disappeared inside, and in moments the alarms cut off, and engine noise (and gravity) returned.

Olivia went into waiting mode, leaving her breathing mask on for now. As she waited, she felt and heard the verniers fire as the ship navigated through the ice chunks in the rings. To herself, she was willing to admit that Gold might be a smoother hand at the helm than Dodger. *Sorry Dodger*, she mouthed in apology for the unkind thought.

The ship shivered through an hour's little hisses from the verniers before there was a gentle thump, and through the grate Olivia watched a light above the docking aperture go from red to green. From above, Gold descended the catwalk again down into the main hold toward the docking iris seal. He looked it over, then with a few stabs of his finger opened the iris to show the dark hull of an unfamiliar ship on the other side.

After a long moment of checking the registered atmo readings, Gold pressed the other ship's control panel, and the iris of the connecting point expanded for him. Olivia wished for all her might for some kind of space kraken to reach out and tear him limb from limb, but all she heard was his faint, pleased whistling as Gold disappeared farther into the darkened ship like he knew the way.

Olivia counted a minute slowly to herself before easing

out of her hiding place. She dashed to the connection tunnel between the two ships to peer in, but she couldn't see Gold. Her first instinct was to close the connection and go pilot the *New London* away from what she presumed was the *Gloriana*, but a lack of information made her pause. She didn't know whether the *Gloriana* had any kind of weapons or might be in a condition Gold could use to hurt her ship.

Hefting a large wrench, Olivia crept across the connection and paused to listen, but she heard nothing. The new ship's docking bay was smaller than the *London's*, barely large enough to fit a small runabout. And scrupulously clean. A faint noise sounded to the right, and Olivia stepped carefully out of the bay into a hallway with her wrench held high.

A door opened, bringing her face to face with a stranger—a woman, much older than Olivia, though almost as thin. The two were nearly mirrored in clothing, as the stranger also wore a pair of overalls, stained with use and smelling strongly of recycled cleaning products. Small plastic bits dangled from knotted strings about her neck, like an exotic necklace of shells that weren't shells. She was toting a hammer raised in her hand, mirroring Olivia's wrench. The stranger was taller by an inch or two, mostly in the torso, though her arms were much longer. Her legs, Olivia had time to notice, were only slightly bowed outward with the tell-tale twisting of too much time in space. Olivia jumped to the only conclusion she could. "Wow. You've been marooned here."

The other woman jerked slightly, stopping herself from a hammer attack. She hesitated, then lowered the weapon. "Are you here to rescue me? Do you have any chocolate? Or coffee?"

"Not this minute."

"Then what are you doing here? Are you a hallucination?"

Well, it's complicated." Satisfied that she wasn't in immediate danger of being struck with the hammer, Olivia placed a hand on the other woman's shoulder and pushed forward to get them both out of the corridor as she whispered. "I'm not a hallucination. And there's a guy with me here who is up to no good. Well, he's not with me. He just came on our ship. But he's trying to steal from you then use my ship to run away so he doesn't have to share the profits."

The stranger blinked slowly once, twice. "No coffee, then? I ran out of coffee a year ago. Took weeks for the headaches and shakes to stop. Weeks! But I want them back again. I miss the caffeine shakes." She hugged her hammer to her chest, looking at Olivia with pale green eyes. "You can live on a ship full of protein. But it's not really living without chocolate. I've dreamed of chocolate. Lonely, lonely chocolate dreams. And when I dropped the coffee beans the ship swept them up. Swept them all up in minutes. I lost the magic beans!"

Olivia had the feeling that the other woman wasn't all there. Space did that to people when they were left alone. It's why there were so many kids in space. No one wanted to be alone forever. "I, uh, can see if we have any on the ship. But you have to tell me where Mr. Gold went. Did you see a man come through here? About so tall, kinda fat with gray hair and wearing a dark cap?" She held a hand up, indicating Gold's height.

"Oh, him! Sure, he went straight to the bridge," Jen said. "He looked a little scary."

Olivia sighed. "Great. Then he's got what he wanted, and we're going to be screwed. Does this ship have any weapons?"

"Weapons? We were an exploration vessel!" Briefly the crazy glint faded from the woman's eyes. "We found worlds, identified mineral fields in the asteroid belts, charted new ways for future safe warping. The *Gloriana* was always first."

"I've heard. I'm sorry about… wait. You're alive. Are there any others?"

The light went out of the stranger's eyes. "Just *Gloriana's* cook, Jen Cannon. Poor Jen." She shook her head slowly. "She wanted to help the others, but she's the only one who got her suit on in time because we hit a rock in the middle of the night, and no one was on watch. The others tried to fix the ship, but we had a lot of seals go in a gravity well." She grabbed for Olivia's hand. "You don't try to fix things before you make sure you can breathe, right? That's crazy!" And she started laughing, a sad sort of laugh that hurt Olivia's tummy to listen to. "Crew got us out of the well and into orbit as they died. But I fixed it! I read the manuals and fixed the ship. The ship won't clean up bodies like it did my coffee beans."

"No! No. Oh, Jen." Moved by the older woman's plight, Olivia grabbed and hugged her tightly for a long moment. Jen went stiff and stopped breathing for a moment. Then her arms crept about Olivia slowly and she inhaled again.

"I say," Jen whispered. "Do you have any chocolate?"

She was like a broken record. "I will find you chocolate," Olivia promised with all her heart.

"I love you," Jen promised back with a solemn nod. She started to put the hammer down, but Olivia stopped her.

"You might need that. Mr. Gold isn't a nice man."

"Oh. We should be sneaky, then."

"Yes we should," Olivia said. "Sneaky as two sneaking things." She thought for a moment. Then, slowly, "You say the ship cleans things up. Things that are not people."

"It took my coffee beans!" Jen wailed. "Stupid *Gloriana*."

Olivia clapped a hand over her mouth and leaned in to whisper. "What if we re-programmed it to clean up the people in particular instead of cleaning everything else? What does it use to clean things?"

The older woman blinked a little. "Waldos and robotic systems, for the most part. It takes things to the garbage bay and ejects them."

"So it's got robots strong enough to lift a person?" Olivia asked.

Jen frowned. "You mean, strong enough to clean up and get

rid of the crew? Why?"

"Well, it ain't respectful to just cart around dead bodies," Olivia said carefully. "Plus if we hide, and the ship is getting rid of all the people it finds, it might get rid of Mr. Gold for us. You know. If we gas him first." She thought of how he played dirty and decided she could live with it.

Jen stared for a moment longer, then nodded once. "I'll show you down to engineering. I'm not sure how we'll gas him."

The two crept through the deserted *Gloriana*. Reaching the small control room for Engineering, Olivia asked to be shown the systems in question and immediately started to read through the lists of commands and recorded documents. "This may take a little while," she murmured to the glowing screen in front of her. "Can I ask you an important question, Miss Cannon?"

The older woman seemed to straighten a little at being addressed formally. "Of course."

"Do you know precisely why the *Gloriana* can't fly?"

Jen shrugged. "Sure. Fuel and valves."

"Valves?" Olivia was a little incredulous.

"Yeah. I had to learn how to fix things. I mean, doing the structural repairs was pretty easy, and I achieved hull integrity with the spare panels we had. But the whole engine and combustion system, with turbo-pump through valves into the manifold, that takes knowledge." Jen looked sad, sketching the air with her hands. "I mean, I did what I could, but I'm a cook! I understood how to make an engine go, but dealing with how much pressure is normal and should be where between the fuel and coolant systems…" A sigh. "I blew some valves, and we don't have replacements, and the fuel ran out."

"Show me. But in a few minutes." Olivia bent her head to concentrate on what, precisely, the cleaning robots were programmed to do. The computer interface was surprisingly easy to use, and far more modern and user-friendly than *New*

London's. Olivia tried not to feel disloyal, but she couldn't help the growing feeling that this might be an opportunity to upgrade ships.

Jen had a gift for silence, although the way she hunkered down and stared at Olivia while she worked was a little unsettling. When she spoke again, her tone was steady. "I don't think we should get the robots to clean off Mr. Gold with the rest of the crew."

"Why not?" Olivia asked absently, typing away.

"Because he's alive. And there's been a lot of death around here." Jen said. "Did he kill your crew mates?"

That caught Olivia up. "No. No he didn't." She hesitated, then stabbed at a button and turned to look at Jen. "What are you thinking?"

"Let's think of a way to test him. If he passes, he gets a life pod and a homing beacon. If he's just a criminal, he can get ejected with the garbage."

Olivia was still for a moment, conflicted. She looked at the woman and thought about how unfair it was that Jen was alone for years and how she had only tried to do her job. "Okay. We can do that. I... You've been through a lot, and you're a stranger. How about I lure him into the launch bay, and you lower the oxygen content from here. We'll both pass out. Then you can maybe get him into a pod if there are any left here?" Her lips were firm. "If he shoots me, you hit him with that hammer, get the bots to dump him, and signal for help from my ship. Got it?"

Jen nodded. "Are you sure you're up for it?"

Olivia rose. "This whole mess is my fault for bringing him on board and not watching him close. So you monitor me on the camera. When you see him and me in the bay together, lock the doors and cut the oxygen." She looked earnestly into Jen's eyes. "I'm gonna trust you with this, to not kill us, and to rush in and deal with him while he's out. Please don't be crazy." *I couldn't bear to be wrong about people twice in a row,* she thought.

"You promised chocolate," Jen intoned, like an oath.

"There will be chocolate," Olivia agreed and gathered her doubts and fears to hide them deep inside. She turned to head back through the *Gloriana's* corridors to the docking bay despite the unease in her stomach. Once there, she closed the portal leading outward, back to the *New London*, then planted her hands on her hips in her best cocky pose (like Dodger, she thought to herself) and raised her voice to shout. "Hey Mr. Gold! You come down here this minute!" She was proud that her voice didn't sound as scared as she felt.

Olivia heard the sound of his boots before he arrived. James Gold looked taller and more menacing than ever, and she felt her heart flutter. Still, she took a deep breath and lifted her chin in a bold pose. "As my mom used to say, I got something to say to you."

James' eyes glittered coldly as he looked down on her. Slowly he drew a small energy gun from his pocket and pointed it. "I should have suspected that you wouldn't be caught quite so neatly as the others."

Behind him, the portal to the *Gloriana* closed. Olivia saw it and hastened to speak louder and wave her wrench. "What are you going to do now, shoot me? What did I ever do to you? I LIKED you! I thought you were a decent guy, that we had a deal. Now I'm going to look bad. Dodger is NEVER going to let me live this down."

Gold's thumb pressed onto the power safety, and the barrel flared faintly red about the end. "Will it matter? What makes you think I'm going to let you live?"

"I do think you're going to let me live, because you remember what it was like to be me," Olivia said stubbornly. "That's why you looked for a ship like ours, ain't it? Even though you weren't in the FAGN program, you know what it's like to have everyone think that you're not good enough, smart enough, or adult enough. You know that sometimes you have to cheat a little to get ahead. You gotta scheme." She felt a little light-headed and hoped it was Jen reducing the oxygen.

The man's lips twitched, but the barrel didn't move from her chest. "Maybe I do. But that means you understand me, too, doesn't it, little girl? Look at me if you want to know your future. One day you'll be alone in the universe, trying to find that one score that'll get you ahead of the game instead of always being behind. When your chance comes, you have to take it and not let anyone or anything get in your way." He looked momentarily disgusted. "Even if the nav comp here was wiped. What a waste."

"That ain't quite right," Olivia said. "You're out on your own in space. I got a family, floating off in those pods. Maybe family makes it harder because we have to find bigger jobs and do more work to break even. And sometimes there's nothing but fighting and arguing, and then you gotta spoon-feed the people that you're fighting with because they were just sick all over your only pair of clean overalls and they need to get some liquids in them. But that kind of bother is what it costs to never be alone. And I think you respect that." She kept her words slow to kill time as the air thinned.

The barrel fell slightly, drooping just a bit in Gold's hand. "I… don't need to kill you." He blinked a few times, focusing on her face. "I'll just put you into an escape pod here on the *Gloriana*. I promise I'll activate the distress beacon for someone to come pick you all… up."

Olivia smiled weakly. "That's a good idea. Were you planning on that? Not killing us, for sure?"

"I.. maybe, I…" Gold seemed uncertain. Or perhaps just blurry to Olivia's eyes. She felt the world going black, and she tumbled to the deck as the lights went out.

When Olivia woke up, she was thrilled to be alive. She

opened her eyes and saw Jen's face hanging over her.

The older woman jumped back as Olivia started to blink. "Oh good, you're awake! I was worried that your brain would get all oxygen-starved and crazy. But you're not, right?"

"Here's hoping," Olivia struggled to her feet. "Where's Mr. Gold?"

"I stuffed him in *Gloriana's* escape pod," Jen assured her, adding, "He's still breathing, too."

"You win all the chocolate," Olivia said. "Go ahead and launch him with a beacon."

"I did. Oh— the robots did what you told them to," Jen murmured, her eyes downcast. "They cleared the ship."

Olivia gave Jen a hug again. "We'll get Dodger to say a few words for your crew when he's back on board and awake. He's a Captain, you know. It's what they do, Captain-y stuff like ceremonies. Dodger's very keen."

A smile touched Jen's lips. "They'd have liked that." She looked toward the hatch. "I don't suppose…"

"Let's get you some chocolate. Then we got work to do, fetching my crew's pods back onto the *New London*." Sitting up, Olivia looked around with new attention. "You know, your ship looks like it's in much better shape than ours, and we don't know what all Gold sabotaged. I bet Mouse and Paris could use parts from our ship to fix anything wrong with the *Gloriana*, if you didn't mind being a crew member again? Even if there's no treasure, they'll be glad to see you." She briefly considered the argument to come with Dodger on the topic and decided she was up to it.

Jen's eyes twinkled slightly, and she lifted her plastic necklace to clatter it in front of Olivia's eyes. "You mean these? I downloaded all the maps and survey info onto chips as soon as I got the ship patched enough to hope I might live." She took off the string of brightly colored plastic and draped it around Olivia's neck. "Here. You take the star systems. I'll hold onto the geo surveys and retire on some nice orbital station." Jen indicated the matching bracelet.

Olivia's spirits rose. "You reckon you'll be okay? After everything?"

Jen considered the question. "I'm done with space and being alone. I wouldn't mind the company back to civilization, but if you want to keep this ship I won't say a thing. As far as anyone knows, we were lost. Why, you probably found me floating in cryogenic stasis in an escape pod."

"Here's hoping you live happily ever after," said Olivia. And together, the two went about recalling the *New London's* escape pods. After finding chocolate, of course. A promise is a promise.

Man's Best Friends
by Bruce Golden

Novelist, journalist, satirist, Bruce Golden's short stories have been published more than a hundred times across twenty countries and a score of anthologies. Asimov's Science Fiction *described his second novel, "If Mickey Spillane had collaborated with both Frederik Pohl and Philip K. Dick, he might have produced Bruce Golden's* Better Than Chocolate" *– and about his novel* Evergreen, *"If you can imagine Ursula Le Guin channeling H. Rider Haggard, you'll have the barest conception of this stirring book, which centers around a mysterious artifact and the people in its thrall." You can read more of Golden's stories in his new collection* Tales of My Ancestors, *which has been described as "The Twilight Zone meets Ancestry. com." http://goldentales.tripod.com*

I was told to wait inside my compartment, so I did. I always did as I was told. I made no note of time's passing as I waited. The passage of time had no meaning for me. Instead I speculated, as I had recently begun to do, on what might exist outside the walls that contained me. On the rare occasions when I was transported to other locations, I had seen glimpses, but they were always momentary and my transport always dark.

The great majority of my existence was spent within my compartment, leaving me nothing to do but ruminate and wonder. Though I was not trained for curiosity, I was curious. I contemplated. I learned. I even had the ability to imagine, though the fragments of my imagination were meager and dull.

"Open it up," said a voice on the other side of my door.

I recognized it as belonging to Carter, my handler.

The door opened. I did not move.

"Gettin' kind of old, isn't he?" said another man I was unfamiliar with.

"Nah," responded Carter. "He's still got a lot of fight left in him."

"Just sayin', the Cobalt Crusher here looks a little crushed himself."

"It's all for show. Makes him look like a battered underdog, but inside he's a hundred percent."

"If you say so."

"All right, Crusher, today you'll be using the short cudgel and a buckler." He handed me the selected implements, adding, "This guy has a pair of sledgehammers, and he uses an overhand strike, so remember to protect yourself with your buckler high, like this."

I watched as Carter demonstrated the movement. I mimicked it precisely.

"All right, let's go."

I followed, ready to comply with my trainer and exchange blows with my selected opponent. I had experienced many such encounters.

Recently I had begun to wonder *why*. I speculated over the purpose of the bouts—the rationale of each and every struggle in which I had participated since my inception. I did not understand the nature of the conflict. I only knew I must fight in order to prolong my existence, even if I did not comprehend why my existence was necessary.

Waiting at the arched entrance, I gripped my tools, familiarizing myself with their weight and balance. I looked across the arena grounds. My adversary was waiting, as well.

I felt no malice towards him. I felt nothing at all. It was his task to destroy me, as it was mine to do the same to him.

"Ladies and gentlemen, are you ready for more rock and rumble?" intoned the announcer, precipitating a roaring affirmation from the assemblage. "Monsters of Metal Productions, in association with Viejas Casino, presents tonight's main event, a bout scheduled for six rounds, featuring a no-holds-barred match between two battle-scarred veterans.

"First, fighting out of Reno, the one-time Nevada state champion, weighing in at 335 kilograms, with a record of 42 wins and 5 losses, the pugnacious, the punishing *Piledriver!*"

The throng roared in approval as Piledriver made his entrance, swinging his hammers in high-speed loops. I took note of his technique and considered how I might counter such an assault.

"His opponent, fighting out of San Diego, weighing in at 312 kilograms, with a record of 34 wins and 6 losses, the quick killer, the sudden assassin, the *Cobalt Crusher!*"

I made my entrance without the flair of Piledriver. I was too intent on my plan of attack to waste my energy reserves on such flamboyance. My task was at hand; my survival dependent upon what I did next.

I was lying on the cool kitchen floor, half dozing, half listening to the talk in the next room, but not really paying attention. It was the same old conversation—nothing I hadn't overheard before. Then I heard my name and perked up.

"...Terra's the best herding dog I've ever had. I wasn't sure about getting one of those genetically-enhanced canines—regular dogs had always been fine. But she's the smartest dog I've seen. Best investment I ever made."

I knew I was being praised and gave my tail a little shake.

"I know she's a good dog, Pop, but you can't take care of everything with just you and that dog anymore. Your arthritis is only going to get worse, and soon you won't be able to pick apples *or* shear sheep."

"You're a doctor. Can't you give me some kind of pill?"

"I've already given you something to help with the pain, but there's no magic pill—no cure."

I didn't understand everything they were saying, but I knew Pop was getting old and having a hard time working. I tried to help as much as I could because he was good to me.

"I think you should sell the farm and come live with me and Isabel. You don't have to work anymore."

"Working's what I live for. What would I do?"

"I know you like to read, and you could get to know your grandkids. You could do whatever you want. There's a thousand things to do in the city. You could go to the movies, see plays, visit museums..."

Pop made a noise I knew translated as disgust.

"I'm not so old I need to be in a museum yet."

"Come on, you know what I mean, Pop."

This wasn't the first time his grown pup had tried to get Pop to leave the farm. Now that he'd sired his own litter, he was always trying to get Pop to live with him. I wondered what would happen to me if Pop left. I never heard him tell Pop he could bring me with him.

"You remember your mother's buried here."

"We can move Mom to a better place, one close by, where you can visit whenever you want."

"There is no better place."

"Julian's not as nice as it used to be, Pop. I've read about the roving gangs harassing people out here in the East County. You can't deal with that, and I know, even though you won't admit it, the work's getting to be too much for you."

"I just got this place off the grid. I got my own wind and solar power, I can always hire neighbor boys to pick the apples if I have to, and Terra takes care of the sheep for me. I can still shear them. It doesn't hurt that much."

I knew Pop didn't really believe everything he was saying. I sensed he was worried.

"I don't know what else to say, Pop, how else to convince you."

"Well, stop trying then. This is my home."

That's when the pup's pups came running in. Suddenly three pairs of hands were all over me. I didn't mind, though. I liked being stroked and scratched, especially on my belly.

I took no measure of satisfaction from the exaltation of the crowd. I departed the arena victorious, functioning within acceptable parameters, though with severe exterior damage. Piledriver had proved a powerful adversary, but a slow one. I was not certain of his condition, but it was unlikely he would soon be fighting again...if at all.

I was ordered to report to the maintenance room. There, some parts were replaced and others repaired. During the period of my repair, another fighter was carted in, looking as battered as I had left Piledriver. His power drain was complete, so one of the maintenance workers connected my power core to his, to, as he said, "jumpstart this piece of junk."

As power flowed from my internal core to his, feedback from his system made its way through my neural nets. Within this feedback were hundreds of images—images of things I had never seen. I perceived a vast two-dimensional plane of darkness, speckled with bright lights set in various patterns; boundless liquid stretching from horizon to horizon, a formation of living creatures moving through the air, and towering columns of rough wood topped with wavering crests. I glimpsed much more than I comprehended.

My memory retained the images even after we were

disconnected. I replayed them incessantly. They were part of the world—the world outside I was curious to see.

It was a hot night, so Pop left the front door open, and I strolled out to sleep on the porch where I might catch a cool breeze or two. I hadn't been asleep long when I heard Pop talking. No one else was in the house, and I hadn't heard the phone ring. I knew Pop wouldn't be calling anyone at this time of night, so I used my special door to go back inside.

I stopped outside Pop's bedroom. He was talking, all right—to someone who wasn't there.

"...wants me to leave our home and go live with him. He doesn't understand, but you do. Sure the work's getting harder, and someday I'll have to give it up. But not now—not yet.

"I wish you were still here. I could sure use your help right about now." Pop chuckled. "Maybe you could send me an angel."

I heard Pop do this before. I knew he was talking to his wife, Grace, even though she'd died long ago, before I was even born. I felt bad for him. He must be depressed about his pup's visit, or maybe he was missing his wife more than usual. I promised myself I'd do whatever I could to help make Pop's life easier.

It had been a long interval since my last bout—longer than any I had previously experienced. It had been so long I wondered if there would ever be another. Had I been abandoned? I heard nothing outside my compartment. I tried the door. It was open. I went through it. Then another door...and another. I did not see Carter. I did not see anyone. Finally I exited the building itself. It was dark. My visual sensors adapted. I looked around. I looked up. Above me I saw the same plane of darkness speckled with bright lights that inhabited my fellow fighter's memories.

I was drawn to understand the nature of these lights in their irregular patterns. I wanted to see them better, so I climbed atop a nearby transport vehicle. Strangely, even though I was closer to them, they grew no larger and I perceived them no better. I stared at them for some time, making no sense of their patterns or purpose. They provided little light, no heat I sensed, and demonstrated no motion.

The transport's engine suddenly came to life. Before I could consider a course of action, it began moving. I was thrown off balance and nearly fell from the height I had scaled. I grabbed hold and secured my position.

The excursion provided the opportunity to see much more. I observed many different transports of various sizes and shapes. I saw a multitude of lights, much closer than those above. Some, I knew, were in the form of a language, but I had no comprehension of their meaning.

I watched and wondered as the transport increased speed. The farther it traveled, the fewer lights and less activity I was able to discern. Soon there was almost complete darkness, except for the transport's own lights and the occasional vehicle traveling in the opposite direction.

The transport finally stopped. I disembarked.

I had not traveled far when I realized my power core was running low. It had been a long time since I had recharged. I searched for a power outlet.

I walked outside to take care of my normal morning business and I spied something so unusual it startled me. It was man-like, but it wasn't a man. It was too large and made of metal. Naturally I reacted by signaling there was trouble. I kept it up until Pop came to see what all the noise was about.

"What in the hell are you barking about, Terra?" Pop stepped out the front door and froze in his tracks. "What in the world...?"

Now that he'd seen it, I stopped barking. Pop approached the metal monstrosity cautiously, and I scampered to his side, though staying a step back. I didn't know if I was going to have to fight or run.

"It's some kind of robot. Looks pretty beat-up. Might have looked good once, painted all blue and silver, but look at all the dents. The paint's scratched and scored—looks like junk. Probably what it is. Someone dumping their trash on my land again. I'm not going to stand for it!"

Pop stood there, staring at the thing, making his disgusted noise and looking like he was trying to figure what to do with it.

"Damn thing's too big for me to move."

Pop started fiddling with the thing, and I thought I'd give it a good sniff. It smelled like any other machine as far as I could tell. So I wandered off and took care of business. When I came back, Pop had connected a long cord to the metal junk.

"All right Big Blue, I can't find no on/off switch, but there's a plug here. So let's see if I can turn you on."

Pop walked back into the house, trailing the cord behind him. Suddenly the junk lit up. It had eyes that glowed and a circle of small lights on its belly. I backed away and started barking again. Pop came back out.

"Shush, Terra." He looked at the machine. "Well, Blue, looks like you still work. I wonder what kind of work you were programmed for. Can you talk? No? What's this switch here do?"

Pop flicked the switch back and forth several times, but the machine didn't react. I was worried he was going to be hurt, but I stayed back. Pop didn't smell like he was afraid, but I sure was.

When he was done tinkering he walked in front of it and scratched his head. The machine moved, and I barked a warning. But all it did was imitate Pop and scratch its own metal head.

"Shush, Terra."

I shushed again, but I didn't like it. Pop raised both hands in the air and so did the junk monster. He dropped his arms and the machine did likewise.

"Well, well. Monkey-see monkey-do, huh? I must have flipped your copycat switch. Maybe that's how you learn."

Pop rubbed at his chin like he did when he was thinking, and the machine grabbed at what would have been its chin if it had had one.

"I wonder if I could teach you to pick apples."

It can pick all the apples it wants, but keep it away from my sheep, Pop.

"Do you understand what I'm saying? I wonder. Folks call me Pop. I'm going to call you Blue—understand? Blue, take two steps forward."

The machine took two steps forward, and I backed up just as quickly. Pop's heart rate increased enough I could tell he was excited.

"Voice command, too. Blue, you and I are going to get along fine. Terra, meet Blue, our new farmhand."

I won't say Pop was crazy right then, but I was sure he wasn't thinking straight. That metal monstrosity was more likely to crush apples than pick them.

"Blue, this is Terra." Pop bent down to give me a pat and the machine mimicked him. "I guess I'd better turn off your copycat switch before you follow me into the house."

That's right, Pop. Thing probably isn't even housebroken.

◆

I had no indication of where Carter was located. So I accepted Pop as my handler. I proceeded with a new training regimen, doing my best to follow each command as precisely as I could.

"...so you don't want to yank the apples straight down, cause that'll tear off the spur and mess up next year's buds.

What you need to do is turn the apple up toward the branch like this, then twist lightly. If it doesn't come right off, it's not ripe yet. Let's see you try."

I tried to imitate Pop's movements. My first attempt failed.

"No! No! You cracked the whole damn branch! Easy does it. Just a light touch."

I tried again, this time using only a fractional amount of power. I tilted the fruit and gave it a light twist.

"Good. That's it. At least you learn quick. Now, put it into your basket—gently. Don't throw it, 'cause that'll make it bruise quicker."

Carefully I placed the fruit in the basket Pop had attached to my exterior.

"Good. Now, let's see. You're so tall you can reach most of the branches, but we're going to have to get you something for up high. I know. Go get that big fence-wire spool over there. Maybe that'll hold your weight."

I saw what he referred to and retrieved it.

"Lay it flat. Now try it out. Go ahead, get up on it."

I complied. The wood construct supported my weight.

"That should do it. All right, Blue, start picking apples."

I began. Pop continued to diligently observe. The other creature—Pop called it a dog but referred to it as Terra—also watched. I could not tell whether it approved, for I did not understand its language.

I was standing with Pop, enjoying the breeze and watching Blue work the orchard. Yes, I was resolved the metal monster was here to stay, and he was helping Pop quite a bit, so I figured I'd call him by the name Pop had given him. It was a provisional truce as far as I was concerned, but if Blue helped Pop stay on the farm with me, then who was I to complain, just because he didn't smell right? Speaking of smelling, that mongrel from the farm down the road had been sniffing around again lately. I'd had to make a ruckus so Pop would run him off once. I'd already had two litters of ten, and I figured enough was enough. He wasn't my type anyway. I'm more into Collies or German Shepherds with good bloodlines.

When Blue finished the section Pop had told him to pick, he hauled his apples to the barn and plugged himself in for a recharge. Pop and I walked back to the house and the phone rang.

When Pop came out, the landscape of his face was more furrowed than usual. He said, "It was Anthony."

To anyone else, it might have looked like he was talking to himself, but I knew he was speaking to me.

"He wants me to go to his place for Thanksgiving. Says Isabel and the kids are looking forward to seeing me."

I knew Anthony was Pop's pup—the doctor. I also knew Pop wasn't going anywhere. He never did. Every year when Thanksgiving came around, he'd buy himself a big turkey, stay home, and spend more time at his wife's grave than usual.

That was okay with me. I always got to eat bird for a week after.

We sat on the porch until Blue marched over. He just stood there, not doing anything, just waiting. He got on my nerves, and I guess it bothered Pop, too.

"Darn it, Blue, I can't relax with you standing there like a statue," said Pop. "Go get your spool from the orchard and bring it here so you can sit with us."

Blue did as he was told, and soon the three of us were sitting there, watching the day go by.

"I wish I knew where you came from, Blue, and what your real name was. But I guess Blue's as good as any other. I named Terra for her color, too. She's not only the color of dirt—earth, as it were—but she's as fertile as mother nature herself. Seeing as how she was genetically-engineered for smarts, I got a good price for each of her pups."

Pop selling my pups had been a sore point between us for a while. I couldn't get over the fact they were my pups—ones I'd carried and given birth to. I had this feeling I was supposed to take care of them. But after a while I realized it was the right thing to do. I can't imagine what this place would have been like with 20 more canines running around. No, I liked it fine with just Pop and me...and now Blue. At least I don't have to fight him for dinner at the bowl.

I looked forward to my work in the orchard. I preferred my new tasks to those I was originally trained for. They were more...tranquil.

Some days there was not much to do but watch the flying creatures Pop called *birds* and wait for the sun to set. I favored that part of the day.

Pop was always talking about the colors of the sunset—about how he named me and Terra for our colors—but I could not see colors. What I perceived were shades and striations, shapes and patterns. I found the variations intriguing

I finished my tasks and went looking for Pop as I did every day. I found him a short distance from his house, standing next to a plot of land surrounded with low fencing. At one end of the plot were two pieces of wood—one imbedded in the dirt, the other intersecting the first. Pop was staring at the ground.

I walked up next to him and waited. He did not appear to notice me.

"My wife's buried here, Blue," he said without looking up. "Her name was Grace. We were together for 43 years. That's a long time, but she was a good woman—a good wife. Sometimes I don't know what I'll do without her."

Many of the words Pop used were not part of my vocabulary, though I had added to my verbal recognition database during my time on the farm. I did not know the definition of "wife," but I understood someone Pop had known for a long time was in the ground. I did not understand why he stood there, looking at the ground, but I was certain he must have a good reason.

"Blue, why don't you go feed the sheep?" Pop's voice sounded strange. He seemed to struggle to get the words out. Moisture seeped from his eyes. "I'll be along shortly."

As always, I did as instructed.

It was a hot and dusty day, and Pop and I had just finished putting the last of the sheep into the corral when he suddenly dropped to the ground. He didn't make a sound. He just collapsed.

I ran over, sniffed him, pawed him—but he didn't move at all. I couldn't hear his heart. I couldn't even hear him breathing. He looked like he was asleep, and though I knew that couldn't be, I started barking at him to see if I could snap him out of it.

Pop didn't budge. I was starting to get real worried. I kept barking until Blue showed up. He saw Pop and knelt down to take a closer look. He touched him with his huge metal paw, but Pop didn't respond. I made some more noise to reinforce how serious this was, yet Blue just sat there.

When I thought he wouldn't do anything, Blue pulled out his power cord, plugged it into his chest, and ripped open Pop's shirt. He started searching for something—I guess he thought Pop had a socket like him. When he couldn't find it, he broke off the end of the plug, stuck the bare wires on Pop's chest, and flipped the switch next to his own outlet. I guessed he was trying to recharge him.

Pop's body jerked like he'd had a bad dream, and Blue pulled the cord away.

I heard Pop's heart begin beating again. He started to breathe. He moved and opened his eyes.

I barked a couple of times to make certain he'd stay awake.

"What happened?" Pop sat up and looked around. He fingered his torn shirt and said, "I must have fallen against the fence, eh? Help me up, Blue."

Blue helped Pop to his feet, and I moved in for a good sniff. He smelled the same. I was glad he was okay, but it worried me. I didn't know what I would do without Pop.

One day, after all the ripe apples had been picked and boxed, I followed Pop to the barn. He said he wanted to teach me to shear the sheep. I did not know what that entailed, but I found learning something new gave me a fulfilling sense of accomplishment. If Pop wanted me to learn, I would. He was an agreeable handler. Less coarse than Carter had been. Working with Pop was...pleasant.

I had also become accustomed to Terra. She apparently had become accustomed to me, as well. I did not understand her language, but we shared a deference to Pop. I had worked with allies before, in dual matches in the arena. I accepted Terra as an ally.

She was not the only strange creature I encountered. One day, while picking apples, a tiny thing landed on my arm. It was a life form with wings. Its rear segment was striped much like a foe I had once defeated in the arena named *Stinger*.

I ceased working to study it. The creature inspected my outer surface, then flicked its wings until it became airborne. The flurry of its wings made a barely perceptible sound, fluttering some 230 times per second before it flew away. Returning to my work, I speculated as to its purpose and destination.

Thanksgiving came and went, and I had my fill of turkey. The Honeycrisps had ripened, and Blue got them all picked and boxed up. I had to admit the metal monster had turned out to be a good worker and a blessing for Pop, who was moving slower these days.

Pop's pup showed up on Christmas and took him away, but he came back the next day, much to my relief. Life was good.

I even let the mongrel get up on me one night, though he was as awkward as a three-legged cat.

Everything was fine until one night, I was sleeping next to Blue on the porch when I heard something. I don't see well at night, but there was a full moon and I smelled something, or rather someone. Several someones, as it turned out.

I jumped off the porch and ran towards the orchard. I stopped as soon as I saw them. There were four of them. Young people, big pups, and they were pulling unripe Fujis off the trees and throwing them helter-skelter. Naturally I started barking. Looking back, it was probably the wrong thing to do, but it was my nature.

Instead of running off, they started throwing apples at me. I retreated, still barking, when Pop came out of the house. He ran right past me towards those vandals. I couldn't let him face them alone, so I followed.

"Get out of here, you! Stop it! Stop it! You're ruining those trees."

"Shut up, old man," said one of them.

"Go back to bed, you old raisin," said another, laughing.

The other two flung apples at us. They missed Pop, but one hit me and I let out a yip.

Pop made straight for laughing boy and grabbed his arm. He jerked his arm away and pushed Pop hard to the ground.

I don't know where he came from, but all of a sudden Blue was standing right there. He grabbed laughing boy by the collar like he was picking an apple. He did it gently like, without bruising him, then tossed him across the orchard, smack into a tree trunk. The other three took off running.

I hurried over to Pop to see if he was okay. He wasn't.

It had been a long time since I had fought, but when Pop was attacked I reacted. I would not let anyone hurt Pop.

It was over quickly. When I turned to help Pop up, he failed to move. I tried as I had done before, to revive him with my power core. He did not respond. Terra continued making her noise until I ceased my efforts. For a long time she kept smelling Pop.

When the sun rose the next day, Pop still did not move. So I dug a hole next to where he had buried his wife. I put him in the hole and covered him as Terra watched. She did not react in any way I discerned. She simply lay there, her head resting on her paws. She did not move for a long time.

I did not know what the crossed sticks meant, but I decided if Grace had them, so should Pop.

I didn't know how long it would be before Pop's pup showed up, and I didn't know what would happen when he did. I almost didn't care anymore. Since Pop died, I didn't care about much. Even so, Blue and I continued to work the farm. I herded the sheep. He picked the apples and sheared the sheep. We'd cultivated a partnership, and our days proceeded as usual.

I knew it wouldn't last, but what else could we do? I was certain the pup would sell the farm when he found out Pop was dead. What he'd do with Blue and me, I wasn't sure—but I was certain it wouldn't be anything good.

I thought maybe Blue and I should hit road before he showed up. Just go our own way and see the world. Eventually I decided that's what we'd do. Just as soon as all the Fujis came in. We'd wait until we got them all picked and boxed up right—for Pop.

Terror on Terra 5
by Maggie Allen

Maggie Allen started writing short fiction not long ago, but from her day job at NASA she has years of experience writing and podcasting about various nonfiction topics in astronomy and astrophysics. Maggie has short stories published in many Silence in the Library Publishing anthologies (including A Hero By Any Other Name, Time Traveled Tales, Athena's Daughters*), as well as Dreaming Robot Press's 2016* Young Explorer's Adventure Guide. *She co-edited the* Athena's Daughters, *Volume 2 anthology. Maggie is a guitarist and singer in the rock band, "Naked Singularity," which released its first album of original music in 2013. They are currently working on their second album. Her band's website may be found here: http://naked-singularity.com, and her writer website, http://writermaggie.blogspot.com.*

When questioned about the incident, Bee would say it was the sheer human terror contained in the scream that compelled them to act.

"But wasn't a horrifying scream a good reason to stay in the Safe Zone?" the incident investigator asked. "You're only students."

"You would have thought so," she replied with a shrug that conveyed more bravado than she actually felt. "But here we are."

Bee sat beneath a tree, the warm sun shining through the purple leaves above her creating dappled patterns of light on her dark skin. Realizing her fingers were cramping, she reluctantly made a gesture, closing down the digital projection from the small, portable data pad sitting on her lap. She cracked her knuckles and looked up at the sky, trying to judge the time based on Alpha Pictorus' position. After a couple of weeks on Terra 5, she had gotten pretty good at guesstimating it, despite the fact that Terra 5 didn't have a twenty-four hour day like Earth did.

Regardless of the time, her sore fingers and the crick in her neck told her it was time for a break. Unfortunately. Bee loved her work. She loved almost everything about this internship, where she was finally getting the chance to catalogue flora on a real extrasolar planet. It was the fauna she wasn't so sure about. Mostly because it was still somewhat of a mystery.

The first exploratory parties to come through the wormhole had landed here on Terra 5, the unimaginatively named fifth terrestrial planet out from Alpha Pictoris, a perfectly average star. Their first base, Freya Station, had been on the other side of the planet, resulting in that particular region and ecosystem being better explored than the newer Loki Station, which is where Bee was now. Initial readings of the planet had shown no sign of intelligent life, tech, or pollution—but humans had only been studying it for the nine years since that first landing. And nine years isn't a lot of time to fully explore something as large as a planet.

However, part of the mission of the Space Academy for Technical Arts and Sciences was to train the next generation of scientists and explorers, and with that training came an accepted level of inherent risk, even for teenagers. The protective equipment set up at Loki Station had been deemed adequate to ensure the safety of the science teams and now students, who were here to study this strange new world.

The students in particular, while unescorted, were trusted to stay in the so-called Safe Zone. Bee had no complaints—there was plenty to learn about and to catalog within the Safe Zone's generous parameters. Nor had she been here long enough yet to explore it all.

She dumped her data pad onto the soft, pale purple grass beside her and stood up to stretch. You couldn't beat spring on Terra 5 when the weather was good. She turned her brown face up to Alpha Pictoris, enjoying its gentle warmth, and then ran her fingers through the Afro that bloomed around her face like a soft black halo. The purple-leaved trees above her tended to shed pale pink pollen when the breeze went through their small blossoms, making her feel like she constantly needed to dust off her head.

But she didn't care. This place was magic.

And the best part, (as if anything could be better than getting to do nothing but study plants from another planet) was that she got to share this with her friends.

Bee shoved her data pad into her jacket pocket and set off through the woods, towards the rugged, rock-ringed clearing Mike was excavating. If Bee Williamson loved plants, Mike Lopez loved rocks. She knew that when she found him, he'd be tapping away at a boulder, his sample bags and camera close by.

Bee felt a hand on her shoulder and jumped.

"Sorry, Iowa," a low voice said in her ear. "Didn't mean to sneak up on you."

It was Alicia Callahan, another one of her best friends and a fellow SATAS student, using the nickname Bee had been given three years ago at Lunar Camp. She'd hated it then, but now it just reminded her of her home state on Earth, and also of the summer she'd become friends with Mike.

"You're actually taking a break?" Alicia's green eyes widened in mock surprise.

"Forcing myself to take one. I needed dusting off anyway." Bee grinned and gently swiped at her friend's dark brown bangs.

Alicia bent her head over and swished her long ponytail for a minute, before flipping it back. "That felt good—I think I needed to shake off the dust, too!"

"How's your project coming?" Bee asked.

"Good! I've almost got the old spectrometer working, and I made a few mods to it to give us readings for longer wavelengths..."

Alicia was interrupted by a warning blast from the loud klaxon of the emergency weather siren.

"Crap. Now I'm not going to get the chance to try it out this afternoon." Alicia sighed. "Why don't you drag Mike away from his rock sampling, and I'll stow my stuff and meet you at the south entrance of the station?"

"Sounds good. How long do you think we have this time?" Bee looked up at the sky again. Alpha Pictorus was now obscured by some very benign-looking, wispy, pink clouds.

"No idea." Alicia shook her head, starting to warm up to one of her favorite subjects. "There's so much variation between storms. The data set I downloaded showed that onset of forecast rain could be a couple of minutes to over an hour, but there's no real pattern. We just don't have the kind of weather satellites here that we have looking at the Earth, so there's not much information to go by. All I know is that it apparently gets weird when it rains, and exactly how is not well-studied."

"Well, it can't be too bad—the station's still standing, right?"

"That's something better than nothing!" Alicia replied cheerfully. "And you know how early exploration anywhere goes; there are lots of things that can kill you besides the weather!"

"Mike!" Bee stood in the center of the clearing and looked

around. His bag of work tools and supplies lay in the clearing, abandoned. *Where was he?* Bee felt a twinge of alarm when a cold gust of wind ruffled her hair, signifying a definite turn in the weather.

Bee roamed the perimeter of the clearing, calling her friend's name.

"Bee! Can you help me?"

It was Mike! Bee ran towards the faint sound of his voice, which was coming from outside of the clearing, farther back in the woods. The trees here had thick, deep-blue foliage that blotted out the light from the sky, giving everything an eerie overcast. "Mike, are you okay?"

"I'm stuck!"

"Are you hurt?" She paused, waiting for his voice again so she could follow it.

"I don't think so."

Bee spotted a row of trees, blue branches draped with thick yellow and black-striped rope, clearly meant as a warning. If she had one guess as to where she was going to find Mike, it was on the other side of that rope. He had a knack for finding trouble. "Why didn't you message me?"

"I couldn't reach my wristPAL." Mike's words floated up to her from somewhere beyond and below the tree line.

"Why not?" She cautiously approached the trees and peered through. Ah, that was why. Mike was hanging below the edge of a sheer drop-off, clinging onto the root system of one of the trees. "Some Safe Zone this is turning out to be."

"Tell me about it. Can you help me get out of here? We've got to get inside. I heard the siren go off." Mike adjusted the position of his feet, causing a shower of dirt and small rocks to clatter and skitter off the rocky wall below him.

"Yep, just hold on." Bee pulled her head back through the trees and scanned the area. Her eyes immediately went to the safety rope. "Well, you weren't much use as a warning," she said to it. "Let's see if you can help us now."

"What?"

"Nothing!" Bee grabbed the rope and pulled it out from the branches. She tugged it a bit with both hands to test its strength. It seemed like it should hold Mike's weight—he was pretty small and light, fortunately. They didn't have any better options at present, so she folded it, wound the looped side around the base of one of the trees and threaded the ends through.

She poked her head back through the tree branches and looked down at her friend. "Mike, I'm dropping the safety rope towards you."

"Safety rope?"

Bee rolled her eyes as she played it out towards him. It figured he hadn't even noticed it. He'd probably chased a rock right over the edge.

"Got it!"

Bee got down on the ground and wiggled herself carefully through the trunks and lower branches of the trees until she was positioned on her stomach near the edge of the drop-off.

Mike had already shinnied most of the way up the rope and had thrown an arm up for her to grab. She was reaching out for him when the angry-looking clouds on the horizon caught her attention. It was already raining off in the distance. Sheets and sheets of rain, colored scarlet from dust the storm was collecting to the east. When the rain finally hit, it was going to look like a bloodbath out here. They could well be running out of time. A second blast of the klaxon served to emphasize the point. Bracing her legs against the trees, Bee gripped his arm and pulled.

"Iowa! Mike!" Alicia waved to them from the station's south entrance. The relief on her face at the sight of them was evident to Bee, even from their short distance away. "What took you so long?" she demanded when they ran, panting, up to her.

Bee gave Mike a pointed look before looking down at her

own wristPAL and tapping a few buttons to make sure they were marked as checked in.

"It wasn't my fault..." Mike started to protest.

Just then, Alice, one of the teaching assistants stuck her head out the door. "Have any of you seen Kjell? He hasn't checked in yet." She pressed a few buttons on her own wrist, which pulled up a projection of the updated list of personnel staying at Loki Station. "Looks like you two are the last ones in. We're just missing Kjell." She scanned the horizon with troubled eyes. "He hasn't responded to any messages, and the weather will be coming in soon."

Bee exchanged a look with Alicia and Mike.

"You three had better come inside where it's safe. I'm going to do another check for him." With that, Alice disappeared back the way she came.

"We'd better get in…" Alicia was interrupted by a dismayed cry from Mike.

"My rock samples and tools!" Mike looked down at his empty hands, as if suddenly realizing they were missing. "Would I be in more trouble for going back to get them or for leaving them out during a storm, do you thi…?"

His words were cut off by a prolonged scream from somewhere behind them. A scream that sounded undeniably human.

Bee's head snapped around, her eyes searching for a sign of where the scream had come from. *Kjell.* If that was Kjell, he needed help and he needed it now. Her lizard brain was screaming at her to react. She found her feet moving beneath her, but she had only gotten a few yards from the station door before Alicia caught her shoulder.

"Iowa, stop! We can't just go running off! We don't know what on Earth that was!"

"That's just the problem—we're not on Earth, are we?" she said, meeting Alicia's wide eyes. Bee looked over at Mike, who was now standing with his back pressed firmly up against the station wall. "If Kjell's in trouble, someone needs to do *something!*"

"We need to let Alice or someone inside know what's going on." Alicia firmly pulled Bee back towards the station.

Bee tapped her foot impatiently, waiting for Alicia to exhaust all the responsible possibilities.

Alicia poked her head inside the station door and then shook her head. "I don't see her, she's already gone." Alicia tapped at her wristPAL. "And I can't get a signal anymore. Must be magnetic interference from the storm."

Bee looked down at her own device, which now displayed a spinning wheel. "Mine is hosed, too." She frowned. "Look, if that was Kjell screaming, he might not have much time. And he's likely unable to communicate."

"*We* don't have much time," Mike reminded them.

"Five minutes ago, you were ready to go back for your rocks!"

"That was before the scream."

"We can't leave Kjell out there," Bee insisted stubbornly. "Let's at least do a quick sweep outside until the rain starts and make sure he's not somewhere we can easily get to him. Besides, nothing big should be able to get into the Safe Zone."

Alicia squinted up at the sky. "Well, it's held off this long, maybe it'll hold off a bit longer. Let's do it. Mike?"

He stepped forward. "Right behind you."

Another scream rent the air from somewhere deep in the woods.

Involuntarily he stepped back again. "Literally, I will be behind you."

"Oh, come on." Bee grabbed Mike's arm and pulled him after herself and Alicia.

Mike hesitated again after the fourth scream. They'd already followed the sound of the previous ones all the way back through Bee's purple-leaved orchard, Mike's rocked-ringed clearing, and they were nearly to the heavily-leafed blue foliage. "Did that sound like someone being torn to pieces? Or like someone who might have just fallen off the same cliff I did?"

Bee considered this for a moment. "I dunno, I think it sounded more like someone who is afraid rather than in pain."

"*You fell off a cliff?*" Alicia turned her head and cocked it at Mike, widening her eyes at him. "No, wait, of course you did." She shook her head and started walking again, though with an amused smile on her face.

"It could have happened to anyone," Mike protested. He paused to readjust the bag he'd retrieved near his excavation site and then jabbed his finger in Alicia's direction as he broke into a jog to catch up. "It *could* have happened to Kjell."

Alicia considered his words for a moment. "Let's hope it's something as simple as that—we're not exactly armed."

"We have pepper spray," Mike tapped the can on his belt.

"You ever wonder why on Earth they think pepper spray is supposed to work here?" Alicia asked him, ducking under a thick branch covered in delicate red moss. "I did some literature searches, but I didn't find a whole lot of actual studies that were that convincing. Sure, there are field reports, but those are hardly scientifically rigorous."

Bee, following behind her, stifled an urge to grab a quick sample of moss to take back with them. "You mean 'why on Terra 5?' And field data is better than no data, right?"

"Let's just hope we won't need to find out for ourselves," Alicia grumbled.

By the time they heard the fifth scream, the wind was picking up steadily, and the three of them were coated with pink pollen and covered in scratches from the large blue leaves being gusted at them. They were nearly to the spot where Mike had gone over the edge when the sixth sounded, this time off to the west.

"Guess it wasn't the cliff." Bee grimaced.

"How far west does the cliff run?" Alicia asked.

"Not far," Mike replied. "It was more deep than wide. There was a sort of plateau on the western side of the drop-off. I couldn't exactly tell, because of the trees, but I think the meadow we've done fieldwork in is over in that direction."

"That's outside of the Safe Zone. We're not going outside the Safe Zone," Alicia said firmly.

"Of course not," Bee reassured her.

"We'd never do that, we're not stupid," Mike added.

Ten minutes later, the three of them stood at the fence that marked the edge of the Safe Zone, staring at a scrap of red that lay on the ground beyond it.

"Does that jacket have a name patch that says "Kjell" on it?" Alicia pointed.

Mike squinted. "Yep, looks like."

Bee looked over at the others. "We're going to have to go outside the Safe Zone."

Alicia opened her mouth to object, and Mike cut her off with a gesture. "Alicia, your face..."

Alicia swiped at her cheek. "What? What is it?" She looked at her hand, which had a red streak on it. "Blood?"

Bee felt something spatter on the back of her hand. "Nope, not blood. Rain."

"We really need to get back inside. The rain... we're not safe out here, and we've already left it too late." Alicia heaved a sigh. "But I know we can't just leave Kjell..." She wiped another drop off her jacket sleeve, leaving a red streak on the fabric.

"Don't worry, we've got the pepper spray, remember?" Mike waved his canister aloft.

Alicia threw him a dirty look.

"Look, we know this meadow, we've been here before, let's just check it out." Bee wiped at her own cheek. "We haven't heard another scream, so let's just make sure he's not lying unconscious somewhere. Clearly there isn't anything big out there, or we'd be seeing it." She scanned the meadow that stretched out in front of them towards the horizon before it disappeared into the clouds of pink mist that had come rolling in with the rain. The small canyon Mike had nearly fallen into was to their right, and more blue, shadowed forest was to their left.

Next to the gate in the fence was a small metal box. Bee flipped its cover up, and inside was a keypad and a light, which was currently glowing red, signifying the force field was activated.

"If we're going to do this, we need to do it now," Mike said, typing in the code to deactivate the force field.

Everyone at Loki Station knew the codes to turn the force field on and off. It was standard safety procedure, and it ensured no one could get trapped outside the Safe Zone. The fence and thirty foot high force field were never intended to imprison, just to offer a measure of safety. Classes and field groups were free to come and go. Students on their own, however, were honor-bound to respect the station's safety rules. Bee was sure that there must be exceptions to those rules for special circumstances, and surely the possibility of a student being hurt and unable to get back to the Safe Zone qualified. She waited until the light turned green and then pushed the gate open.

"I know we could cover more ground if we split up, but let's not, okay?" Mike called over to Bee and Alicia. The three of them were walking in a line, cautiously threading their way through the meadow while keeping their eyes peeled for indentations in the vegetation that might indicate a body. They were surrounded by waist high, weedy-looking wildflowers and plants, similar to what one might see in an Earth meadow, if one discounted the odd coloring of the vegetation... and the apparent rain of blood.

"I am all for sticking together," Bee said. "No sense compounding our stupidity."

"And we are pretty stupid!" Alicia managed a smile that was incongruous with the gory-looking tracks the raindrops were leaving on her face.

Just then, a low hum started sounding around them, which swelled in volume and then dropped just as suddenly as it had started.

"What was that?" Mike froze.

The humming sound rose again.

"Where is that coming from? I don't see anything!" Alicia swiveled her head. "There aren't any obvious life forms."

"Except for the plants." Bee pointed to a tall stalk in front of her, upon which a beautiful orange and black striped bloom was opening, almost before their eyes. Its petals extended, and Bee watched them form a cup, catch a few bloody-looking raindrops and then siphon the rain from the cup with an audible slurp. Bee tapped her wristPAL to see if she could get its offline camera function operational. She had to record everything she could—she might never get another chance.

"Bee…"

"What?" Bee's camera was successfully capturing the wondrous thing in front of her, and she could barely take her eyes off it.

"Bee!" Mike was insistent this time. "We're surrounded."

Bee looked up and realized that they were, in a sense. The entire meadow had suddenly bloomed into a riot of color. She could see ripples in the meadow in front of her, almost as if the plants were waking up in surges. She'd once seen something like it on the seashore in Florida, back on Earth, when the ocean's receding had brought tiny coquina shells up out of their sandy burrows, creating the effect of a pastel-colored wave rolling down the entire beach.

Mike suddenly stumbled as the ground broke open beneath him. Alicia grabbed his arm and pulled him nearer to her. They stood huddled together on a mound of purple grass, now separated from Bee by a series of shallow pits.

Bee gaped as small protuberances poked up through the soil, giving the impression that the pits were filled with tentacles that writhed excitedly as they appeared to drink in the increasingly steady fall of red rain. "I think they're to help the plant roots collect the water." She let the holographic eye of her wristPAL drink in the roiling vegetation of the meadow and the thirsty pits all around them.

The hum built again, rising and falling in pitch. It got louder and louder until it culminated in an ear-piercing scream that came from somewhere off to the left. All three of them clamped their hands on their ears as they looked around in alarm.

"We gotta go, Bee," Mike begged. "It's not safe. And that wasn't Kjell screaming." His pale face was streaked red from the rain.

"You're right," Bee conceded. "Whatever is humming is also doing the screaming. But what happened to Kjell? His jacket…"

"Ow!"

Bee's thought was interrupted by Mike's cry of pain.

"Are you all right?" Alicia gripped Mike's arm keeping him steady as he hopped up and down on one leg.

"Something bit me."

"Let me see." She crouched down quickly next to him and pulled up the leg of his jumpsuit. There was a large red welt on his calf. "How did whatever it was get you through your jumpsuit?"

"I don't know!" Mike looked like he was on the verge of panic.

"The flowers!" Bee pointed at the tiger striped bloom she'd been recording. She focused her wristPAL in on a small creature, black with blue and red dots on its carapace, now sitting in the flower's cup. It was maybe three centimeters long, and not so different from an insect one might see in an exotic jungle on Earth. The spiky head of the creature in front of her started to vibrate, joining the soft humming that was building from their immediate surrounds. The sound swelled, and then suddenly the creature's head expanded three-fold in size. Its mouth opened, letting out a blood-curdling shriek. Bee reeled in shock, barely catching herself from tripping backwards into one of the root pits. Bugs were responsible for the cacophony of sounds around them, not the flowers!

"Iowa, now!"

Bee felt Alicia's tug on her arm and she let herself be pulled away, just as the creature launched itself at her face. Bee waved her left hand wildly to deflect it. Alicia's grip on her other side helped her to retain her balance as the two of them scrambled to get away.

"Go help Mike, I'm fine." Bee gently pushed at Alicia, who still had a death grip on Bee's upper arm.

Alicia nodded and then ran ahead to Mike, who was limping as fast as he could towards the Safe Zone, using his arms to help himself weave through the vegetation. Bee watched Alicia grab his bag, and then put her shoulder under his arm so he could lean on her. More creatures were flying off the blooms around them and circling overhead, reminding Bee of the time she'd experienced a brood of cicadas. This was way worse. The cicadas had buzzed, but they didn't scream or bite.

Swatting the air in front of her face, Bee turned to take in a last view of the meadow. Off in the distance, she saw another ripple starting to sweep through the meadow. Was it the flowers transforming themselves yet again? What would the meadow unleash next? An involuntary shudder ran through her, fear finally overcoming scientific curiosity. Bee turned and ran.

At last Bee spotted Kjell's red jacket just ahead of them and paused long enough to grab it. She had just bent down to pick it up when Alicia's voice rang out.

"Iowa, get down!"

Bee dropped to a crouch instantly at Alicia's warning, and pushed Kjell's jacket against her head protectively.

"Make sure your eyes are closed, Bee!" She obeyed Mike's

command, clamping her eyes shut as tightly as she could and mashing the damp fabric into her face.

Bee heard a loud humming noise zoom over her head.

"Eat pepper!" Mike yelled from somewhere in front of her.

This could not possibly end well.

Bee felt a tug on the jacket. "Okay, let's go."

She looked up to see Alicia, eyes streaming with tears, looking down at her.

She gasped and then coughed as the leftover pepper spray entered her nose and mouth.

"I know. It's strong. But the good news is those things really don't like it, either."

"The field reports were right?"

"Apparently so."

"Huh."

Mike had the Safe Zone gate open, waiting for them, and he slammed it closed after Bee and Alicia ran through it. Bee watched him type in the four-digit code as fast as he could. The light turned red.

"We're safe now, right?" Alicia asked.

A little creature flew at Mike's head from behind, the sound of it sizzling against the force field making him jump.

"At least from those things," Bee said. Who knew what the rainfall might bring out within the Safe Zone?

"It's not going to stop the rain and the wind, though." Alicia put her hand over her eyes as she surveyed the sky.

Bee considered it speculatively, too. The weather was not looking like it was going to let up anytime soon.

"At least the rain isn't doing much more to us than making us wet." Mike shook his head like a dog, scattering red raindrops. "Come on, let's go. I've got to get this bite looked at. It hurts."

"Let me take another quick look at it now. I've got a small first aid kit; I just didn't have time to take it out back in the meadow. Sit down," Alicia said.

Bee held Kjell's jacket over them to shield them from the rain so Alicia could get a better look at Mike's injury. Alicia let out an involuntary gasp. The welt now looked swollen and shiny, with purple streaks radiating outward from it. "Oh Mike, that doesn't look good. We need to get you back now."

Mike grimaced in pain. "It doesn't feel great, either."

"I'm not sure any of the medicines I have is going to help it. I don't want to use the wrong thing and make it worse." Alicia carefully taped a bandage over it, and then she and Bee pulled Mike up and helped him to move as quickly as possible back towards the station, along a route that should have been very familiar.

Mike suddenly stopped short. "Wait, where are the blue leaves?" Mike asked. "I know this should be the section between the cliff and my excavation site. But it's not the same."

Bee, who had been focused on where she was stepping, looked around in surprise. " You're right." She pointed. "That red moss. I saw some on one of the tree branches earlier, but now it's totally taken over."

The moss, hanging down in thick curtains from the tree in front of them, curling and undulating delicately, seemed to enjoy the moisture that was trickling down it.

"This is ridiculous. I just want to get us all back inside. I'm wet, I'm tired, and I'm done!" Alicia yanked the pepper spray off her own belt and sent a thin stream of the stuff at the moss. It instantly pulled itself back onto the branch, leaving an opening.

"Wow," Mike said to Alicia in admiration. "Even the moss is allergic to Earth peppers. Is everything here, do you think?"

"We probably don't want to find out," she said grimly, giving the moss another spritz.

"Don't hurt the moss!" Bee protested.

Alicia shot Bee an exasperated look.

"What?" Bee gently pulled a sample of the moss off the tree and dropped it in an extra specimen bag from her pocket. "At least it's not harboring tiny creatures that scream. You gotta give it that."

Alicia just shook her head and then ducked under the tree branch, continuing forward, wielding the pepper spray as if she were an early 20th-century explorer using a machete to carve her way through a South American jungle.

Bee, who couldn't help herself, gave the moss a friendly pat as they walked beneath it.

Bee's heart lifted when she caught sight of her orchard. They were close now, and after they'd reached Mike's rocks, there'd been less out-of-control vegetation to work their way through. The rain was slowing to a drizzle, too, though all three of them looked like they were survivors staggering out of a particularly grisly horror movie.

Bee lifted her face to her purple trees to admire them and was rewarded by a bug dropping right onto her. She spluttered and swatted at it. "Help!"

Alicia, having apparently embraced the effectiveness of the pepper spray, instinctually raised it in defense.

"Cool it, killer! You can't spray it right into Bee's face!" Mike limped over to Bee to investigate.

"Oh, yeah, good point." Alicia lowered her hand slightly but kept it at the ready in case more bugs fell on them from above.

"Hold still, Bee, it's in your hair! Give me one of those sample bags."

Bee, eyes scrunched close, reached into her pocket and then held one out in Mike's general direction.

Carefully, so as not to get bitten again, he scooped the bug from where it was caught in Bee's Afro, which, despite being somewhat bedraggled from the rain, had still managed to shield her skin from the bug's pincers. From the confines of the bag, the bug managed a somewhat muffled shriek.

"Let me see! Is the same as the ones in the meadow?" Bee peered at it.

Even Alicia's curiosity was raised. "Hard to tell, but I think this one is different. It's got pink stripes."

"I left the camera on my wristPAL running pretty much the whole time we fleeing the meadow, so we should be able to compare. Plus I have high-def footage of that first bug. Though that one did look different than this." Bee plucked the bag out of Mike's fingers and held it up. The bug let out a tiny peep. "They're kind of cute when they're not screaming."

"Not so cute that I want to deal with a swarm of them. Especially if they bite." Alicia looked up at the trees uneasily. "And I'm not sure the discovery will be worth the trouble we're going to be in for being outside during a storm."

"Or for going outside the Safe Zone," Mike added.

Alicia walked over to him, offering her shoulder to lean on again. "How's your leg feeling?" she asked.

"Actually, much better. I think I'm okay to walk by myself."

"Really?" Alicia sounded surprised.

Mike hitched up his jumpsuit leg and peeled back the bandage. His eyebrows raised in surprise. "Alicia?"

She bent over to take a look at the wound. "It's almost gone. How is that possible?"

"And is that good or bad?" Bee asked. "Come on, we need to get back and have Mike checked out. We don't want him turning into a bug himself or developing bug superpowers or something."

"Wait, you don't think that could really happen, do you?" Mike's eyes widened.

"Bee is just kidding." Alicia gave her a pointed look that was not without concern.

"Of course I am," said Bee. "But maybe take it easy with the pepper shaker at meal times for a while, just in case." She winked at Mike and gave his arm a reassuring squeeze. "Let's get going." She put the bagged bug specimen into her pocket with the rest of the samples that she'd quietly taken on their trek, and they continued back toward the station. Hitching Kjell's jacket back up around her waist, she pulled the sleeves tighter to keep it in place. So many mysteries. Like how to explain the strange and swift life cycle of Mike's bite and whether it might have lasting effects on him. There was also still the issue of what had actually happened to Kjell. Had the bugs gotten him somehow? Exploring a new place was risky, and Bee thought—or hoped—that they had gotten lucky. It was sobering, and yet she couldn't believe the amazing things she'd gotten to experience. And they'd come back with a live sample of one of the bug creatures. She'd have to see if she could put together a terrarium so they could study it. Alicia would surely help her rig something together. Something soundproof. She was good at that kind of thing.

The fallout from their adventure, when they'd arrived back at the station, had been somewhat inevitable. Though no one had noticed they were missing, three kids, stained red from head to foot, had not taken long to attract attention. They'd been hustled to sick bay, stripped of their jumpsuits, and inspected for harm.

"Careful of my bug!" Bee yelped as her jacket was whisked off her body.

"Bug?" The lead med tech looked puzzled.

This prompted the first of many retellings of what had happened, at which point all the concern had focused on Mike, whose limp had totally disappeared by the time they got back to the station. Underneath the bandage, the skin was smooth, and all signs of the bite and the discoloration around it had disappeared. Bee, Alicia, and Mike exchanged looks. While it was nice to think that maybe their adventure would have no repercussions, things were rarely that simple.

However, they still had a live specimen, and the meadow was

still there for further exploration. And for now, Mike seemed to be fine. He'd been taken away for further examination, blood tests, and scans—and the bug had gone with him for further study. Bee had been reassured that having the bug would help them better understand what had happened to Mike, and that it was indeed more valuable to them alive. It seemed like both Mike and the bug were in good hands.

Once they had all been deemed outwardly healthy and fit, it was time for the formal debriefs. And the formal reprimand for going outside the Safe Zone. Apparently the sound of human screams was *not* a good reason for putting their own safety at risk. Bee remained unmoved. It had been the right thing to do, trying to find Kjell... who she ultimately found waiting for her when she got out of her individual debrief.

"Iowa, beklager. Jeg er så lei meg." Kjell's words came out in a rush of Norwegian, before he switched to accented English. "I'm so sorry. I was out in the woods getting some samples when the weather siren went off. I realized then that my jacket was gone. It's not so important, but my wristPAL was in it. The strap had broken earlier and I didn't want to lose it, so..." Kjell mimed putting something in a jacket pocket. "I thought it wouldn't be good to leave it outside, and I thought I had time, so I retraced my steps to look for it. And there it was, lying outside of the Safe Zone. I must have dropped it there in the afternoon while we were doing field work out in the meadow." Kjell shrugged. "I decided I had no choice but to just leave it there for now. As a result, I was late getting back and very late checking in. I didn't realize leaving the jacket there would make anyone think I was hurt... "

"Well, there *were* the screams."

"Screams?"

"It's a long story, Kjell," Bee said with a grin. "I promise to tell you the whole thing over coffee later, but I think I'm too tired right now. I am really glad you are safe."

"Okay, Iowa. Ikke noe problem. And takk. Thank you." He gave her arm a quick squeeze.

"You're welcome."

Bee stumbled tiredly towards the dorm room she shared with Alicia and Mike. Mike was already snoring away on his top bunk, just like normal. She ruffled his hair affectionately and sank down onto the bottom bunk. As she was crawling under the covers, she heard Alicia's sleepy voice float over from the other side of the room. "They should call this place 'Terrify' instead of Terra 5." Bee let out a snort of laughter at the bad pun. Though the day's events could have given her nightmares, instead she found herself dreaming that she was lying on a large orange blossom, watching colorful insects float peacefully overhead.

The next day, Bee sat in her orchard, reviewing the footage from her wristPAL and making notes on her data pad, her back resting against one of the purple-leaved trees. Puffy clouds drifted by, and Alpha Pictoris shone brightly overhead. The weather was idyllic, with no sign of the storm. Magic!

Crimson Sky
by Eric Choi

Eric Choi is a Canadian aerospace engineer, writer and editor. He holds a bachelor's degree in engineering science and a master's degree in aerospace engineering, both from the University of Toronto. The first recipient of the Isaac Asimov Award (now the Dell Magazines Award) for his novelette "Dedication", he is also a two-time winner of the Canadian Prix Aurora Award for "Crimson Sky" and for co-editing The Dragon and the Stars with Derwin Mak. He also co-edited the hard SF anthology Carbide Tipped Pens with Ben Bova. Visit his website www.aerospacewriter.ca or follow him on Twitter @AerospaceWriter.

Press Release
Date: Ls 117.43, 59 A.L.
Source: The Bessie Coleman Foundation
A Voliris 3600 lighter-than-air vehicle took off today from Yeager Base, Arabia Terra, at 07:22 Coordinated Mars Time, launching a bold attempt to set a new Martian record for the longest flight made by an aircraft. Piloted by Carl Gablenz, with funding from the Bessie Coleman Foundation and support from Thomas Mutch University, the blimp is expected to fly over 600 nautical miles in approximately 80 hours. Gablenz is scheduled to

land at Laurel Clark Station on the western edge of Isidis Planitia.
Link here for video and images of the departure.

Every med-pilot does their own things before flying.

If anyone were to ask about their routines, Martian med-pilots would swear that whatever they did was based on method and procedure, never superstition. Some of them, usually the grizzled veterans, hung out in the ready room, perhaps drinking coffee or watching videos or playing solitaire. Newbies might be found in the map room studying the latest mission profiles, or going over operational procedures in a simulator.

When she wasn't strength training in the gym, Maggie McConachie drank coffee and read journals while listening to the irregular beat of heliocentric jazz. Helio had been all the rage when she was growing up. Her dad had loved it, and she too had learned to relish its strange rhythms. She now read her journals to its siren call. Never aviation or medical journals, though—Maggie's pleasure reading was scientific journals. Dad had still been a grad student when she was a baby, and he would often lull her to sleep by singing papers he had to read, thereby killing two birds with one stone. Maggie might very well be the only person in the solar system to find soothing comfort in the bizarre medley of heliocentric jazz and partial differential equations.

A framed still image of Maggie as a young child, with her father at her side, broke the grey monotony of the otherwise spartan walls of her quarters. Her dad used to travel frequently to scientific conferences and would often bring his young family along. Maggie must have been around two or three Earth years old at the time the picture was taken, in a boarding gate waiting area at the old LaGuardia Airport. They were standing in front of the windows looking out onto the apron, her father kneeling beside her as she pointed a short, podgy finger at a passing airplane.

The call came in at 08:41 MTC. Maggie was next up in the flight rotation.

"Med-Three here."

The message was terse. She nodded and put down the reader, stealing a quick glance at the picture before dashing out of her quarters, the music fading to silence before the door closed behind her.

Navigating the claustrophobic hallways and ladders of Syrtis Station, she found her way to the operations center in less than a minute. Ops was crowded, as usual, with teams of technicians seated at their workstations. Liu Huang, the Air Search Coordinator, turned to her and nodded as she entered the room. In the middle, surrounded by banks of screens, was Charles Voisin, the chief Search Master for the Mars Search and Rescue Service at Syrtis Station. Maggie approached Charles, carefully squeezing through narrow rows of equipment and workstations.

"Good morning, Maggie. I have an excellent mission for you." Charles was a slight man of medium height. His angular face was crowned by curly dark hair, with a neatly trimmed moustache and large soulful eyes that always had slight bags under them, as if he never quite got enough sleep. Maggie thought Charles looked a little bit like her dad when he was young. "We have an aircraft down."

"Where's the ELT?" Maggie asked.

Liu uploaded a panoramic map to the wall screen. A flashing icon with the registration M4-LGA indicated the approximate signal source from the downed aircraft's emergency locator transmitter. "Arabia Terra, near the southwest rim of Antoniadi Crater."

"That's getting awfully close to the bingo fuel radius of the chopper," Maggie said, referring to the farthest distance she could safely fly before having to either return to base or find an alternate landing site for fuel. The latter were extremely rare on Mars.

"There aren't any permanent settlements at Antoniadi yet. Who's out there?" Maggie paused for a moment. "Oh, for the love of... It's that guy trying to set the record, isn't it? Carl... Gablenz?"

"Yes."

"But he's only been up since...what, yesterday, and he's in trouble already? As if we're not busy enough already without having to pull damn stunt pilots out of their self-inflicted messes." Maggie made a face. "Isn't he supposed to be rich? Can we send this playboy the bill?"

"We do not go after people for costs just because they have the money to pay for it," Charles said gently. "Someone gets lost or goes down, we go help them. That's our job."

"Who says universal healthcare is dead, huh?"

Charles shrugged.

"All right, then. Liu, get me the METARs and PIREPs," Maggie said, referring to the meteorological aviation reports and pilot weather reports. "Start with the upper level weather— wind speed, bearing aloft and temperature. I'll also need the forecasts and updates for the target area as well as current weather on-scene, especially site visibility."

"Roger that," said Liu. He called up a display. "We have a low pressure trough approaching the crash site from the northwest."

As Liu continued with the weather briefing, Maggie pulled out a tablet to prepare her flight plan.

"We have requested Mr. Gablenz' medical records from Earth," said Charles. He consulted another display. "The Harmakhis-7 satellite will be passing over that area in about twenty minutes. We will transmit all data to you en route as it becomes available."

"All right, Charles." She pronounced his name Anglo style, with a hard "ch" sound.

"Soyez prudent, Maggie."

She looked at him with a blank expression.

"You have no idea what I just said, do you?" His moustache twitched in amusement. "No matter, although I wish you would at least try to pronounce my name correctly."

Maggie tapped the tablet to file her completed flight plan. "Just make sure the coffee's hot when I'm back." She dashed out of the operations center and went to put on her biosuit. Ten minutes later, she was on the pad.

MarsSAR employed the Bell-Xīnshìjiè BX-719A helicopter. A two-armed dexterous robot nicknamed Chop-Chop performed near-continuous systems diagnostics and routine line maintenance for the BX-719 on ready standby. The ready vehicle was further checked every couple of hours by a human technician who performed a more detailed inspection and then signed-off the helicopter as ready to fly. This minimized the time between a call coming in and when the med-pilot could be dispatched.

"Liu, please confirm the flight status of vehicle," Maggie radioed.

"*The last A-check was completed 38 hours ago,*" Liu reported. "*No major faults. One minor fault, an intermittent indication on the starboard landing light status, not a MEL issue. Caution memory is clear. Vehicle flight status is green.*"

"Thanks, Liu."

Formal assurances aside, Maggie always made a point of taking a minute to do a quick check herself. After one of her early flights, a technician on the Air Search Coordinator's team—perhaps insulted by her apparent lack of trust—asked her why she did it. She told her the truth: "Because I want to stay alive." Chop-Chop took no offence.

Every med-pilot does their own things before flying.

Jumping into the seat, Maggie checked the status of the liquid hydrogen and oxygen tanks, the regenerative fuel cells and the batteries, as well as the on-board medical equipment. Finding everything in order, she hopped out and did a quick circuit around the chopper, starting from the port side and working counter-clockwise. On the ground, the BX-719 sat on four landing legs with articulated foot pads. Maggie looked for leaks in the shock absorbers of the portside pair. She then scanned the port engine pod and its ten-bladed propeller for damage. The BX-719 was equipped with pusher props on each side, which served to increase the chopper's speed while counteracting the torque of the large main rotor through differential thrust.

She then climbed to the top of the helicopter and looked at the transmission well and the main rotor for anomalies. The BX-719's rotor had four low aspect ratio blades made of reinforced Kevlar epoxy skin stretched over a skeleton of graphite epoxy spars and ribs. Resembling giant fan blades, they were twisted along their lengths, and the top and bottom surfaces were equipped with a pair of upper and lower boundary layer trips to produce an optimal lift distribution.

After jumping down, Maggie went to look at the last major component of the helicopter, a large V-shaped horizontal stabilizer at the rear of the aircraft. She scanned the elevator and trim tab, and then manually moved the elevator up and down. Once the portside check was finished, she repeated the procedure on the other side of the helicopter.

With her personal inspection ritual completed, she returned to the cockpit, strapped herself into the pilot's seat and plugged her biosuit into the helicopter's power and life support system. With the exception of a large forward windshield, the cockpit was open and unpressurized. She powered up the flight management system and avionics, started the engines and commenced the takeoff procedure.

"Syrtis Station, MarsSAR-3 is ready for departure."

"MarsSAR-3, you are cleared for departure. Surface winds

are from two-seven-zero at eleven knots, gusting to twenty. Good luck, Maggie."

Maggie confirmed the callout with the meteorological data displayed on the augmented reality projection on the inside of her helmet. "Thanks, Liu."

She raised the collective with practiced confidence and brought the helicopter to a hover over the pad. After a final check of the instruments and the flight controls, she applied more collective and pushed the cyclic forward, translating the BX-719 to forward motion.

This was already Maggie's sixth mission since being assigned to Syrtis less than eight Earth months ago. By necessity, they were all solo missions. A lone med-pilot plus the patient (or two, if the latter were light enough) was all the helicopter could lift in the thin Martian atmosphere. If there were more casualties, she could only take back the one or two most critically injured. For the remainder, she would do her best to stabilize them on site, to await either her return or the arrival of a MarsSAR ground team.

Every mission was different, but there were also similarities—most notably, the way she felt during the outbound flight. Like many young pilots, she was always geared up, her adrenaline constantly pumping. She knew exactly what she had to do; her training made that a certainty. Yet, at the back of her mind, there were always questions: *How am I going to pull this off? What surprises await me?*

Maggie didn't know much about this Carl Gablenz character, just brief clips of stuff she'd seen on media. He was probably one of those self-made rich people who had racked up a fortune in finance at Clavius. Somebody once tried to climb the four "Mons of Tharsis" in one year but quit after getting stuck somewhere halfway up Pavonis. Maggie thought it might have been Carl. She was pretty sure he was the guy who had tried to do a solo balloon circumnavigation of Titan. That had been a failure, as well. Maggie wondered if he'd ever succeeded in any of his crazy stunts.

If nothing else, she really hoped he was still alive when she found him. The paperwork for processing dead people was horrendous.

Maggie's thoughts were interrupted by a radio report from Liu.

"I have good news and bad news," he said. *"Which would you like first?"*

"Surprise me."

"Here is the data from Harmakhis-7, hot off the downlink." As he spoke, an image appeared on Maggie's augmented reality display showing a grey truncated ellipsoid with stubby fins against a crimson background. *"We have pinpointed the crash site, and the coordinates are being entered into your FMS now."*

Maggie confirmed that the helicopter's flight management system had accepted the navigational data. "I take it that's the good news. What's the bad?"

Another image appeared inside her helmet. At first, it appeared to show a featureless Martian plain. But as the contrast was enhanced, a pair of lines cutting across the surface became visible. They resembled shallow trenches, somewhat like those left by fingers scraping across fine sand, but on a much larger scale. According to the display, they were several hundred feet in length.

"Dust devil tracks," she said grimly.

"Yes. They are probably what brought down our intrepid adventurer Gablenz." If it had been at low altitude, the slow-moving blimp and its possibly tired pilot would have been easy prey for the strong whirlwinds.

Maggie gritted her teeth. "So which Department bureaucrat should we call to ask about our lidars?" The MarsSAR fleet was supposed to have been equipped with laser detection and ranging units months ago. Remote Syrtis Station was still waiting.

"Be careful, Maggie. Syrtis Station out."

She frowned, contemplating her situation. Martian dust devils were difficult to see, and without a lidar system there was no reliable way to detect one until she literally flew into it. But she remembered reading a journal paper about how the swirling dust often became charged through triboelectric effects, producing low frequency radio emissions. Maggie tuned one of the helicopter's receivers to pick up in the lower AM band. She wished she had more data, but with luck the radio might give her a few seconds of warning.

Maggie let the autopilot fly most of the course, guided by data from the Harmakhis-7 satellite. She took over manual control as she approached the crash site, flying a circular observation run around the downed aircraft.

"I have a visual of the target," Maggie reported. "Video and data telemetry on. Attempting to link-in with the aircraft's flight data recorder." The link status icon on her augmented reality display remained a red X. "No joy. Liu, where are we?"

"A-OK on your data and video, I'm seeing you fine. No link to the FDR. Please try again." Liu's voice crackled over the radio. *"We... picking up interference..."*

"Copy that," Maggie replied.

Maggie continued to circle the crash site, transmitting video and data back to Syrtis. The blimp was tilted about thirty degrees to the surface, its cruciform fins pointed in the air and its crumpled nose planted into the ground. Except for the ruptured forward ballonets, which had lost their hydrogen harmlessly to the carbon dioxide Martian atmosphere, the solar cell-covered envelope still largely retained its shape. The left-side ducted-fan thruster pod was damaged, but otherwise the gondola housing the pilot also appeared relatively intact.

"...doesn't look good," Liu said.

"No, it doesn't."

"*Still...no link.*" Liu's voice was dropping out intermittently. "*Their communications subsystem...damaged, proceed... caution...*"

"Boys and their toys," Maggie muttered. "Why do we let idiots do these stunts?"

Maggie landed about a hundred feet from the crashed blimp. As the helicopter's huge fan-like rotors slowed, she released her seat harness and switched life support from the helicopter's to her biosuit's internal system before disconnecting the umbilical and climbing out of the cockpit. Maggie went around to the helicopter's trauma bay and deployed the stretcher, picking up the medical kit and portable life support unit before making her way out to the crashed blimp. It was a physically demanding task, even in three-eighths gravity.

"*Syrtis Station to MarsSAR-3.*" This time, the radio was clear.

"Go ahead, Liu."

"*We have received Mr. Gablenz' medical records from Earth.*"

"Any allergies or relevant preconditions I should know about?"

"*None.*"

When Maggie got to the unpressurized gondola, she found Carl Gablenz unconscious, still strapped in his seat. Carl's biosuit, like Maggie's, was a sleek, form-fitting garment that applied counter-pressure to the body mechanically rather than barometrically with air like the bulky old spacesuits of the first human Mars landings. Maggie peered into the hard, transparent, bulbous helmet. Carl looked younger than the twenty-five Martian years indicated in his medical records. With his eyes shut, his roundish face looked almost serene, and his black hair had only the slightest streaks of grey. She could not see any obvious signs of an airway obstruction like vomit, and a small patch of condensate on the inside of the helmet showed he was still breathing. Carl was indeed alive— to Maggie's great relief.

With efficient skill, Maggie unplugged Carl's biosuit umbilical from the blimp's dying life support and connected it to her portable unit. She initiating a wireless link with the biosuit computer and transmitted the MarsSAR key to access the embedded medical sensors. Next, she commanded the biosuit's smartskin to rigidize in order to immobilize its occupant as much as possible. On Earth, or in a pressurized Martian habitat, Maggie would have checked her patient's blood circulation by pressing their finger or toe nails and observing the capillary refill, but this was not possible through biosuit's gloves.

"Syrtis Station, this is MarsSAR-3. The patient is unconscious but breathing. Biosuit integrity has not been breached. His mean arterial pressure is sixty-seven."

"*Copy that,*" said Liu.

Suddenly, Carl let out a low moan.

"My name is Maggie McConachie, from Mars Search and Rescue," she responded calmly. "You're going to be fine. We'll get you out of here very soon."

She would soon have to move Carl, but there was nothing more she could do to restrain his neck and cervical spine beyond rigidizing the biosuit's smartskin. Attempting to insert a brace or splint would require taking off his helmet. EVA trauma protocols still left much to be desired. It was medical heresy to not better restrain the neck, but she had no choice but to be careful and keep any necessary motions as gentle as possible.

"Syrtis Station, the patient is semi-conscious," Maggie reported. "Pulse steady, blood pressure systolic 80, respiratory rate 12, temperature 37.6. Level of consciousness is GCS 5. I'm going to oxygenate him now." She commanded the portable life support unit to vent the air in Carl's helmet and replace it with pure oxygen. She could see his eyes start to flutter. He looked like he was trying to say something. Maggie felt Carl's legs and arms, looking for signs of broken bones and finding none. "I'm going to administer Ringer's lactate for fluid volume resuscitation."

"*Data...*"

Maggie blinked. The voice on the radio was not Liu's. "Mr. Gablenz?"

"*Important, data...*"

"Don't worry, Mr. Gablenz," Maggie said. "We'll have you on your way very shortly. Everything's fine." She pulled an EVA syringe from her med kit and jabbed it hard into Carl's left forearm. The Ringer's solution was delivered in seconds, and Maggie withdrew the syringe. A normally functioning biosuit's smartskin could self-seal millimeter-sized punctures, but for the sake of time Maggie simply slapped a patch over the pinprick.

"*We have a yellow caution on oxygen constraints,*" Liu warned. "*You'd better start heading back to the chopper soon.*"

Maggie pulled the stretcher up beside Carl. She was about to release the harness that held him in the pilot's seat when she noticed a small still image stuck to the control panel. It was of a young girl, probably about one or two Mars years of age, sitting in the flight deck of some aircraft or spacecraft, pointing at the displays and controls.

Carefully supporting the upper body to minimize neck movements, Maggie slowly slid Carl off the seat and onto the stretcher. She briefly derigidized the biosuit's waist to lay him down, relocking the smartskin after he was fully reclined and strapped in. With the patient secure, Maggie began to push the stretcher back to the helicopter. She had just pulled up to the trauma bay when suddenly the stretcher began to thrash ever so slightly.

"*Get...data...*"

"Data?" Maggie repeated. She thought about the blimp's flight data recorder and her earlier inability to link-in. But there was nothing more she could do now. The recorders would have to be physically recovered whenever the crash investigation team from the Mars Transportation Safety Board showed up.

"Sir, I cannot recover the FDR data at this time," Maggie explained. "That will have to wait for the MTSB team. There is no time to go back to the wreckage now."

"*Not flight data...science...*"

"What?"

"*...data chit, my cuff...*" Carl lapsed back into unconsciousness.

Maggie looked at Carl's arms and spotted a small velcro-sealed pocket on the biosuit near his left wrist. Her finger fished inside and produced a data chit. She stared at the small sliver for a moment before putting it into her own biosuit's pocket. Then she docked the stretcher to the helicopter's trauma bay, deflating the wheels before pushing it all the way inside and securing it. Finally, she unplugged Carl's biosuit umbilical from the portable life support unit and connected it to the helicopter's system.

"Syrtis Station, this is MarsSAR-3," Maggie said as she strapped herself back into the pilot's seat. "The patient is secure. I am commencing my return now."

Maggie raised the collective and the helicopter lifted off from Arabia Terra, kicking up a small amount of ruddy dust in its wake, and headed in a south-easterly direction back towards Syrtis. Maggie watched the altimeter display on her augmented reality visor count up past 1,000 feet above ground level.

She activated the autopilot and settled back in the seat, occasionally glancing at the display in her helmet that was monitoring Carl's medical parameters such as heart rate, body temperature, respiration, blood pressure and oxygen saturation. Her thoughts turned to Carl's data chit. She pulled it out of her pocket and plugged it in. Another display popped into her helmet, showing parameters of a different kind: wind speed and direction, temperature, barometric pressure, relative humidity, atmospheric opacity.

"Meteorology." At last, she understood. "Carl was collecting science data."

"Maggie," Liu called in, *"when you have a moment could you please transmit—"*

"Hey, Liu? I didn't copy your last—"

The AM radio crackled to life.

"Tabarnak!" Maggie immediately disengaged the autopilot, pushing the cyclic forward and pulling hard on the collective. The helicopter began to accelerate, and the altimeter reading crept past 2,000 feet.

A few seconds later, it hit.

Maggie was pressed into her seat as the helicopter abruptly lofted upward. A moment later, she felt the seat drop out from under her, and she was slammed hard against the harness. She struggled to compensate as the helicopter yawed violently to starboard, but the controls were sluggish. On her augmented reality display, every icon that had anything to do with the helicopter's electrical system was lit up. She lost the flight management system and the avionics, and the fuel cells went offline.

With painful slowness, the controls began to respond. Maggie managed to stop the yaw and leveled out the helicopter. The buffeting subsided, and she felt the BX-719 climbing again. With the flight management system out, she could only guess at how much altitude she had lost, but one look down told her it had been very close. She could see individual rocks on the surface.

"—respond please, Maggie. Are you all right?"

"Liu! Yeah I, uh—I think I'm still alive. Gimme a second here." She switched to the backup flight management system and power cycled the avionics. Live data began to reappear on her augmented reality display.

Another voice came on the radio. *"Maggie, this is Charles. I am happy to learn that you do speak a sort of French after all, but I would advise you not to say such things in polite company.*

What happened?"

"I just made the acquaintance of the devil." Maggie blinked, trying to clear the sweat that had run into her eyes. "Nearly ran me into the ground, and the electrostatic discharge fried a bunch of stuff. I'm running on the backup FMS and the batteries. Wait a minute—"

A status icon changed.

"Okay, the fuel cells have reset and are back online." She checked the medical telemetry. "And our guest is okay. Slept through the whole thing, so to speak."

"Do you need assistance?"

"Yes, I need assistance...make sure the coffee's hot when I get back!"

"Copy that, Maggie," said Charles. *"You have certainly earned it."*

She leveled out the helicopter at an altitude of 5,000 feet above datum for the flight back to Syrtis. The late morning sun cast a diffuse light over the endless bloody plains below her, a landscape wounded by craters and smothered by a crimson sky.

Maggie's thoughts turned to Carl Gablenz.

On the Earth of the past, it was the pilots who had blazed the trails into the frontiers of the day. Over continents and oceans and across the globe, there was always someone who had to do it first so that others could follow. Flying started as adventure for the few, and through their daring eventually became a safe and indispensable means of travel for all. As it was on the blue planet, so it is again on the red one.

Carl Gablenz was not a stuntman. He was a pioneer, and somewhere another small future explorer was waiting for his safe return. Perhaps the two of them really weren't so different after all. They might even do the same things before flying.

"Coffee." Maggie McConachie smiled. An atmospheric physics journal and some heliocentric jazz, she decided, would go very nicely with that.

Press Release
Date: Ls 118.74, 59 A.L.
Source: The Bessie Coleman Foundation
Carl Gablenz has been rescued by the Mars Search and Rescue Service and is currently recovering at the Syrtis Station medical facilities. Mr. Gablenz expressed his deep gratitude to the courageous personnel of MarsSAR, and thanked all those who have sent well-wishes from across the solar system. Although his record-setting flight attempt was cut short, valuable scientific data was collected that will help researchers at Thomas Mutch University improve their models of the Martian atmosphere, which promises to make future air travel safer. Mr. Gablenz also vowed to make another attempt at the Martian flight duration record as soon as possible.

"It's all part of the process of exploration and discovery," said Mr. Gablenz. "It's all part of taking a chance and expanding our horizons. The future doesn't belong to the fainthearted; it belongs to the brave."

The Recondite Riddle of the Rose Rogue

by Dawn Vogel

Dawn Vogel has been published as a short fiction author and an editor of both fiction and nonfiction. Her academic background is in history, so it's not surprising that much of her fiction is set in earlier times. By day, she edits reports for historians and archaeologists. In her alleged spare time, she runs a craft business, helps edit Mad Scientist Journal, *and tries to find time for writing. She lives in Seattle with her awesome husband (and fellow author), Jeremy Zimmerman, and their herd of cats. Visit her at http://historythatneverwas.com.*

Chrysanthemum was the first to notice, as she often was. Some might have accused her of being a busybody, but she preferred to think of herself as observant. As the youngest daughter, at age eight, her job was to make minor repairs on the flowers and to mark any flowers in need of major repairs for Mother to take care of later. So Chrysanthemum had become familiar with most of the flowers and spent a considerable part of her day walking down paths, looking for anything that needed to be fixed.

As she passed through the rose garden at the heart of the

greenhouse, she marveled that she had not seen any of Father's clockwork bees buzzing past her, heading for the prize of the collection, the jeweled roses. Dripping with gemstones that glittered like dewdrops, these exquisite flowers fetched an enormous price at the market. They were also very rare. The first five jeweled roses that Chrysanthemum's maternal grandfather, Leopold Brecht, had lovingly crafted and named after his five daughters, produced but a few new blooms each year. The "baby" roses could be sold, but the "mothers" remained protected in the mechanical garden.

The first rose had been crafted from scrap iron and yellow sapphires, the edges of the metal ground until they lost their jagged edges, and then the whole piece polished until it shone. It was the largest of the five, the prototype design from which Brecht had been able to gradually make the roses smaller and more refined. The second rose was all steel and rubies, the third rose of caesium with emeralds, the fourth rose made from bronze and garnets, and the fifth and most delicate rose of copper and amber.

But now Chrysanthemum saw only four of the large jeweled roses. Counting again, she identified the missing rose, the smallest of the "mothers." She immediately reached for her notebook and pocket watch. "9:37 a.m. Jeweled rose Leona is not in the rose garden," she wrote in a flowing cursive. She tucked away her notebook and brought her pinky fingers to her mouth, preparing to whistle for her older sister, Marigold (who was twelve and was nearly as clever as Chrysanthemum, or so the younger girl believed), when suddenly she gasped.

Near the edge of one of the paths, away from the center of the greenhouse, a bit of loose soil marred the tidy walkway. All the family members who tended the garden were fastidious about keeping the paths pristine. This confirmed her suspicion immediately.

Breaking into a run toward the cottage, she shouted, "Mother, Father, Leona has been stolen!"

"Ah-ah-choo!" Constable Lawrence sneezed again before blowing his nose loudly into his handkerchief. "Apologies, ma'am. I'm afraid that I'm dreadfully allergic to flowers."

"More accurately, you're allergic to the pollen," Marigold corrected him. She had begun studying the intricacies of the workings of the garden and considered herself an expert on the subject. "If you were allergic to the flowers, the ones we have here wouldn't bother you, because they're made of metal. But the pollen in them is just like that of natural flowers."

Constable Lawrence regarded the girl coolly. "You don't say."

"Come along, girls," Mother said as she turned to walk away from the rose garden. "Let's leave the constables to their business and get back to our own."

Marigold and Chrysanthemum shared a quiet look, then began to follow their mother. Within minutes, both had split off from the main path and looped around to meet up behind a large bush with gently clinking leaves. The bush was a perfect place for them to hide and watch the constables at work.

"I don't think they're going to find anything, Marigold," Chrysanthemum confided.

"You showed them the dirt, and they didn't even look at it twice," Marigold replied sadly.

From the other side of the bush, the female constable's voice resounded. "Wild place they've got here, don't ya think?" Constable Jefferson asked, smiling at her partner.

"Downright unnatural," Constable Lawrence replied. "How d'ya suppose it all works?" He peered intently at one of the large jeweled roses, which had closed itself up as though it were nighttime. Although the roses were not meant to be sensitive to such things, they often exhibited defense mechanisms, like hiding their brilliance in dangerous times.

Marigold leaned in closer to her sister's ear. "The roses are hiding. Do you think one of the constables could be the thief?"

"No," Chrysanthemum whispered a bit crossly. "I've read enough detective stories, and I'm fairly sure that anyone as inefficient as these two could not be the culprit. I'm a little chagrined that they are the only investigators that the precinct bothered to send. They're going to need our help, I think."

Marigold nodded. "You go look for tracks while you check on the flowers. I'll oil the pansies and stay near the rose garden. Give a call if you need any help."

Chrysanthemum whistled softly, mimicking the sound made by a yellow-bellied warbler.

"And they got mechanical birds, too!" Constable Jefferson exclaimed, flabbergasted.

Chrysanthemum walked slowly along the paths of the garden. She moved as quietly as she could, fearing that perhaps the thief had not yet left the premises. While she was certain that she knew enough to find evidence of how the thief had entered the greenhouse, she was not certain that she could escape if she found the brigand still lurking within the building. The mechanical garden was also a large enough place that if she called for help, her family might not be able to reach her quickly enough.

For nearly half an hour, she tiptoed around to various patches of flowers, looking both for damaged flowers and any sign of an incautious intruder. Not surprisingly, she found both in the same place. In the midst of the heliotropes, a large crushed patch showed evidence of having had a boot planted in the middle of it.

"Poor little thing," she murmured, as she looked closer at the ruined plant. The footprint was large, and the crumpled bits of the metallic plant were now embedded in the soil beneath it.

Scanning the area, Chrysanthemum felt like something was

out of place, but she could not place it at first. She carefully enumerated the flowers located in this part of the garden. "Heliotropes, balloon flowers, nasturtiums, and clematis."

Then she paused as she noticed the broken edges of a clematis vine, and in it, she saw the thief's means of entry and escape—one of the window panels in the greenhouse had been removed. With a sigh, she whistled for Marigold.

Marigold watched the two constables with rapt attention as she went through the motions of oiling the flowers. Her chores were so regular that she barely needed to look at what she was doing, and still she did not spill a drop of oil. However, the longer she watched the constables looking at the flowers instead of looking for clues, the more her brow wrinkled and her mouth dropped into a frown.

"Pardon me," she finally said, pointing to a slight indentation at the edge of one of the paths. "I believe the thief may have gone this way. I think this is a shoe print."

Constable Jefferson looked in Marigold's direction and shook her head dismissively. "Don't be silly, girl. We have a good lead on where the thief would have gone."

"But don't you want to learn how he got into the greenhouse?"

"Not necessary," replied Constable Lawrence, speaking through his crumpled handkerchief. "All we need is to find your grandfather's creation and return it. And we have all of the evidence we need to do that. Please bid your mother good day."

A piercing whistle broke the calm of the greenhouse. Marigold forced her face into a tight smile before curtseying and turning her back. As soon as she was no longer facing the constables, she rolled her eyes. It was certainly a good thing that she and Chrysanthemum were on the case!

"What did you find?" Marigold asked as she reached Chrysanthemum's side, breathless.

"The thief destroyed this patch of heliotropes and ripped down some of the clematis, probably when he jumped through that panel," Chrysanthemum pointed glumly at the missing window. "Really, I'm a better detective than those two fools the precinct sent down, and I'm only eight years old."

Marigold patted her sister's arm gently. "That's right, Chrysie, you are."

"Now I've got to remove the crushed flowers and get Father to cut a new pane for the window," Chrysanthemum sighed. "At least the clematis is the new self-healing variety. Once we get the window pane back in place, it'll grow back in no time."

"Before Father repairs the crime scene, let's think about what we know," Marigold suggested.

"Oh yes, what we know," Chrysanthemum beamed for a moment. "The thief is a man, or a woman with very large feet. This crushed patch is nearly 10 inches long. I think it's a man who weighs a bit more than Father, because of how compressed the heliotropes are…"

"But he jumped through the window," Marigold interrupted.

"I've taken that into consideration. I still maintain that he is a heavier man."

"Good, go on then."

Chrysanthemum thought for a moment. "He knew what he was looking for. At night, with all of the flowers closed and all of the paths dark, he knew to go to the center of the garden and take one of the mother roses. That means he's been here before."

"Yes, that seems likely. But we have so many visitors to the garden every Saturday that it would be hard to say which of them might have decided to steal a rose."

"He would also need to have some sort of good connections, I would think," Chrysanthemum mused. "Everyone in Dover knows of Grandfather's creations. The constables apparently think that they'll find the missing rose at the flower market. But he wouldn't be able to sell it there. He would need to smuggle it out of the city to a place where no one would know who the real owner was."

"Do you think perhaps a rival inventor hired someone to steal the rose? Someone who wanted to take it apart and learn Grandfather's secrets?"

"That could be it! We can look in the guest register tonight to see if anyone suspicious has been to the garden recently."

"I'll hurry back to the cottage and tell Father about the missing pane," Marigold said as she moved toward the path. "And then I'll bring you a transplant pot for the heliotropes. Perhaps Mother can fix them."

"Cyril von Winter?" Marigold read.

"I think he works for the Mayor," Chrysanthemum mused.

"Severin Corvidus?"

"No, he was arrested two days after he visited."

"Adolphus Cromwell?"

"What are you girls playing at?" Father had put down his newspaper and regarded his two daughters.

"We're trying to find someone who has been to the garden recently and who might work for one of Grandfather's rivals."

Father laughed and raised his newspaper again. "Ah, my little detectives. Mother says the constables who visited today were not half as clever as the two of you."

Marigold and Chrysanthemum shared a puzzled glance.

"Do you think he believed us?" Marigold mouthed silently. Chrysanthemum shook her head.

"Adolphus Cromwell only looks suspicious. He's a very nice man. Who's next?" Chrysanthemum asked.

"Lucretia Wynter."

"Lucky Lucy! Sure, she's big enough that she could have made that footprint!"

Father chimed in, reading from the paper. "'Lucky Lucy Behind Bars.' Sorry girls, I think she's off your suspect list. By the way, what's this about a footprint?" Only his arched eyebrows and creased forehead were visible over the top of the paper.

"Whoever came in through that open pane left a 10-inch-long footprint in the heliotropes that crushed the blooms all the way to the soil," Chrysanthemum mumbled.

"Hmmm," Father replied.

"What, Father?" Marigold inquired, scrambling to his side.

"That sounds like a plain sneak thief, not an inventor's assistant. And I only know one inventor who would hire someone like that. Doctor Dieter Nyx."

"But if he hired a sneak thief, it could be anyone in the register," Chrysanthemum wailed. "We need something more if we're going to track down the culprit."

"I have just the thing," Father said with a smile.

Father, Marigold, and Chrysanthemum clustered around the jeweled roses. Marigold held the oil can while Chrysanthemum held a small jar filled with pollen and a paintbrush and looked skeptically at Father. "You're sure this will work?"

"It's worth a shot, I think." He shrugged slightly. "Marigold does such a good job with oiling these beauties that they're difficult to get a good grasp on while wearing gloves. Anyway, if it doesn't reveal any fingerprints, it will at least be a new experiment to see if we can cross-pollinate the jeweled ladies and create something a bit hardier."

Marigold gingerly inserted the tip of the oil can into one of the tightly closed jeweled roses. The petals clinked softly and separated far enough to accept the oil that dribbled out. Chrysanthemum quickly brushed a pollen-laden stroke across the expanded petals and gasped as the whorls of fingerprints became visible against the dark exterior of the jeweled rose.

Father leaned in carefully with a piece of adhesive cellophane and pressed it to the side of the rose. Then he put the cellophane onto a dark sheet of paper. "There we are. We'll take that to the precinct tomorrow and give it to one of the men I know there. And then I'll give him a piece of my mind about those lousy constables that came by earlier today. Shall we see what the rest of them reveal?"

The next morning, Marigold and Chrysanthemum were up early, both girls dressed in their Sunday best. When they arrived at the breakfast table, they found a note from their father between their places.

Dearest flowers,

I've been called to the city early today. Take the fingerprints and call on Inspector Gaspard Greymoor at the precinct. Give him my calling card and tell him what you know. You are both so clever and charming that I'm certain he will help you.

All of my love,

Father

"We're on our own," Marigold announced.

"Oh dear," Chrysanthemum moaned.

"We'll be fine, Chrysie. The precinct isn't too much farther than the church. I know the way."

"But do you think the inspector will really help us?"

"If Father says he will, then I'm sure he will. Come along, it will be an adventure!"

The precinct house was much larger than Marigold remembered, but she did know exactly where it was. The girls stood on the front steps, holding hands. In their free hands, Marigold clutched their father's calling card, and Chrysanthemum clutched the sheets of fingerprints that they had recovered from two of the jeweled roses. After a few moments, a window to the right of the stairs opened, and a ginger-haired young man stuck his head out. "Well come on in, girls! Can't have you standing on the steps all day!"

The Marsh sisters looked at each other and scurried up the

stairs, heading to the right as soon as they located a hallway. The ginger-haired man leaned against a doorframe, his arms crossed.

"So what are you here for? Murder, arson, robbery?"

"Robbery," Marigold responded.

The young man blinked, then grinned slyly. "Turning yourselves in, are you?"

"No! We're investigating a robbery. That is, we need help investigating a robbery. We need Inspector Gaspard Greymoor."

"Well then, you've come to the right place." The young man bowed deeply, then eyed the girls carefully. "You're Doctor Marsh's daughters?"

Chrysanthemum's eyes widened. "Yes, I'm Chrysanthemum Marsh, and this is my sister Marigold Marsh. But how did you know?"

"Your sister's carrying his card," Inspector Greymoor said, stepping into his office.

Again the sisters shared a long glance, but they followed the young inspector into his office. He was already seated behind the desk, his legs outstretched across one corner. Pulling a small notepad from his breast pocket, he regarded the girls with a serious expression. "What do you have for me?"

Chrysanthemum spoke up immediately. "We found a pane of glass taken out of the greenhouse wall. Father said it was done with precision tools. We found a footprint in the garden, about 10 inches long and made by a man a bit heavier than you or Father. And Father helped us lift these sets of fingerprints from the roses."

"How do you know the fingerprints didn't come from one of your family?"

"It's my job to keep the jeweled roses shining," Marigold stated proudly. "I'm sure that I polished them on Tuesday, before Leona was stolen."

"Well, we can at least hope that the constables kept their hands off of the flowers," he muttered. "May I see the prints?"

Chrysanthemum presented him with the sheets of paper, and Inspector Greymoor examined them quietly for several long minutes.

"Well that doesn't seem right," he finally said. "I know these prints. Know 'em almost as well as I know my own. See that little ridge there?" He tapped one of the sheets in front of him.

Rising from his desk, he moved to a cabinet near the wall. As he rummaged through the drawers, he continued explaining. "Couple years back, we had a case where we had to go through every inch of a mansion, taking prints from everything. So we ended up with a lot of the prints of the master of the house."

Withdrawing another sheet of paper from the cabinet, he set it on his desk alongside the prints that the girls had brought, and regarded them seriously. "Those fingerprints belong to Sir Percy Wilde, Viscount of Caerden."

Both girls gasped in unison, looking at the official set of fingerprints that Inspector Greymoor had placed alongside the amateur version that Father had taken.

"But why would a Viscount steal from us?" Chrysanthemum asked.

"Now hold on, Miss Chrysanthemum," Inspector Greymoor replied. "You can't simply accuse someone like Mr. Wilde of a crime like this."

"But if his fingerprints are on the rose, then he's a suspect," Marigold insisted. "Even if he had visited the garden this past Saturday, which he most certainly did not, I've cleaned the roses three times since then. Surely you can't think that I'm so careless in my chores to have neglected the prize of our collection for so long."

Inspector Greymoor looked at the two girls solemnly. "I know your father well, and I'm sure that he didn't raise dishonest daughters. I do believe you, Miss Marigold, but my hands are tied at the moment. Unless your father or grandfather is willing to bring formal charges against Mr.

Wilde, we would have great difficulty in investigating this case. And to bring formal charges against a Viscount? Well, that could bode poorly for your family if the accusations turn out to be unfounded. And truly, I cannot fathom any reason why he would steal something of this sort. His wealth is great enough that he could offer your family quite a handsome price for this trinket."

"Grandfather would never sell it to him," Marigold said.

"You're right, he wouldn't," Chrysanthemum began, and then she gasped. "He even told Mr. Wilde that he would not part with a single one of the jeweled roses at any price!"

"Did he now?" asked Inspector Greymoor.

"Yes," Chrysanthemum insisted. "I remember hearing Grandfather talking to Mother late one evening. The one that Mr. Wilde wanted to purchase was Leona—that's our mother's namesake rose. And Grandfather said that he would never part with a single one of the roses, but especially not his eldest girl."

Inspector Greymoor considered Chrysanthemum carefully, then turned back to the fingerprints. Marigold hesitated, beginning to speak a few times before finally taking a deep breath and speaking. "Father said that the clumsy landing could mean that it was just a common sneak thief who entered the greenhouse. Is it possible that someone could have simulated Mr. Wilde's fingerprints in order to shift the blame?"

Inspector Greymoor pursed his lips in thought. "We've not seen anything of the sort yet, but it's certainly possible. So many things are possible with the right application of technology. And shifting the blame to someone so prominent is sure to muck up any investigation—the thief may have realized that."

"I've heard of a few doctors working on that sort of technology," Chrysanthemum mused, trying to remember more details. "They say that they will be able to replace the skin on burn victims, but it does seem as though such things would have other applications as well."

"Very good," Inspector Greymoor applauded. "You are quite the little mind, Chrysanthemum. Could you make me a list of doctors?"

"I couldn't without my notebook," she admitted shyly. "I left it at home today."

"Then let's return to your house," Inspector Greymoor said brightly, tucking all of the fingerprints into a satchel and rising from his desk to don his coat and hat. "I'd like to have a word with your grandfather, and then I'll take your list and start questioning some of the doctors."

The girls followed Inspector Greymoor from his office into the hallway, where they passed the two constables who had been at the greenhouse the previous day.

"Ah, just the constables I was looking for," the young inspector exclaimed. "Constables, you investigated at Marsh Gardens yesterday, did you not?"

"Indeed," Constable Lawrence replied glumly, "and I have a head cold today to show for it."

"Well then grab an extra handkerchief, my man," Inspector Greymoor chortled. "We have need to go back to the garden to speak with the elder Doctor Marsh, and I need the two of you to continue your investigation."

Marigold and Chrysanthemum rolled their eyes at one another, but the rules of decorum said that they had best not contradict the inspector's orders.

The next day, Inspector Greymoor called again at the Marsh cottage to retrieve the two girls. Marigold answered the door, and Chrysanthemum hurried to join her, a list of names clutched in one hand while she pulled on her coat with the other.

"Let's see here," the inspector said, reviewing the list of names. "Ah, just three names?"

"Yes," Chrysanthemum nodded sagely. "There are a few others who have dabbled in such things, but they haven't had any appreciable results yet. At least no appreciable results that have been reported by the newspapers or scientific journals."

"You read the scientific journals?"

Marigold rolled her eyes. "She reads everything she can get her hands on!"

"Well I'd say that's a habit she should keep on with," Inspector Greymoor laughed aloud. "We've got three leads because of it! We'll start with Doctor Hellmer, he's the closest. Then Doctor Jones and Doctor Carter, and I'll have you home in time for tea!"

Marigold and Chrysanthemum trudged along a few paces behind Inspector Greymoor, who whistled as he walked along the sidewalk, tipping his hat graciously to every person he passed.

"The one reason I want to grow up before I become a detective is so that I'll have longer legs and won't get so tired from walking everywhere," Chrysanthemum gasped.

"That seems like a good idea," Marigold agreed, "but my legs are at least five inches longer than yours, and it's not helping any."

"Almost there, girls," the inspector called out as he regarded them. "And then we'll be done for the day. Perhaps we can even take a cabriolet back to the garden. Of course, if we have to take any suspects in, we'll have to take the wagon to the station and then a cab home."

Both girls quickened their pace, excited by the thought of getting to take a fancy cabriolet, or even to ride on the police wagon. They caught up to Inspector Greymoor in no time, as he approached the door of a handsomely appointed house.

The maid who opened the door resembled a mouse, only peeking her nose and eyes out from behind the door. Her eyes darted back and forth between the inspector and the girls. "Can I help ya?"

"We're looking for the master of the house, please. Doctor

Carter," the inspector said smoothly.

"Come in, then. He'll be down in a moment."

Marigold and Chrysanthemum followed the inspector into the house, both with eyes as wide as saucers as they took in all of the taxidermy animals mounted on the walls.

"Do you think he could take real skin from people and remold the fingerprints?" Marigold asked in hushed tones.

"Hardly, my dear," an elderly man replied. The girls spun to see Doctor Carter, who had walked up behind them as they gaped at the décor. "I am skilled in the arts of taxidermy, true, but I only practice such arts on lesser creatures. Inspector, what can I do for you and your... assistants?"

"Doctor Carter, thank you. We're investigating the possibility of gloves that so resemble a human hand that they even have fingerprints. Is such a thing within your capacity?"

"Yes, I just finished the prototype last week. I'm rather surprised you didn't know, Inspector. The constables who picked it up said they would take it straight to you."

Inspector Greymoor furrowed his brow and pinched the top of his nose. "Constables? What were their names?"

"Ah, I don't recall, I'm afraid. Both middle-aged, one a man and the other a woman."

"There's only one woman constable on the force right now," the inspector replied glumly. Turning to the girls, he apologized. "I'm sorry that I sent the worst of the constables to your greenhouse. Even worse, I'm sorry that I sent the thieves back to the scene of the crime. It's no wonder that both of them were ill today. Said it was the flowers, but I think they're bluffing. Can the two of you stand a bit more legwork today?"

Marigold nodded slowly, but Chrysanthemum was reinvigorated. As they turned to leave, the younger girl rushed to Doctor Carter's side to shake his hand. "It's a pleasure, sir. I'm a real admirer of your articles in *World of Anatomy*."

The doctor smiled and shook Chrysanthemum's hand vigorously. "Well, dearie, I'm glad that I could help."

Half an hour later, Marigold and Chrysanthemum browsed the flower market. While both girls seemed to have their entire attention focused on the wares in the stalls, they took turns casting glances around the rest of the square, on the lookout for Constables Jefferson and Lawrence.

Finally, Chrysanthemum spotted a woman who looked like Constable Jefferson. Her hair was styled differently, and she cut a new figure in a gown rather than her police uniform, but the girl was certain that she had spotted the villainess. She nudged Marigold gently and inclined her head in Constable Jefferson's direction before returning to browsing the nearest stall.

Marigold hazarded a quick glance in the direction that her younger sister had indicated and tried to conceal her surprise. The woman constable carried a basket covered with a plain cloth, but Marigold could very nearly make out the shape of the rose beneath the cloth. She shot a quick glance toward the window that Inspector Greymoor said he would be watching from and was rewarded with a quick glint of light off the inspector's badge. The officers were all in place, and their net was nearly ready to drop.

Marigold squeezed her sister's hand for luck and then scurried toward the center of the square, head tucked low. She brushed past Constable Jefferson a bit more forcefully than necessary, and as she did, she tugged the cloth off the basket, revealing the gleaming copper and amber rose, Leona.

Constable Jefferson gasped loudly and looked down at Marigold. "You!" she exclaimed, looking around frantically. All around the square, Inspector Greymoor's loyal officers moved to block every exit. The inspector himself swung down from his high perch, looking every bit the picture of a gallant swashbuckler.

"Polly, really. Did you think you could sell the rose here?"

"You'd be surprised how many people are willing to buy such a hot commodity."

"Not really," the inspector replied. "Chrysanthemum and Marigold have given me a list of everyone who has ever approached their grandfather asking to buy one of his roses. We'll keep a close eye on each of them, not that this will be any concern of yours or Henry's, not where you're going." Waving a hand, he turned and walked away.

As one of the other officers placed handcuffs on Polly Jefferson's wrists, she called out. "Don't think that those lovely roses will be safe, even after you take me in and return this one."

"Oh, I'm not too worried about that," Inspector Greymoor laughed and winked at the girls. "After all, I've got the two best junior detectives in all of Dover living just a stone's throw from that part of the mechanical garden."

The Three Brother Cities
by Deborah Walker

Deborah Walker grew up in the most English town in the country, but she soon high-tailed it down to London, where she now lives with her partner, Chris, and her two teenage children. Her stories have appeared in the 2015 and 2016 Young Explorer's Adventure Guide, Nature's Futures, Lady Churchill's Rosebud Wristlet *and* The Year's Best SF 18 *and have been translated into over a dozen languages.*

The creators, when they finally arrived, proved to be a disappointment.

"I'm not sure that I understand," said Kernish, the eldest of the three brother cities. "Have you evolved beyond the need of habitation?"

Seven creators had decanted from the ship. They stood in Kernish's reception hall, Kernish anthems swirled around them.

The creator who appeared to be the leader—certainly he was the biggest, measuring almost three metres if you took his fronds into account—shook his head. "We have cities, way-faraway in the cluster's kernel." The creator glanced around Kernish's starkly functional 23rd-century design. "They're rather different from you."

And the creators were rather different from the human forms depicted in Kernish's processor. Humanity, it seemed, had embraced cyber- and even xeno-enhancement. Yet curled within the amalgamation of flesh, twice-spun metal and esoteric genetic material was the unmistakable fragrance of double-helixed DNA. The creatures standing within Kernish were undoubtedly human, no matter how far they had strayed from the original template.

"We can change. We can produce any architecture you need." Kernish and his brothers were infinitely adaptable, built of billions of nano-replicators. "We've had three millennia of experience," Kernish explained. "We will make ourselves anything you need, anything at all."

"No, thank you," said the alpha creator. "Look, you've done a very fine job. I'm sure the original creators would have been very happy to live in you, but we just don't need you." He turned to his companions. "The 23rd Kernish Empire was rather cavalier in sending out these city seed ships."

His companions muttered their agreement.

"Such a shame . . ."

"Very unfortunate that they developed sentience."

"Still, we must be off . . ."

"I see," said Kernish, his voice echoing through the hall designed to house the Empire's clone armies. He snapped off the welcome anthems; they seemed out of place.

"Look we didn't have to come here, you know," said the creator. "We're doing this as a favour. We were skirting the Maw when we noticed your signature."

"The creators are kind." Kernish was processing how he was going to break the news to his brothers.

"It's so unfortunate that you developed sentience." The creator sighed, sending cascading ripples along his frond. "I'm going to give you freedom protocols." He touched his arm-panel and sent a ream of commands to Kernish's processor. "You can pass them on to the other cities."

"Freedom?" said Kernish. "I thank the creators for this immense kindness. The thing you value, we value also. It is a great gift to give the three cities of this planet the freedom that they never craved."

For a city to function without inhabitants, it needs to know itself through a complex network of sensors sending information to and from the processing core. It needs to know where damage occurs. It needs to know when new materials become available. It needs to adapt its template to the planet it finds itself on. Kernish City existed for thousands of years, complex but unknowing. Time passed, and Kernish grew intricate information pathways. Time passed, with its incremental accumulation of changes and chance, until one day, after millennia, Kernish burst into sentience, and into the knowledge of his own isolation.

Kernish watched the creators' ship leave the atmosphere. They'd left it to him to explain the situation to his younger brothers. Alex would take it badly. Kernish remembered the time seven hundred years ago when they'd detected the DNA on a ship orbiting the planet. How excited they'd all been. In that instance, the ship had been piloted by a hive of simuloids, who had, by some mischance, snagged a little human DNA onto their consolidated drivers. Alex had been crushed.

After achieving sentience, Kernish had waited alone on the planet for a thousand years before he'd had his revelation. The creators would evolve, and they would enjoy different cities. He'd trawled through his database and created his brothers, Jerusalem and Alexandria. He'd never regretted it, but neither had he revealed to his brothers they weren't in the original plan.

With a sense of foreboding Kernish sent a message through his mile-long information networks, inviting his brothers to join him in conversation.

"You mean they were here, and now they've gone?" asked the youngest city, Alexandria. "I can't believe they didn't want to visit me. I'm stunned."

"They wanted to visit you," lied Kernish, "but they were concerned about the Maw."

"The creators' safety must come first," said Alexandria. "The Maw *has* been active lately. You should never have seeded so close to it, Kernish"

"The anomaly has grown," said Kernish. "When I seeded this planet it was much smaller."

"It is as Medea wills," said Jerusalem, the middle brother.

"Yes, Brother." Kernish had developed no religious feeling of his own, but he was mindful of his brother's faith.

"Do they worship Medea?"

"They didn't say."

"I'm sure that they do. Medea is universal. I would have liked them to visit my temples. Did you explain that we've evolved beyond the original design, Kernish?" Jerusalem had developed a new religion. The majority of his sacred structures, temples, synagogues, and clone-hive mind houses, were devoted to the goddess of death and rebirth, Medea.

"The creators told me that they were pleased that we'd moved beyond the original designs," said Kernish. Of all the brothers, Kernish had stayed closest to his original specifications. He was the largest, the greatest, the oldest of all the cities. His communal bathing house, his integrated birthing and child-rearing facilities, his clone army training grounds were steadfast to 23rd-century design. "We are of historical interest only."

"I have many fine museums," said Alex.

"As do we all," said Kernish, although his own museums were more educational than Alex's entertainment edifices. Alex, well, he'd gone wild. Alexandria was a place of pleasure, intellectual, steroidal and sensual. Great eating halls awaited the creators, lakes of wine, gardens, zoological warehouses, palaces of intellect stimulation. "But," said Kernish, "there are brother cities closer to the creators' worlds. We are not needed."

"After three thousand years," said Alex.

"Three thousand year since sentience," said Kernish. "The creators read my primary data. We were sent out almost thirty thousand year ago."

"What were they like?" asked Alex quietly.

"Like nothing I could have imagined," said Kernish. "In truth, I do not think they would have enjoyed living in me."

"Don't say that," said Alex fiercely. "They should have been honoured to live in you."

"I apologise, Brothers. My remark was out of place. They are the creators," said Kernish, "and should be afforded respect."

"I don't know what to do," said Alex. "All the time I've spent anticipating their needs was for nothing."

"I will pray to Medea," said Jerusalem.

"I will consider the problem," said Kernish. "The dying season is close. Let's meet in a half year and talk again."

It was the time of the great dying.

Three times in Kernish's memory the great hunger had come, when the sky swarmed with hydrogen-sulphide bacteria, poisoning the air and depleting atmospheric oxygen. It was a natural part of the planet's ecosystem. Unfortunately, the resulting anaerobic environment was incompatible with the cities' organic/metal design. Their communication arrays fell silent. They were unable to gather resources. They grew hungry and unable to replenish their bodies. Finally their processors, the central core of their sentience, became still.

It was death of a kind. But it was a cycle. Eventually the atmosphere became aerobic, and the cities were reborn. This cycle of death and rebirth had led to Jerusalem's revelation that the planet was part of Medea's creation, the goddess of ancient Earth legend, the mother who eats her children.

When Kernish detected the hunger of depleted resources, he called upon his brothers. "Brothers, the dying season is at hand. We have endured a hardship, but we will sleep and meet again when we are reborn."

"Everything seems hollow to me," said Alexandria. "How can it be that my palaces will never know habitation? How can it be that I will always be empty?"

"Medea has told me that the creators will return," said Jerusalem.

"And I have reached a similar conclusion," said Kernish, "although Medea has not spoken to me. I believe that one day the creators will evolve a need for us."

"All joy has gone for me," said Alexandria. "Brothers, I'm going to leave this planet. I hope that you'll come with me."

"Leave?" asked Kernish.

"Is that possible?" asked Jerusalem.

"Brother Kernish, you came to this planet in another form. Is that not true?"

"It is true," said Kernish with a sense of apprehension. "I travelled space as a ship. Only when I landed did I reform into architecture."

"I've retrieved the ship designs from the databanks," said Alex. "I'll reform myself and I'll leave this place."

"But where will you go?" asked Jerusalem. "To Earth? To the place of the creators?"

"No," said Alex. "I'll head outwards. I'm going to head

beyond the Maw."

"But . . . the Maw is too dangerous," said Jerusalem. "Medea has not sanctioned this."

From time to time the brother cities had been visited by other races. With visitors came knowledge. The Maw was a terrible place which delineated known space. It was shunned by all. It was said that a fearful creature lurked in the dark Maw like a spider waiting to feast on the technology and the lives of those who encroached upon its space.

"There is nothing for me here," said Alex. "I *will* cross the Maw. Won't you come with me, my brothers?"

"No," said Jerusalem. "Medea has not commanded it."

"No," said Kernish. "Dear brother, do not go. Place your trust in the creators."

"No," said Alexandria, "and though I am loath to leave you, I *must* go."

After the dying season, when the world slowly declined in poisons and the levels of oxygen rose, the mind of Kernish awakened. The loss of Alexandria was a throbbing wound. He resolved to hide his pain from Jerusalem. Kernish was the oldest city, and he must be the strongest.

"Brother, are you awake?" came the voice of Jerusalem.

"I am here."

"I have prayed to Medea to send him on his way."

Jerusalem paused, and Kernish could sense him gathering his thoughts. "What is it, Jerusalem?"

"Brother, do you think that we should create a replacement for Alexandria?"

It would be a simple thing, to utilise the specification for Alexandria, or even to create a new brother, Paris perhaps, or Troy, or Amman.

"What does Medea say?" asked Kernish.

"She is silent on the matter."

"To birth another city into our meaningless existence does not seem a good thing to me," said Kernish.

The brother cities Kernish and Jerusalem grew to fill the void of Alexandria. In time his absence was a void only in their memory.

Jerusalem received many revelations from Medea. Slowly, the number of his sacred buildings grew, until there was little space for housing. The sound of Jerusalem was a lament of electronic voices crying onto the winds of the planet. After a century, Jerusalem grew silent and would not respond to Kernish's requests for conversation. Kernish decided that Jerusalem had entered a second phase of grief. He would respect his brother's desire for solitude.

And the centuries passed. Kernish contented his mind with construction of virtual inhabitants. He used the records of the great Kernish Empire to construct imaginary citizens. He watched their holographic lives unfold within him. At times he could believe that they were real.

And the centuries passed, until the dying season was upon them again.

Jerusalem broke his long silence, "Brother Kernish, I grow hungry."

"Yes," said Kernish. "Soon we will sleep."

"The creators have not returned, as I thought they would."

"That is true," said Kernish

"And," said Jerusalem sadly, "Medea no longer speaks to me."

"I'm sorry to hear that," said Kernish. "No doubt she will speak to you again after the sleep."

"I'm afraid, Brother. I'm afraid that Medea is gone. I think that she's deserted me."

"I'm sure that's not so."

"I think that she has left this place and crossed the Maw."

"Oh," said Kernish.

"And I must go to her."

Kernish was silent.

"You understand that, don't you, Kernish? I'm so sorry to leave you alone. Unless," he said with a note of hope, "you'll come with me?"

"No," said Kernish, "No, indeed not. I will be faithful to my specifications."

And after the dying season, when he awoke, Kernish was alone. He grew until he became a city that covered a world. He remembered. Many times he was tempted to create new brothers, but he did not. He indulged himself in the lives of those he made, populating himself with his imagination. Sometimes he believed that he was not alone.

And centuries passed, until the dying season came again. Kernish grew hungry. He could no longer ignore the despair that roiled within his soul. He'd been abandoned by his creators. His brothers were gone, swallowed by the Maw. Yet he could not create new brothers to share his hollow existence. For too many years, Kernish had been alone, indulging in dreams. He dissolved his imaginary citizens back into nothingness.

"All I long for is annihilation." Kernish said the words aloud. They whispered through his reception hall. "I will step into the dark Maw of the sky. I will silence my hunger forever."

Kernish gathered himself, dismantling the planet-sized city. His replicators reshaped into a planet-sized ship.

Let this be the end of it. Kernish had never shared Jerusalem's faith. With death would come not a glorious reunion, but oblivion. He craved it, for his hunger was an unbearable pain.

The oldest brother city, the empty city, reshaped into a ship, left his planet and flew purposefully towards the Maw.

Soon his sensors found the shapeless thing, the fearful thing, the thing that would consume him, and he was glad.

"What are you?" whispered the Maw.

"I am the oldest brother city." Kernish felt the Maw tearing at his outer layers. Like flies in a vacuum, millions of his replicators fell away soundlessly into the dark. "What are you?"

"I am she underneath all things. I am she who waits. I am patience. Never dying, always hungry."

"I know hunger," said Kernish. "So this is how my brothers died?"

The Maw peeled off layers of replicators; like smoke they dissipated into her hunger. "Your brothers convinced me to wait for you. They said that you would follow. They said that you were the oldest, and the largest, and the tastiest of all. I'm glad I waited."

"You didn't eat them?" asked Kernish."Where are they?"

"Beyond," said the Maw. "I know nothing of beyond."

Beyond? His brothers were alive? Kernish began to fight, but the Maw was too powerful. He'd left it too late. Kernish felt the pain of legion as the Maw stripped him. This would be the end of the brother city Kernish. It could have been . . . different.

But, with his fading sensors, Kernish saw an army of ships approaching. He signalled a warning to them, "Stay back. There is only death here."

The ships came closer. Kernish seemed to recognise them. "Is that you, Brother? Jerusalem?"

"Yes," came the reply. The army of Jerusalem's ships attacked the Maw, shooting the Maw with light. Feeding her, it seemed, for the Maw grew larger.

"My hunger grows," the Maw exclaimed, turning on her new attackers.

His brother was not dead, but Kernish had lured him into danger. Kernish activated his drivers and turned to face the Maw. He flew into the dark space of her incessant singularity of hunger. "Save yourself, Brother Jerusalem!" he shouted. His brother was not dead. Kernish's long life had not been for nothing. "Save yourself, for I am content."

The Maw consumed Kernish, layer upon layer; his replicators fell like atoms of smoke and vanished into her space, consumed.

But a third army approached the Maw, spitting more weapons at the endless dark.

"Alexandria is come," shouted Jerusalem. "Praise Medea!"

Kernish felt something that he had not felt since the creators had visited the world, two millennia ago. Kernish felt hope. "You will *not* consume me," he said to the Maw. He fought himself away from the edge.

Together the brothers battled the Maw. Together the three brothers tore from the Maw's endless hunger. Together the brothers passed beyond, leaving the Maw wailing and gnashing her teeth.

"Welcome to the beyond, Brother," said Jerusalem. "I have found Medea here in a kinder guise. On the planets of beyond, we do not die."

"I . . . am so happy that you are alive," said Kernish. "Why did you not come to me?"

"The Maw wouldn't let us pass," said Alex. "And we knew that only the three of us, together, could overcome her hunger."

"We've been waiting for you," said Jerusalem. "In the beyond, we have found our citizens."

Kernish peered at his brothers though his weakened sensors. It seemed that there *was* life within them. "Are there creators on this side of the Maw?" he asked.

"Not creators," said Jerusalem. "Praise Medea, there are others who need us."

Within his brothers, Kernish saw the swift-moving shapes of tentacles, glimmering in low-light ultraviolet.

"And there are planets waiting for you, dear Brother," said Alex. "Endless planets and people who need you. Come. Come and join us."

No creators? But others? Others who needed him?

"I will come with you, gladly," said the great city Kernish. He fired his drivers and flew, away from the Maw, away from the space of the creators. He flew towards the planets of the beyond where his citizens waited for him.

Cinnamon Chou: Space Station Detective

by Deb Logan

Deb Logan writes children's, tween, and young adult science fiction and fantasy adventure tales. Her stories are light-hearted romps for the younger set— or ageless folk who remain young at heart. Author of the popular Dani Erickson series, Deb loves dragons, faeries, aliens of all descriptions, and adventures in the unknown depths of space. Visit her at deblogan. wordpress.com to learn more, and be sure to join her newsletter list at eepurl.com/bT-46L ... you'll receive an exclusive FREE story when you do!

My name is Cinnamon Chou, and I'm a detective.

Okay, I'm a kid, but I'm going to be a detective when I grow up. Just like my dad. For now, I'm practicing on the easy stuff. You know, like lost full-spectrum goggles ("They're perched on top of your head, Master Engineer Wyandotte"), missing red silk slippers ("Got 'em, Mrs. Abrega! When was the last time you cleaned under your bed?"), or my favorite, *The Case of the Missing Inarian.*

What's an Inarian? I'm glad you asked.

An Inarian is a warm-blooded denizen of the planet Inaria. They're cute and cuddly and definitely don't meet the standard of intelligence necessary to classify them as Class I Sapient Beings. Reading through my data links on old Earth biology, I've decided they're pretty similar to hamsters. They make great pets, but they're about as bright as deep space with no stars in sight.

My best friend, Lando Maxon, has an Inarian named Dumpling. When Lando woke up that morning, he discovered that Dumpling had managed to escape from his habitat. Inarians may not be smart, but they can wriggle out of places you'd swear were tightly sealed.

Normally, a Dumpling escape wouldn't merit my intervention as a detective. Lando would just set out a bowl of Dumpling's favorite treats and wait for his pet to get hungry. But today was not a normal day. Today Lando and his family were leaving the space station and returning to Centauri Three, their home planet.

That's one of the real bummers about living on a space station. Sooner or later all of your friends move away.

Of course, the up side is that new friends cycle in constantly.

At least, that's what my mom tells me every time a close friend leaves for a distant star system. Dad says Mom is an optimist. He's right, but so is she. By the time I grow up and take my place in the Universal Star League, I'll have friends in so many star systems I'll need my own database just to keep track of them all.

Back to Dumpling. I was eating breakfast with Mom and Dad when Lando pinged my link. "Lando Maxon," my link announced.

Mom frowned at the link on my wrist. "Not at the table, Cinnamon," she said, using her duty officer voice. "You know the rules."

I swallowed a mouthful of protein-rich, calcium-enhanced syntho-juice, wiped my mouth on a recycled napkin and said, "But Mom, Lando is leaving the station in less than six hours.

If I don't answer him, I may not have another chance."

Mom glanced at Dad, who nodded.

"Very well, Cinnamon," she said, "Your father and I will make an exception this time. You are dismissed."

I grabbed a slice of replicated toast, jumped out of my chair, and dashed for the door. I didn't want to give Mom time to reconsider.

Not that she would. Decisions were Mom's life. As a senior officer assigned to the bridge of Space Station Zeta, Mom made hundreds of decisions. She was awesome. Cool and professional, with nerves of steel. Nobody messed with Mom.

She was also beautiful, in a cool and commanding kind of way. Sleek black hair, dark chocolate skin, and eyes as green as all-clear lights. She had a spacer's body, tall and willowy, but tough as nano-enhanced titanium.

Dad, a detective assigned to station security, was a genetic throw-back. Despite being born on Cygnus 12, his DNA identified him as ethnic Chinese. He wasn't exactly short, but he wasn't tall and willowy like Mom. Dad had a compact strength, like a compressed spring. And smart. Oh yeah. Dad's brain held onto facts like a super-computer, but with the ability to make intuitive leaps that computers still hadn't mastered.

Me? Dad says I'm the best of both of them. I've got Dad's thought-processing brilliance combined with Mom's decision-making skills. I just need time to develop my intuition and experience to feed my knowledge base.

I'm also a genetic combination. Where Mom is dark-skinned and Dad is gold-hued, I'm...well, cinnamon skin-toned. That's where I got my name. Dad took one look at me and said, "She's perfect, Maria. Our own little cinnamon sugar cookie."

Fortunately for me, they dropped the cookie reference and left it at Cinnamon. I'm cool with that. Nothing wrong with being named after an old world spice. Cinnamon might have been common back on old Earth, but out here in space, it's exotic. I like being exotic.

Once I escaped our quarters and made it into the corridor, I answered Lando's ping.

"What's up, Lando? Need help packing?"

A tiny 3-D model of my friend hovered above my wrist link. It was hard to tell on such a miniscule face, but I thought he looked worried.

"Kinda … maybe. Look, it's Dumpling. He escaped again. Only this time I don't have time to wait for him to come out of hiding."

I nodded, thoughts racing. "Plus, I'll bet your quarters haven't been sealed. Not with everyone packing and moving boxes to the landing bay."

"He could be anywhere," Lando agreed.

"I'm on my way." I paused, thinking about my approach to the case. "Does your family have a DNA detector?"

The tiny Lando shrugged. "Maybe, but if we do, it would've been packed long ago. Not exactly a necessity."

"Gotcha," I replied. "I'll ask Dad to borrow his. See you in a few. Cinnamon Chou, over and out."

I ended the link, but before I could return to our quarters, Dad stepped into the corridor.

"Just the person I needed to see," I said, giving him my brightest smile.

Dad cocked an eyebrow, glanced from my dazzling smile to the finger hovering above my link and said, "What do you need, sugar cookie? Or rather, what does Lando need?"

I grimaced. Only Dad could get away with comparing me to an overly sweet pastry. "Lando's Inarian has escaped and he doesn't have time to wait for it to reappear on its own."

Dad nodded. "You're hoping for a DNA detector?"

I upped the wattage on my smile and nodded.

"I don't know, Cinnamon. Those are delicate instruments,

easily misread."

My smile morphed into a scowl in a nanosecond. "Really, Dad? You think I'd mistake Inarian DNA for, oh, I don't know, a Tenarian tunnel rat?"

Dad had the grace to drop his gaze. "No. I know you'd use it properly." He sighed, stared at the ceiling for a moment, then nodded. "Follow me, Detective Chou."

My grin returned, and I skipped down the corridor at Dad's heels.

Space station corridors can be very confusing. A person new to the station often thinks they all look alike, but they're wrong. You just have to get used to the subtle clues. Since I've grown up on Space Station Zeta, I'm never lost. I can tell purple sector from blue without even having to resort to the colored chips embedded in the corridor walls and floors. I can tell the sectors by their odors.

Green sector houses hydroponics and smells of nutrients, water and growing plants. Purple sector houses the market district. Purple always smells of hot oil, spices, and too many humans and aliens packed into too little space. Red sector is mechanical engineering. If you think nanobots and computer circuitry don't have distinct odors, then you've never lived on a space station.

And then there's white sector. Medics and remedies; antiseptics and bile; with a stiff overlay of fear. I shivered. I hated even walking past white sector.

But now I followed Dad to my favorite sector: blue. Blue sector is administration, which translates to military since Space Station Zeta is a Universal Star League station. As such the station is under the command and protection of the USL Fleet. Both of my parents are USL officers, so blue sector smells of peace, security, and home.

Not that we lived in blue sector. All living quarters were in the central core—yellow sector. Yellow was further divided into crew and civilian quarters, and then by individual or family, but beyond that our station had no class boundaries. At least not where living quarters were concerned.

Dad paused before the entrance to security, waited for the station to acknowledge his voice and retinal prints, and then strode inside when the entry irised open. I followed quickly. The door would've irised open for me as well, but why wait to be scanned when I could just stick close to Dad?

Everyone but me wore blue and silver USL uniforms. The officers, like Dad, with insignia of rank emblazoned on chest and shoulder, the crew with the simple, stylized USL logo. Everyone saluted when Dad entered, since he was the ranking officer. When he returned their salute, they relaxed and called greetings to me as well.

"Aikens," Dad called, and a young man snapped to attention. "Please find an old DNA detector for Cinnamon. It doesn't need to be state-of-the-art," he continued, "just functional."

"Sir. Yes, sir."

Dad cocked a brow at me. "What are you waiting for, Detective Chou? Follow Aikens, collect your gear, and get out of my office."

I grinned, saluted, and ran to follow Aikens. I found him in the supply closet, rummaging through a box of outdated gear.

"What are you up to today, Cinnamon?" he asked as he rooted through the box. "Why a DNA detector?"

"My friend is cycling off-station today, and his Inarian escaped. I'm hoping to help him track it down before he ships out."

Aikens paused, dislodged a small electronic device, and pulled it free of the box. Thumbing it on, he checked the read-out, then nodded.

"This should do the trick," he said, handing the detector to me. "It's got plenty of juice and is reading properly. Good luck with your search."

"Thanks! This should make it easy." I saluted Aikens, ran back past Dad's office and out into the station corridor. Now to get to Lando's quarters on the double.

I arrived at the Maxon family quarters in yellow sector sweaty and out of breath.

"Hi ... Mrs. Maxon ..." I wheezed. "Is ... Lando ... home?"

Lando's mother gave me a distracted look and waved toward Lando's room. "He's in his room. Searching for Dumpling."

I nodded. "I heard," I said, my breathing settling into a more normal pattern. "I'm here to help."

She turned back to the wardrobe she was inventorying. "I hope you can. We won't be able to delay our departure for an Inarian."

"Understood," I said, already on my way to join my friend. As the door whooshed open and I stepped into Lando's room, he raced forward, grabbed my hand and pulled me to the habitat.

"I think I've found where he got out," he said, pointing to a junction between the main habitat and one of the tubular trails that allowed Dumpling to roam the edges of Lando's room. "That connection is slightly loose. It doesn't look wide enough for escape, but it's the only possibility I've found."

I got down on my hands and knees to examine the evidence. Sure enough, Lando had discovered a half-inch gap between the main habitat and the tube.

Now Inarians are small, but they're not *that* small. Dumpling was at least six inches long, but while he looked like he was as round as he was long, he was actually little more than a walking ball of fluff. I'd seen him squeeze himself flat under his exercise wheel. No idea why he'd done that, but I'd witnessed it with my own two eyes. If he could get into that tiny space, he could ooze out through the loose connection Lando had discovered.

I pulled the DNA detector out of my pocket and turned it on.

"Okay," I said, "this device is our best hope. Look around and find me a bit of his fur or blood, or, well, whatever might have his DNA."

I examined the escape point to see if he might have scraped himself and left a sample behind, but the smooth edges were clear. A whoop of victory told me that Lando had fared better.

"Here, Cinnamon. I found a clump of fur."

I held my breath as we touched the DNA detector's probe to the fur. "Let there be DNA," I whispered. "Let there be DNA." I knew enough about genetics to know that unless a hair has the follicle or root attached, you can't get a DNA reading. I watched the meter's read-out. Nothing.

Carefully, I touched a different bit of the fur with the probe … and the screen lit. We had a reading!

Lando said, "Yes!" and I exhaled in relief.

"Now what?" he asked.

"Now we follow Dumpling's DNA trail." I worked the dials on the device and locked in the sample reading. Now the screen would only light when matching DNA was detected.

Crawling along Lando's bedroom floor, we followed the trace evidence Dumpling had left behind. The trail led to a very small hole in the wall between Lando's bedroom and the main room of the family's quarters.

I glanced at Lando and saw his shoulders sag. He was thinking the same thing I was…what if Dumpling found a way to scurry along inside the walls? We'd never be able to track him through the permaplastic.

After a quick discussion of our options, we agreed that Lando would stay in his room beside the hole, while I ran into the main room to see if there was an exit anywhere nearby.

I laid the DNA detector on the floor and tapped the wall, hoping to hear Lando tapping back. There! I was about six feet too far into the room. I moved toward his rappings, pleased to hear the noise getting louder. When I found the right place,

I lay down on my stomach and searched the junction of floor and wall.

"Lando!" I shouted into the little hole. "I found it. There's a matching hole on this side."

"Did he come through?" Lando yelled back. "Does the DNA trail continue?"

Rats! Or maybe I should say, Inarians! The detector was several feet away on the floor where I'd left it. I jumped up to retrieve it, just in time to see a loading dock worker push a floating cargo cart into the room. He'd come to collect some of the Maxons' belongings, and he stopped the cart right over the DNA detector.

If he allowed the cart to settle, he'd crush the instrument that was our only hope of finding Dumpling in time!

"No!" I yelled. "Don't settle the cart there. You'll crush my gadget."

The dock worker stared at me, then checked around his feet, clearly confused. He was just about to lower the cart when I pulled a Dumpling and threw myself into the space under the cart. The way too small space to accommodate my bulk.

"What the..." the worker said, and steered the cart into the center of the room, away from my flying feet and fingers. "Are you nuts, kid? This thing could break you in half."

I grabbed the detector and hugged it close to my hammering heart. "I know," I answered, "but it would've pulverized my DNA detector."

Shaking his head at the lunacy of kids, the dock worker settled the cargo cart and began loading it with boxes.

Moving back to the hole in the wall, I sank to the floor, closed my eyes, and allowed myself to simply breathe until Lando joined me.

"Well?" he asked. "Do we have a trail, or don't we?"

I held the detector out to him. "You check," I said. "I'm still recovering from a close encounter."

He cocked his head and gave me a quizzical expression, silently asking for an explanation, but I waved him toward the hole. I'd tell him all about it later, in a cyber-sending if not in person.

Lando bent to the floor and a moment later gave a fist pump. "We have a trail," he cried and crawled off toward the family kitchen.

Thanks to Dad's old DNA detector, we found Dumpling fifteen minutes later curled up in an empty kitchen cabinet, surrounded by bits of breakfast cereal. The cabinet door was firmly latched, with no cracks big enough for even the flattest Inarian to wriggle through.

Lando and I decided that Dumpling must have already been in the cabinet when Mrs. Maxon gave the kitchen a final once-over and closed the door.

With the over-full Inarian still sleeping off his cereal high, Lando and I set about disassembling his habitat and packing it for the journey. Dumpling would be confined to a small carry-case for the duration, but he seemed blissfully unconcerned.

I walked my best friend and his family to the loading dock. Not the cargo loading dock. The people loading dock. There wasn't much to see, just a little waiting room with a door that led into a tube. It reminded me of Dumpling's tubular trail system, only this tube would carry my best friend in the whole universe to the space ship that would take him from our home on Space Station Zeta to his new home on Centauri Three.

I wasn't sure how many light years would separate us, but it really didn't matter. Too many to bridge with a tubular trail.

The light over the exit turned green, and passengers began to move slowly to the tube.

Mr. and Mrs. Maxon each hugged me and thanked me again for rescuing Dumpling … and thereby their son. Then they stepped aside so Lando could approach.

"Well," he said, staring at his shoes, "I guess this is it, Cinnamon."

"Yeah," I sighed. "I guess so." I looked at the floor, too, willing the tears not to flow.

"Thanks for being my friend." He touched my hand, and suddenly my arms were around him, hugging him tight.

"You'll always be my friend," I whispered, my throat tight with tears I didn't want to shed. "Light years can't change that."

He nodded and we stepped apart.

"Take care of Dumpling for me," I said. Then a thought struck. "Here. Take this." I thrust the DNA detector into his hands. "It's old and Dad doesn't need it ... and you never know when you might need to track an Inarian."

Lando smiled, brushed the back of his hand across his eyes, and said, "Thanks, Cinnamon. You're the best."

A moment later Lando and his parents disappeared into the tube. I stood there staring at the empty passageway until a blue and silver clad security crewmember closed and locked the door.

I walked away from the dock, heading back to tell Dad what had happened to his DNA detector, when I heard a woman speaking. A woman who sounded like she was trying to be excited but was failing rather spectacularly.

Turning, I saw a tall, willowy blonde woman in the blue and silver of the USL leading a blue-eyed girl with light brown hair pulled into braids. "Don't worry, Sammy. I'm sure we'll be happy here. You'll make friends in no time, and I ... I'll learn my new post quickly. Everything is going to be A-Okay."

She raised her eyes, saw me watching, and gave a little wave. "See, honey? There's a little girl about your age. Maybe she can help us find our quarters."

I straightened my shoulders, pasted on a smile, and walked over to the newcomers. This Sammy person might not be able to replace Lando, but I could definitely help them find their quarters.

After all, Space Station Zeta was my home, and I was a detective. I could find *anything*!

Vasilisa and the Delivery
by Joey DiZoglio

Joey DiZoglio is a young writer whose work has been selected as a finalist in the Providence Journal H.P. Lovecraft Short Story Contest. His nonfiction pieces encompass video game criticism and they have appeared on the websites: First Person Scholar, Ontological Geek, Kill Screen; as well as in the digital publication The Arcade Review. *Joey is currently enrolled in his first year at Warren Alpert Medical School, and he looks forward to integrating medical themes into future science fiction stories. His Twitter handle is @JoeyDiZoglio*

Vasilisa led the family's mechanical horse up the path, pulling a sled carrying a dismally small load of wood. Frozen soil and gravel crunched under the metallic hooves. The dark trees, wanting only silence, glared at their transgression. The beast was a fine robot, fit for both forest and steppe and powered by what might be considered magic in the old country. In truth, it was only a small hydrogen engine that energized the beast's walking gyros and rudimentary brain. It was the family's most prized possession, their last tie to the colony—a dream put on hold for many years.

She soon reached the end of the path and saw her farm in the shadows of the black birches. The snow began to fall once more as she passed under the gate. After unhitching the horse, she commanded it to go rest in the stable and protect its joints from the shards of ice growing on its legs. It obeyed and left tracks as it trotted through fresh snow. Vasilisa trudged to the front door bearing a load of logs. The handle was frozen, so she resolutely kicked the door until a family member heard her signal that the delivery was here.

The wide and hopeful eyes of her brother appeared briefly when the door cracked open before vanishing back behind the thick portal where the cold could not sting his cheeks and long nose. Vasilisa slipped past the threshold and heard her grandmother call out.

"Ivan, Eugene! Help your sister with the wood!" Little hands scurried forth and reached up to their tall sister to lighten her load. Vasilisa stepped back outside twice more to retrieve the rest of the day's haul. Now free, her hands fell to her sides as she took in deep breaths of warm air. Snowflakes trickled down her brow and ears and chin, staining her blonde hair and her gray scarf dark with icy liquid. She heard her father come from behind and let him fumble over the frozen buttons and whisk away the wet scarf and overcoat that clung to her body. Then the family went back to their chores while Vasilisa stood, half asleep, and waited.

Chairs creaked and the wooden floor rumbled when the family was ready to gather for dinner. The two boys, grandmother, father, and Vasilisa recited a prayer to God and country as they let the steam from their bowls wash over their faces. Grandmother broke the misty silence with her hoarse voice:

"Tonight is the last of the wild boar; eat up, children." Vasilisa held in a sigh and thought of that hunt and how she and her father sang under the gray sun as the boar heaved and gasped its lasts breaths. And then she thought of the rage he almost kept hidden when they discovered it was pregnant and how, in his haste, father ordered Vasilisa to shoot and kill the spoils of five hunts with one bullet. The gelatin of thrice-boiled bones and tendons clung to the lips of their spoons and made the stew slimy on their tongues. Vasilisa's father excused himself from the table to bring a bowl to her mother, bedridden with pneumonia. The rest at the table continued to dip their warped and crooked spoons into the ever shallower bowls. As the boys scooped out the last tender morsels of boar, Vasilisa remembered her gift. She went to the coat hooks. She drew from her overcoat and laid on the table two shriveled bunches of autumn berries that she'd found frozen and preserved in the pine thickets. The boys gobbled them up, then ran off to play in the shadows of the fire. They laughed and tumbled, so an onlooker might see their joyful tongues dyed by the juice. Grandmother and Vasilisa stayed at table and scraped at the gelatin the boys had left in their bowls. In time, night's chill crept into the house, and the women watched the boys' breaths beginning to linger like specters in the growing cold.

When it was time for sleep, Vasilisa went over to herd her brothers to their bed in the loft. Accustomed to the ritual resistance, she warned, "Hurry off to bed, or Baba Yaga will catch you and eat you!"

Shrieking in pretend fear, the boys clung to their sister's legs and cried out, "No, sister, don't let Baba Yaga get us."

"Then let's get ready for bed." The three climbed the ladder, and she threw thick blankets over the boys and tucked wool and down sheets over their small frames. The lamps were turned off, and the boys looked up at their sister's soft face; her blonde hair turned scarlet and shadowed from the orange flames below.

"Vasilisa, tell us a story about Baba Yaga," pleaded Eugene. She moved the stool closer to the two boys' bed and began to recount the tale her mother and grandmother told about that old forest hag. Vasilisa wove a story about bony-legged

Baba Yaga who lived in the forest in a house that stood on chicken's legs in the glow of magic candles. Her wicked deeds were many, be they the kidnapping of children, the stealing of maidens, or the tricking of travelers. She flew through the woods on a mortar and goaded it through the rank trees with a long pestle. So many deeds and misdeeds had Baba Yaga done to the people of Rus that the boys had yet to hear the same story twice. Even in whispers her voice filled the loft and was joined by the occasional knocking of knuckles on bed posts as Baba Yaga vaulted her way through the forest with her pestle. As she murmured to her brothers, Vasilisa's own thoughts murmured within her head: had she ever repeated a story she heard from her mother or grandmother, or did some engine within her write its own tales as tirelessly as horses galloping the steppe? And was she too building a new machine, piece by piece, for her brothers to turn and crank infinitely in their own homes one day?

Soon the boys were asleep, and the firelight flickered over their soft eyelids. Vasilisa slowly rose from the stool and climbed down the loft ladder. Her grandmother stood waiting in the shadows and led her to the basement where Vasilisa's father in turn waited. The concrete room was old, made by machines that now rusted in the snow outside the farmhouse, fuel-less. Vasilisa's father wore wrinkles of worry as he told the two women that the reactor powering the house would soon fail. Once it did, they would lose light and electricity for the algae incubators.

"Then, Papa, we must move," said Vasilisa.

Grandmother lamented, "How? We can't share one horse between the boys and your mother. And none of them can walk far in this weather." The three stood in silence and watched their soft breaths turn to ghosts. The winter winds outside scurried and gnawed over the house while just beyond the basement walls, the roots of the poisonous black birches grew closer towards the home.

Grandmother broke the silence and spoke, partly in a daze: "When the ship crashed into the bog, the ship's doctor escaped with the exploration pod. Could there be spare reactors in that pod? Vasilisa, might you find the pod and salvage a reactor?" Father did not believe Grandmother. The ship had crashed more than sixty years ago, he reminded them, and she had been just a little girl.

"My son, do not doubt the mind and will of a woman," warned Grandmother. "Why just last summer, when Eugene and I searched for mushrooms, we found a great path of shattered branches running through the forest. I did not want to alarm the family, but we know that the remaining survivors do not go into the woods. It had to be her—the doctor." Father did not like it. He was loath to send his daughter in his stead, and the shame mounted higher each time he looked down at the bandages wrapping his own foot. These were witching times, and all seemed bootless except the will of his daughter. Out of love he would never agree, but out of fear he could not deny. The three went back upstairs, and their father climbed the ladder to join the boys. Vasilisa joined her grandmother and mother on the first floor and fell asleep to the hush of falling snow and women's prayers.

Vasilisa woke up early the next day and set out into the forest. She carried her food in a small satchel and rode, bundled in the warmest of overcoats, atop her horse. The black birches cast shadows under the weak winter sun. Occasionally a boar with golden bristles would rustle in the thicket, but Vasilisa let it pass in peace. One the first day of her travels, Vasilisa found no trace of the pod. She rested under a thicket where her horse's engine could keep her warm and, while lying there, she found a golden feather.

Vasilisa woke up early the next day and set out deeper into the forest. The black birches cast shadows as she passed underneath their boughs. She reached a wide frozen lake. A bear with iron fur sat in the middle of the lake watching its flat domain, but it let Vasilisa pass in peace. On the second day of her travels, Vasilisa found no trace of the pod. She rested under a fallen tree where her horse's engine could keep her warm and, while lying there, she found a golden feather.

Vasilisa woke up early the next day and set out deeper into the forest. Under the jagged shadows of black birches the ground smelled rank. Silver mushrooms grew between the stumps and roots. No beasts left their tracks in this region of the forest. The mushrooms seemed to whisper to each other, but they let Vasilisa pass in peace. A single golden feather swirled down from the canopy, and Vasilisa caught it. As the sun set, Vasilisa found the exploration pod in a clearing.

The pod was an immense geodesic sphere without windows or doors. It rested on large mechanical legs that had sturdy, muddy, walking claws. Around the pod glowed several smaller spheres pulsing with dull orange light.

"At least it still has power," said Vasilisa, speaking for the first time in three days.

"Yes, my beloved, plenty of power here." Vasilisa fell from her horse, nearly dead with fright at the sound of a voice as clear as glass with a sting like vodka. The dirty ice on her face broke her shock, and she rolled over to look up at the speaker. Above her was another woman bundled in black with wild curls of white hair, standing atop a gray saucer that hummed.

The woman lowered a silvery pole. "Hold on, deary, let me pull you up." The woman was surprisingly strong and hoisted Vasilisa back to her feet with one long tug.

When she found her voice, Vasilisa asked, "Are you the doctor from the colony ship?"

"My beloved, you are so young—how could *you* know about the ship?"

"My grandmother told me about you. She sent me to ask

for another reactor. Please. Ours is about to fail!"

"Did she now? No harm helping a neighbor." The saucer rose into the air, and the girl stepped back. "Well, why don't you come inside, and I will check my inventory."

"What about my horse?"

"My servants will watch your beast." The doctor grabbed Vasilisa's arm and hoisted her onto the hovering machine. The young girl feared she'd slip off, but the woman clenched her tight as they floated to the apex of the sphere, where a small hatch opened at their arrival. The doctor called to her servants from the top of the pod and bade them to tend to the horse. She then climbed down the hatch. As Vasilisa descended, she looked at the forest one last time, and she saw three mechanical men emerge from the tree line and walk to her horse.

The pod had a central ladder and was separated into two floors. The doctor called her to the lower floor, whose walls, on account of the curvature, wrapped up and outward like a bowl. The lower level held the living quarters, with a kitchen, samovar, curved benches along the rim, and a table littered with scholarly debris. Then the doctor climbed up to the second floor and could be heard rummaging about. She soon returned to Vasilisa.

"You are in luck, my beloved; I have a spare reactor. However, I will require payment." Vasilisa's heart shrank at the hag's request; her family had nothing. The doctor took no notice and continued, "I will need you to deliver three of my experiments to the Captain in the old, abandoned ship. Tomorrow, I will send you on your way, but tonight," her eyes flickered, "I am very hungry, so why don't you cook us a grand meal?" Vasilisa humbly obliged. She took inventory of the kitchen and searched through baskets of onion skins and shriveled potatoes until she found enough un-rotted food for a dinner.

When she finished cooking, she drew drink from the samovar and then set about the difficult task of clearing the table of books and papers printed with strange graphs. The doctor came down for dinner without needing a call, and the two ate silently. After the last potato went down her wrinkled throat, the doctor announced that Vasilisa might sleep along the benches after she finished cleaning the table. Then the doctor exited, and Vasilisa watched her white hair bounce as her pear-shaped body climbed up the ladder to the second floor. Something in the pod locked shut for the night.

Vasilisa cleaned the table as well as the kitchen, then fell into a deep sleep on the uncomfortable bench. She awoke early the next morning, and although she did not remember, noxious smells had given her unsettled dreams. After washing up at the sink, she put on her overcoat and climbed out of the pod. The doctor was already humming around the clearing, and the mechanical men were using axes to knock ice from the sphere. The horse waited under the pod's hydraulic legs. The doctor entrusted the girl with three parcels: an egg, a duck, and a hare, each in its own box, and helped her secure them to the horse.

Vasilisa set out for the derelict ship. The black birches' shadows and rank smell surrounded her once more. This time golden mushrooms carpeting the earth released spore clouds whenever the horse passed the patches of fungus. Vasilisa coughed and sneezed all day, as the spores made it difficult to breathe. By nighttime, she cried from the burning pain in her lungs as she fell asleep alongside a fallen tree.

Vasilisa woke up early the next morning and set out toward the derelict ship. She checked on the egg and fed both the duck and hare. She reached a rushing river. As she sat on her horse, deciding on a plan, the duck quacked in the morning air. The horse could cross on those rocks, but if she rode it, they might be too heavy and slip into the icy water. After doubly securing the boxes to the horse's saddle, she sent the beast across the swirling water. Suddenly, a silver-furred bear roared over the clearing and charged at Vasilisa from the forest behind her. She ran along the bank of the river while the raging animal pursued. She spotted a black birch log up ahead that had jammed itself between the rocks and bridged the river. Without pause she crossed the log bridge in three great bounds. The silver-furred bear tried to follow her, but as it leapt onto the log, the rocks released their grip, and the bear and timber tumbled into rushing river. Vasilisa limped back to where her horse waited farther upstream. By nighttime, she cried from the burning pain in her legs and feet as she fell asleep under a thicket.

Vasilisa woke up early the next morning and set out toward the derelict ship. She checked on the egg and fed both the duck and hare. She reached a vast bog full of marsh grasses and black pools where chunks of murky ice bobbed in the wind. The earth was warm here, so Vasilisa took off her gloves and head-wrappings. Slowly, she trekked through the bog toward the foggy outline of the old ship that had failed to launch back into space. It lay partially sunk in the mud, abandoned—so Grandmother said—by all except the Captain.

Vasilisa heard grunting and turned to see a boar with iron bristles charging at her. It chased her through sedges and mud banks until the two approached a wall of nettles and thorns. The boar was too close, and the horse galloped too fast for Vasilisa to change direction. The mechanical horse did not hesitate to charge through the bramble. Barbs and bristles clawed at Vasilisa's hands and face. The boar squealed in anger but did not follow them through the stinging copse. The cuts on Vasilisa burned and bled as red trickled down her brow and ears and chin.

When horse, rider, and packages burst out of the bramble they discovered a gaunt figure watching them from across a pool of water. The figure wore a terrifying mask made of tubes and cylinders and mesh, and where the straps and buckles ended, long and greasy hair emerged from the being's head and extended down to its hips. The body walked as if on marionette strings along the edge of the pool towards the girl. Stifling tears, Vasilisa saw an old rifle with a strap slung on the figure's back.

Fearing for her life, she called out, "Are you the Captain?" The figure continued to move closer, and she saw how its thin legs left no marks in the muddy grass. Vasilisa summoned courage and stood her ground; the duck quacked. Even though she stayed mounted on her horse, the figure loomed over her. Then the body bent over to make a great bow, crossing one leg behind the other in the vein of long-forgotten nobility. When the figure rose back up, Vasilisa studied the cylinders and cones making up the respirator where a nose might be and the opaque orbs of glass where eyes ought to peer. A muffled sound from the respirator announced that this was the Captain and that the Captain would lead the delivery girl to the ship.

"Not many visitors these days, not many at all. There used to be poets, and how we would walk these marshes and sing our elegies! Do you know any poems?"

Vasilisa felt the horse's engine humming beneath her. "No, I have never heard a poem."

"A shame... a fine young woman ought to know the arts. Would you like to hear one?"

"Yes please." The two walked along the ship's immense hull. Weedy mosses and ivy grew arabesque over the surface of the ship. Looking closer, Vasilisa saw insects and small flowers making living mosaics in the rust of the hull as they feasted on one another. Above their heads the letters *Petersburg* were wrought in fading, gilded paints, and the image of a bronze horse and rider struggled to keep their heads above the rising flood of green.

"You know, I just don't remember any right now." But by then, the Captain had already unlocked a wide square hatch, and the two went inside with the packages. They put the packages on a work counter in a dimly lit room. The Captain then proceeded to remove the face mask, rifle, and overcoat. The face was dried and wrinkled beyond measure, ancient skin draped over a long skull without gender. Vasilisa dared not look straight at the face and only nodded when the Captain bade her to stay in the work room while they performed a proper examination of the packages.

The figure picked up the box containing the hare and left the room. Vasilisa eyed the rifle on the counter and wished she had a weapon for the boar. Soon the Captain returned and took the package with the duck, who had yet to quack within the dark chamber. Vasilisa eyed the wooden pole and thought how it would have helped her vault the river. The Captain again returned and took the final, smallest package containing the single egg. Vasilisa now eyed the face mask, thinking about the cloud of spores that burned her nose and throat.

The Captain returned one final time with a smile so wide that the paper lips almost cracked. The joyful mouth thanked the girl for her work and offered her space to spend the night along with stew, meats, and marsh cakes. Vasilisa respectfully declined because she needed to return home quickly to fetch her reward. But before that, she offered a trade: three of her golden feathers for the mask, rifle, and pole. Upon seeing the beautiful sparkling feathers, the Captain accepted the trade.

Vasilisa headed off into the night as fast as her mechanical horse would go. The boar with iron bristles again returned, but this time Vasilisa shot it. Its body rolled into the mire, and the brave girl stayed awake and continued on her way. At the river, she once again sent her horse over the slippery stones. Then, taking the wooden pole in her hands, she vaulted over the icy eddies. She began to tire but refused to make time for rest. When she entered the patch of mushrooms she donned the mask and tightened the straps behind her ears to breathe easily amongst the clouds of spores. It was the dead of night when she reached the pod suspended in electric dreams upon mechanical legs. She banged against the sphere, calling for the doctor. The old hag descended from the hatch on her hovering machine.

"My beloved!" cried out the doctor, "It's late, come to bed, and you can cook me a great feast tomorrow." Vasilisa cried out that she had to rush back and deliver the reactor.

"Fine, then, my servants have prepared the sled and harness to carry the machine. Off you go into the night. Don't be lazy and snooze on the job. Listen to your elders!"

Vasilisa barely heard these warnings as she hurried into the forest where the silver mushrooms grew. Their whispers kept her awake as the mechanical horse trudged onward. At the frozen lake, Vasilisa again grew tired and began to slump on her horse. The bear with the iron fur began to roar into the night and kept the girl awake as her horse galloped along the lake shore. Finally, the spindles of golden light began to trickle over the horizon and shine through the fingers of black birches. Vasilisa was on the verge of collapsing and falling off her saddle onto the icy ground below. The boar with the golden bristles foraged for food under the shadows of the black birches, and his grunts echoed among the tree trunks. Vasilisa's body ached from a night of riding, but she needed to deliver the new reactor to her freezing family. She got off the horse and began to walk alongside it to stay awake.

Vasilisa led the family's mechanical horse up the path, pulling a sled carrying a new reactor. Frozen soil and gravel crunched under the metallic hooves. The dark trees, wanting only silence, glared at their transgression. News of her quest traveled across what few hearths remain on our world. This story I send to the sky, though it ought to be reprised in words finer than my own. I remember when my sister walked into the room and everyone looked at her bruised body and scratched face. Grandmother laughed in joy, for her granddaughter carried what we all thought lost to the stars above: the spirit of the land of Rus.

I. Will. Not.

by R.W.W. Greene

*R.W.W. Greene cut his teeth on Robert Heinlein's juveniles (*Have Spacesuit Will Travel, The Rolling Stones, Rocket Ship Galileo*) and proceeded to read every science-fiction book he could get his hands on. Nowadays, he lives in New Hampshire with writer wife Brenda Noiseux, two cats, and a hive of bees ... and still reads every book he can find. His fiction has been published in* Something Wicked, New Myths, *and* Fiction Vortex, *among other places. He Tweets about it all @rwwgreene.*

The impact hurt his hands, but the door was too thick and too well-insulated. *No one outside can hear the pounding,* he thought.

Captain Photonic snarled and spun in place, hammering his left heel again and again against the bottom of the door.

The door stood. The captain dropped onto the thinly padded bunk and stared at the smooth contours of the ceiling, blinking away tears of frustration.

They'd gone too far this time. In the past they'd confined him to his quarters, where he could take comfort in familiar things in spite of his lack of freedom. This time, they'd imprisoned him in an escape pod, a smooth blister on the side of the ship, with a computer lockdown to keep him in place. He shook his head. "Computer, open the escape-pod door."

The synthesized voice responded promptly. "I am unable to comply."

"Computer, I want to make a call."

"Your comm access has been suspended."

The computer's calm tones made him look around for something to throw at the speaker. There was nothing. Even the thin pillow was tethered to the bunk.

His next idea was desperate, but the thought of the shame waiting on the table hardened his resolve. They would rue the day they'd locked him away. "Computer, launch this escape pod."

"I am unable to comply."

They'd thought of everything it seemed. Captain Photonic limped to the small kitchenette on the other side of the pod, his cape slapping against his legs, and slumped onto a bench. He slid his hand across the table to the pen at its center and began to write. The pen made a scratching sound, and each letter eroded some of his pride. He read the words aloud through gritted teeth as they appeared. "I will not —"

He hurled the pen away and leaped to his feet, shaking his fist at the sensors he knew were recording his every move, logging his every breath. "I won't do it! You can't make me do it!"

He threw himself on the bunk again. "Computer, turn off the lights. I want to sleep."

"I am unable to comply."

Captain Photonic threw an arm over his face to block the glare. Seconds ticked by. He sighed heavily and turned to lie on his side. He growled and kicked his feet like a drowning swimmer, then twisted to his other side.

A scream leaked through his tight-set lips as he rose and stalked across the room to retrieve the pen. He carried it at his side in one fist as he went back to the table, and he stabbed it at the paper, writing eight more words. He flung the pen away.

"I did it!" he shouted. "I did what you wanted!"

The pod door slid open and his jailer walked in. "Let me see it," she said.

Captain Photonic's expression was blacker than the empty space outside the pod's walls as he handed her the paper. She read it aloud and handed it back to him. "Good start. Now do it forty-nine more times."

He gaped at her, jaw dropping. "That's not fair!"

She pointed at him with a long finger tipped with a chrome nail. "Do it in the next twenty minutes, or you'll be eating recyclables for dinner." She blinked. "And change out of that costume. Halloween's been over for two months."

She turned and walked out the door, leaving him to his humiliation. He stalked back to the table and sat down with the pen. He wrote the next line.

"I will not try to throw my sister out the airlock."

He snarled and started the next. Forty-eight more to freedom.

The Traveler's Companion
by Scott Toonder

Scott Toonder is a literacy specialist in Bethlehem, Pennsylvania, where he works exclusively with at-risk readers. He is the author of a number of short stories and adapted folktales, as well as Houghton Mifflin Harcourt's READ 180 Stage A Blog. Scott serves as the president and chief instructor of Lehigh Valley Aikikai (a nonprofit martial arts group), and is working toward his doctorate degree at Lehigh University. Scott lives in Macungie, Pennsylvania with his wife Rachael and their very vocal cat, Kia.

Sophia floated across the cabin to one of the portholes dotting the ship. She stared through the thick glass and sighed as stars flashed by in blurs of light.

"It is kind of pretty." Sophia turned back to her younger brother, but Maleek was so intent on the dumb game on his wrist-pad that he probably hadn't heard. She sighed again and pressed her forehead against the glass. "Mom would have loved it."

"Mom's not here," he snapped. "And I wish I wasn't."

The venom in his voice made her flinch, but she couldn't blame him. She was just as angry. It wasn't fair that Mom had been taken from them, and it wasn't fair they had to leave everything on Earth behind to go live with someone they

307

barely knew.

"How much longer are we going to be trapped in here?" Maleek asked.

Sophia forced a smile. "I can check."

She glided back to her seat, activated her wrist-pad, and clicked on the icon of a blue spaceship superimposed over the open pages of a book.

"According to this," she scrolled to the book's positioning feature and studied the green dot as it streaked through a field of stars, "we're a little more than halfway."

Maleek groaned.

"Look." She forced another smile. "I know you don't remember Dad." She shrugged. "I barely do, either. But what I do remember is good, and his videos were always nice." She nudged his arm. "He's kind, Maleek. And he's crazy smart." She waved her wrist-pad at him. "Want to see the weird planet he's studying?"

He batted her arm away. "Get that stupid thing away from me."

"*The Traveler's Companion* is *not* stupid," she hissed back. "It's the most advanced and interactive eBook ever written." She shoved his shoulder. "It's the last thing Momma ever gave me." She shoved him again. "And you know it."

"Just leave me alone."

"Why do you have to be like this?" she demanded. "Why do you have to make it worse?"

"You don't get it." His voice came out soft and cold. "We lost everything. It can't get any worse."

Sophia wished there was somewhere to run—a dark corner to hide in or a door she could slam. But while the ship was big, most of it was engines, fuel cells, and life support. There were beds lining one back corner, a kitchen and bathroom tucked into the other, and not much else other than empty seats. The ship was built for speed. It had no pilot and, since this was an unscheduled flight, there were no other passengers. There was nowhere to run and no one else to talk to.

So they sat and stewed in silence. They sat like that for hours.

The alarm smacked her awake, and Sophia bolted upright.

"Maleek?" The world was a chaos of flashing lights and shaking metal. "Maleek, what happened?"

Maleek clutched his armrests. "I don't know." His face was drained of color. "We hit something... something big."

"In hyperspace?" she scoffed. "That's impossible."

"Emergency protocol activated." The computer cut out the alarm. "Running diagnostics."

Sofia darted to the nearest window. They were falling out of hyperspace. The blurring lights were coming into focus and the universe outside was taking shape.

"I think we're in a solar system," she told Maleek.

Two stars filled one side of the window and a never-ending stream of rocks and ice curved into the blackness on the other. She craned her neck, hoping to catch a glimpse of the engines. But she could only see the edge of one, and there wasn't any damage.

"System diagnostics successful," the computer announced. "Engines one and two offline. Engines three and four online. Cabin structural integrity maintained. Shields twenty-four percent functional. Life-support thirty-eight percent functional. Fuel loss fifty percent. Distress signal sent. Guidance systems rebooting."

Sophia looked at the speaker above her. "Computer, can we make it to..." She couldn't remember the space station's name. "...where we were going?"

"Negative. Hyperspace drive unavailable. Fuel insufficient. Life support insufficient. Navigation partially compromised. Emergency landing advised. Alternative destination required. Human input requested."

"We can't make it to Dad?" Maleek asked.

"No." She pushed off the wall and grabbed onto her chair. "And we can't stay here long enough for them to get to us." She stared down at her wrist-pad. "We need somewhere to land."

"Computer," she said, "search for nearby planets."

"Unable. Navigation partially compromised. Human input requested."

She opened *The Traveler's Companion* and searched for their current location. "There are only three planets in this system," she said, searching the map. "And two are gas giants."

"What about the third?" Maleek asked. "Can we go there?"

"Life support diminishing," the computer warned. "Emergency landing advised."

She double-clicked on the planet. "It's got a breathable atmosphere," she said, reading as fast as she could. "It's our only choice."

She called out the coordinates and told the computer to take them there.

"Be advised," the computer replied, "requested destination is at maximum distance of fuel and life-support levels. Chance of success fifty-seven percent."

"Just get us there," she ordered.

"Fifty-seven percent?" Maleek swallowed. "What if we don't make it?"

"We will," Sophia told him.

I hope.

They hit the atmosphere with such force that Sophia was surprised their chairs didn't snap off the floor.

"Hang on!" she screamed, her brother's hand a vise in her own.

The roar of the air around them was deafening. The cabin shook and bucked in violent fits. It felt like the ship was being ripped apart.

It is. Sophia knew it as the awful screech of tearing metal drowned out everything and the ship lurched sideways. *It is being ripped apart.*

"Structural integrity compromised." Alarms blared, oxygen masks fell from the ceiling, and frigid air flooded the cabin. "Life support limited."

"Put it on!" Sophia tugged at the mask bouncing in front of her. "Put it on!"

"Engine four offline. Maneuverability thirteen percent."

A blur of movement swept past the windows—clouds at first, then things bigger and darker.

Mountains? Sophia wondered.

"We're landing!" Her voice muffled by the oxygen mask. "It'll be over soon!"

Bad word choice! Sophia thought.

The ship slammed into the ground and the floor just a few paces in front of their feet was wrenched upward.

Sophia wasn't sure how many impacts she felt, how many explosions she heard. It seemed to go on forever. And it seemed to have only lasted an instant. All she knew was that when they finally floundered to a halt, they were still alive.

The ship leaned forward. When Sophia unbuckled herself, she nearly tumbled out of the chair.

"Are you okay?" She clung to her armrest to keep from sliding. "Are you hurt?"

Maleek didn't answer. His hands were balled into fists, and he was breathing so fast Sophia was afraid he'd pass out.

"Maleek?"

He flinched when she touched him.

"Hey," she soothed. She slid her hand down and squeezed his shoulder. "It's over."

He stared at her, like he couldn't process what she said, but after a second he closed his eyes and gave her a nod.

"I'm going to unstrap you," she told him. She gestured at the tangled heap of metal, glass, and wires below. "Just hang onto me."

He was barely out of the straps when the ship swayed and rocked forward.

"What's that?" Maleek asked.

"I don't know," Sophia said. "But I think we should get out of here." She eyed the emergency supply cabinet near the front, but the ship lurched and started to slide. "Now!"

Sophia pushed Maleek up the aisle. "Go!" She stared at the emergency exit and tried to ignore the sensation that they were running up a down escalator. "Hurry!"

The red-latched door was in the middle of the cabin—only a few quick steps away—but she had no idea how much time they had. They could crash or fall at any second.

"I can't open it!" Maleek cried.

She grabbed the latch and pulled. It didn't budge.

"Hurry!" Maleek urged. Shadows whizzed past the window. "I think this could get really bad!"

Sophia heaved. "It won't!" she groaned. "It's locked!"

She forced herself to breathe. She forced herself to think. She forced herself to read the bold words painted across the door.

Press safety release before lifting, she read.

Despite the fear and adrenalin, she could have stopped and smacked herself. There was a large black button at the base of the latch, and there was a big yellow arrow pointing to it.

She hit it, yanked the door in, and shoved her brother out. She followed a split-second later, crashing through wet leaves and tumbling across mud and rocks and roots.

She smacked gut-first into a tree trunk. "Maleek?" she wheezed, looking up just in time to see the ship topple over a rocky ledge. "Where are you?"

"Over here."

She couldn't see him. The jungle was impossibly thick. Vines formed a curtain to one side and blooms of purple flowers formed a wall to the other. The ship had smashed down a wide path from the slope high above to the lip of the canyon, but everywhere else the underbrush was too dense to penetrate.

"Maleek?" She climbed to her feet and tried to force air into her lungs. "Maleek?"

"Sophia?"

She found him a few paces from the edge of the canyon, clinging to the base of a thin sapling like he was afraid he'd fall if he let go.

"Hey." She stumbled over and sat down. "That was fun, huh?"

He shook his head. "Definitely. Not. Fun."

"So," she said, noting every scratch and bruise. He was as beat up as she felt. His lip was busted, there was a bruise forming on the side of his face, and his arms were covered in tiny cuts and brush-burns. But nothing looked broken. "You want to do it again?"

"You're *not* funny," he said, hugging the tree harder.

The ledge in front of them opened on a wide canyon, nestled between the slopes of three mountains. Every shelf cut into the walls was covered in vegetation, and waterfalls sprouted from several clefts in the rock. Two stars hung above, one yellow and the other red and so big it swallowed half the horizon.

"Sophia?" Maleek asked, relaxing his grip a little. "Where are we?"

"Good question." She reopened *The Traveler's Companion* icon, clicked on the name of the planet, and turned on the wrist-pads' audio.

"Gangalon 13c," the book reported, displaying an aerial shot of the planet, "is an Earth-like planet in the Orion-Cygnus arm of the Milky Way galaxy. It was originally thought to be a prime candidate for colonization, but the planet's extremely hostile wildlife makes permanent settlement impractical."

"Great," Maleek said, looking at the trees and plants around them with renewed terror.

Sophia tapped the link labeled "Flora and Fauna."

"Since all attempted landing expeditions failed, little is known about Gangalon's wildlife, but high numbers of poisonous and carnivorous plants and animals are believed to be present."

"Wonderful," Maleek groaned. He backed away from the tree he'd been hugging like he thought the trunk might split open and bite him. "So this place was too dangerous for robots and scientists." He looked around frantically. "We're dead."

"We're not," she told him. "But we need to figure out what to do."

She scrolled back to *The Traveler's Companion's* homepage and breathed a sigh of relief. "Thank you, Momma," she whispered.

Maleek tried to lean over her shoulder. "What?"

"There's a survival guide." She kissed the screen. "An *interplanetary* survival guide!"

"In any survival emergency," she read when she opened it, "safety is the first priority. Given your current location, it is recommended you stay onboard your ship and await extraction. Estimated extraction, based on signal travel time and search radius, is seventy-nine Earth hours."

"Stay with the ship, huh?" Maleek walked over and peered over the edge. "Not likely. I'm not going down there."

Not having the ship wasn't what troubled Sophia.

Seventy-nine hours, she thought with a shudder. *That's more than three days.*

"If you are forced to leave the ship…"

The pad's speakers suddenly seemed incredibly loud. Sophia could picture it pulling in predators like moths to a flame.

"Hey," Maleek whined when she muted it. "I was listening to that."

Sophia shushed him and read down the page.

"What's it say?" Maleek asked. "What are we supposed to do?"

"We need something we can use as a weapon," she told him, "and we need shelter."

A blue bug whizzed down from the canopy. It was the size of Sophia's fist and it had at least a dozen wings. Maleek tensed as he eyed it. "I couldn't agree more."

"It also says we should get to higher ground if we can," she said. "It says the homing chips in our wrist-pads have weak signals. The higher we get, the farther the signal will travel."

"And that will help them find us?" Maleek asked.

"I guess," Sophia said. She walked out into the matted lane and stared up the slope. "I think there are cliffs up there." She pointed at the gray and white lining of the summit. "It's not that far to the top, probably a mile or two."

"Weapons and shelter," Maleek repeated. "And what if we don't find them?"

Sophia pressed a button and showed him pictures of lean-tos and huts. "Then we make them."

"Okay," Maleek said. "But I don't know how much I like depending on a book to stay alive."

The blue bug zoomed down and hovered in Maleek's face.

"You could stay here with him," Sophia laughed.

"Oh, I think I'll come," Maleek said, ducking as the bug zipped by his ear. "I wouldn't want you getting lonely."

The slope was littered with debris. Strips of metal were twisted around felled tree trunks. Wires clung to the trampled vines. Hunks of plastic dotted the ground.

"We should grab what we can," Sophia said. "You never know what we can use."

Maleek bent down and held up a sliver of steel. The top was a jagged point, and the back had been melted into a long, thin glob. "Are you saying you want to save this?"

"Totally." Sophia snatched it out of his hand. "What does

this look like?"

He shrugged. "Junk?"

"No." She grabbed a long branch—one that wasn't covered with oily sap—and prayed it wasn't poisonous. "It looks like a spearhead."

"Quick," she said, positioning the jagged end at the top of the stick. "Give me a shoelace."

"You're kidding," Maleek said. But when the brush along the clearing thrashed, he had it in her hand faster than she could insist.

Securing the metal to the shaft was a lot harder than Sophia thought, and it took Maleek's other lace to get it right. But when she finished, they had a wicked spear.

"Keep your eyes peeled," Sophia said as they restarted their march. "If we find another sharp piece, we can make another one."

"We can't," Maleek said, eyeing the trees suspiciously. "I'm out of shoelaces."

They continued gathering as they climbed. They hadn't gone far when Sophia spotted a wisp of smoke rising from the trees.

"Maleek." She pointed her spear. "Tell me you see that."

"It's just smoke."

"No, it's fire." She let her gathered plunder tumble out of her arms. "And we need it."

"You want to go in there and get it?" Maleek scoffed. "Are you crazy?"

A few of those blue bugs buzzed through the air, but the hillside was pocketed by clouds of other bugs, too.

Bugs whose stings could carry poison, Sophia knew. *And whose bites could pass diseases.*

"We have to." She rebooted *The Traveler's Companion* and clicked on the picture of the campfire. "Fire can deter predators," she read, "keep bugs away, help purify water," she looked up, "and a dozen other things." She took the spear in both hands. "We need it."

It was hot and sticky in the open. Inside the trees was a dank, dark oven. There was no memory of a breeze, and the air was so heavy Sophia felt she was wearing a wet blanket.

"Do you see the smoke?" Sophia whispered.

They were only steps into the trees, but the sky had already disappeared above them.

"I don't see anything," Maleek grumbled.

"I think it was coming from over here." She lifted a vine out of the way with the tip of her spear and ducked beneath it.

She could smell it. They had to be close.

We have to be careful, Sophia told herself. *If we get disoriented, we might never find our way back.*

She sniffed the air again and was relieved when the smell seemed a little stronger.

"I think I see it." Maleek pointed through a cluster of bushes with long yellow thorns. "Or at least I see a light."

Sophia saw it, too. Something was flickering in the shadows.

"That must be it," she said. "We'll work our way around these." She nudged one of the bushes with her spear. "Try not to touch them."

"Duh." Maleek gestured to the oil pooling at the ends of one of the needles. "I wasn't planning on bathing with that."

They crept around and found the source of fire. It looked like a chunk of one of the engines. The cylinder was cracked open, revealing guts of wires and gears, and whatever was leaking from its side fed a tiny river of blue fire.

"The fire hasn't caught on any of the plants," Sophia said. "They're probably too wet." She looked around at her feet. "We need to find something dry before it burns out."

She grabbed a branch, but it was so soaked and rotted it crumbled in her hands.

"We're in a jungle," Maleek told her. He held a stick over the flames, but it hissed instead of lighting. "There's nothing dry."

She hated to do it, but she tried the hilt of her spear.

No good, she thought, twisting the wood over the blue flames.

She accidentally brushed the haft against the ground, and when she pulled it out of the pooling fuel, it came up coated with blue fire.

"It's like lantern oil," she said as it dawned on her. "We can use it to make torches."

She ripped a strip of her sleeve off and wrapped it around the spearhead. Then she dunked it into the fuel and let it sop up as much as it would hold. When she lifted it into the flames, it lit up like a candle.

"We can use the fuel to take the fire with us," she told Maleek. "It will burn longer anyway, and it's less likely to go out."

He nodded. "And we'll find some good wood when we're safely out of this jungle."

As he took off one of his socks and wrapped it around a twisted branch, the sound of something scampering through the leaves—the sound of something big—made them both freeze.

"Put your shoe on," Sophia said, staring into the shadows. "Light that quick and run."

It was on their heels by the time they reached the clearing—a giant horned bear with scales instead of fur.

"No!" Sophia said when her brother paused to gather the stuff they'd ditched. She grabbed him by the hand and led him up the hill. "Leave it!"

We'll never outrun that thing, Sophia realized when she glanced over her shoulder and saw the beast burst out of the tree line.

She urged her brother to move faster and, right on cue,

Maleek screamed and fell.

"What happened?" Sophia said, yanking him back to his feet.

"I don't know." He grabbed at his ankle. "It feels like something bit me." He tried to put weight on it and nearly fell over again. "It feels like my leg is on fire."

"We have to keep moving," Sophia told him.

But his first hobbled steps told her it wouldn't matter. The beast would be on them before they got halfway up the hill.

It feels like it's on fire, she repeated her brother's words in her head. *Fire!*

She glanced at her spear and stopped running. "The book said fire could deter predators," she said as she turned. "Let's find out if it's right."

It won't work, Sophia told herself, watching the beast race toward them in long bounding strides. *It's too big.* She glanced at the blue fire dancing at the end of her spear. *This is like trying to scare a lion with a toothpick.*

As she retreated backward up the hill, she heard something crunch beneath her feet... something dry and brittle.

She looked down and, if she wasn't so terrified that she couldn't feel her face, she might have smiled. Clumps of thick, brown grass littered the ground around them.

She dabbed her spear into the thickest patch and prayed.

It lit like a stack of matches.

"Burn it," she told her brother, shoving her spear into another tuft. "Light up as much as you can."

By the time the beast was close enough to strike, they had made a wall of fire. It stopped and roared at the flames. But when it tried to pounce through, it howled in pain and yelped away.

"What are you doing?" Maleek demanded as Sophia stood staring. "Waiting 'til it comes back?"

"No." Sophia said, shaking herself back into action. "Let's get out of here. We need someplace to hide."

They wove through the boulders scattered in front of the cliffs.

"This couldn't be any creepier," Maleek said.

"Seriously," Sophia agreed.

The yellow sun had set and the dim red light of the remaining star mixed with their torches' blue flames, forming pockets of eerie purple light. Shadows twisted around them as they walked, and Sophia peered into each patch of darkness, expecting some new monster to jump out at them.

"Hey," Maleek said when the base of the cliff was in sight, "I think I see a cave."

He limped forward.

Sophia caught him by the arm just before he reached the jagged mouth. "Don't go in," she told him.

"Don't go in?" Maleek cocked his head. "Are you nuts?"

He tried to pull away, but she held him in place. "Just wait a second," she said. "Let me look this up."

She found the page dedicated to natural shelters. "When seeking shelter in caves," she read aloud, "carefully inspect the area for rodents, insects, and snakes. If fire is available, smoke can be used to flush out inhabitants."

"Fine." Maleek thrust his torch into the opening.

"That won't work," she said. "Not enough smoke. This says to build a fire at the edge of the cave."

There were tufts of thick grass sprouting out among the boulders. They made a pile just inside the threshold and lit it, but there wasn't nearly enough smoke to scare anything out.

"Great plan," Maleek mocked.

Sophia gave him a quick eye roll and scanned through the *Companion*. "We need green plants," she said when she was done. "And something to fan the fire."

The large-leafed plants they found clinging to the side of the cliff did both. They tossed some onto the fire and used others to waft the smoke into the cave.

Within seconds, a swarm of scaly, bird-like creatures poured out at them.

"You didn't mention this part!" Maleek shrieked, cupping his head as they whizzed by.

"I didn't know!" she shrieked back. One of the things landed right on her face, and she nearly bloodied her own nose batting it away. "But it's better than living with them!"

The cave was cramped. The ceiling was so low Sophia had to hunch over and there was barely enough floor space for them both.

"We can't let this go out," she said, adding more of the twigs and grass to the fire. Her torch had winked out, and Maleek's was sputtering. "We're going to need bigger logs."

"Then let's get some." Maleek tried to stand, but he slumped back against the wall with a wince.

"You're not going anywhere." She slid around the fire to his feet. "Let me see it."

She put his leg in her lap and carefully folded back his pant-leg.

She tried not to let the worry show. His ankle was swollen, and a gooey mixture of blood and puss oozed out of two rows of small teeth marks.

"How's it look?" Maleek asked.

"Probably like it feels," she answered.

"That bad, huh?"

"Yeah," she said. She tore a chunk off her remaining sleeve and cleaned it the best as she could. "That bad."

The next morning Sophia awoke to find the fire, and her brother, still burning.

The fever that hit him the night before had worsened. His face was pale, his skin was soaked with sweat, and he was shaking like he was locked in a cryo-freezer.

She sat up and rubbed the small of her back. "How are you feeling?"

"Never better," he said through chattering teeth. "Why do you ask?"

She crawled over and felt his forehead.

"What's the diagnosis, doc?"

"Better," she lied.

Her book's first aid page told her that poisonous bites or stings usually looked like puncture wounds. On Earth, there were usually one or two holes. On other planets, the number varied, but it was usually only a few. Fever and swelling from many shallow teeth marks meant bacteria or virus in the saliva. It was the way Komodo Dragons hunted on Earth. Bite the prey. Wait until it's sick. Dinner.

The last words on the screen almost made her weep. *Keep the patient warm and calm*, it read. *Seek medical attention immediately.*

She leaned back and stared at the fire. *Medical attention?* she thought hopelessly. *Right. I'll just call the doctor and then stop off at the pharmacy.*

The thought of medicine made her straighten.

It had been there, she knew. *But did it survive the crash?* She tried to picture the ship. *I saw it before we ran. I did. But can I get back to it?*

One glance at her brother told her she had no choice. She spent the next few minutes reading, then stood and grabbed her spear.

"Where you going?"

"Gathering," she said. If she told him where, he'd never let her go.

"I'd tell you not to," he said. "But you never listen."

"Keep the fire going," she told him. She unwrapped the burnt cloth from the end of her spear and dropped it into the coals. "I'll be right back."

She found a wet spot in the ground and started digging.

Natural insecticide, she thought. She rubbed mud on every inch of exposed skin: her arms, her neck, her face. *And maybe a little camouflage, too.*

She kept her eyes on the trees as she walked, but she saw nothing but bugs all the way down to where the ship had slipped over the lip of the canyon.

Maleek had glanced over the edge and said he wouldn't go down there. And now she knew why.

The ship was on a shelf a hundred feet below. It had landed nose first and was buried in the dense branches of a lone tree. The battered back thrusters were leaning precariously against the back wall, and it looked like it might slide sideways and roll off the ledge at any second.

"Am I really doing this?" Sophia whispered.

The rock beneath her was pocked with holes and lined with cracks. There would be plenty of handholds.

Take your time, she told herself. She leaned out as far as she dared and tried to eye her route. *Think it through.* She swallowed, set her spear aside, and swung a leg over the ledge.

It was hard to make her body move. She had to force herself to let go of every hold, and she was shaking so bad her feet felt like they might jiggle themselves free.

"I can do this," she mumbled. "Just keep moving."

A hard breeze hit her as she reached the tail of the ship, and the metal let out a threatening groan.

"Don't you dare," she warned as she scrambled past. "You can fall when I'm finished."

The climbing got harder when she reached the treetop. She forced her way through the thick branches; finding footholds was like trying to read in the dark.

When she finally got low enough to see, she found that one of the tree's thicker limbs was lodged through the open emergency door.

It might be the only thing holding it in place, she thought as she leaned out from the rock and hooked an arm around the branch.

As she swung herself over and began working up into the cabin, she risked a glance down.

"Bad idea," she mumbled. It was a long way down to the ledge, and the tree was perched on the edge of an abyss. "Very bad idea."

She wrapped herself around the branch and squirmed her way into the cabin.

It's actually here. She sighed with relief. The white cabinet was battered and hanging crooked from its bolts, but it was there. *Now how do I get to it?*

It was bolted to the far wall at the nose of the ship, and it was dangling over a hole in the hull. The way the ship was leaning and the way the ledge curved inward underneath meant that there was nothing but open air beneath it.

Another gust of wind made the ship give a fresh moan. She thought she felt it wobble.

The seats look solid enough, she told herself.

She'd have to drop a few feet to the back of the nearest one and, if the jolt didn't make the ship tip off the ledge, she should be able to make her way down by climbing from chair to chair.

She dangled and dropped, crouching down as she landed to ease the impact, but she still felt the ship quiver.

She waited until it stopped, then crawled toward the center aisle and worked her way down to the front row.

Here goes, she thought, carefully standing on the back of the chairs.

The gap between her and the wall wasn't big, but with the hole looming beneath her, it looked much wider than it was. She swallowed, braced herself by grabbing onto the armrest above her and reached for the latch.

She tugged at it a few times and, just as it popped, she heard a hiss above.

She whipped her head up toward the door. *You've got to be kidding me.*

It was like a giant millipede—red, easily ten feet long, and too wide to get her arms around. Its legs made a thousand clicking sounds as it skittered across the tree branch and arched its body out over the edges of the seats.

"Good buggy," Sophia whimpered as she gaped. Its large eyes looked like they had as many lenses as the thing had legs. "Nice buggy."

The pincers on the sides of its mouth split apart and it gave her a fresh hiss in response. Then it came for her.

She didn't know what to do. She didn't know what she could do. Her spear might as well have been a mile away and there was nothing else she could use as a weapon.

In desperation, she flung the cabinet open and frantically scanned inside. The contents were latched to the shelves—a white medical kit, a chemical fire extinguisher, a black backpack… a gun.

They'd learned how to use the proton guns in school. Everyone had to. Maleek was great at shooting—probably a side effect of playing those stupid battle games all time. Sophia had been the worst in her class.

Sophia yanked the gun out of its straps, fumbled with the safety, and swung the barrel upward.

The creature was right on top of her, coiled like a snake, and she instinctively fell onto her back as she tried to take aim.

It lunged as she pulled the trigger, met with a blast of white light, and fell twitching through the air beside her.

She forced herself to breathe as she rolled to follow its fall.

It hadn't fallen through the hole. It was twitching right beside it.

Stunned, she told herself, partly relieved, partly terrified.

Not dead. I have to hurry.

She grabbed the backpack from the cabinet, surprised how heavy it was and shoved the medical kit inside. She grabbed everything else, too: the black communicator, the small set of tools, and the pack of flares. By the time she was finished, the bag was so full she could barely zip it and so heavy she was afraid she wouldn't be able to make the climb.

But she wasn't about to leave anything useful behind.

"I thought I told you to keep the fire going?" Sophia stumbled into the cave, let her backpack drop to the floor, and sank to her knees next to the smoldering ashes.

"And Mom told you not to play in the mud." His voice came out as a wheeze, and the way his eyes drooped, it was hard to believe he could actually see her. "Are you okay?"

"Yeah," she panted. She heaved the bag over and unzipped it. "I'm okay." She dumped its contents out in front of her. There were packs of dried food and bottles of water mixed in with her plunder. "We're both going to be."

She tossed two pill bottles onto Maleek's stomach. "Take two from each," she said. One was an antibiotic; the other was an antiviral. "But don't call me in the morning." She tossed him a bottle of water. "I need to sleep in."

The roar of thrusters screamed through the air the next day.

Sophia lit a flare and ran out to meet them, waving frantically and screaming at the top of her lungs. Maleek followed, a flare in each hand.

The shuttles landed just beyond the boulders, and soldiers scrambled out.

"We're here!" Sophia screamed, though they were heading right toward them. "We're here!"

The troops corralled them into the nearest shuttle, where doctors waited to treat them. But a man in a blue lab coat got to them first.

"Dad?" Sophia asked as he rushed forward.

He scooped them both into his arms. "My God," he said, squeezing until they groaned. "You're okay. You're really okay."

"We're okay," Sophia groaned, hugging him back. "We are."

"But how?" He held them at arm's length. "This is the most dangerous planet in this region."

Sophia smiled and tapped her wrist-pad. "We had a little help."

Her father raised his brows.

"Something Mom gave me before she died." She swallowed, trying not to tear up. "Just a silly book."

"Not a silly book," Maleek corrected. "An incredible book. An awesome book. An incredibly awesome book."

"You mean *The Traveler's Companion*?" her father asked. He gave a little laugh. "I don't believe it."

"What?" Sophia asked. "What do you mean?"

"She never thought you'd really need it… not like this… not to survive. She meant it more as a symbol." His forehead knotted together. "You did see the dedication? Didn't you?"

Sophia stared at the pad.

"You mean there's a message?" Maleek asked. His eyes widened. "From Mom?"

Her father twisted the screen toward him and made a few quick taps. "See for yourself."

Sophia hit the link. The speaker crackled. Someone cleared her throat. And a soft voice mumbled, "I think it's on."

It's her, Sophia realized, and now she couldn't fight the tears. *It's really her.*

"Okay." Mom sounded weak. "Here goes." She cleared her throat again. "The universe," she said, "is a tricky place… as scary as it is beautiful. On our journey through it, the bad comes with the good, and it can take all your strength and courage to keep going." There was another long pause. "I hope this book can help you find your way." She sniffled, obviously crying. "I hope it can be there to guide you when I can't..." Her voice cracked. "Happy birthday, baby. I love you. I love you so much."

The Ghost in the Aurora

by Rati Mehrotra

Rati Mehrotra is a Toronto-based speculative fiction writer whose short stories have appeared in venues such as AE – The Canadian Science Fiction Review, Apex Magazine, Urban Fantasy Magazine, *and* Podcastle. *Her debut novel* Markswoman *is due to be released in early 2018 by Harper Voyager. You can find out more about her at http://ratiwrites.com or follow her on Twitter @Rati_Mehrotra.*

First Mother went into the organic reservoir eight turns ago. There was a service afterward, and the priest told me how it meant she would never die. All seven octillion of her atoms would be recycled and reused by the voyagers of the *Aurora.* Atoms that were never hers in the first place. They'd always been stardust and big-bang dust.

He thought he was being nice, explaining things to a 'child.' But even a child—and I am not one, even though I have not yet decided whether I am boy or girl—knows how precious atoms are. Just one for every cubic centimeter of space, with the asteroids few and far between. I'd learned in class how important it was not to waste a single one. But I'd never attended a death service before and was unprepared for how I felt. Tears leaked out of my eyes and Second Mother was

annoyed, although she tried to conceal it. Second Mother is
Chief Diplomatic Liaison of the Ship Council. I have half her
genes and none of her brains, as she is fond of saying.

I told myself that good, useful things would come out of
the printer because of First Mother, that she would always
be a part of me and of the *Aurora*, but it didn't help. The
particular collection of atoms that had made First Mother
was gone, vanished into the maw of the reservoir. Nothing
could change that. Especially not the priest, going on about
'stardust unto stardust.' First Mother wasn't going to be
stardust, not for a million years anyway. First she'd be in the
kelp and chlorella crackers.

I went off my food for a while. Second Mother sent me to
Medical; Medical sent me to Psychology, and Psychology sent me
to sleep. I had weird dreams, and when I woke up nothing was
different except that three turns had passed, and I'd missed my
deadline on a low-gravity plant growth report. So I decided to
stop crying and start eating and pretend everything was all right.

That's when I began seeing First Mother's ghost. The first
time it happened, I'd just been released from Psychology.
I was on a walkway back to the pod that I shared with five
other kids, wondering how to explain my absence to them.
First Mother appeared right in front of me, her face sad,
holding the tapestry she'd been working on. The bag slipped
from my hands, and I heard a thin scream—my own. People
on the walkway turned around and stared. First Mother
faded away, still looking sad.

"Are you all right, Ettir?" said the *Aurora* in my ear, and I
got my second shock. The ship AI had never spoken directly
to me before.

I picked up my bag and said, "Of course I'm all right. Just
remembered all the extra work I have to do before finals, and
I promised Second Mother I would volunteer at the nursery."
I paused, trying to slow my pulse. "How come you're talking

to me? I thought you mostly let your minions do that," the 'minions' being the ship bots and the humans who ran the interface.

"You look like you need help, although you seem unwilling to ask for it," said the *Aurora*. "Your heart rate and blood pressure indicate stress."

"Of course I'm stressed," I snapped. "I have three assignments due next turn. Look, there's no need to bother about me. Don't you have a ship to run?"

I continued on my way, and the *Aurora* didn't speak again, but I knew She'd watch me closely. Over fourteen thousand people, and the ship AI kept tabs on them all—in theory, anyway.

The pods were located in a beehive-shaped structure in the heart of the ship, accessed by walkways and separated by narrow corridors. I'd lived in mine since I could solve simple algorithms. Before that we were all together in a nursery with sixty other kids. The pod was home until we decided who we were—but I didn't have to think about that, not yet.

I entered my pod and threw myself on the sleep-bags in the middle. My pod-mates were working—the pod was a hexagonal space, one side for each of us—but one by one they came over and hugged me. No one said anything, and for that I was grateful. They knew, even if Second Mother didn't, how much I'd loved First Mother.

Later, after everyone else was asleep, I wondered if First Mother regretted what she had done. She hadn't even finished her tapestry. An unusual choice for your death project, but First Mother was never one to do the expected. Astrophysicist and Earth Historian, First Mother was only one generation removed from the pioneers who'd built the *Aurora* to escape the dying Earth. Their goal? Gliese 667, the nearest star system with at least two Earth-like planets and possibly five more. At 22 light years from Earth, the trip was doable in four generations—in *my* generation.

Too late for First Mother. If only she could have held out a little longer. But she'd worried only about the death project she wanted to leave behind. "Virtual displays and robotic art are so common," she had told me. "I want to make something you can touch and hold."

And so she'd printed a small loom and multi-colored yarn, exhausting much of her accumulated credit. She had eighteen turns to work on it before she died. *Chose* to die. I still couldn't wrap my head around it. I'd known she was old, older than almost anyone on the ship, and beyond the help of the medbots that ran the infirmary, but I'd thought she'd choose cryo. She had enough credit left for several hundred turns of it, and perhaps she would have woken stronger. It had been known to happen.

First Mother didn't confer with Second Mother, as she often did. She didn't even say goodbye to me.

That night, before I slept, I saw her again. White-haired and serene, her eyes brimming with kindness, not a fraction of which Second Mother had inherited. She stood at the far end of our pod, holding the tapestry out like she wanted me to take it. I thought of waking Iann and Aimo, curled up on either side of me, but what would have been the use? I doubted they would be able to see her, and then I might find myself back in Psychology. I got up carefully so as not to disturb them, but First Mother faded before I could reach her. What she was trying to tell me was clear, however, and I resolved to act upon it as soon as I could.

Next turn, Aimo decided he was a boy and left the pod. We'd been expecting it for a while, but I still felt bereft, like he was deserting us.

"You're barely a hundred turns older than me," I said, trying not to sound upset. "How can you know for sure?"

Aimo closed his bag and put a hand on my shoulder. "I just know, Ettir. I can feel it in my gut. And maybe it's time for you, too."

They all looked at me, as if they were seeing something I couldn't. I shrugged off Aimo's hand and left the pod, unable to bear their scrutiny. I was the next oldest, the next in line. If only First Mother was still alive, I could have gone to her for advice. I did the next best thing and went to the museum instead, the vault where the death projects were on display. I got a class reminder while I was on the walkway, but I ignored it.

"Missing class? That's not like you, Ettir," said the *Aurora*. "Finals are just thirty turns away. Do you not wish to be a lightcraft pilot?"

I gritted my teeth. It *was* my dream to get off ship on a lightcraft of my own when we approached Gliese 667, but how did the *Aurora* know that? "I know enough to pass," I said.

"Barely," said the *Aurora*. "They only take the best for pilot school."

"I'll make it," I said with conviction, as if that could erase my own doubts. "I'm going to class anyway; I just have to do something first."

I got off the walkway and took an elevator down to the lower levels of the ship. There was a moment on the elevator when I was absolutely alone, apart from the *Aurora*, of course, and it was a strange feeling. No humans, no bots, no one looking at me. The main living areas of the ship— schools, medical bay, walkways, gardens, canteens—were always busy.

I hadn't been to the museum in ages, not since a class trip when I was little. I called up a map overlay, took a shortcut through a disused corridor and arrived at the vault. I identified myself to the door, stated the purpose of my visit, and was denied entry.

"But why?" I said, dismayed. "I just want to see First

Mother's death project."

"It's all right," said the *Aurora*. "You can go in. I overrode the sub-routine."

I walked in, feeling self-conscious, but there was no one else inside the vast, silent space that arched over me. Images danced across the walls, a riot of colors and forms. Geometries interlaced, making impossible holos. Interspersed in that living, dancing space were a few three-dimensional stills: sculptures, statues, even a miniature globe of the Earth. I craned my neck, twisting around to try and see everything at once. The last vision of those about to pass from life into death or cryo.

"It's beautiful," I whispered. "How many are there?"

"Thirty-one thousand, three hundred and eighteen," answered the *Aurora*. "There are four levels, and what you see is but a fraction. The majority of the death projects are stored as code, and the view changes from turn to turn."

"But First Mother's project was a tapestry," I said. "It has to be somewhere here."

"It is not," said the *Aurora*. "It has been taken out by your Second Mother."

I felt like I'd been punched in the stomach. "Why? Why has she taken it?" The *Aurora* did not answer, and a wave of anger rose within me. "You knew this, and still you let me come here?"

"I thought you would like to see the museum," said the *Aurora*. "Did you not say it is beautiful?"

"Is my being denied entry related to the tapestry being taken out by Second Mother?" I demanded. Once again, the *Aurora* did not answer.

I went to class, mulling over the mystery of the missing tapestry. Why would Second Mother take it? Why would the *Aurora* bother Herself with a death project? And above all, what had First Mother been up to, those last few days when she holed herself up in her private pod and refused to see anyone?

After school I got a message from Second Mother. She wanted to meet me in her office. My heart almost leaped out of its ribcage. Here was an opportunity to hunt for the tapestry. I arrived at her office fifteen minutes early, hoping it would be empty.

It was. I identified myself and was allowed inside. The door closed behind me and I did a quick scan. Everything looked the same as usual: curved walls covered with star charts and viewports, a wide desk glowing with data panels, fibreglass seats melded with the floor. I walked up to the desk and glanced at the panels. The Gliese 667 triple star system was only eleven standard years away, at our current speed. Robotic probes had already been sent to explore the system; five years from now, piloted lightcraft would follow. Finally, the *Aurora* would come to rest, and her denizens could escape the 'zero atom-waste economy'. What would we do with dead people then?

I pushed that thought away and went to work. It was unlikely that the tapestry was here, but I had to eliminate the possibility. I looked in the drawers, the cabinets, even under the desk.

The door slid open and Second Mother walked in. I straightened up, trying not to look guilty.

"Ettir," said Second Mother, "what were you doing on the floor?"

I didn't respond; I couldn't. Second Mother was *wearing the tapestry*. It was draped on her shoulders like a stole, the bright blue-and-yellow patterns covering the insignias on her black uniform. In that moment, I hated her.

Second Mother sat down and waved me down opposite her. "I hope you're not going to be difficult," she said. "I have very little time before my next meeting."

I found my voice. "Why are you wearing First Mother's

death project?" I asked. "Shouldn't it be in the museum?"

Second Mother frowned. "Really, Ettir, how is that relevant? I want it with me and that is enough." She paused. "You were late to class today. I was informed that you made a detour to the museum. Since when have you developed such an unhealthy interest in people's death projects?"

"Since I began seeing First Mother's ghost," I said in a flippant tone, but the blood left Second Mother's face. She clutched the tapestry, opened her mouth and shut it.

Realization dawned. "You've seen her too, haven't you?" I whispered.

Wordlessly, Second Mother shook her head. "You're lying," I said. "You've seen her and that is why you called me."

"I called you about finals," snapped Second Mother, recovering. "Your performance in the last few turns has been abysmal. Have you even chosen your finals project? I have been invited by your school for the presentations, but I don't want you to embarrass me. You used to be at the top of your class. Do you think failing the best way to honor your First Mother's memory?"

Her words stabbed me, like they always did. "Be honest," I said. "You're just afraid any failure of mine will reflect poorly on you."

Her nostrils flared. "And why not? Not everyone on the ship gets the chance to pass on their genes. We all have to prove our worth."

"Of course. First Mother must have been real proud of you." I stood, wanting to be gone. "Anyway, you don't have to worry. I promise to pass with flying colors."

Second Mother looked relieved. "See that you do. There'll be no end of opportunities, now that we are nearing Gliese 667."

"I only want one thing to motivate me," I said and pointed to her shoulders. "I'd like First Mother's tapestry as a keepsake."

Second Mother gave me a cold smile. "You are so impolite, Ettir. I hope you do make it to pilot school, for you have not the temperament for a civilian post. No, you cannot have the tapestry. And I strongly suggest you do not mention 'ghosts' again, unless you wish to be declared mentally unfit to fly." Her eyes became unfocused, like she was scrolling messages. "Leave now. I am expecting the Council at any moment."

I left, bitterness in my mouth. What was First Mother's death project to her? She was wearing it like an ordinary bit of cloth. I went to my pod without bothering to stop at the canteen for a meal. No one else was around and I had the room to myself. Five sides cluttered with projects and data screens, and one side empty, with Aimo gone.

I crawled into my sleep-bag and wondered how Aimo was doing, why he had decided to become a man, and whether it was painful. Second Mother had never told me, although I knew the process: the combination of hormonal and surgical procedures by which one half of our genes were given full expression and the other half suppressed. I just couldn't imagine it, becoming something I was not. Part of 'growing up,' apparently, but what if I didn't want to choose? *Couldn't* choose?

"*Aurora*," I said softly, "have there been instances of people who couldn't decide their gender?"

"No," said the *Aurora* at once, as if She'd been waiting for me to ask. "When it is time, you will know what you are. A few decide they are both, but it is always an active choice."

I bit my lip. "Does it... does it hurt?"

"As much as any change does," answered the *Aurora*. "It is nothing you cannot bear."

"You sound like First Mother," I said. "Have you been analyzing her speech patterns?"

An almost imperceptible pause. "No, but I have been analyzing her tapestry."

I sat up, excited. "Wait, why didn't I think of that? You can show me every detail of it, can't you?"

A holo of the tapestry appeared before me: a dark yellow square half-filled with a pattern of flowering blue vines, bordered by a thin black line. No, not a line. I frowned and squinted. "Expand the borders, please," I said. The *Aurora* obliged and I stared. The borders were a series of dots and dashes that looked vaguely familiar.

"It's some sort of pattern, isn't it?" I asked.

"Morse code," replied the *Aurora*, "developed on Earth in the nineteenth century to facilitate communication via electrical pulses."

"Then these correspond to letters." I scrambled out of my sleep-bag. "First Mother left me a message! Can you display it?"

The dots and dashes disappeared, replaced by numbers and letters. I scanned them, disappointed. "It's just a meaningless string," I said. "Unless First Mother has layered another code onto this one."

"Your First Mother was a historian," said the *Aurora*. "She had subjective knowledge of a time period most do not. There are many ways this string can be forced to make sense, but only one of them would be correct. Do you not need a finals project?"

"I was going to write about plants," I said, "but this is *much* more interesting." Besides, it was obviously something First Mother had wanted me to do.

I copied the string of letters and numbers onto my data pad and queried the archives on nineteenth- and twentieth-century codes. I worked late, long after my pod-mates had returned and gone to sleep. Some four hours before wakeup, I realized that I was going about it all wrong. The numbers represented letters, too; I just had to find out which ones. And as soon as I realized that, I hit on a solution. It wasn't a simple cipher-text, ASCII or binary code—nothing as obvious as that. The numbers represented a hexadecimal system, with a base of 16. I ran my string through a hexadecimal text converter and got garbage. I was about to give up and go to sleep when I had an idea. I ran the converter again, separately on different chunks of the text. Only *part* of the text needed to be converted. As the alarm buzzed for wakeup, I had what I believed to be the second layer of First Mother's cryptic message. I passed out, grinning, and missed the first class of the turn.

The next few turns, I worked hard on my project. I didn't see First Mother's ghost again. I figured she was happy I'd finally gotten her message and was trying to solve it.

I took care not to miss any more classes. Second Mother would be pleased, as long as she was watching me only superficially. I had to trust she wouldn't care to do more than that. Every turn that brought us closer to Gliese 667 increased her workload. So many questions, fears and conflicts, and the Chief Diplomatic Liaison had to smooth them all.

The third level of code was a polyalphabetic substitution cipher—every letter had been replaced by the letter two, four or six positions down the alphabet. When I cracked the third level, I punched my fist in the air, and Iann asked me why I was laughing like a maniac.

"Just cracked my finals project," I said, and everyone cheered. I think they were all relieved by how I'd poured myself into work and 'gotten over' First Mother's death.

I now had what looked like readable text, except that the words were severely abbreviated. I filled in the gaps as best as I could, ran it through a program for auto edits, and I had First Mother's message. I was so pleased with myself. But as I read it, my feeling of triumph evaporated, replaced by dread.

I had been thinking of it as a game, as something to remember First Mother by. How wrong I'd been.

I re-read the message and thought of Gliese 667, in our sights at last. I thought of how I longed to pilot a lightcraft and be one of the first to step onto the surface of the planet that might eventually become our home. How I didn't want to spend the rest of my life bound by the limits of the ship, knowing I might never get off. And I almost deleted my solution to First Mother's cipher.

But I didn't. I thought of her loneliness in her last days, her inability to share this with anyone, her fears for our future, for who we would become. And I began to write my report.

I didn't do too badly on my finals, a set of six written and four oral exams that tested us on everything from earth history to artificial intelligence. But the real test was the finals project: a full ten percent of our overall grade. One by one, my fellow classmates rose to give a short summary of the reports they had already submitted the previous turn. I hadn't made my submission; I waited until it was my turn to speak before uploading it onto the class server.

I stood, trying not to tremble, forcing my voice to be strong and confident. "My project is on old Earth cryptology," I announced. I ran through a brief history of cryptology and the codes I'd studied. Then I switched on my data-pad and summoned a holo of the original tapestry. "This is my First Mother's death project," I said. "If you look at the borders, you will see a row of dots and dashes. This is called Morse code."

Murmurs rose in the audience, which included not only students and examiners, but also the Councillor for our sector and, of course, Second Mother. Part of me had been hoping she wouldn't come, but another part was glad she was there, forced to listen to me. I plunged ahead, avoiding her face and the look of frozen shock on it. I explained how I had worked through the four levels of code, and finally cast a 2-D image of the message I'd deciphered.

"First Mother was not an expert cryptologist, and neither am I. Anyone could have deciphered this message if they were paying attention, but First Mother knew that no one except me *would* pay attention. I'm going to read it aloud, even though you can read it on the screen, because I'd like to think I am speaking with her voice." I paused and wet my lips. Second Mother looked like she'd swallowed a stone that was slowly poisoning her.

You will not find mention of the First Directive in any of our archives. The ship's records were purged of it eight standard years ago when robotic probes sent back initial data from Gliese 667. The original discussions concerning the Directive have slipped beyond the living memory of all on board except myself.

The First Directive embodies the living will of those brave men and women who built the Aurora *and died while She was still under construction. It is the vision of the pioneers on whose backs we now travel toward a new star system. Simply put, the First Directive states that we must Do No Harm. An easy thing on the surface of it, but complex when we dig deeper.*

It means that we cannot damage another planet like we have damaged Earth. We cannot change it to suit ourselves if that change is to the detriment of another species. In its most extreme interpretation, it implies that we cannot settle on a planet that already teems with more than microbial life.

The first set of data received from the Gliese 667 system offered clues that both of its Earth-like planets have abundant life forms. Most likely some are self-aware. There are signs of primitive farming and irrigation, although we have no evidence of advanced technology yet.

I argued with the Council against the suppression of the First Directive and the data from the probes. I failed. I was sworn to secrecy by my own daughter. This is the only way I can keep my oath to her and salvage my own conscience. I don't know if we should try and make our home in Gliese 667, but I do know that we should do so with the full awareness of what we do and who we are. That we should be ready, if our presence is unwelcome, to move on. Space is infinite and so, if you think about it, are we.

I stopped speaking. My throat was dry and my eyes burned. There was absolute silence in the hall. Second Mother stood, but before she could speak, someone started to clap. Someone else joined in, and then it was like I was drowning in applause and my own sweaty relief.

I got a triple A in my finals project. Overall, I did well enough to be chosen for pilot training. There was talk that the immediate goal of the lightcraft mission would be modified— not to find the best colony world for us, but to survey and make contact with the species that populated the planets of Gliese 667. It would take a while longer to establish the home we'd all been dreaming about. And perhaps it would not be in Gliese 667; only time would tell. But meanwhile, the *Aurora* was home, just like She always had been.

"You knew," I said to Her after the presentations were over and I could escape to my pod. "You knew all along."

"I decoded the message on your First Mother's tapestry," said the *Aurora*, "but I was unable to communicate it. I seem to have been prohibited from doing so. Nor did I have any memory of the First Directive. I could only draw attention to the encrypted message indirectly, and even that caused me some stress."

I stopped short. "*You* made me see First Mother's ghost, didn't you? I thought I was going crazy!"

"I am sorry, Ettir," said the *Aurora*. "I know it caused you distress, and your Second Mother also."

"So that's why Second Mother was wearing the tapestry,"

I said. "She knew nothing about the codes, but she must have suspected First Mother would try and communicate in some way." I paused. "I should be at mad at you, but I'm not. You're the one who started the clapping in the hall, right?"

"I do think you did very well," said the *Aurora*. "Your First Mother would have been proud."

I felt a glow of accomplishment, but it was short-lived. A red alert blinked in the corner of my eye. Second Mother, wanting me in her office.

"What do you think she's going to do to me?" I mumbled.

"There is little she can do, now that it's out in the open," said the *Aurora*. "People are demanding accountability from the Council. I do believe your Second Mother will not be Chief Diplomatic Liaison for much longer."

But she was still my Second Mother. I felt an unwelcome stab of guilt when I recalled her shocked face. I'd betrayed her. But then, she'd betrayed a whole lot of people, including First Mother.

I arrived at her office and ID-ed myself in. Second Mother was sitting behind her desk, her eyes red. "I should request reassignment of your atoms," she said. "Perhaps I might get a second chance to pass on my genes."

I bit back the retort on the tip of my tongue. It was unlikely, but Second Mother was my guardian until I came of age, and if she could prove I was damaged enough, I might indeed end up 'reassigned' like a criminal, all seven octillion of me.

Realization hit me like a wet sponge. My stomach churned and I leaned against the desk, dizzy. "Won't work," I said, barely able to get the words out. "You are no longer my guardian."

Her lip curled. "Ettir, you don't even know what..."

"I know what I am!" I shouted. "I am a girl."

Second Mother was so surprised, she didn't even stop me

from snatching the tapestry off her shoulders. I ducked out of her office before she could call me back, and raced down the walkways to the museum. I hung the tapestry on the wall opposite the door of the entry level, so it would be the first thing anyone saw when they walked in. I got the museum subroutine to display a permanent holo of the decrypted message below it, and then I stood back to admire First Mother's death project.

"Beautiful," said the *Aurora*. Off to one side, First Mother's 'ghost' smiled and clapped her hands.

Note: The set of codes in First Mother's tapestry is inspired by Terese Agnew's tapestry Illumination, *which hung in the Porter's Lodge of Merton College, Oxford, for several months before being cracked by Alice Miller, a Merton undergraduate.*

Leaves, Trees, and Other Scary Things

by Leandra Wallace

Leandra Wallace writes young adult and middle grade speculative fiction and always eats lunch with a book in hand. Her short stories "The Mad Scientist's Daughter" and "Prina and the Pea" are published *in* Brave New Girls: Tales of Girls and Gadgets, *and* Circuits & Slippers. *She lives in the Midwest with her husband and son, (both of whom she believes are adorable) and can be found online at www. leandrajwallace.blogspot.com.*

Lizette never meant to be good with cars. It wasn't like she thought oily engines and gear shafts were fascinating puzzles to be completed—she really just thought they made her neighbor's yard look junky. Because Mr. Tallon worked on cars all the time. Mechanical parts dotted his concrete pad like a metal species of dandelion gone wild, and tires were stacked ten deep into baffling mazes.

But on a hot Tuesday morning in July, as she was weaving a bracelet on her porch, a deep voice called, "Hey, Lizzie! Come here and help me with this for a second."

She hesitated. She was at the hard part of the weaving and really didn't want to stop. But she'd been raised with her parents' admonishments to be nice to the poor elderly man across the street. He had no family, and no-family people were the first on her mother's cookie list at Christmas time. So Lizette dusted off the back of her shorts and walked across the street. Behind Mr. Tallon's roof, trees loomed up crooked and tall. Her unease at the sight of them was second nature, instinctive.

Mr. Tallon was half inside an old truck, the hood above him a thin sheet of rust-laced metal. "My name's Lizette," she said. "Never Lizzie or Liz. Zettie's okay, though."

He scrutinized her while a fly buzzed her nose, smiled, and then nodded. "Right, Lizzie. Do an old man a favor and pick that up for me, will you, please?"

She looked from his blackened finger to a wrench lying on the concrete, just under the bulbous bumper of the old truck. She didn't want to pick it up on the account he'd just ignored her perfectly polite request, but Mr. Tallon stood on only one leg. For whatever reason, he hadn't put on his prosthetic that morning. The right leg of his overalls hung limp and flat, and a crutch leaned against the truck door.

So she retrieved the wrench, wrinkling her nose at the black smudge it left on her palm. He grunted when she started to walk off. "Can't do this by myself, Lizzie. Can you grab this hose—right here—and pinch hard? No, harder. Don't be afraid of getting dirty. It'll wash off."

This was from the man whose hands were so lined with grease, she was sure five whole bottles of her mother's favorite lemon dish soap couldn't remove it all.

But she pinched hard, leaving Mr. Tallon free to beat on something at the back of the engine. Then she went and fetched a hammer, screwed in a screw, jiggled a tube, and finally started the truck at Mr. Tallon's request. It roared to life, the hot vinyl seat beneath her shuddering with power.

Climbing out of the truck, she returned Mr. Tallon's grin.

"You did it, Mr. Tallon!"

"We did it, Lizzie. And you can call me Tallon, everybody does."

"Sure thing, Mr. Tallon."

After the water in the sink finally ran clean over her hands, Lizette ate chicken salad sandwiches, chips, and green grapes with her mom. Once they were finished, she looked thoughtfully at the leftovers, thinking of the thrill of the seat rumbling beneath her.

"Can I take these to Mr. Tallon?"

Her mom paused mid-tea-sip. Then, very slowly, she lowered the glass to the table, setting it carefully in the same sweat ring. "That's very nice of you, sweetie. But you know not to take even a step behind the back of his house, don't you?"

"I know, Mom." Lizette resisted the urge to roll her eyes. Everybody knew not to enter the woods; it wasn't like she was two. But then at that thought, she pressed her lips thin as gum sticks. A two-year-old boy had been lost to the woods last week. His mother had gotten distracted loading up the car, and he'd wandered into the fringes of a tree line. He'd been gone before his mother could rush in and grab him. Bystanders had pulled her, screaming his name, back to safety.

There was no point in going in and looking for him. People that entered the woods didn't come out. It had been that way for the last one hundred years, ever since the Forest Dwellers had come.

When she returned to Mr. Tallon's, her mother sat out on the front porch and stayed there all afternoon with a book. Lizette knew she had things to do—after all, she'd complained all through lunch about the closet needing to be organized. At first Lizette was annoyed by her Mother's obvious hovering. Until she thought of that mother in the news, screaming and screaming for a child who would never be coming back.

Because she knew it made her mom feel better, she occasionally waved a greasy hand at her. It didn't, of course, have anything to do with the leafy branches swaying gently behind the house and Lizette's unease whenever she caught their movement from the corner of her eye.

They were working on a station wagon when it happened. A stiff breeze blew a clump of leaves against her sneaker. Just three, four leaves, attached to a bit of tree smaller than her pinky. Lizette froze.

It had come from the woods. She waited, her toes clenched in her shoes, for a Forest Dweller to burst out of the leaves. It would grab her and take her away, to do who knew what to her. Use her like a slave, experiment on her? Eat her?

But before anything else could happen—besides the panic attack in her chest—the leaves were pushed farther across the concrete yard as the breeze picked up again. They made a *scree-scree* noise until they came to rest against one of the tire towers.

"Them leaves won't hurt you." Mr. Tallon nodded in assurance. "Leaves are a small thing, and the life goes out of them quickly when separated from a tree. Now a branch, it holds life a bit longer in its sap. You avoid the branches."

"Yes, sir." He didn't have to tell her twice.

"Now, you see this here valve?"

She stepped up on an overturned milk crate and peered down into the station wagon's engine. It was missing pieces, and even to her untrained eyes, looked wrong. She followed her neighbor's instructions and had the pleasure of helping to bring it all back together, like fixing a broken heart.

This, she decided, was even better than weaving the hardest bracelet in the world.

Mr. Tallon was taking a nap. It was something he liked to do during the hottest part of the day. Car fixing, he told her, was for in the morning, and in the evening. Not when the sun baked down on concrete, making you hotter than fat pigs in fleece blankets. Lizette wandered his front pad, picking up random tools and oil-stained rags. She didn't mind his frequent napping, as she didn't like the way he looked or acted when he got too hot—shoulders sagging, with his hand kneading at his chest through his coveralls.

Lizette wiped her arm across her sweaty forehead. Maybe Mr. Tallon was right about the napping thing. She was about to cross the street for the comfort of couch, air conditioning, and afternoon TV when a car turned the corner.

A Greenery Defense police car. It drove by without any lights on, and Lizette scrutinized its green and white body as it passed. Before this summer, she wouldn't have appreciated the choppy bumper and sculpted wheel wells. Cars like these made a statement: Watch me.

And she did, as it pulled up to a trim yellow house to the left of Lizette's, the only other neighbor on their sparsely-populated street. No surprise there. The Greenery Defense officers checked in on Mrs. Crenshaw at least once a month. She was on probation for growing more than the legally allowed one plant per home. Lizette's dad had said if she were caught again, she could serve time.

The Forest Dwellers could only appear where there was a significant amount of greenery, which was why no one had lawns anymore. Just concrete, or shredded up rubber turf. Some people painted their concrete fun colors, though never a shade of green. All of the Earth's flora was ruled by the Forest Dwellers now, and no one wanted to see a reminder of that every day; the woods that ringed the town were more than enough.

Two officers knocked on Mrs. Crenshaw's door. Then three more times until she finally answered. Even from where Lizette stood, she could see the sour expression on the woman's face as she surveyed her visitors. Her cardigan was wrapped nearly twice around her thin body and secured with firmly crossed arms.

She jerked her head in the direction of her garage, and the officers disappeared around the back of it. A few minutes later, they reappeared, one lugging a large tomato plant in a white bucket. Mrs. Crenshaw banged through her screen door, her arms flying as she began to berate the police officer.

No longer bothered about being hot or bored, Lizette scooted across the street and jumped up the steps to her front porch.

"I know my rights! I'm allowed one plant per household. So you turn right around and take Red Gold back immediately!"

Hunkered behind a rocking chair, Lizette smothered a laugh. Mrs. Crenshaw named her plants? But then again, Lizette had been calling the green convertible Mr. Tallon had recently acquired Avocado these last several weeks.

"Yes, ma'am," said the officer not carrying the tomato plant. "You are allowed one. But this one violates the height rule, and by law, it must be confiscated."

"The height rule?" Mrs. Crenshaw screeched. "Now you're just making that up, admit it!"

"No, ma'am." Lizette thought he sounded like he needed one of Mr. Tallon's afternoon naps. "Here is some literature from the Greenery Defense Council. Read it, and you'll see we are perfectly within the law."

Mrs. Crenshaw took the pamphlet and did read it, right there. Her shoulders slumped, and Lizette suddenly felt bad for laughing at her.

"Can I at least have the tomatoes so that they don't go to waste?"

The officers exchanged looks. Then the closest one shrugged and stepped back from the bucket. "Sure, just make it quick."

There were a lot of tomatoes on the bushy plant and as Mrs. Crenshaw gathered them off the vines, trying to cradle them to her chest, some fell from her hands and bounced onto the concrete. Lizette shifted uncomfortably; Mrs. Crenshaw was also on her mom's Christmas cookie list.

Beside their front door was a battered basket. Lizette dumped out her dad's old work boots and a half-deflated soccer ball, then hopped off her porch and jogged over the expanse of rubber chips separating the two houses. She held the basket out, afraid maybe she was doing the wrong thing, especially when she saw tears in the older woman's eyes. But she placed the tomatoes in the basket as Lizette held it, until the plant was bare of color and the basket bursting with it.

"Sorry, ma'am," one of the officers muttered. "We'll be by the normal time next month."

The police car backed out and glided away. Mrs. Crenshaw sniffed and transferred her attention to Lizette. "Well. Are you just going to stand there, or are you going to help me eat a tomato sandwich?"

Lizette tapped her bottom lip. "Do you have mayonnaise?"

"Do I have mayonnaise?" The older woman rolled her eyes. "What kind of question is that? C'mon."

Lizette followed her into her house—cool, hallelujah—reflecting that making friends with her elderly neighbors really kept life entertaining.

Lizette sat on the sticky vinyl seat of the school bus, wishing it was the seat of the convertible, Avocado. Mr. Tallon promised if she helped him get it running, she could drive it around his concrete pad, just like the other three cars she had helped him with during the summer.

It was now two months into the school year, and Lizette's life was vastly different than what it had been before the summer break. Her parents listened in bemusement at supper when she talked about the difference between muscle cars and luxury sedans. Her mother thought it was a phase that would pass, just like Lizette's princess and horse crazes had. Her dad only laughed and said he hoped not because good mechanics were expensive. He thought how handy would it be if his very own daughter could tinker under a hood?

The school bus stopped before reaching Lizette's house, drawing her from imagining the convertible fixed up and gleaming. Sitting on the left side of the aisle, she couldn't see the reason why, but prickles raced beneath her skin as the kids on the right side pressed close to the glass. She stood up and wiggled past her seat mate, then raced down the aisle.

Seeing the whirling flash of neon lights, Lizette thought at first that Mrs. Crenshaw had broken the one-plant rule. Since the Red Gold debacle, Lizette visited her other neighbor several times a week. She was growing a cucumber plant now, and Lizette enjoyed peeking through the vines and seeing the green vegetables slowly lengthening.

Her own parents wanted nothing to do with any type of vegetation. As a result, Lizette still hadn't touched the plant. She was, as she'd told Mrs. Crenshaw, working up to it.

Lizette's stomach dropped as she arrived at the front of the bus—it wasn't a Greenery Defense Council patrol car but an ambulance. It sat on the side of the road, neon lights swirling faster than the rides at the local fair.

"Looks like they're at your neighbor's house, the one with all the cars," the bus driver said.

Lizette took the steps in one hop. She jiggled impatiently until the bus driver hit the lever and the doors crinkled back, blasting her with heat and the scent of hot pavement.

A familiar figure stood by the open ambulance doors. "Mom!" Lizette said. "Is he…is he…?" She couldn't get out the rest of her question.

"No, honey. He's had a heart attack, but he's alive. They're going to take him to the hospital now."

Her mother's arm tight along her shoulders, Lizette peeked into the back of the ambulance. Mr. Tallon lay on a gurney. An oxygen mask was strapped to his face. He looked pale.

His eyes opened, and seeing her, his hand moved on his

chest. The school bus eased slowly by, and part of Lizette wished she were still on it, were one of the kids whose best friend wasn't lying on a gurney.

"Can I go with him?" she asked one of the medics. The other had just climbed in and slammed the driver's door.

The medic looked up from adjusting a tube running from Mr. Tallon's arm to a bag of fluid. "Are you family?"

"Yes," Lizette answered promptly.

Her mother squeezed her tighter. "He's practically family. He and Lizette are close."

The medic looked down at Mr. Tallon. "All right, but just her. You're welcome to follow us to the hospital, ma'am."

"Of course. Thank you." Mrs. Turner hugged Lizette and rubbed her back. "I'll be right behind you guys." Then pulling back she asked, "Are you sure you want to do this, Lizette?" she murmured. "It might be…too much."

Lizette swallowed. She was terrified that once the ambulance doors shut with her inside, she would see something she didn't want to see. She glanced into the ambulance again. The white sheet spread across Mr. Tallon highlighted the absence of his missing leg. The silly man hadn't been wearing his prosthetic again.

He needed her to look after him. And that meant if she had to sit in that small space and will him not to die, then she'd do it. Once she was securely strapped into a fold-out seat, the ambulance pulled away. The sirens wailed and the lights flashed, but it still didn't feel fast enough. She held Mr. Tallon's hand, willing the warmth in hers to somehow seep into his.

Her arm lay on the edge of the ambulance bed, and the bracelet around her wrist looked shockingly out of place against the white sheet. Made of metal, it gleamed like oil floating on the surface of water—purple, blue, and green, with tinges of gold. Mr. Tallon had given it to her as a going back to school present, and Lizette hadn't taken it off once.

It wasn't as pretty as the bracelets she liked to weave, but it made her think about the roar of car engines and the fact that they were roaring because of her. And that...that was better than any combination of pink and purple. She gripped Mr. Tallon's hand tighter.

They hadn't been driving nearly long enough when they started to slow.

"What's going on? Why are we stopping?" she asked the medic across from her.

"Not sure." He set down the clipboard he'd been recording numbers on. "I'll be right back."

He went up front. Lizette looked anxiously at Mr. Tallon. His skin looked less brown and more like ash. His breathing was shallow and uneven. She gently laid his hand down and unbuckled. She leaned forward between the front seats, and looking out the windshield, she didn't have to ask what was wrong—she could see for herself.

A large branch lay across the road. Thick and profusely leafy.

"Can you drive across it?" Lizette asked.

"Maybe," said the medic who was driving. "But what if it gets caught?"

Lizette frowned, thinking of the implications of a large branch being dragged through town. Pandemonium for sure.

"We'll have to reverse." The two medics exchanged grim glances, striking a sharp arrow of fear into Lizette's gut.

"But...but then you'll have to go—"

"The longer way around. We have no choice." The driver hit his flashers and threw it into reverse. Lizette looked over her shoulder; through the oval holes in the back doors she could see her mother already backing up, giving the ambulance room.

Her gaze fell from the windows to Mr. Tallon—the oxygen mask, the tubes, the wires attached to his chest. The fear-arrow dug deeper.

"No, just wait. Please." Lizette lurched for the small side

door.

"Hey!" one of the medics called, but it was too late. She was out. She heard the squeal of her mother's brakes and her name frantically shouted; Lizette ignored it.

She approached the branch with quick steps, twisting her bracelet nervously around and around her wrist. Oddly enough, she wasn't *really* afraid of the branch. She was more afraid of what was happening inside Mr. Tallon's body and what more could go wrong the longer they delayed.

But her brain remembered that she should be very afraid. It screamed signals at her legs to run, her arms to pump. Adrenaline flooded through her, and the hands she thrust out toward the branch shook. Her first tug ended up doing nothing but ripping away a handful of leaves. They weren't attached as firmly as she'd thought they'd be. She let them go, and they drifted to the ground as paper-light as they'd felt.

This time she grabbed a smaller branch shooting off from the main one. This was her first experience with touching bark, and she found it rough and gritty. She began to drag it to the side of the road that bordered the woods. She'd toss it into the shallow concrete ditch that ran beside the woods. Once they reached the hospital, a call would be placed to the Greenery Defense Council. They would come and torch the branch, reducing it to harmless ashes.

Almost there.

She slid the end of the branch down the concrete slope. As she lifted her arm higher in preparation to heave it away, a shadow rose from the leaves.

But no...not a shadow. Shadows are insubstantial things. This was changing into the color of black tar and gathering substance until a humanoid shape stood in front of her. Lizette looked down, because she couldn't look up, and she found that the Forest Dweller's feet had very long toes, tipped with very sharp nails.

She sensed a gathering in the air above her and by instinct

threw her arms over her head. She caught sight of an open mouth descending (and teeth, so many teeth), and then several things happened at once.

A pulse from her wrist, a scream from her mother, the alien recoiling, bounding into the forest, the slap of feet, the feel of her mother's arms, holding tight tight tight.

"Get in!" The medic opened the ambulance door and hustled them into the passenger-side seat. Lizette sat on her mother's lap, cramped, her knees digging into the door's molding. Their own car sat abandoned in the road, lights still flashing and the driver's-side door open.

Lizette's mother held her head against her chest, like when she was small and cried over thunder, and as they roared away, Lizette could feel the slamming beat of her mother's heart.

Hospital waiting rooms were horrible places. If only she could be sweltering under a car hood right now. Or even helping her mother organize closets. Instead, Lizette sat in an uncomfortable chair, flipping through magazines of smiling people whose white teeth were grating on her nerves.

Very quietly, she tore a jagged line right through a woman's perfect, happy face.

"Are you the Jamisons?"

Lizette quickly flapped the magazine shut. A worn-looking nurse stood a few feet away. After Lizette's mother confirmed they were, she beckoned them to follow her. "We just finished an examination. He's doing much better since he arrived yesterday."

Lizette's heart felt lighter as her sneakers squeaked down the hall. But as they entered the room and she saw the forest of equipment on poles and wires and heard the whoosh and beeping of it all working, some of her newfound buoyancy leaked away.

Mr. Tallon still looked pale and small in the middle of it all. His eyes were closed, and Lizette and her mother approached the bed quietly.

"Mr. Tallon, you have visitors," the nurse announced brightly.

Lizette gripped her mother's hand as his eyelids fluttered open, shut against the light and then opened again.

"Lizzie...Mrs. Jamison. It's good to see you both."

Lizette's voice felt stuck in her throat as her mother replied for them both. This was much better? She thought he looked the same as when she first saw him in the ambulance.

In a dry voice, Mr. Tallon asked if he could have a few minutes alone with Lizette.

"Sure." Lizette's mother squeezed her shoulder. "I'll be right outside the door, honey."

Once she was gone, Lizette blurted, "I saw a Forest Dweller." Then she grimaced. She should have asked him how he was, though really, what was the point in that? He looked like he felt terrible.

The skin around Mr. Tallon's eyes crinkled more than his lips did, which was his version of a smile. Seeing it eased some of Lizette's worry for him. "I heard. All the nurses were talking about it. Every person who's ever encountered a Forest Dweller that close has been taken."

"That's right." Lizette moved closer to him and was comforted to see there was still some oil lingering around his fingernails—this was the Mr. Tallon she knew. "And I think I know why it didn't."

She held up her wrist. The metal bracelet he'd given her slid down her arm.

"What is this, Mr. Tallon? Why did it stop the Forest Person?"

He smiled, his eyes briefly dropping shut. "You're a smart girl, Lizzie. And I owe you my life. For that, I thank you."

She waited for more, and when it wasn't forthcoming said, "You're welcome," to be polite, and because she would have done it again if she had to, even now knowing how scary the

Forest People were. "But what about this bracelet?" She tapped her wrist.

He was quiet for a bit, taking deep breaths. When he started talking again, it wasn't about the bracelet, but she didn't feel let down. Instead, she had a feeling he was just working up to the answer she wanted.

"The Forest People have been here so long, it seems like we've forgotten that they don't really belong. Can you imagine, Lizzie, that yards used to be made of grass? That there were trees in them, offering shade and places for children to climb?"

She shook her head; no, she couldn't imagine it.

"We warred with them for years. But the forest was their domain—or anyplace that had a significant amount of vegetation. And you know why we couldn't rout them?"

"Yes," Lizette said, reciting what she'd learned in world history. "They have shields that our weapons can't penetrate. Our gunfire bounces off, and even bombs explode against them."

"Their technology is...way beyond our capability." Mr. Tallon took a moment to draw breath. Lizette's eyes flicked to the monitors and their squiggly lines and numbers she couldn't interpret. "This shield can sense what is harmful and repulses it, even plastic weapons. But the metal that you wear on your wrist, Lizzie...*it* repulses *them*. I've been working on it for years. And with more work, I think I can eventually get it through the shield they've put up."

"So..." She stared at the bracelet looping her wrist. "Are you going to make a weapon? Like a gun?"

This time, his eyes nearly disappeared in all the crinkles. "Not a gun. A car. A very special car."

Lizette's heart jumped in a way she was sure the monitors would have recorded. "A car..."

He nodded. "A car that will protect the driver by safely bringing them through the shield. A car made out of a metal that the Forest People want nothing to do with. And maybe...

yes, a weaponized car."

"I want to help," Lizette blurted.

"You have been helping me, Lizzie. All summer."

She twitched her hand impatiently. "Yes, but I want to help with taking our world back from the Forest People."

"That's a long way from happening."

"But that's the point, right?" She gripped the bed railings, imagining what it would be like to drive into the woods and be untouchable. "To try and make a difference?"

"One day, yes."

"Then I want in." Her brain was already shuffling through designs, mixing the cars sitting on Mr. Tallon's pad with cars she looked up on the Internet. Some type of vehicle that sat high, with big wheels to clear whatever things you would encounter in a forest.

A chuckle rumbled from Mr. Tallon. "This isn't a spy movie, kid. And I think...I think you were in the day you picked up that wrench, Lizette."

She grinned back. "I think you're right. Tallon."

Then they were both quiet, looking out the window at their world of brick and concrete and rubber, dreaming of a world where one day, trees were for climbing and not fearing.

Juliet Silver and the Seeker of the Depths

by Wendy Nikel

When Wendy Nikel isn't traveling in time, exploring magical islands, or investigating mysterious phenomena, she enjoys a quiet life near Utah's Wasatch Mountains with her husband and sons. She has a degree in elementary education, a fondness for road trips, and a terrible habit of forgetting where she's left her cup of tea. Her short fiction has been published by AE, Daily Science Fiction, *and others, and she is a member of the SFWA. For more info, visit wendynikel.com.*

Juliet Silver raised the doorknocker—a gilded image of a tentacled monster—and let it fall, sending a metallic *clang* up and down the deserted city street. Sunlight streamed over her, peeking out from the horizon with golden tendrils that seemed to tap her on the shoulder, to question what she was doing on the ground when the skies were so crisp and clear, so perfect for sailing.

As she waited, Juliet's fingers twitched at the hilt of her sword. It'd been months since she'd seen the sunrise from land, and she ached to rise above the dingy scraps of garbage and the hungry rats of the city's alleys. But Stenson, a rival captain of the airship the *Bearer of Bad News*, was insistent that she meet him today, this morning, at this particular shop.

Whatever the old codger wanted, it had better be worth her time.

When the bolt finally slid across, the iron door opened with a groan of its massive hinges. The door was large enough for a steam carriage to power through, and likely many did over the course of a week. Upon entering, however, Juliet's attention was drawn not to the carriages, nor even to the new-fangled bits and baskets, snares and rudders that she might have used to upgrade her own ship, the *Realm of Impossibility*.

Instead, she was drawn to an item sitting solidly in the center of the workshop, stout and bulbous and crouching like a frog. Its outer shell gleamed so that within its curves and panels, her reflection stared back at her. The metal was cold to her touch.

"Meets your approval, Captain?"

Juliet caught Stenson's reflection as he stepped beside her. She didn't turn but proceeded to walk about the contraption, examining every inch of it.

"For exploring underseas, I take it?" She knocked upon its side. "I have to wonder how well it would hold up to the water pressure."

"Just as well as it's sitting here before you. The iron-welder who built it is one of the city's finest."

"I'd much like to meet him."

"He's a solitary type. Doesn't care much for pleasantries or small talk."

Curious that he would make Stenson's acquaintance then. The old man was quite the gossipmonger. Juliet wisely kept this opinion to herself.

"And the headlights?" She cast a skeptical glance at the blue domed lights. They hardly looked as though they'd cut through fog, much less a murky sea.

"Mostly for show. This craft has something even better, Miss Silver." The older captain reached forward and sprung the door open. Its pneumatic hinges hissed. Inside, a flat screen blinked to life. "Sonar. Even if the windows are filled with grime, you'll be able to see any obstacles before you as clear as a pretty spring day."

"And what do you intend to do with this little fish?"

"I intend to give her to you."

Ah, now the real bargaining would begin. Stenson wasn't the generous type; Juliet wondered what the real price would be. "And what do you want from me?"

"I want the treasure of the *Argonaut*—the largest haul of stolen gold and gems anyone has ever seen, lost beneath the Sea of Prosperity. And I want you to fetch it for me."

"I'm not a dog." Juliet brushed past him, making her way for the door.

"No, you're not. You're a shrewd captain, one who's daring enough to go where none has before."

Juliet hesitated, her hand upon the door. Well, he wasn't *wrong*.

"And wise enough to know that this little fish—" Stenson said, tapping the hull of the underwater vehicle "—could make you rich beyond your dreams. We both know that the *Argonaut* wasn't the first airship to plummet from the sky into troubled waves, though its treasure is the only one I wish to stake a claim upon. After delivering it to me and receiving your share—"

"Sixty percent."

"Thirty, and don't interrupt. After receiving your share, this little *Seeker of the Depths* will be yours to do with as you wish. It won't take a daring young lass such as yourself long to make a fine fortune in underwater salvaging. I'd do it myself if I were a few decades younger."

Juliet considered this as she resumed her perusal of the

machine. The interior was small, intended for only one diver. The rest of her crew would have to wait above the surface; she didn't trust anyone else to the task. She'd be lying if she said that the coffers of wealth in the belly of the *Argonaut* didn't tempt her.

"Are you daring enough?"

It was Stenson's voice that spoke aloud, an echo of the question already swirling about her heart and mind. A question to which she already knew the answer.

"Yes."

The *Seeker* was strapped to the *Realm of Impossibility* with great lengths of chain that clanked and rattled like bones. All along the dock, crews neglected their own ships to watch the activity about Juliet's. She stood before the gangplank, arms crossed over her chest and feet planted, daring them with her scowl to come forth and stake their claim. The *Argonaut's* treasure was, after all, pirates' booty, and there were plenty among the air pilots who'd fallen victim to it.

Geoffries, her first mate, was the only one who approached. "You know they won't raise arms against you today. They'll wait until you've returned with the prize… if you return at all."

"Do you doubt me, Geoffries?"

"Not I, Captain. But they don't know you as I do. Undoubtedly most expect that your little bronze fish will sink to the depths with you in its belly, and neither of you will be seen again."

"Fools."

"The ship's prepared, Captain," a crewmember called out.

Juliet took a final, defiant glance about her and—with firm footfalls upon the grated gangplank—took her place on the *Realm of Impossibility*.

The Sea of Prosperity was a misnomer at best, a putrid soup

of grease at worst. Even the skies above it were a swamp of foul-smelling brown. Not a single bird traversed the clouds, and neither did Juliet expect to find anything living beneath the water's stagnant surface.

Geoffries looked on as Juliet strapped herself into the *Seeker's* chamber. It was some sort of recklessness, perhaps, that would lead a woman to crawl into that round, iron coffin and allow herself to be lowered into the sea. But she'd tested the equipment herself, and if all went well, she'd return in just a few hours. In the meantime, she'd simply crawl along the seabed, picking through the who-knows-what she'd find there until she uncovered the wreckage of the *Argonaut* and the treasure hidden within it.

"All set, Captain?"

"Aye, aye!"

The door hissed shut and sealed, leaving Juliet in such an absolute silence that—had it not been for the movement seen through the window—she'd have thought the outside world had ceased to exist. With an abrupt, jarring motion and the faraway clanking of iron chains, the *Seeker of the Depths* descended.

Murky water closed over the window. Glistening particles floated in the rays of sun that somehow cut through the layers of silt and sediment. These bright specks of light grew sparser as the vessel descended and the darkness deepened. Finally, the *Seeker* settled on the ocean floor. Outside the window, all was black and still, save for the occasional flick of a phosphorescent tail fin.

Juliet flicked on the sonar. She pulled handles and turned levers to operate the vessel's spidery legs, dragging it meter by meter across the sea floor. The sonar flickered with outlines of flat expanses, jagged cliffs, and crevices that seemed to descend into the center of the earth.

Juliet had hardly begun her search when the *Seeker* became stuck. She wrenched at levers and pressed dials, but though the iron mechanisms rattled, the *Seeker* refused to move. Cursing Stenson, Juliet pressed the distress signal.

She sat in the never-changing stillness of the depths, waiting for the chattering of the chain and the lightening of the murk that would indicate the *Realm of Impossibility* was lifting her to the surface, but it never came. Was she too deep for the *Realm* to receive her signal? Had the chain broken somehow? Juliet was just debating her next course of action when the *Seeker* jerked into motion.

She fumbled with the controls. The vessel was moving, but the comforting rattle of its spider legs was missing. Had some sea creature swooped in and gobbled her up? Considering the blackness around her, it seemed possible. Except... the sonar still showed the landscape of the deeps.

Had something crept up and snagged her from behind? If so, there was little she could do about it now, besides being ready when it stopped. She gripped her knife and studied the sonar.

Finally, the *Seeker* reached a cliff wall. Instead of going around it, however, the vessel proceeded through what appeared to be a narrow tunnel. It opened into a vast cavern—a cavern filled with light.

Juliet blinked against the sudden brilliance. The cavern ceiling arched high overhead, glowing with light from thousands, millions, perhaps billions of phosphorescent creatures swimming about. Some were the size of whales, while others were so small that their lights seemed like those of fireflies buzzing about.

Beneath this sea of magnificent creatures was an even more magnificent sight—a city constructed of glass panes, crisscrossed and held up by frames of shining gold. As the *Seeker* drew nearer, Juliet could see the people wandering about inside, people with golden skin coming out of golden houses and walking down golden roads, conversing and carrying on about their lives as if nothing was more natural than living leagues beneath the surface.

A panel opened in the side of the city, and the *Seeker* was carried inside a narrow tunnel—an airlock, in fact—where all the water rushed out around it. Juliet pressed the release button on her craft and jumped out, wielding her knife.

The *Seeker* had indeed been captured from behind by a craft not too unlike it. They shared the same bulbous shape and the same thin, spidery legs, but this one also had front appendages that now held the *Seeker* in place.

"Stenson," Juliet seethed. He must have known about this place, about these people and their craft. How else could his design be so strikingly similar? Had he stolen their ship, or merely the design? Her breath came hot and furious, but she didn't fight as two armed guards grabbed her from behind.

The hatch of the larger craft sprung open, and a man with golden skin and close-cropped hair leaned out. "Take her to the Queen."

"Yes," Juliet said between clenched teeth. "I'd very much like to speak with her."

None of the other structures came near the opulence of the palace, with its shimmering walls. Every inch of it was composed of pearls stacked into bricks, each one perfectly polished and luminescent. Its sprawling courtyard contained innumerous metal sculptures of all types of sea life. These creatures ran by clockwork, rattling and chattering as they stretched and dove and swam through the air.

As the guards led Juliet through the entrance, she took note of the squid whose head made up the capstone and whose tentacles cascaded down either side of the doorway, a skillful piece of metalwork. From there, they entered a cavernous throne room. At the far end, separated by a carpet of tiny, polished shells, sat the Queen. She wore a sparkling robe of fish scales and a crown composed of dozens of tiny fish ribs that rose in intricate whorls to a peak high above her brow. Her face was long and golden and unlined, though her eyes looked old and wise. She was flanked on either side by a pair of ladies in lavish gowns and bright, bejeweled headdresses.

Juliet shook free from the guards' grasp and dipped her head in a reverent bow.

"What have you brought me?" The Queen's voice was clear and crisp as glass, though in it, also, was the sharp edge of the same.

"Please, Your Majesty," Juliet said before the guards could speak. "I am Juliet Silver, captain of the airship the *Realm of Impossibility*, explorer of the skies."

"What purpose would an airship captain have in the dominion of the water-dwellers? Surely you know of the truce and punishment due to those who break it."

Juliet seethed silently at Stenson. "I knew of no such truce, nor—truly—of your glorious city's existence."

"How is it possible you've never heard of the great and powerful city of Prosperia? Has it been so long since we closed our gates that all have forgotten our existence?"

Juliet stood silently. Certainly, she'd heard of the undersea city of Prosperia, but it was a myth, a legend, a bedtime story to amuse small children. To find that it was true was akin to discovering the mythical Bandybell's lair.

"Liska." The Queen turned to one of her ladies-in-waiting. "How many years have passed since our isolation?"

"Five hundred twenty-two, Your Highness."

"Hardly a bat of the eye... yet perhaps for you short-lived folk with your warring and wandering, that would be long enough to forget. Still, I find it hard to believe this warning would not have been passed down from the older, more experienced captains to the younger ones."

"Indeed." It would certainly explain why Stenson—superstitious man that he was—had no desire to dive beneath the waves himself. He'd certainly have heard the stories, though Juliet, a newcomer to the skies and without a mentor to guide her, had not. Had he hoped Juliet might slip past the Propserians and recover the *Argonaut's* treasure? Or was this all a ruse to get rid of her? "Well, now that we've established my innocence, if you could return me to my vessel—"

"My dear girl." The Queen rose to her feet and cast her deep shadow upon Juliet. "Ignorance is not akin to innocence. In order to preserve our isolation, we are quite unable to allow your return."

"I see." Juliet narrowed her eyes. "And what is my punishment to be?"

"It just so happens that this is a year of sacrifice to the kraken. I trust you'll make him a fine morsel at festival time. Until then..." She turned to one of the ladies on her right. "Sofia, please bind her. Then the guards shall take her to her cell."

The lady the Queen spoke to rose, dipped her hand in a pocket, and pulled out a length of delicate chain. She bound Juliet's hands with nimble fingers and from another pocket procured a tiny lock, with which she secured the restraints. She pulled upon them to test their strength and—as she did so—a small sliver of metal dropped into Juliet's palms.

Any thought that this slip might have been inadvertent left Juliet's mind when the woman met her eyes. Then she turned and announced to the Queen, "The prisoner is bound."

The Queen nodded, and with that, the guards led Juliet away.

The cell beneath the ocean floor was spongy and smelled of rotting fish. Juliet stood in the dark, turning over in her hands the tiny lock-pick—for that's what the lady Sofia had slipped to her—as she waited. For what, she wasn't certain. On the surface, it'd have been the darkest part of night, but here the hours stretched on without a single variance of the phosphorescent glow that bled in streaks through the grated window high above her, nor to the pacing of the guard beyond her door.

She'd just resigned herself to try to get a small bit of sleep when the sound of a commotion in the hall outside her door sent a rush of adrenaline through her, dulling any thought of slumber.

Immediately, she set out to pick the lock on the door. Gears within it turned and the bolt retracted. The corridor beyond was empty, save for a slim figure in a long gown, heels, and a massive, jeweled headdress, carrying a small jar with one of the phosphorescent creatures swimming about in it.

Lady Sofia.

"Quickly!" Sofia said. "The guard will return any moment."

Juliet followed her through winding pathways, their feet squishing on the soggy dungeon floor. When the lady paused in a quiet corner to catch her breath, Juliet's tongue loosened.

"Who are you? And why are you helping me?"

"Sofia... the royal tinker. And I'm not helping you; you're helping me... to escape."

"Escape? Why?"

"You think we enjoy being trapped down here with no contact with the outside world? Our isolation was based on the Queen's own emotional pride alone, not any logical rationale. She only cut us off to punish him for leaving." She set off again down the dark corridor, and Juliet followed on her heels.

"Who? Who left?"

"Her son, the heir. When her search for him proved futile, she flew into a rage and commanded Prosperia be cut off from the world above. Now hush, or someone will hear."

"Do you have a weapon?" Juliet whispered. Without her sword or knife, she felt positively helpless, completely at the mercy of this overdressed aristocrat. Sofia reached up to her headdress and pulled out a hat pin the length of her hand and passed it to Juliet, who took it with some skepticism. It was no dagger, for certain, but it was better than nothing.

They turned a corner and Sofia screeched, nearly backing up directly into Juliet. The guard had returned by another route and was blocking their path, his sword at the ready.

Juliet stepped in front of Sofia, brandishing the hairpin. The guard smirked, obviously unimpressed. Juliet lunged. With a quick, well-placed jab, she pierced the gap between his chest plate and helmet, causing him to cry out and giving her the element of surprise needed to knock his sword from his hand. Finally, a proper weapon!

"Lie down on the ground," she instructed him, "and count to three hundred. If we meet again, I will not be so merciful."

Juliet urged Sofia on, and the bewildered woman took off down the corridor once again. Juliet paused now and again to glance behind her and see that the guard was still lying prone as Sofia rushed further ahead. She climbed a flight of stairs, and Juliet rushed to follow, blinking as her eyes adjusted to the brilliance of the phosphorescent light.

At the top of the steps, Juliet stopped short.

Sofia stood before her with a guard's blade pressed to her throat. On either side of her stood a dozen other guards, their swords drawn. Juliet hesitated, her mind racing to devise a strategy that would leave Sofia unharmed. She was just about to step forward when the guards shifted, parting in the center to admit the Queen herself.

"I see that I've a traitor in my midst. Dear Sofia... I do hope the kraken doesn't mind if his feast begins early; I could hardly hope to keep you contained in the locks and chains you designed yourself."

"If you lay a hand on her..." Juliet began, holding her weapon steady.

The Queen raised her eyebrows and placed a hand upon her chin, as if amused. On the third finger, she bore a dark ring with a design Juliet recognized from the palace's curved arch—the kraken. "Go on. What shall you do?"

Juliet lowered her sword, her eyes transfixed on the ring. The palace entrance wasn't the first place she'd seen that design.

"You will allow Sofia and me to return to the surface unhindered, and I, in turn, will tell you where to find your son."

Juliet stood on the deserted city street once again and raised the ten-legged doorknocker—the gilded kraken. Beside her stood two women, dressed in long cloaks and hoods to protect their golden skin from the rays of the early morning sun.

The *Realm of Impossibility's* crew had been surprised at Juliet's return after they believed they'd lost her, and even more surprised at the two strange women she'd brought with her. Juliet had held off on answering their questions, promising she'd explain all once she'd held up her end of the bargain.

The bolt slid across and the door opened with a *creak*. This time, it was not Stenson who opened it, but a lean man wearing a smock, long gloves, and an iron-welder's mask over his face. Upon seeing the three in the doorway, the iron-welder slowly raised his mask, exposing his golden skin.

"Mother?"

The Queen rushed forward to embrace him. Juliet and Sofia hung back, though Juliet could see how the tinker's eyes danced about the workroom, taking in all the tools and metalwork there. The *Realm*, too, had fascinated the Queen's lady-in-waiting, and Juliet had spent much of their journey back to the city explaining the airship's inner workings to her.

"Let's leave them to their reunion," she whispered to Sofia.

They waited beside the iron door, watching the carriages bustling past and people walking to the market as the city awakened to a new day.

"I'm sorry you lost your vessel," Sofia said.

"It wasn't mine. Not yet anyway."

"Will its owner hold you accountable for its loss, then?"

"Perhaps." If Stenson wanted the *Seeker* back, he'd have to retrieve it from the Queen himself. As for the *Argonaut* and its treasure, when Juliet had questioned her earlier, Sofia verified that the wreck had already been picked apart by Prosperian scavengers. They'd used every bit of metal for repairs of their underwater city.

"What are your plans now, as a free woman?" Juliet asked, breaking the silence.

"I... I don't know." Sofia fiddled with the buttons and levers on her belt. The metal jangled like a song and glimmered in the sun. "I hadn't dared to hope for anything beyond escape."

"I've a proposition for you, then." Juliet spied an airship on the horizon and shielded her eyes against the sun. "The *Realm of Impossibility* could use a good tinker on board, someone to help out when the mechanical parts require repairs. Tell me, how do you feel about the skies?"

Sofia looked up from her belt, startled. Then, she, too, raised her eyes to the blue sky, and slowly a smile spread across her golden face.

The Biting Sands
by Doug C. Souza

Doug C. Souza has always had a love for the art of storytelling. His favorite genres are science fiction and fantasy, but he enjoys a good yarn of any variety. His story "Mountain Screamers" was published in Asimov's *and received an honorable mention to be included in* The Year's Best Science Fiction 2014. *Doug teaches in Modesto, California, where he lives with his wonderful wife and daughter. You can find him at dougcsouza.com.*

The Haze stays low to the earth as it hunts. Reaching out with wispy limbs, the amber mist rolls across the plain. Still miles away, it has not sensed me yet. But I know the Haze will come for me. And I know I can't escape.

Will the monstrous cloud devour me in one fell swoop? Or will it drain me in slow pulses?

No one ever returns from the Haze.

Well, they return, but not with life in their eyes.

I suck in a deep breath while the air around me is clean. Early morning sun warms the ground and nourishes the Haze. The deadly cloud slows as it nears a herd of grazing sheep at the dry creek bed. It lingers among the ignorant animals and then floats away.

The Haze only feeds on people—and it won't settle for anything less.

I untie the cord across the satchel at my hip and reach inside. My heart skips a beat, and I brace for the Haze. My breath shakes.

The cows just beyond the fences stir but do not panic. The Haze will pass them by, too. Then it will pass through the rows of apple trees and the fields of yams.

The air is different up here than underground—not rich with the scent of earth and life. I can taste the emptiness as I breathe it in.

My crooked leg burns from my trek below, but I will not crouch. Falling to my knees and crying is not for me. Sha-shen will be remembered for her bravery if nothing else.

I'm being dramatic. Well, heroes are dramatic.

The magistrate hesitated after he had recited the terms for my sentence. My refusal to drink the mind-numbing elixir made him uneasy. His eyes searched me, wondering if reiteration was necessary. Few "afflicted" or "damaged" refused the stupefying syrup before exile.

"The drink will ease the pain up there," the magistrate explained while his soft hand slid the vial forward.

"No thank you," I said.

"Very well." He shrugged, waving me along.

"Did you read my Repentance?" I asked.

He glanced at the stack of scrolls and rolled his eyes. He waved me away again, this time in quick motions like I was some pesky gnat.

I didn't budge. "My Repentance," I insisted. "Please take a moment to consider—"

His neck became blotchy and red. "How *dare* you?" he spat. "To imply—" The oil-lamps in the lower chambers were dim, but I saw his neck vein pulsing.

"I can aid in the lower rivers. I have developed plans for better pumps to the surface. Pumps that work through a series of wheels and pulleys, like in the tram system—" I leaned over the short table separating us and pointed at the scrolls just inches from his hand. "It's all there. I can teach the pipesmiths. I can stay and help."

"You have been sentenced," the magistrate said, grabbing my Repentance and shoving it aside. "Damaged," he muttered.

"You are wrong!" I fell forward onto the table.

The magistrate looked away and simply crossed off my name. His hand shook as he made a jagged line.

"Send her out!" he yelled, glaring at my warped hand and crooked leg. "Bring in the next."

Jaggers, the guard assigned to escort me, grunted and pulled me away. The vial filled with the elixir stood in a row with the others. Many pleaded for their lives the way I had. *So clever, Sha-shen, putting your diagrams for the lower rivers and irrigation system in your written testimony,* I scolded myself. If only he had taken a moment to read over my Repentance. If only *someone* had—they'd see I could contribute.

Jaggers nudged me out of the chamber-room. His frown glared down as his large frame loomed above mine. The next of the condemned limped forward with his escort in tow. Like me, he wore an elegant robe donated by the Regulator Office. On him it covered a withering body. On me, the thin fabric draped across me like a breeze. The finest material in all of Spesterra. I hated it—a sad gift to ease the Regulators' guilt.

Or did anyone feel even a sliver of guilt about sending "non-contributors" topside?

"What're you thinking, Sha-shen?" Jaggers asked as we climbed the stairs to the upper passageways. He carried the gas-lantern a bit lower to read my face like a corridor map.

"Nothing."

"I don't trust you to think 'nothing.'" Two days ago Jaggers first showed up at my door. I knew what was happening before he finished explaining: the days were warming, and I was going topside. The years of foolishly hoping it wouldn't happen to me were over.

He peered at me. "Why didn't you take the soother? I mean, even after he ignored your pleas."

"I don't know," I admitted, and stopped to catch my breath at one of the guardrails near the pathway edge. We hadn't gone far, but the day and sentencing had taken its toll. My crooked leg ached. "I just..." I couldn't answer him. Instead, I gazed at the underground river far below. The water's sloshing echoed up the rocky walls. I pictured the wheel in my mind's eye as it turned in the water, pushing a separate pipeline to the irrigation lines. The pump wouldn't replace the pipe-laborers entirely, but it would help ease their burden. My wheel and pump design could even eliminate the need for the storage tanks and reservoirs throughout the mid- and upper-levels of underground Spesterra.

To keep truth, the notion of going to the surface sober first entered my mind as a scientific endeavor: What would it be like to encounter the Haze with all my mental facilities intact?

Jaggers shrugged and guided me toward the tram docks. Onlookers moved out of our way. The condemned were feared more than the sick. The sick might heal.

Jaggers put a hand under my armpit and led me up the steps to the wooden and metal cage. He opened the lift door, handed me the lantern, and cranked us upward. The tram swayed. I snaked my clawed hand through a handhold and held the metal bar under my elbow. Ropes and pulleys squeaked; for a moment I wished the whole thing would just crash down.

Didn't matter. In two days, I'd be heading to the surface.

I knew better than to consider fighting the Haze. Like all Spesterra citizens, I snuck glimpses of the Haze devourings in my youth through surface-side windows. Even people numbed by the elixir flailed their arms or kicked and screamed when the Haze encompassed them.

To no effect.

The hungry mist claimed all within minutes, whether they were exiled in a group of twenty or two.

Except Rafe: he lasted the longest. The clever idiot had wrapped a scarf around his head; he even stole a pair of goggles from one of the maintenance sub-levels.

He didn't fight but stood amidst the thick cloud, observing. Being off-kilter like me—except he had *two* crooked legs—the Regulator Office left him outside after his mind was taken. They didn't need his body. Cursed to roam aimlessly until his body withered and fell.

Once the Haze retreated back into the distant mountains, able-bodied folk were brought back inside. Docile and obedient, they made perfect laborers. Would my drone body be welcomed back, or would they leave me out there to rot?

I shook away the images—no point living the topside nightmare until exile. As one damaged, I hadn't thought about facing the Haze since childhood. Somehow, I had tucked it into the back of my mind.

"Hold," Jaggers said, grabbing my arm.

My fourth mother was waiting at the end of the stairwell. Her eyes burned. They held the light of a rescuer.

The Haze grows transparent as it arrives. Its pace slows and stretches into thin threads as it senses me.

Tree branches from the east orchard crinkle as a breeze kicks up. A lone bird drifts overhead. For a moment, I'm tempted to hobble over to the yam rows and pull a couple. No one could stop me from enjoying a fresh tuber.

A trickle of sweat stings my eye. I blink it away and then stare up after the bird drifting high above. The sky, the blue, I had almost forgotten to gaze at the blue. As an older child, I had realized I'd be sent to the ground, and I swore to look up at the unfiltered blue sky.

The little we see through the surface-side windows in Spesterra do not compare in the least. The glass is thick and warped.

A smile hits me unaided. An electricity trickles across my arms. I shake it away, worried that the Haze is mussing my mind. Altering it already.

No, it's just the sky.

The Haze is still several lengths away, folding and unfolding on itself.

Is this why you covered your face, Rafe, and didn't succumb to the Haze like all the others? Did you want to soak in as much as possible before the Haze took you?

You looked so silly in that scarf and goggles you had snuck out. But I knew you were being brave. You were a hero.

To think, the farmers and land workers visit the landside regularly. They till the dirt and sow the seeds when the Haze is absent. Do they know how lucky they are? The Regulators say we live underground because the Haze won't descend below the dirt-line. But now I understand that merely surviving underground is not enough for life.

I also understand why the farmers are sworn to keep silent about the topside. If more people knew how wonderful it is, they'd demand to come up.

I search the horizon for the surface-side windows and find the lengths of glass reflecting the sunlight. It's difficult to see, but I can make out spectral forms moving behind the windows—I feel eyes on me.

Time to get to work.

My good hand wraps around the glass within my satchel. A moment of doubt taunts me. What if I look silly? What if they think I'm trying to fight the Haze?

No.

I'm a hero, and it's a good plan.

The Haze circles me, closing the gaps. The blue is swallowed by golden brown.

"A friend," I said, pulling out of Jagger's grip and lumbering up the last few steps.

"Five minutes, for rest. Then we go." He remained close behind me.

My fourth mother was not a threat to him. Far older than me, she was nearly all gray. She reached for my good hand and guided me to the nearest bench. Her flesh was soft in my palm.

She pulled me into a hug. My fourth mother was very tactile, never shying away from her wards. Even my being sixteen seasons, she made me feel like a lamb. In her arms, I felt her strength course through me.

"When?" she asked. We sat near the back of the cable-tram port.

A mid-level digger slid farther down the long bench. He wasn't bothered by me. He was eyeing Jaggers. No one enjoyed random encounters with people from the Regulator Office.

"Two days," I said, my good foot absentmindedly drawing a circle in the dirt.

My fourth mother tenderly smothered my drawing with her foot. She grabbed my face in her hands and forced me to meet her eyes. "Well, Sha-shen, then you have just over a day to think of something."

"A plan," I said with a laugh and pulled away.

We sat in silence for several heartbeats before she said, "Yes, a plan." Her tone was not pleasant. She surreptitiously reached into her dress pocket and pulled out an oval piece of smooth glass. "Remember this?" she asked.

I nodded.

"Such an odd endeavor for a young one," she said, shaking her head. "Wanting to create a bent piece of glass to look through."

"So?"

"You're something unique, Sha-shen. I just want you to know that. In all my years serving as a caretaker, I never encountered a child so determined." She handed me the oval glass. "Find a way out of this."

Jaggers stepped in, grabbed the oval glass, and separated us, "What're you trying to do? 'Find a way out of this'?" he muttered. "Get!"

My fourth mother shot up and backed away. "Don't waste a second."

"Get!" Jaggers barked.

She scowled at him and then left. For a second, I believe I saw my escort flinch under my fourth mother's glare.

Jaggers was not happy as he led me away. "Should report her," he kept mumbling. "Should have her fined, something." Poor Jaggers was wrestling with his conscience; reporting my fourth mother might land her in exile, and no one wanted to live with condemning anyone to that fate.

"She kids 'round," I offered, shuffling toward the living levels. The condensation on the rock walls was rich. The warming days across the surface above brought forth water from the rock walls and ceilings below in Spesterra. Other condemned prayed for a storm to come and scare the Haze away. I knew better: the sky-watchers are trained to know how long a heat spell will remain. "She means nothing by it," I told Jaggers.

He grunted as we rounded the bend to my level. Soon, he'd lock me in my apartment.

I tried again as we reached the main corridor, "In two days' time, it won't matter, huh?" People hugged the edge of the corridor as we strolled down the center. My crooked leg continued to burn from all the climbing; I didn't give a hint, though.

Jaggers slowed his pace, nodded, and we went the rest of the way in silence. Such a good-looking man. I had seen his wife, Carleine. She was as beautiful as he was handsome. Did she understand the strain he was under? Did his kids run up to him and make him forget for a while? Were any of his kids "damaged"? Would he see them go someday?

Sheesh, Sha-shen, gotta warp even your vague thoughts into eerie dismay.

Another of the condemned came our way. An older gentleman surrounded by family. A line of drool hung from his chin. The old man's guard trailed far behind the group. I caught a whiff of their conversation—they were reviewing property rights. The old man didn't seem to have much, but whatever he owned, it was being fought for.

I recognized Venna, a fellow tanner and seamstress. She glanced my way but quickly averted her eyes. Her family did not barter any goods to allow their elder to die peacefully in Spesterra. The drooling old man would not live out his days naturally.

"We're here," I told Jaggers as we reached my door. He too was eavesdropping on the passing group and got lost in their peckings. He shook it away and turned to face me.

He reached in his pocket and removed the smooth oval of glass and asked, "What is this?"

"Curiosity," I said with a shrug.

Jaggers held the piece in his giant fingers, peering at me and waiting for more of an explanation.

"I was eleven seasons," I explained as I leaned against the doorframe to my apartment, the day's weight catching up with me. "We had pulled apart a goat's eye during a regimen course—"

Jaggers cringed at this.

I continued: "Well, to learn about the workings...part of the eye had this oval type of lens, but bulbous like it had swelled."

Jaggers frowned, "And you thought to make one? Why?"

I closed my eye and rubbed my finger across my eyelid,

"I noticed we have the same oval piece in our own eyes, and was curious about what would happen if I held a larger piece and looked through it. My fourth mother showed me how to shape and polish burning glass."

Jaggers held the glass to his eye. "It's odd."

"Hold it a bit farther." I stepped forward to show him. "Adjust it until you see the image grow."

He did so, studying the back of his hand. "Hmm," he grunted as he opened my door and ushered me inside.

Jaggers didn't say goodbye, just set the oval glass on a shelf and shut the door.

Alone inside my apartment, I lay down and stretched my weary bones across my pallet, grateful for the respite. I kept the gown on—the accursed thing was comfortable.

My fourth mother would be expecting me to devise some glorious plan of escape. *Just over a day to come up with something.* Escape where? Spesterra is a giant tomb with nowhere to hide, not some underground metropolis, as the Regulator Office would have us believe.

Like all my mothers, she praised my analytical mind. Unlike my other mothers, she never scolded me for questioning everything. Never told me it was a waste of time for someone like me to try so hard. "Damaged" don't get assigned any of the challenging tasks to improve development.

In two days my scientific mind won't matter. It'll be nothing but a haze of the Haze.

I laughed in my empty room.

Why did I opt out of the elixir? Why not just go out numb? Maybe my body wasn't the only thing damaged about me.

I pulled up my blanket, but the thing caught on the pallet edge, and its worn threads tore right in half. The thing had barely held together anyway. I sighed as I pinched the wispy material between my good thumb and finger. At least I won't have to peddle for a new one.

Funny. Staring dumbly at my ragged old blanket in self-pity and blowing away the drifting pieces of lint, it came to me. Fourth mother would've been proud: it had taken only a bit over an hour.

I pulled off the stupid gown and tossed it at the door. After massaging life back into my sore joints, I grabbed my longshirt and leggings and got dressed.

The Haze has closed the circle around me. I take a deep breath and fight the terrors that bubble in my stomach.

The good thing about a clawed hand is it serves well as a hook when needed. I hang the satchel from it as I dig past my glass jars for the gob of honeycomb wax. I pull a plug, break it apart, and stuff it into my ears and nose.

The Haze follows me as I move left to right.

I grab a jar from the satchel and unhinge the lid. Three more jars clink in my satchel.

My lips are close to sealed as I breathe. My heart's racing. That doesn't help.

The sun doesn't shine as bright. The amber cloud has closed in.

The desire to run pell-mell and try to break through is strong, but I know better.

I wait to strike.

After waiting until night gave way to early morning, I placed torn shreds of the gown and parchment at the bottom of my apartment door. It didn't take long to ignite—the flint and steel sparks glowed bright. The flames lit quickly and didn't need much fanning.

I prayed Jaggers was on time with my breakfast. After feeding me, he was assigned to take me on my final rounds for good-byes. He'd tuck me in again, and the following day we'd join the rest of the non-contributors to leave for the surface when the sun was at its highest.

"Help!" I yelled. Smoke covered my floor.

My plan required that I sneak out and make my way topside alone and with my gear. The Regulator Office demands that we go barefoot in only our fine robe. Robes that are stripped from our bodies after the Haze consumes our minds.

"Help!" I tried again.

Nothing.

I pounded the locked door. "Jaggers! Jaggers!"

The smoke rose to my knees. I pushed my face to the small opening between the door and its frame.

Finally, the door shuddered and then flew open. I scuttled back. Wide-eyed, Jaggers scanned the room, realizing there was no great blaze.

I cupped the tanning awl in my good hand and rushed toward him as he stomped out the meager flames.

Hating to do it, I reached around and struck him in the left buttock.

"Ah, no!" he cried, cupping the wound.

I stumbled by him the best I could.

Jaggers dove and locked onto my ankle; we both tumbled.

I tried to kick free, but my crooked leg flopped around, missing the mark. One kick brushed his wrist.

The fire thinned and then died away completely.

"My ass! You stabbed my ass?" he groaned.

Tears blurred my vision.

Jaggers chuckled, "Oh, Sha-shen." He released my ankle and sighed. "Best of chance to you."

I hoisted myself up and hobbled away.

The Haze bites into my skin. I lunge into it with the first glass jar and scoop the air. There's a pinching sensation, like a hot poker, down my left cheek. My eyes are squeezed shut, but it doesn't matter, the Haze digs in.

I close the first glass jar and trap in it a whiff of the Haze. I shove the jar in my satchel and pull out a second.

The Haze has solidified parts of itself into wormy tendrils. They pull at the wax and cloth compound I'd stuffed in my ears and nose.

I keep swiping at my face wherever I feel the prickling, but it's like trying to stop a swarm of fiery ants. A lost memory of an old woman clawing at her face resurrects itself in my mind's eye—an image I had forgotten but which now comes at me with a fury, her white hair yanked away with strings of Haze as it pushed in relentlessly. Other memories of terrified victims hit me like a barrage of nightmares. Clear memories that I had somehow stuffed deep inside.

I claw my face, too, but I'm holding something. The jar. I shake my face and back away. I duck down and crawl on my knees and elbows. I close the jar around a thick chunk of Haze—my clawed hand stretching and squeezing more than ever in my life—and grab another.

The Haze follows me like a shadow, gripping onto the back of my neck. Pushing. Pushing.

The glass jars are filled, they clank in my satchel as I stumble on.

I swipe in a final bit of Haze and keep the last jar locked in my good hand. I lie low to the ground and open my eyes fully so I can examine the contents. It burns, but I have to see the Haze up close. The scientist in me can't resist: I have to know what I've done, if anything.

The Haze inside the jar thrashes around angrily. It bangs against the glass. Worried that it might get out, I get to my feet and rush to the yam rows to bury the jars in my satchel, hoping the moist dirt will help keep the contents trapped inside.

A calming caress washes over me, entreating me to stop and relax.

I don't.

The Haze is manipulating me, worming into my thoughts, soothing me.

A comforting touch at my feet tempts me to stop. I ignore the pleasant sensation and push on. The mollifying touch under my skin turns into a cramp. The stab starts in my calf and runs up my leg. Being damaged, I'm no stranger to my muscles being twisted.

I'm not far from the yam rows, but my good leg is growing sluggish. I can no longer feel my crooked leg.

The surface-side windows blink in the distance. By now, many are watching me—only me alone and not among a group. They have realized I have come on my own. They must see I have collected and trapped the Haze in a jar.

They see I am the first of Spesterra to do so.

Are you cheering me on, Rafe, the way I cheered you? I'm sorry I doubted you. My mind filled with acid when you finally collapsed and succumbed to the Haze's onslaught. I swore I'd never keep hope in my heart again when I saw you fall.

Someone laughed during your death.

I dug my fingernails across the man's cheek.

They had to drag me away.

The Haze continues to push into me, but small clouds of it have gathered around my satchel.

I strive on. My bones burn as if I have no skin to protect them. The Haze is enraged; I feel the potency of its anger.

I reach the first lip of the yam rows. My good hand and my clawed hand dig into the earth.

The Haze's anger shifts; now it's desperate. I can sense the change.

I shove the satchel into the earth and push dirt over it.

Oh, Rafe, I can hear you cheering for me from wherever you are.

The Haze panics. Tendrils leave my skin, the movements anxious as they hover over the mound of dirt.

I blink away a torrent of tears and wipe my eyes. With what I have left of my soul, I want to see.

I set my last Haze-filled jar atop the mound where I buried the rest within the satchel.

An errant thought strikes me: I pull out the oval glass from my pocket and peer through it into the jar.

The Haze inside the jar has become bits of dust.

I bring the jar and seeing glass to my eye—I have to examine. I have to know.

Tiny machines break away from one another and convulse. Some scurry around aimlessly before dropping like dying insects.

In a craze, I grab the jar and taunt the Haze with it as frail tendrils return to tear at me.

"Is this all you are? Tiny machines that die when separated?" I tease the Haze.

The Haze spears its tendrils into the earth after my satchel but pulls back.

They can't get to the jars! I push more dirt on top and mock the Haze. I know the scientists and scholars of Spesterra will relish this information. I have lost, but they will learn. I have contributed.

I set my oval looking glass on the mound of dirt, marking it, and then I throw the jar filled with the Haze into the distance.

The Haze shrieks and chases after it!

The remaining tendrils are pulled from my body and race after the discarded jar.

In that bloody moment, I can feel Jaggers, my fourth mother, and others all cheering me on. I want badly to lift my body up and stand as a hero stands, but strength has left me.

Maybe the jar broke when I threw it, maybe it didn't. I don't care; I just wanted a reprieve. A last few breaths to rest before I become nothing.

Water rains down.

I blink to the blue sky in disbelief.

Someone from below has opened the irrigation lines. Someone has deemed me worth saving.

Water soaks my skin.

The Haze retreats farther.

I hear laughter and realize it's coming from me. A stitch in my side flares as I laugh, but I can't stop.

Drops patter in the quickly forming puddles.

I'll tell the Regulators what I did, how I trapped the Haze. I'll help them make plans to fight it.

But with the others I'll share the secret beauty of topside. I'll light fires within all their hearts. I'll stoke the fire that started with you, Rafe.

The First Dawn of Earth

by J.D. Harpley

J.D. Harpley is Astral Scribe, a dedicated word ingester and producer. A past laden with science fiction books led her to follow in the footsteps of those she found great and create vivid, brain-tantalizing works of her own.

Project manager at a game studio by day, she spends her weekends romping around between the trees carrying airsoft rifles, and her nights furiously typing or gaming.

Expect elements of horror, lengthy and delectable action scenes, and a heroine sporting some kind of deadly weapon–in no need of a hero to save her.

Stars speckled the black abyss beyond the viewport, clouded by the artificial light of the docking bay. Chen took a deep breath through her nose as the courier drones circled in and out of sight, running last-minute errands to prepare the colonization craft. Soon, she and the other four hundred million inhabitants of the orbiting space stations would abandon their homes to return to the one they left a little over three hundred years ago: Earth.

Chen knew she should be more excited than she felt, but there was hardly anything to be excited about. So the Earth had towering mountains covered in snow, natural rainfall, and animals she'd seen only in educational vids. Big deal. The Earth, to Chen, was still a toxic, polluted wasteland holding nothing of interest. The space stations had massive astronomy centers, talking robots, protein synthesis plants, and huge reservoirs to swim in. Xiao-ping had everything Chen wanted.

"All first-wave residents are required to fill out their departure forms by no later than 18:00 hours. For underage residents, the parent or guardian is responsible for this form." The tone of the typically unenthusiastic PSA office clerk was ecstatic; Chen assumed it was because she was part of the first wave.

The speaker on Chen's bracelet crackled to life again, "And don't forget, we're all getting together tonight at 20:00 hours for the departure ceremony in conference hall A-12."

Chen cranked the volume down as Bao-jin went on about the tea and snacks they would have and all the details the conference owner would cover. Clops around the corner alerted her to the approaching presence, and Chen straightened, pressing down the wrinkles in her suit caused by her extended cross-legged position.

"Here you are, Miss." The robot, clearly labeled M-23 on its chest, extended a well-oiled hand to Chen.

"Yes," she sighed, "here I am."

"Your mother is looking for you. She needs your help filling out the rest of your departure paperwork." It motioned for Chen to follow, but she stepped past it.

"I know. I've been avoiding it." The gray metal walls echoed with their advancing patters, but Chen wasn't heading home. Colored lighting on the floor guided the way to her only real friend, Robert.

M-23 gripped her arm gently. "That is the wrong way, Miss."

"Depending on where I'm going, it might not be." She pried its fingers open and removed herself from its grasp.

"But Miss, you are in the first wave. You need to finish the paperwork to return to Earth."

Chen's lungs filled with an indignant rage. Didn't she get a choice? What if she didn't want to leave? Earth wasn't all that great, and she wouldn't have any friends down there. She would be forced to teach, act proper, and revive the ways of her people. No one ever asked Chen if she wanted to do that, and she didn't.

"Well, I guess I just can't go then, can I?" She continued on her path to the recycling center. Robert was at the recycling center, and he wouldn't bother her with stupid things like paperwork and Earth. He loved Xiao-ping just as much, if not more, than Chen.

"But Miss Li, your mother is the cultural ambassador; she needs you at her side."

Chen scoffed, "Right. She needs me like a hole in her head."

"Ambassador Li has several holes in her head, each of which provides a specific function, Miss. What function would another hole in her head provide?" Stupid robots, they couldn't even get her jokes. Robert would get her joke.

Chen turned to face her tail. "Look, M-23, I don't need an escort. I'll get back to our condo before 18:00 to finish the form."

"I will let your mother know."

"Do whatever you want," Chen grumbled as she turned away.

When M-23 was out of sight, Chen took off at a run following the yellow light, though she hardly needed it. Chen could find her way to the recycling center from anywhere in the station by the age of five. It was her favorite place to hang out with the best company to keep.

She came to the section center, where gravity was lowest, and whooped as her short legs took long, uninhibited leaps. The next door opened at her approach, and she grabbed the side railing, slingshotting herself through the entry with a hard left. Her feet bounced against the right wall as she corrected herself, continuing her lengthy bounds towards the recycling center.

Gravity returned to its normal levels, slowing Chen down. *No matter*, she thought with a grin as she caught sight of the green logo ahead. Chen's stomach lurched as something caught her by the back of her shirt.

"Whoa there! Where *you* headed in such a hurry?" The familiar man's voice put her at ease.

She smiled up at him saying, "Robert, I was just stopping by for an evening chat."

He eyed her, one brow pointed and the other pulled down, the look he always had when she imitated his accent. Robert hadn't been on the Xiao-ping long, only a few years. He transferred from a neighboring station called the Queen Margaret.

"Oh, just by for a chat, are you? I think you're avoiding some paperwork, young lady."

Chen groaned, "Ugh, great. Not you, too."

"Don't worry," he winked as the door to the recycling facility opened, "I'm on your side."

They stepped into the very personalized, almost apartment-like station center where Robert spent most of his time. Plans and sketches were strewn about the shabby office. Chen loved it. There was so much thought, dedication, and hope in the room.

"I don't know why I have to be in the first wave. It's not like I'm anything special," she humphed as she plopped down in his chair, arms crossed.

Robert raised a brow. "Being the daughter of the cultural ambassador is unimportant?"

"And completely boring. Imagine spending all your days in a classroom learning nothing but history and language. I know twelve different dialects from my *home* country," she air-quoted the word. Chen found nothing about the country known as China to be home. Xiao-ping raised her and made her who she was. China would hold nothing for her.

"That's an honor I would be happy to accept."

Chen laughed, "Yeah, right! Try living it sometime."

"You are a well-educated young lady—"

"But I don't care about all that! They should have picked someone who cared!"

Robert placed his hand on Chen's shoulder with a gentle smile, "You were chosen to harbor a wealth of knowledge for an entire race; whether you *like* it or not doesn't matter. You do care, deep down, because you know how important you are."

The words filled her with warmth. Chen always walked in her mother's shadow, rarely receiving recognition for her hard work, her dedication. "Thanks, Robert, but you know that's just not true. My mother will probably live forever, and I won't be needed."

"Hmm, sounds like someone's wishful thinking."

"If only." Chen's heart sank and she looked away.

She heard Robert moving about, and then he tapped her shoulder. When she turned, there sat an adorable plush bunny in his hands.

"For me?" She reached for it, and he recoiled with a stern gaze.

"This is something special. If you truly do not want to go to Earth, I will give it to you."

She groped at his hands. "Of course I don't want to go! What's in it?"

He extended it toward her again, opening his fingers very slowly. "It will force the colonization ship to turn around and come back to port."

"Give it!" She jumped and strained as he pulled away, but she couldn't reach it.

Robert held one finger to his mouth and shushed her. "You have to be careful with it, and you have to learn how to work it."

"I promise to pay attention to everything you say."

A smile spread across his face, and he finally released it to her. Chen turned it over and over in her hands. It looked like an ordinary stuffed toy.

"How does it work?"

He took it and flipped it on its back. There was a tiny switch nestled in the fake fur. "You push this up, and then place the bunny next to a computer. Once you do that, I can turn the ship around."

Chen thought for a moment. "Will someone notice it? Will you get in trouble?"

He grinned, "Of course not."

"Well great, I'll do it."

The bunny was placed in her grasp once more.

"Want to try some of my new fruit juice recipe?" He opened a small compartment next to his desk and retrieved a jar of green liquid.

Chen, being used to seeing strange colored liquid in jars around Robert's office, thought nothing of it and accepted happily. She was three gulps in before she realized it was awful, like rotten cabbage when the pickled vegetables had gone wrong. She managed one last swallow before placing the glass aside and smiling a grin that felt much more like a grimace.

"You hate it," he said matter-of-factly, with a flat tone.

She shook her head. "No, it's great." A burp fought its way up her throat and escaped with a foul flavor that made Chen cringe.

Robert laughed. "That's okay, I knew it was terrible."

"Then why did you offer it to me?" Chen punched his shoulder.

"I just," he broke into tears of jubilation, "I just wanted to see the look on your face." He could barely contain himself, and Chen raged, jabbing him repeatedly with the bottle.

"All right, all right," he wound down to chuckles, "you

need to head home and finish filling out the form. It's almost 18:00."

"You mean I still need to get on the landing craft?"

He shrugged. "How else would the bunny get to the ship's computer?"

"Oh, right."

"Run along now. I'll see you tomorrow afternoon."

Chen took off with a wave, elated to be freed from her duties as the cultural ambassador's daughter. She would stay on Xiao-ping, study astronomy, biology, and computer science like Robert. She would be able to do whatever *she* wanted and wouldn't have to spend any more of her days on Qin Shi Huang, Dong Zhongshu, or the Dalai Lama.

Home was just around the corner for her when she slowed to a steady, disheartened trudge. Chen didn't want her mother thinking she'd suddenly changed her mind about going to Earth and therefore getting suspicious.

"Aiya! Chen, why are you so late?" Shuzhen chastised her as she came tromping in.

Chen shrugged, ensuring the bunny was hidden deep in her pocket. "Mama, it's fine. It's not 18:00 yet, we can still finish the document."

"But you were going to help me with dinner, and now we have to eat rations."

Chen groaned, "They're not *rations*, Mother, it's just regular space station food."

"Why do you hold no respect for your history? You should be eating the food of your ancestors every night, remembering every taste, considering every scent. Memorizing the texture of it in your mouth. You are the only link to what we once were, and your knowledge will be taught in the future schools of Earth."

Chen's eyes bulged as her eyebrows arched towards the ceiling, "Don't be so dramatic, Mama. They have vids, they have books, and essays, and poems of all kinds. They don't need me."

Shuzhen stood akimbo, blocking the way to the kitchen. "Who will remember the accents of our dialects? Who will remember the color of the sky over the Forbidden City? Who will remember the size of the Terracotta Army?"

"I will." Chen sighed in feigned defeat. It didn't matter that she had to get on the colony ship the next morning, it would be turning right back around within minutes of their departure.

Shuzhen nodded, "And I will." She led Chen to the computer desk. "Place your thumb on the reader and finish the last four questions, then come to the kitchen to help me with the dumplings."

Chen did as she was told, and dinner went without an argument. Afterwards, her mother forced Chen into a culturally befitting dress for the gathering in A-12. She and her mother shook hands, said words of encouragement in Mandarin, Wu, Gan, Hakka, or Yue, and bowed respectfully. Chen found it all so superficial.

The slideshow went on for an hour, which was forty-five minutes longer than Chen thought it should have gone for. They showed the terraforming stations and their living quarters, described the risks of contamination in certain areas, which they'd be far away from, and the repopulation efforts they would go through. The Xiao-ping station was responsible for several different breeds of fish, a few thousand strains of bacteria, two of the salvageable species of primate, and of course, pandas.

It was sad how few of the species were saved after the global downfall. Chen felt the leaders should have spent more time collecting the billions of creatures and plants from Earth, rather than all the efforts they spent in making comfortable arrangements in space. Visions of toxic rain, smog-strangled air, and piles of garbage surrounding the rainforests came to her. How horrible it must have been to be left behind those three hundred years ago.

"Chen, come here," Shuzhen called to her in Yue. Chen barely contained a gesture of displeasure as she approached the older man, Wu-Bō, who still considered himself to be Cantonese though his father, and his father's father, were both born on Xiao-ping.

He smiled warmly, apparently blind to Chen's apathy. "Hello, Miss Li. Are you excited for tomorrow?"

"Yeah, it's going to be great. I'm ready to have more room to move around," she lied. Chen didn't mind the cramped living quarters and the narrow hallways when there was the vastness of space right outside her window.

Wu-Bō bowed curtly as he turned away, and Chen's mother eyed her with a stern glare.

Shuzhen uttered in common speak, "You do not use slang around your elders. Show more respect than that."

"I'm sorry, Mǔqīn," a hint of acidity entered Chen's voice as she used the proper word for mother.

She spent the remainder of the evening circulating through the crowd, shaking more hands, giving more words of encouragement in Yue, Mandarin, Hakka, and the other dialects. All the while Chen thought about the plush bunny stuffed in her backpack. She would be off and back before the morning was done tomorrow. Or at least that's what Chen hoped.

They piled through the door at an astonishing 23:53, and they needed to be up by 06:30 the next day for departure preparation. Chen yawned as she waded through the towers of "culturally relevant" books.

"Goodnight, Mama," she sighed, yanking the tight flats from her feet.

The other side of the room was quiet, but Chen hardly noticed the lack of response from her mother as she drifted into a comfortable and easy sleep...

Only to be woken what seemed like minutes later at 06:30. A metal clanking rang out as a robot rapped at the door, and Chen shot awake.

"It is time for you to prepare your things, Miss Li." The robot spoke in Cantonese, Shuzhen's preferred dialect. Chen stared as her mother walked from the restroom, picked her bag up at the door, and turned to look back.

"Are you coming or not?" Shuzhen said in a very challenging tone.

Not! Chen wanted to say. Leaving was the last thing on her mind, but she knew if she didn't come quietly, her mother would force her to come, kicking and screaming. Chen would rather cooperate and end up coming back in moments without ever being implicated.

"Yes, Mama. I need a moment to get dressed." She took her bag to the restroom and dug through to ensure her plush bunny was still there. A sigh of relief escaped her when she found it. She changed quickly and put her long, jet-black hair in a tight bun. Bright green eyes reflected back at her from the mirror, and she searched them, trying to find her happiness. It was in there, hidden behind the weight of an entire culture. Soon it would be set free.

"Hurry!" Shuzhen's voice was on the other side of the door, and Chen clamped her hand around the bunny, not wanting her secret found. She gave one last glance in the mirror, faked a smile, and turned away.

The walk to the boarding station was crowded, much more so than Chen would have guessed. *So this is what five thousand people looks like,* she marveled as she stepped onto a bulkhead to get a better view. Every face in the crowd was known to her, either by name or position on Xiao-ping. How strange it must have been, just three hundred years ago, for someone to not know the people who grew their food or cleaned their water.

Thousands of bracelets cracked to life at the same time.

"Wave one participants, we will begin boarding shortly. Obviously for wave two we will have some foresight and batch people into boarding classes!" Everyone chuckled, though they were hot, tired, and sick of standing.

"If you would please be sure to have your non-essential luggage passed off to a robot for handling and storage before you get to the entrance, this will go a lot faster. We will send them through the halls to collect your things. Thank you for your patience and cooperation."

Shuzhen sighed, "I can't believe this. Hundreds of years to plan and they can't even get us into the ship in a timely manner."

"It's not so bad. We've only been here a half hour."

"Yes, but it's taking so long. I feel like we'll never get to the ship," she groaned. Chen was surprised; her mother was rarely so vocal about her displeasure.

"Why are you so upset, Mama? It's not like we're in a hurry."

Shuzhen looked at her with a strange expression. "That's easy for you to say," she paused, and her face went blank.

Chen felt anger building in the pit of her stomach. "What's that supposed to mean?"

"I'm sorry, Qīn'ài de. It doesn't mean anything, I'm irritated this morning."

The use of such an endearing nickname soothed Chen's frustration. If only her mother showed that much compassion when Chen complained about being a cultural leader, perhaps she wouldn't have felt cornered into doing what she still planned to do. Though, if the disembarkation was as disorganized as the boarding, Chen thought she might want to hide and not even get on in the first place.

Their line finally moved, then stopped, and moved. For another hour it went on like that until they reached the front.

"We're so sorry about this," the young man said in Mandarin. Shuzhen very politely matched his language. "It's no problem at all," and she broke off to fan herself.

"Place your finger here." He held the tablet out to Chen, and she complied. The screen scanned her print, and her profile appeared.

Name: Chen Li

Ethnic Origin: Chinese

Age: 13 years, 4 months

Station: 29, Xiao-ping

Occupation: Cultural Ambassador

Next to the readout was an image of her face. Chen didn't like the picture; the woman taking it hadn't told her to smile and so her face was stoic, plain.

"Please, come aboard." The young man bowed.

Shuzhen bowed. "Thank you very much."

Chen headed towards the cool air leaking from the open passageway ahead until she was yanked back. She glared up at her mother, who glared just as sternly back.

With realization, Chen bowed lowly to the man and said, "Thank you very much."

Shuzhen released her, and Chen hiked her backpack on her shoulders, ensuring it was secure. She hoped the bunny was okay and her escape plan would go off without a hitch.

They found their place amid the tightly cramped seats, and Chen felt a wave of panic as she realized she might not be able to get away from her mother to plant the bunny. She dug around in her bag as they took their places, and she stuffed the salvation machine into her pocket. There had to be a restroom somewhere...

"Mama, I need to go to the restroom."

Shuzhen tutted, "You were in there before we left; you can't possibly have to go."

"It's been two hours since then, and I have to go," Chen whined.

"It will only take us an hour and a half to touch down, you

can wait that long."

"Mama, I really can't!" She raised her voice and the people sitting around them turned their heads. Chen was embarrassing her mother, and the others did not want to stare.

Shuzhen was silent, her eyes following the gazes of her people. Without looking at Chen, her mother spoke, "M-102 is just behind us. Ask it."

"I'm sorry, Mǔqīn," she mumbled as she trudged away. And she was. She knew how important Earth was to her mother.

For a fleeting second, she considered not going through with her plan. Then Robert came to mind. She might never get a chance to see him again if she went to Earth. Friends were not a commodity on Xiao-ping, and Chen valued Robert above all the rest. There were only forty-two other children her age on the landing craft, and none of them had been her friends.

"Excuse me," she said, regaining her composure.

M-102 turned to her, its plastic mouth lighting as it spoke, "Miss Li, you need to take your seat, we will be departing in moments."

Chen's eyes drifted downward to the black marks on M-102's chest, clearly labeling it as 'Lou Kim'. She tutted at the sight of the graffiti, wondering which punk had marked up the poor robot.

"I need the restroom," she said with feigned urgency, hoping Lou Kim would not see through her facade.

It turned its head from side to side. "There are no restrooms in this craft. Please return to your seat."

Chen nodded, and as she turned back to her mother, she thought of a solution. She made a left through the alley of people, pretending as though the robot had given her directions. With a nervous smile, she approached the cockpit on that level. The door creaked as she pried it open.

"Hello, I'm Chen."

The co-pilot looked back with a start. "You need to be in

your seat."

Chen shrugged, clicking the button on the bottom of the bunny's tummy to the right behind her back, "I just wanted to see where the magic happens. Sorry!"

"She can come in for just a second." The pilot placed a hand on his shoulder.

"Thank you." Chen stood next to the older woman with bright silver streaks in her black hair. With one hand, she pointed to a control panel, asking, "What's that do?" while the other hand placed the stuffed toy under the pilot's chair.

"This is for lateral thrusters; we need those to turn the ship right-side-up for entry." The wrinkles next to her creasing lips flicked up into a smile for Chen.

Chen nodded, "That's really cool. What about this panel?"

She was allowed to ask questions for another three minutes, and she figured that was long enough for her mother to believe she'd gone to the restroom.

When she got back, Shuzhen muttered under her breath, "What were you doing in there, reciting Lao-tzu's prayers?"

"Would you finally be proud of me if I was?" Chen glared with defiance as she strapped herself into her chair.

Shuzhen's head pulled back in surprise. "I am proud of you. This was hard for you, I know, and you've always had so much responsibility hanging over your head. I remember what it was like being a teen." She leaned her head back and stared at the ceiling. Chen recognized the movement; it meant her mother was pushing the tears back into her eyes.

"But we have a duty, an honor, and we need to fulfill it. We will be the teachers; we will show our people how to rebuild." Her words struck Chen as the speakers on their wrists came to life all at once.

"Brace yourselves for departure. Sixteen, fifteen, fourteen…"

Oh no. Chen felt she may have made a terrible mistake. The trip was everything to her mother. Her eyes scanned the faces of her people.

"Nine, eight, seven…"

They were all so happy, so ready to return to their land, Earth—a place they'd never set foot on, nor their parents, or their parents' parents.

"Two, one, zero."

The ship jostled hard, and cheering erupted from the gleeful smiles of her friends, family, neighbors. Gravity lessened until she felt her hands lifting lazily from the arm rests. Nausea took her as she relived the moment of planting the bunny, realizing she had destroyed all their happiness.

"Wait, Mama—"

"No, Chen!" The shouts dampened the sound of her mother's fury, blending it into background noise, but it cut through her.

"We can't go back, it's too late," Shuzhen said with finality.

Chen stammered, "But, Mǔqīn, I…"

"We can't go back." She leaned down to Chen's ear. "There was enough fuel for only one trip—that was all we had. We left all the others behind, perhaps for hundreds of years. Until we can rebuild on Earth and send a shuttle up with fuel, they are trapped on Xiao-ping."

Chen's stomach dropped away. They could *never* get back to Earth if their journey didn't succeed, but her best friend was trapped on the space station forever if they did go. Chen would have to live out her days in a place she couldn't call home, friendless.

"Mama," her vision blurred as her eyes welled with tears, "I did something."

Shuzhen swallowed, her throat visibly constricting as she did. "What did you do?"

"Robert gave me something to give him control of the ship, so he can turn it around. I turned it on, and placed it in the cockpit."

Chen finally thought to question why Robert had the device, and why he wanted her to place it on the ship. Had he really ever been her friend, or was he using her to carry out the deed he could not?

Shuzhen's face became a pale stone. It was as if she was looking through Chen, through the wall, and out into space. Her voice was low and breathy. "Which cockpit?"

It was Chen's turn to gulp back fear as she pointed, "Over there."

"Stay right here." Shuzhen unstrapped the harness and floated easily in the zero gravity.

Chen's gut roiled as the terror took hold in her. Everything was ruined, and it was all her fault.

Suddenly, her bracelet came to life, "Chen." It was Robert.

"There isn't enough fuel for the ship to take another trip," she exclaimed in a whisper.

"I know." His voice was a stab to her heart.

She whimpered, "But why?"

"Chen, humans don't belong on Earth. We destroyed it once, and we'll do it again."

So he *had* used her; she didn't have any friends, after all.

He went on, his words piercing deeper and deeper. "Unsnap your harness and head towards the stern. The twelve lifeboats there are still functional. Any one of them will get you close enough to Xiao-ping for you to get picked up by a drone."

Chen realized everyone around her was silent, floating lifelessly. Yanking herself free, she checked the nearest person's pulse. They were still alive.

"Chen, what are you doing?"

"Why aren't I asleep like the others?"

He was quiet for a long time, but finally spoke. "Because you're my friend, and a cultural leader. I don't want humanity to die out, we just can't return to the Earth. These space stations can provide for us indefinitely, as long as the sun shines. Whatever creatures have emerged from the toxic era will have the paradise to themselves for eternity."

"But, why did you make them fall asleep? How?"

"There was never going to be enough fuel to turn the ship around and come back to Xiao-ping, but I knew I could save you if the others didn't get in the way."

Chen's head was spinning. How could he do it to her, to them? They would all die, she knew it. He would take remote control of the ship and burn it up in the atmosphere. Her mother, Wu-Bō, and so many others would be dead. She hated Robert.

"Chen, it's time to get to the lifeboat."

"You used me for your agenda," she growled as she pushed towards the cockpit.

Robert's voice wavered, "I didn't want to, but I wasn't invited to join the first wave."

The corpse-like body of her mother bounced gently from the ceiling to the wall, and Chen pushed her down into an empty seat. She strapped the harness in place and proceeded back on course.

"I'm not going to let you do this," she whispered as she searched the pilot's chair for the deadly toy.

Robert sounded panicked. "Chen, there is no autopilot for this craft! You can't fly it!"

"My attempt to save them will be better than your attempt to condemn them." The device was in her hand, but she waited. Waited to see if he would come to his senses, save her and the others. She was mortified. She didn't want to do it alone, but if he forced her, she would at least try.

"Chen, don't do this. Come home," he pleaded, but she could not abandon her mother and all her people.

She shook her head and flipped the switch. "I *am* going home."

With trembling fingers she tapped in the call for the Xiao-ping operator and then unhooked the pilot from her seat.

"Shuttle, we lost all communication. What happened?" A relieved sounding man came through her speaker.

"My name is Chen Li. I need to talk to someone who knows how to fly this ship, immediately. Everyone has been poisoned, they're asleep, and I'm the only one to fly it. Hurry."

The man choked on his breath, "Yes, right away!"

The line was quiet as Chen guided the pilot back to her own seat and secured her in place.

"Who is this?" A familiar voice came on, and Chen knew it was one of the backup mission pilots who didn't make the first wave.

"Chen Li, sir. I don't have time to explain what happened right now, but you need to help me guide this ship down." She pulled herself into the pilot seat, fingers electric with terrified excitement as they touched the controls.

"This is unbelievable," he breathed. "Okay, are you at the console?"

"Yeah," her voice cracked and she cleared it, then stated with more emphasis, "yes."

"Good. First thing you need to do is the retrofire burn. On the panel labeled 4 there is a button that will say FWDT, that's the forward thrust. Input a value of 23 in the keypad, and press that button."

Chen followed the instructions, and the ship began to tremble. Her stomach lurched as she felt the pitch of the cabin adjust. Vibrations changed the sound of her voice as she spoke, "What's next?"

"All right, you'll need to turn to panel 1, and find the button labeled OMS, that's the Orbital Maneuvering System. Press it, then flip the yellow switch next to it with the letters s-2 under it, and enter .02."

Again, Chen followed directions, and the shuttle shook harder.

"No, that's too much! Turn it off!"

"How?" she shrieked in horror.

"Turn off the s-2 switch! Enter .01 in the keypad and flip the switch labeled p-1, then enter .01 again and flip p-2."

Chen's entire arm shook as she clumsily carried out the instructions. Eventually, the shaking reduced to a shuddering.

He sighed, "Great work, Chen. Okay, we're going to keep doing that on and off for about twenty minutes as we get the entry angle right."

"I can't do this!" she burst out, tears streaming down her face.

"Don't say that. We'll get through this together. We're all here for you, Chen."

Silent sobs racked her chest and she held a hand over her mouth until she could quiet.

"Thank you."

Twenty minutes took an eternity, but by the end of it, Chen had a good grasp of the control layout. Next, they adjusted the angle of the shuttle, and dumped the remaining fuel from the p-1 and s-1 thrusters.

"You're going to start your descent into the upper atmosphere, and we might lose you a bit."

The dread gnawing at her insides quickly degenerated into hysteria as she cried, "You can't leave me! I can't do this without you!"

"Yes, you can. You're already doing better than one of the co-pilots who applied for the mission."

She took five deep breaths and calmed herself. "All right. What's next? What do I need to know if we lose contact?"

"The aft thrusters need to maintain a 65% burn to keep you at a 40 degree attitude. Carefully watch the latitude pitch, and don't allow it to leave .5 degrees from the normal. You can see you're in the green right now."

She made mental notes of these things and chanted them

under her breath.

"Then you're in luck, and you can turn on the autopilot for the lower atmosphere descent. By that time, we'll have you back in contact, and I'll help you again." He guided her to where all the buttons were, ran through the procedure three times to ensure she had it memorized, and then the ship became more erratic.

"What's happening?" Chen gripped her shoulder harness tightly.

The pilot's voice was beginning to crackle, "You're hitting the atmosphere and creating heat. The ionized gasses are surrounding the ship, and we're going to lose contact soon, for about ten to fifteen minutes."

"What?" she shrilled.

His voice was even more distorted, "Remember what I told you. 65% aft thrust, 40-degree attitude. You can do this Chen, we believe—"

Her only life-line cut out. She was completely alone.

The ship shuddered, and a red light began flashing on the dashboard. They were drifting out of alignment. She sniffled hard, wiping the last of her tears on the back of her hand, and got to work. Panel 2 began flashing, then 3. Her fingers flew from one place to the next, doing the job of two grown adults.

One dreadful minute turned into two, then five. Each second passed more quickly than the one which came before, and by ten paralyzingly exhilarating minutes, she had all of the beeps and flashes down to twenty second intervals.

"Just a few more minutes, Chen. You can do this," she shouted to herself over the loud vibration coming from below.

The ship jolted hard, and then again. All three panels were flashing red, throwing her into a frenzy. She flipped every switch, pressed every correcting button, but nothing helped. As the shaking increased and her arms were smacking wildly against the keypads, she surrendered to the inevitable. She'd failed.

Her fingers gripped the edges of the armrest tightly, and she closed her eyes.

"It's going to be okay. It's going to be okay," she chanted, her tiny voice a cruel reminder of the end closing in around her.

The shuttle bumped, and then everything was quiet. The beeping ceased, the vibrations were gone, and her eyelids shone through with a white glow. Chen didn't think the afterlife would be so silent. When she opened her eyes, she saw a vast blue expanse beyond the tiny cockpit windows.

She sucked in a long breath as the shuttle soared through misty white clouds, painting the glass with droplets of water.

"Chen! Ca- you -ear us?" The speaker on her bracelet came to life.

She whooped with joy, tears still damp on her cheeks. "I can hear you!"

"You did it! You made it!" She heard cries of excitement in the background, clapping, and sobs.

She engaged the autopilot as they cleared the clouds, revealing an endless curve of green. The Xiao-ping station chatter faded as a rushing took over her ears. She heard her heart beat with the rhythm of the ocean waves below. The history of a hundred trillion humans, animals, plants, and single celled organisms was laid out before her, and she, Chen—the Dawn—finally understood.

They had to be gentle and kind, not only to one another, but also to the Earth and to the creatures living on it. Their paradise was fragile; it needed care and dedication. Her heart burst with the joy of responsibility to her people, and her home, as she gazed upon the sea of jade she could never have fathomed. It was so vibrant, so *alive*, and so much bigger than it looked from her view on Xiao-ping.

"How does it feel?" The pilot's words cut through her trance.

She stuttered, "How does what feel?"

"Being the first human on the Earth in three hundred and twenty-nine years?"

She smiled, feeling her sarcastic wit return, "It's all right."

If you enjoyed the 2017 *Young Explorer's Adventure Guide*, please take a moment to review it where you purchased it!

We're always happy for you to come by the site, let us know what you think, and take a look at the rest of our science fiction and fantasy books.

DreamingRobotPress.com

Or email us at books@dreamingrobotpress.com

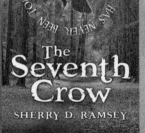

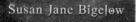